# THE REBEL KILLER

Paul's love of military history started at an early age. A childhood spent watching films like *Waterloo* and *Zulu* whilst reading Sharpe, Flashman and the occasional *Commando* comic gave him a desire to know more about the men who fought in the great wars of the nineteenth and twentieth centuries. This fascination led to a motivation to write and his series of novels featuring the brutally courageous Victorian rogue and imposter Jack Lark burst into life in 2013. Since then Paul has continued to write, developing the Jack Lark series to great acclaim.

To find out more about Paul and his novels visit www.paulfrasercollard.com or find him on Twitter @pfcollard.

Praise for Paul Fraser Collard and the Jack Lark series:

'A thoroughly enjoyable, action-packed read, which brings alive the horror and futility of war' *Historical Novel Society*

'I love a writer who wears his history lightly enough for the story he's telling to blaze across the pages like this. Jack Lark is an unforgettable new hero' Anthony Riches

'Holds the full horror of war, mortality and the depravity of the human condition . . . I highly recommend' *Parmenion Books*

'Plenty of honour and action in a satisfying slab of martial adventure'
*Daily Sport*

'Sharpe fans will be delighted to welcome a swashbuckling new hero to follow . . . Marvellous fun' *Peterborough Telegraph*

'A confident, rich and exciting novel that gave me all the ingredients I would want for a historical adventure of the highest order'
*lights*

*By Paul Fraser Collard*

The Scarlet Thief
The Maharajah's General
The Devil's Assassin
The Lone Warrior
The Last Legionnaire
The True Soldier
The Rebel Killer

*Digital Short Stories*
Jack Lark: Rogue
Jack Lark: Recruit
Jack Lark: Redcoat

The Jack Lark Library
(*short story omnibus including prequel story*, Rascal)

# Paul Fraser Collard

# THE REBEL KILLER

HEADLINE

First published in Great Britain in 2018 by
HEADLINE PUBLISHING GROUP

First published in paperback in 2019 by
HEADLINE PUBLISHING GROUP

1

Cataloguing in Publication Data is available from the British Library

ISBN 978 1 4722 3909 9

Typeset in Sabon by Avon DataSet Ltd, Bidford-on-Avon, Warwickshire

Printed and bound in Great Britain by Clays Ltd, Elcograf S.p.A.

HEADLINE PUBLISHING GROUP
An Hachette UK Company
Carmelite House
50 Victoria Embankment
London EC4Y 0DZ

www.headline.co.uk
www.hachette.co.uk

*To Alec and Sybil Swan*

# Glossary

———◆———

| | |
|---|---|
| abatis | fortification made of felled trees laid lengthwise and facing outwards |
| antebellum | existing prior to the US Civil War |
| bint | British Army slang for a girl or woman |
| broadside | single-sheet advertisement |
| carbine | shortened musket usually used by cavalry |
| columbiad | large-calibre muzzle-loading cannon |
| corned | London slang for being drunk |
| Jack Sheppard | infamous eighteenth-century thief |
| lucifers | matches |
| pannie | London slang for burglary |
| picket | sentry |
| rhino | London slang for money |
| rookery | city slum |
| secher | Northern slang for someone from the South who supported succession |
| talwar | curved native sword |
| turnpike | road on which a toll was collected |

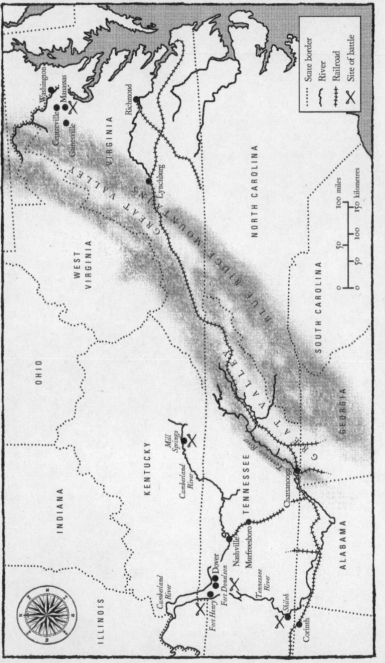

THE EASTERN UNITED STATES 1862

# Chapter One

---

*Virginia, 22 July 1861*

Silence lay over the battlefield like a shroud. The man dressed in the uniform of a Union army officer crept through the early-morning mist like a ghost. He picked his way through the detritus of the fight with care, fearing the noise he would make if he were clumsy enough to kick a fallen musket, or any of the other thousands of items of military equipment strewn across the Virginian grassland that bordered the Bull Run river.

He paused, every muscle tensed, as he heard the sounds of soldiers. It was a reminder that he was treading on ice, not just bloodstained and powder-scorched grass. He waited, concentrating on the noises. The soldiers were close, but not so close as to allow him to be seen.

The mist wrapped around him as he waited, something more than just its cool touch making him shiver. He did not move off immediately. Another sound had emerged from the hushed morning air, the soft groans barely audible above the rasp of his own breathing.

'Help me.'

The words were spoken clearly, and the officer placed their source immediately, the owner of the voice no more than half a dozen yards to his left.

'Please. Help me.'

They came again, more urgent now, the voice cracking as the plea was repeated.

The officer did not move. He was not there to offer mercy. His nose twitched. The smell of burnt powder lingered, the whiff of rotten eggs present ever since he had left his shelter. And now he caught the taint of something else in the damp air. It was a familiar smell, one as common to his trade as the odour of sawdust was to a carpenter. The officer had smelt enough old blood and torn flesh to know what lay hidden in the mist.

'Please. Help me. I beg you.' The voice had changed. Desperation and pain now underscored the words. And there was fear too, the terror only the soon-to-be-dead could know making itself heard in the earnest appeal.

The officer turned his back and moved away quietly, noting the position of the voice only so as to be able to steer a course around it. He felt nothing. There was no shame in leaving. The voice belonged to a stranger, not to a friend or comrade.

He moved more quickly now and his boots scuffed against a fallen ammunition pouch. He kept low, his left hand held out in front of him like a blind man feeling his way forward. His other hand hovered over the holster on his right hip, its flap unbuttoned, the weapon inside cleaned and loaded. He had prepared for this scouting mission as he would for a day of battle. For he was far from home, and far from the men whose side he had chosen. Only a fool faced such a situation without a loaded and primed weapon, and a mind that was ready to use it without thought of compassion.

The mist thinned as the ground under his boots inclined. He slowed, snuffling the air like a hound sniffing a distant fox. The fetid miasma of putrid flesh caught in the back of his throat. It was strong enough to make him want to spit.

Ahead he saw the source of such a foul odour. The corpses lay in a line, their limbs twisted into the obscene shapes only the dead could make. The line stretched on for a hundred yards before its furthest reaches were lost in a denser patch of mist.

The officer recognised the formation of the dead soldiers well enough. The men had been fighting in line of battle, the double-rank formation in which they faced the enemy. The bodies he now looked at were what remained when the survivors had moved away. They lay where the line had fought, their deaths marking the ground where men had fired volleys that could gut an enemy unit in minutes.

He did not try to tally the numbers of the dead, but there had to be at least fifty corpses on ground stained black by their blood. He ran his eyes over the bloated flesh, looking only for a threat. There was no horror at the sight, or widening of the eyes as they gazed upon mutilated flesh and ripped, limbless bodies. It was a sight he had seen on a dozen battlefields, and it looked the same on every continent. Death was death. War was war. He had seen too much of both to be horrified by the sight of the broken bodies.

'Who's there?'

The officer squatted low the moment the challenge came at him. He cursed under his breath, a moment's annoyance at having been seen, then went totally still, his senses reaching out to locate the picket who had spied him.

'Show yourself.'

There was little conviction in the sentry's demand. The

officer heard the weariness in the voice and understood it well enough. The previous day had witnessed a battle the likes of which had never been seen before on American soil. The army of the Union had attacked hard, their ambitious flanking manoeuvre eventually crushed by a Confederate army that had refused to recognise when it was nearly beaten. The officer understood the sentry's exhaustion, for he felt it himself. He had fought for the North, for those seeking to preserve the Union. Like the rest of his chosen army, he had ended the day in flight, his companions killed or otherwise lost to him. Save for one.

'Show yourself or I'll shoot.'

The last demand came with more authority. It allowed the officer to place the sentry. Still crouched, he set off, moving briskly, his tired muscles tensed, ready for the threatened shot. It never came. He was not surprised. Even the most anxious picket would hesitate to fire on a single shadow.

The mist thinned as he retraced his steps. Yesterday had been stiflingly hot, and already today promised to be little different. He could feel the heat beginning to build, the sudorific air already starting to press down on the scarred earth that had been chosen by the generals as the field of battle. The mist that sheltered him would not last for long.

The barn that had been his refuge overnight loomed into view. When he had left it just under half an hour earlier, he could see little more than the doorway. Now the whole thing was visible, a reminder that it was time to leave.

'Rose, are you there?' The officer paused at the door and hissed the question. He might have been dressed in the uniform of the Union army, but his accent came straight from the streets of east London.

'Yes.' The reply was almost instant. Rose stepped into the doorway, a mocking smile on her face. 'Did you think I would've left all by my lonesome?'

'I wouldn't put it past you,' the officer answered, no hint of a smile on his lips. He saw her scowl as she spotted his tension. It was a rare expression. Rose would more often mock than berate; tease when others would complain. It was one of the things he liked about her. The fact that she was pretty merely added to her attraction. At that moment, there was a hint of pink on the tips of her cheekbones, the colour sitting well on her dark skin. Her hair was pulled back, its soft curls tied into a purposeful ponytail. She usually wore it loose, letting it wrap around her face so that it hid the scars that marred one side of her jaw. Now she faced him with her disfigurement on show. She no longer had reason to hide anything from him.

He glanced over his shoulder, wary now that the sun was burning away the mist, then pulled his companion back into the barn and out of sight.

'What did you find?' Rose asked the question quietly, sensitive to his mood.

'They're still all around us. We need to get moving.'

'So be it.' She nodded as she replied. There was no hesitation. She accepted his decision without a murmur. 'We cannot stay here. Those sechers will want the fodder. Are you up to this?'

The officer scowled at the doubt in her tone. 'I'm fine.'

'Are you sure?' Rose stepped closer to him. He towered over her, and she was forced to crane her neck back as she considered his face. She smiled, then lifted her right hand so that she could brush her fingers across his cheek. There they lingered, tracing the thick scar that ran across the left-hand side of his face. It had been left by a mutinous sawar's sword outside the walls of

Delhi four years earlier and was a reminder of failure, of the moment when a woman he had come to care for had been snatched away from him, never to return. It was one of the dark memories, one of the demons that he kept locked and chained in the recesses of his mind where he refused to venture.

'Let's get going.' There was a harsh quality to his voice now.

'I'm ready.' Rose smiled as she heard censure in his tone. 'What are we waiting for?'

The officer bit back a brusque reply. It would be easier if he were on his own, if he didn't have Rose to consider. He was used to fending for himself. He was a wanderer, a man with neither home nor family, his connections in the world little more than fleeting gossamer-thin strands that could be broken at a moment's notice. Yet now he was saddled with a woman. The choices he would make were no longer his alone, and such a complication would surely only serve to make his life harder.

'You can go on without me if you like.' Rose took a pace backwards as if she read his thoughts. 'I can look after myself. I've done it before; I can do it again.'

The officer looked at her sharply. He saw no fear on her face as she suggested that he abandon her. It was a reminder of what had drawn him to this former slave turned housemaid. There was a spark deep in her eyes and devilment in her gaze. She was a challenge that he had been unable to ignore.

'No.' He spoke quietly and reached his hand out towards her. 'We'll walk our chalk together.'

'We'll do what exactly?'

He nearly smiled at her reaction. It was a common enough phrase on the streets of Whitechapel, where he had been brought up, but he was a long way from there, so he tried again. 'We'll go together.'

'You'd better speak clear, else it'll be a long, hard day.' She took his hand as she delivered the rebuke.

'Yes, ma'am.' He squeezed her hand in reassurance. There was nothing else to say.

He led the way outside and into the last of the mist. His early-morning excursion had given him a fair idea where the closest Confederate troops were. He paused, taking one last moment to summon a plan. He thought about discarding the uniform he was wearing. It was the dark blue chosen by his regiment, the 1st Boston Volunteer Militia. Many of the Union regiments had decided upon a different uniform, the army fighting its· first major engagement with many of its soldiers not able to tell friend from foe. This self-created confusion was just one of the many mistakes the inexperienced soldiers had made that day.

Yet there was little point undressing. If they escaped the immediate area then there was every chance they would come across Union soldiers, the broken army sure to have scattered to the winds as it fled the field of battle. His officer's insignia might well save them, and so he decided he would keep wearing it, even though it was filthy, the dark blue cloth stained black with dried blood, and covered with muck and dust from the battlefield.

With Rose's hand held firmly in his, he took them west. Neither spoke as they walked away from the barn that had sheltered them overnight. With the sun on their backs they made for a dense thicket of woodland. It was time to leave the battlefield behind.

They heard the sound of movement at the same moment. Both stilled, with little more than a glance exchanged. Someone was rushing through the wood at speed.

'Just one.' The officer hissed the words at Rose, who nodded by way of confirmation.

He let go of her hand, freeing his own. It moved to his holster. The Colt was cool to his touch as he drew it. It was a beautiful weapon, made to be so much more than just a simple instrument of death. The metal had been polished so that it shone like silver, and the grips on the handle were inlaid with ivory covered with intricate carvings. It was the weapon of a rich man, one the officer had coveted since the moment he had seen it given to another.

The action of drawing the revolver felt good. He switched it to his left hand, holding it just as he did in battle. Its weight reassured him and lent him power; the same power that propelled him into the fight certain of his own ability. He was a man who knew his trade in a way that only years of experience could bestow.

'Stay behind me.' He gave the instruction softly, then took a step forward. The fingers of his right hand flexed as he considered drawing the sabre he wore on his left hip. He would feel better facing any confrontation with weapons in both hands, but he did not yet know what awaited him, and he wanted to keep the hand free in case he had to grab Rose. So the sword stayed in its scabbard.

He felt Rose reach out, her hand resting on his shoulder in a moment's reassurance. The gesture pleased him far more than he could have imagined.

The noise stopped for the span of a dozen heartbeats, then came again, now closer than before. There was time for the officer to take one last deep breath before the figure of a man emerged from the wood no more than six yards to his front.

For a moment, the two men stared at one another. The

stranger wore a dark blue uniform similar to the one the officer wore. Yet it lacked the bright buttons and the sky-blue shoulder straps with their golden thread. Its sleeves were free of the markings of any other rank.

Neither man spoke. The officer stayed stock still, the revolver held low. The stranger stared back at him, his tongue flickering anxiously across his lips. Then he began to move, slowly at first, his body always turned towards the officer. Step by step, he passed across the clearing, his eyes always watching for any sign of reaction. He did not so much as breathe a single word.

He covered a couple of yards, each movement slow and deliberate, as if he were wary of startling the officer into action. Then he bolted away, crashing through the undergrowth like a deer finally awaking to a hunter's approach.

The officer had not moved the whole time. Now he turned, a hint of a smile flickering across his face as he looked back at Rose. 'He was in a hurry and no mistake. The rude bugger didn't even say good morning.' He spoke softly lest his voice carry too far into the trees.

Rose smiled at the jest. 'Well, you don't look none too friendly. I ain't surprised he ran off.'

'You saying I'm that ugly?'

Rose reached out, her hand holding the officer's chin as she made a play of inspecting his face. 'Well, you ain't what I'd call wholesome. You're a little battered around the edges and I reckon you'd scare the hell out of any babes coming your way, but I suppose you're not all that bad.' She chuckled at her own words, then released her grip.

The officer almost laughed. They were far from any notion of safety, yet still Rose could find something to tease him about.

It spoke well of her spirit. His earlier mean thoughts had done her a disservice. She was no burden. He was not saddled with her; he was fortunate that she had chosen to give herself to him. He held the thought close, repeating it in his mind in the hope that it would settle, that it would become an inalienable truth.

'And what are you smiling about? It weren't that funny.' Rose watched him carefully, with the same look on her face a sane person might wear when confronted with someone they suddenly realised was as mad as a hatter.

'I'm happy.' He answered honestly.

'You're happy now? Here? Like this?' Rose shook her head at such a foolish notion.

'I'm with you, love. How can I be anything but happy?' The officer was not lying, but he would never be able to put the feeling properly into words. He was happy because he felt alive in a way that he had almost forgotten. For all its horror, the battle had let him be the person he knew he was meant to be.

'Well, I reckon that makes you a crazy fool, Jack Lark, but I think that's why I like you.' Rose still regarded him warily, but there was a smile on her face now.

Jack looked back at her and wondered again at his own foolishness. Rose might be correct. He may well be a madman. But if he was, then he was a happy one. He might be lost in the woods and be surrounded by an entire enemy army, but at last he was free.

# Chapter Two

---

'**D**o you see them?' Jack whispered the question directly into Rose's ear.

'Uh huh.' The reply was delivered just as softly.

They were crouched in a thicket, deep in a wide swathe of woodland around a mile from the barn where they had sheltered overnight. Jack had brought them to a stop, screening them from view the moment he heard the sounds of more than one man moving through the same trees. He held them there, his hand placed on Rose's back. He could feel the beat of her heart, and her body trembled ever so slightly under his touch. He savoured the sensation, his fingers splaying out so that they could pick up every reverberation.

'Wait here.' He hoped the single command would hold her in place. With reluctance he removed his hand, then drew his revolver before easing himself to one side, both to improve his view and also to give him space to use his sabre should the need arise.

The two men he had spotted were dangerously close. There were no pickets, or at least none that he could see. At first he could not work out what they were up to. Neither wore much in the way of uniform. Both sported a grey jacket and they wore matching trousers made from an extravagant chequered cloth. Jack wondered if that meant they were family, perhaps even brothers, their mother or sister working on the same fabric in the production of their gaudy trousers. He was almost certain that they were Confederates. He had not seen a single Union regiment in anything less than the most splendid uniform. The same could be said of much of the Confederate army, but there had been plenty of Southern soldiers who had turned up to the battle in nothing grander than their ordinary homespun clothes.

The men may have lacked a fine uniform, but both were armed. From his vantage point, Jack could see they were carrying what looked to be smoothbore percussion-cap muskets, a weapon that had little place on a modern battlefield now that rifle muskets were being manufactured that made the older versions obsolete.

The previous day, the Union troops had had the advantage, with many of their regiments armed with modern Springfield rifle muskets. They had decimated the Confederate troops, the powerful rifles vastly more effective than muskets that were little changed from those carried by the soldiers who had fought in the Napoleonic campaign fifty or so years before. Yet not even the superior rifles had been able to secure the North a first, decisive victory, and Jack knew not to take the humble soldiers he was studying lightly.

Both of the Confederate men were armed with more than just muskets. They wore long bowie knives at their waists, and one also carried a revolver. They were well armed and confident, their loud voices and braying laughter a sure indication that they felt no sense of danger.

They were busy with something on the ground, yet Jack could not make out what was holding their attention, his viewpoint only allowing him to observe the men from the waist up. He shifted further to his left, his hand holding the revolver tightly as he moved as quietly as he could. Only then did he get a glimpse of the ground around the two men's feet.

Four bodies were sprawled in the dirt. One of the Confederate soldiers was squatting down as he rifled through their clothing. There was no doubt in Jack's mind that the men on the ground were long dead, but there *was* doubt whose side they had been on. They wore grey uniforms, their colour not dissimilar to the jackets worn by the pair of Confederate soldiers.

As he looked more closely, however, he could see that one of the dead was an officer, the twin gold bars on sky-blue shoulder straps identifying him as a captain of infantry. The rank markers made it certain that the men were from the Union army. A number of the Northern regiments had worn a dark grey uniform, and he was almost certain that the men he was now looking at came from one of the New York militia regiments that had fought close to the 1st Boston.

A series of loud whoops greeted the discovery of something interesting in the officer's clothing. The man squatting over the corpse stood up, a fine gold pocket watch dangling from a chain held up for his friend to admire.

The second man stood and gawped at the find, a look of disgust on his face as he saw his comrade's good fortune, before he bent down and started to go through the clothing of another of the dead men. After a moment's searching, he grunted in disgust, then stood up holding nothing more valuable than a letter and what Jack supposed to be a photograph that he had pulled from the man's pocket.

'Why, look at this fine Yankee bitch!' He leered at the photograph, making a show for the man still studying the pocket watch.

'Let me see!' His companion slipped the looted watch into a pocket, then snatched the photograph. He hooted with glee as he looked at the image. 'Why, she is fine indeed!'

The man who had found the photograph scowled, then grabbed it back. 'That's mine. I think I'll be keeping it for myself.'

'We all know why that is!' His companion raised his voice mockingly. 'I reckon I know you well enough to figure out what you'll be looking at when that little fist of yours gets busy under your bedroll tonight.' He hooted as he finished speaking, his face creased into a smile.

His mockery was enough for the man with the photograph to crush it, then toss it onto the dead officer's chest along with the letter. 'I will not. I ain't interested in no dirty Yankee bitch, so you shut your filthy mouth, Adam Hunt, before I shut it for you.'

The threat was enough to have the man with the looted pocket watch backing away. 'Easy now, Seth, easy. I meant nothing by it.' He bent down to pick up his musket from where he had left it on the ground. 'You know I'll share the money I get for the watch. Ma would tan my hide if I didn't. Now we'd better get out of here and see if we can find ourselves any living Yankees to kill.'

He made to move off, then paused, his head cocked as he listened. He held the pose for no more than a handful of heartbeats before he turned and stared directly at the pair of fugitives hiding no more than a dozen yards from where he stood.

Jack reacted on instinct before any notion of a plan entered his head. He charged at the pair, his only thought to prevent them revealing his presence to any other Confederates in the area.

He drew his sabre as he thrashed through the undergrowth. The blade had been cleaned, but there were still the dark marks of old blood etched into the scars and notches it had taken the previous day. He felt the power in the bloodied and battered steel. It thrilled through him, wiping away the fatigue that only a day's fighting could force into a man's body.

There was barely time for the man who had plundered the gold pocket watch to cry out before Jack was on him.

His first blow was wild. The Confederate soldier threw his musket up in a desperate parry that blocked the cut and knocked the sabre away. Jack saw the flash of joy rush into the man's eyes before he raised his left hand and smashed his revolver into the side of the man's head. It was a cruel blow, the beautifully crafted handgun reduced to nothing more than an expensive cudgel. It knocked the Confederate to one side, the blood rushing from the crack in his skull.

Jack grunted as the blow landed. He felt nothing as he recovered the sword from the man's parry, then slashed the steel into the side of the man's neck. The man tried to scream as the steel drove deep. No sound came. Instead blood filled his mouth, his terrified cries drowned as Jack twisted the steel then ripped it free from the inevitable suction of the man's flesh.

'Adam!'

No more than a handful of seconds had passed since the Confederate with the pocket watch had spied Jack and Rose hiding. In that time, his companion had not moved so much as an inch. Now he stared as his brother fell to the ground, hands clawing at the ruin of his neck, his mouth emitting a dreadful series of gurgles and gulps as blood gushed from the horrible wound.

Jack could see the rabid fear in the man's eyes. It would be easy to gun him down where he stood. The blood-splattered revolver he held in his left hand was loaded and primed for just such a fight as this. Yet he had killed one man in near silence, and he saw no need to open fire and draw the attention of any more enemy soldiers. He recovered the sabre, a grotesque spray of blood and gobbets of flesh flung from the blade as he swung it ready to launch the next blow.

The Confederate soldier named Seth saw the movement. His mouth opened, but no sound came out, any cry of fear or hatred lost as he realised Jack was coming for him. He did not run, but stood his ground, his musket presented forward as he readied to defend himself.

It was bravely done. It was no small thing to stand your ground when a man came at you with a blade dripping with gore. The Confederate braced himself, his knees flexing and his body tensing as Jack swung the sabre at his head. His musket punched up, the wooden stock taking the full force of Jack's first attack. It was there again as Jack recovered the blade and swung it in a second blow, the sabre gouging a thick splinter from the musket's stock.

But Jack was beginning to find his speed. He recovered from the second parry, then lashed out with his revolver. Seth's musket lifted a heartbeat before the weapon would have connected with his skull. It was a good parry, the kind that could save a man in a fight. But not that day. Not against a man-killer like Jack.

Jack thrust his sabre forward the moment he saw the musket move to block the revolver. Even as his left arm rang from the brutal contact, he drove the blade home with his right. It took the Confederate in the chest, the bloodied steel tip ripping through the tawdry grey jacket and deep into flesh.

Seth tried to scream then, but Jack saw it coming and slammed his head forward, smashing it into the man's face. The head butt came straight from the rookeries of London; it broke teeth and filled the Confederate's mouth with blood.

Seth stood there, Jack's sabre buried in his breast, blood dribbling down his chin like red wine from a drunk. Yet he tried to fight on, using his musket as a club and thumping it into Jack's left arm. His wounds stole much of the strength from the blow, but it was still enough to knock Jack away and tear the sword from Seth's flesh.

Jack ignored the flash of pain. He regained his balance and chopped his sabre down. It was a butcher's blow and it took the brave Confederate at the junction of neck and shoulder. He followed it a moment later with another blow in the same spot, slamming the blade down with all the finesse of a slaughterman.

The twin blows drove the Confederate to his knees. He dropped his musket as he hit the ground, so was defenceless as he looked up at Jack one last time. It should have been a moment for pity, for the two men to stare at one another and wonder at the speed with which fate had brought them to this moment.

Jack looked deep into the other man's eyes. He saw the fear there, yet he felt not even a shred of compassion. The moment the brothers had spotted the pair of fugitives, they had become a risk to Rose and to the future he might share with her. It was time to end it. He lashed out with the sabre, bludgeoning the steel into the side of Seth's head and knocking him to the ground. The Confederate fell without a sound.

Jack turned away, searching the undergrowth for Rose. She had not moved during the short, bitter struggle. Now she rose to her feet and stalked forward.

'Are they dead?' She asked the question in a voice quite without emotion.

'One is. One soon will be.' He gave the cold answer, then began to wipe the worst of the gore from his sword on the jacket of the man he had slain. He could not return it to its scabbard until it was clean, lest it stick to the insides.

Rose came to his side. There was no hint of horror on her face; only sadness. She had seen Jack fight before. She knew what he was. She had accepted him.

She looked down at the second man, the one she had heard called Seth. He was still alive, yet it was clear that he would not last long. Already the flow of blood pulsing from his grotesque wounds was slowing, and his skin was the colour of week-old ash.

'Give me your revolver.' She made the demand of Jack in a voice wrapped in iron.

'No.' Jack saw what she intended. 'Shoot him and you'll draw more of them this way.'

'You'd leave him to suffer?'

'He's as good as dead, love.' Jack reached out and took a grip of Rose's shoulder, turning her so that she faced him and no longer looked at the dying man.

'He's suffering.' Rose shook off his hand. 'His name is Seth and he is suffering.'

'Oh, for fuck's sake.' Jack let his exasperation show. He cared for nothing more than keeping Rose safe. Yet he knew her well enough to understand that she would not be swayed, so he stepped forward, hefting his blood-smeared sabre in his hand.

'No.' Rose commanded him with the single word. 'I'll do it. You've done enough.'

Jack stopped in his tracks. He had heard something in her tone. Was there a rebuke in her words? Or was she simply looking to play her part?

Rose crouched down next to the dying man. 'Quiet now, Seth.' She reached out as she used the young man's name, her fingers brushing lightly across his forehead and pushing away a lock of hair that covered his right eye.

Seth whimpered at her touch. His lips moved as he tried to form words, but no more sound came out.

'Hush now,' Rose soothed him, her voice that of a mother to a disturbed child in the dark of the night. Her left hand continued to smooth his hair whilst her right reached down to his hip, where she carefully and slowly eased the bowie knife he wore out of its sheath.

'Sleep now.' She spoke the last words Seth would ever hear, then pushed the knife into his chest.

She had to work the blade as she eased it between his rib bones and then through the thick band of muscle beneath. Seth's eyes widened for the span of a single heartbeat as the tip of the knife pierced his heart, and then he sighed and died quietly.

Rose pushed herself to her feet. Blood covered her right hand, but she seemed not to notice it.

'God rest their souls.' She muttered the well-worn phrase under her breath.

'Yes.' Jack looked down at the two men. He tried to find a moment's pity, or even a flare of guilt. He failed. He felt nothing. 'God rest their souls.'

# Chapter Three

---

Jack stood over the body of the dead Union officer and the cold corpses that surrounded him. He could smell them now that he was closer, the rank odour of their bloated flesh overwhelming the sweeter smell of freshly spilt blood. Yet the stink was no great deterrent, and he scanned around him one last time before he holstered his revolver and laid his sword on the ground.

He looked at the dead officer for the first time. The man stared back at him. His eyes were open. The twin lifeless orbs stared up at the sky, blank and glassy like the eyes in a stuffed animal. His mouth had lolled open and Jack saw lines of white teeth that were still bright and clean. Their colour stood out against the ashy pallor of the man's face.

Jack supposed him to be in his late twenties, perhaps thirty at most. His beard was neatly trimmed, the black hair devoid of even a single rogue grey strand. It made him not that much younger than Jack himself, who was feeling every one of his thirty-one years in the aches and pains that racked his body.

They were men of the same generation, yet now one lay on his back, his hopes and ambitions stolen away along with everything he had ever been and ever would be. Jack's own aspirations had been washed away in the ocean of blood he had seen shed, and he had lost much of himself along the way. Yet he could still feel something of what it was to long for a future. To want something other than what he already had.

He glanced at Rose. She was rifling through the clothing of the two dead Confederates, but he noticed she was still watching him closely. He knew she was the cause of this new-found longing. He had drifted for a long time, letting fate choose his path and allowing it to decide which direction he took. Now he wanted to reclaim his life. He would no longer permit fate to guide him. It was why he had fought, why he had butchered the two Confederates. Fate had placed them between him and this glimpse of a new future. He could not have let them stand in his way.

The wind rustled through the trees. It stirred the letter that the Confederate had tossed away with such disdain. Jack scooped up the pages. He supposed they comprised a final message, written in the days, perhaps even the hours, before the battle. A tight copperplate script flowed across the paper, yet he did not read it. Instead he bent forward and picked up the photograph that had been found along with the letter.

He straightened its edges then smoothed it out on his thigh as best he could. It was a common enough object, especially amongst Union officers, the fashion for *cartes des visites* creating a boon for the handful of photographers able to produce the stiff, awkward images of men in uniform and their proud families.

A flicker of a smile traced across Jack's face as he remembered the one time he himself had been photographed, just a few weeks before. It had been at the behest of a young woman called Elizabeth Kearney, the daughter of the man who had employed him and one of the most beautiful women he had ever met. He still carried a copy of the photograph taken that day in his pocket as a reminder of a life he might once have been able to find.

He glanced down at the photograph in his hand. The dead officer stared out from the image, his face not wholly different to the one now shrouded with death, his eyes just as lifeless as they were at that moment, the photographer unable to capture even a flicker of the vitality that must once have lit them from within.

At his side sat a young woman. Jack could not help a moment's scrutiny of her. He supposed her to be pretty, in a wholesome way. She too stared out from the photograph, but with what could possibly be a flicker of a smile playing across her face. He wondered what her name was. A glance at the letter told him it was addressed to a Caroline, a woman he supposed would now be a widow, although she would surely not know of her loss for some time to come. Her husband would be listed as missing, a common enough fate for a soldier. Jack wondered how long her misery would last; how many weeks or months, or even years, she would jump at every unexpected knock at the door. How many thousands of short-lived flares of hope she would experience in the belief that somehow her husband had returned to her.

'Are you done?' Rose called across to him, interrupting his musing. She pitched her voice low so that the sound would not carry far.

'Yes.' He stood up, trying not to wince as his back protested. He still held the letter. For a moment he was tempted to toss the pages back onto the dead officer's chest, just as the

Confederate had done. Yet his hand would not move. He knew these people now, a thin tendril of shared connection linking him to them. He stuffed both the letter and the photograph into a pocket.

'Are you going to deliver those too?' Rose asked.

Jack understood the reference well enough. He had come to Boston to deliver a number of letters. It had been that particular delivery that had led to his short career in the Union army. 'Maybe I will. If I can.'

'What does that make you then? A delivery boy?' Rose came closer. 'I thought you were meant to be a soldier.'

'I was. I am. But I think I can be something else. There's more to me than just that.' The words formed thoughts that were still building their foundations in his mind. It had taken him a long time to accept what he was: a soldier and a killer of men. The prospect of being something different did not sit comfortably with him. Saying it aloud helped to make the fledgling thought take flight.

'Is that so?' Rose glanced behind her at the bodies of the newly dead. Yet she said nothing about them. 'So what are you going to be, Jack?'

'I haven't figured that out yet.'

Jack made an inspection of the woods around them. It was not just out of concern for their safety. These thoughts for the future were too fresh to sit comfortably now he had released them to the world. He had not yet worked it out, but he did know that *he* would decide what he would do, what he would be; he would leave nothing to the whims of fate. He was still a soldier. It was all he had been, all he had known, for more than a decade. But he was beginning to hope that he could be more than that. Much more.

'Well, you'd better start thinking. We can't just wander around for ever.'

'I know.' Jack felt his determination harden. 'I'm done wandering.'

He reached out, taking her bloodstained hand in his own. He might not have everything figured out, but there were some things that just made sense. Rose was one of them. His immediate future had one certain fixture in it, and for the moment, that was enough.

They walked through the wood in silence, each lost in their own thoughts. Jack led them, Rose's hand cradled in his. The warmth of her flesh felt good against his skin.

He did not set a fast pace. They moved slowly but steadily. Every few steps he paused, straining his hearing and listening for sounds of more soldiers. Only when he was reassured that they were still alone did he continue. As he walked, he reached out with his senses, trying to feel his way through the wood that surrounded him. He listened for sounds other than the breeze rustling through the trees and tried to detect the smell of men against the damp, earthy scent of a wood in summer.

The gunshot came suddenly.

They both flinched, reacting instantly to the sudden explosion of sound. Neither spoke, but they both crouched down, their heads turning from side to side as they tried to find the source of the shot.

'There.' Jack spotted them first. He pointed through a gap in the trees to where he could see a group of men.

'Shit.' He could not help the oath escaping as a second gunshot cracked out. This time it was followed by a dull thump, like the sound a barrel of gin made when it was dumped onto the ground from the back of a brewer's wagon.

'Let's double back.' He twisted on the spot, looking for another way round. He had no desire to fight again. They had not yet been seen, and so he could still search for an alternative route.

'No, stay low. Wait it out.' Rose gave the command.

He saw the sense in her words. Moving was a risk. They were less likely to be seen or heard if they just stayed where they were and waited for whoever it was to move on.

'How many left?' A deep voice barked the order.

The words helped Jack to place the group. They were twenty or perhaps thirty yards away. From what he could make out, they were standing in a small clearing. He heard a voice reply to the question, but he missed the words themselves. He forced his breathing to slow and concentrated on what he could see and hear.

He caught glimpses of men dressed in grey uniforms, moving around busily. He was trying to count their numbers when he saw a flash of blue amongst the grey. At least one Union soldier was in the midst of what had to be a large number of Confederate troops.

'Well, get it done.' The same deep voice came again. There was no hiding the annoyance in the man's tone. 'These whoresons led us a merry dance and we've wasted enough time here. Scouring this wood for yellow-belly Yankee fugitives ain't about to take care of itself.'

'Yes, sir.' A second voice gave a nervous reply. 'Come on, you son of a bitch.'

Jack heard the sounds of a scuffle. He moved slowly and carefully, easing his way forward until he could see more clearly. He did not have to move far.

His first thought had been correct. A group of around twenty Confederate soldiers were gathered in a clearing. Some were standing at ease, leaning on what appeared to be carbines. Those who were in motion were dragging a young man dressed in the dark blue uniform of a Union regiment towards a lone tree that stood within the boundary of the clearing. The Union soldier was not going quietly. He might have been bound and gagged, but he still fought against his captors, his body jackknifing and kicking for all it was worth.

'Come on, you goddam Yankee bastard. There ain't no point in fighting. Why can't you just go quiet like your friend?' snapped the man who had answered the command to get on with it.

Jack looked at the foot of the tree they were headed towards. A body dressed in the same blue uniform lay sprawled on the ground. He did not have to be any closer to know the man was dead.

'Come on now,' the Confederate soldier in charge shouted at the Union man, who was still fighting for all he was worth. 'Do as you are told and make it easy on yourself.'

The man did not quit his thrashing, and it took four soldiers several long moments to drag him to the tree. Only when they had bound him to it with ropes already tied around its stout trunk did they move away, their hands busy rearranging their clothing that had been pulled this way and that by their prisoner's struggles.

The Confederates were quiet now. The only sound came from the Union soldier, who was crying and moaning through his gag for all he was worth. His eyes bulged as the piteous sounds poured out of him, pleading with the men around him to relent.

'Goddammit, why don't you hush now?' The man with the deep voice spoke firmly. 'This ain't a manly way to go.'

Jack saw the owner of the voice for the first time. The commander of the group was a tall man. He wore a light grey jacket, its sleeves decorated in an intricate pattern of golden thread that covered most of the fabric from cuff to elbow. He was tall almost to the point of being gangly, with a long, thin face covered with an unkempt, ragged beard that matched a wild thatch of grey hair so pale it was almost white. In his hands he carried a heavy revolver.

The man stepped towards the prisoner. He walked slowly and calmly, as if he had not a care in the world. For his part, the prisoner quietened, his moans and muffled pleas lessening in volume. He lolled against the ropes holding him to the tree, as if all the strength had been sucked from his body. Only his head moved as he watched the man walking towards him with eyes wide with fear.

'That's better. No sense going to your God whining like a goddam babe.' The man with the revolver stepped closer, then stopped. He stood there holding the gaze of the prisoner. Then he raised the revolver slowly until it pointed directly at the bound man's forehead.

'I'm right sorry to do this to you, but that's the way of it. You killed three of my boys and I ain't about to pardon that, not since you murdered them in cold blood and all.' He paused, his head cocked to one side as he smiled at the man staring back at him. 'Now you give the good Lord my regards, but tell the son of a bitch I don't have no plans to come see him any time soon.' He pulled the trigger.

The gunshot was overly loud in the quiet of the wood, the retort echoing from the trees. At such close range the man with the revolver could not miss, and the prisoner's whimpers were cut off in an instant as the heavy bullet shattered his skull.

'Now that, boys, is how we deal with these whoresons.' The man addressed the troops around him. 'You all take a good long look. Remember this day and remember those sorry Yankees, just as you remember our poor boys they killed.' There was no trace of emotion in his voice, his tone unchanged even after committing cold-blooded murder.

He turned his back on the man he had shot and was about to walk away when he paused to look around him. Jack had a good enough view to see his eyebrows furrow as he glanced over his shoulder, as if becoming aware of a hidden scrutiny. The man held the pose. Jack thought he saw his nose twitch, as if he were snuffling the air like some woodland creature. Then he moved on, holstering the still smoking revolver as he did so.

'Time to move out, boys. We've got a long day ahead of us and we don't want to keep General Forrest waiting at the end of it.' He gave the order calmly. He was clearly used to being obeyed.

The men moved immediately. Not one returned to the two bodies lying in the dirt.

Jack stayed where he was. He was no stranger to executions. He had seen murderers hanged and he had watched a man die in a bare-knuckle brawl. He also understood what it was to want to kill, to need to kill. In the sordid depths of the worst fighting, he had felt the insatiable urge to slaughter other men. And he knew what it was to kill in cold blood.

He turned to look at Rose. She stared straight ahead, still transfixed by the brutal scene they had just witnessed. He wondered what she had felt as she witnessed a man die in such callous fashion. He was learning that there were many sides to her character. She had killed before, he knew that much. She had confessed to it without a hint of shame, the man she had murdered the same one who had put the marks on her face. She had escaped her life as a slave, her journey north accomplished with the aid of the underground railroad, the network of brave men and women who helped thousands of slaves escape from the antebellum South to the free North; a journey only the bravest and most determined could hope to complete. Yet he had also witnessed her compassion. She would not leave a man to suffer, even though she risked her own life in the process. It was hard to reconcile the two sides to her character, and he had a feeling he still had much to learn about her.

For his part, watching the Union soldier die had not moved him. Only the coldness of the man with the heavy revolver stuck with him. The man had killed without a qualm, the act seemingly meaningless to him. To see such a lack of emotion was enough to send a shudder running through Jack's body. It was not because it shocked him; it was because he understood it. He had watched a cold-hearted killer plying his trade, yet he could just as well have been watching himself.

This was fate's way of reminding him what he was. He was no different to the man with the revolver. His hopes for a new future mocked him. No matter what he might long for, no matter what he might try to forget, he would never escape his past.

## Chapter Four

---

*J*ack lay on his back and looked up at the stars. They stared down, serene and peaceful. He liked the stars. For years they had been his only constant companions. It did not matter that they changed; that the stars he looked at now were arranged in patterns so very different to the ones he had looked up at in India, or in Persia, or from the fields of northern Europe. They possessed the same quality of stillness, of being unperturbed by the tribulations of man. It was what he liked about them. They did not care about war or battle. They did not worry about the future or suffer the memories of the past. They just were.

'You asleep?'

'No.' He took a long, slow, deep breath and held it.

'Good. I can't sleep either.'

'Then just rest. You'll surely need your strength.' He was in no mood to talk, but he understood her inability to fall asleep. He was bone weary, yet his mind would not let him find the rest he craved. If there had been more moonlight he might have risked moving on. Yet if they did that, they were in danger of stumbling across a party of Confederates.

That was a gamble he could not take.

They had stayed hidden in the woods until they were certain the party of Confederate soldiers was long gone. Only then had they moved. They had kept the pace measured, wary now that they knew the Confederates were scouring the woods for Union troops. Their progress had been slow and tortuous. Every sound could reveal a threat, and he had lost count of the times they had stopped, hearts in mouths, as they sensed danger. They had spent much of the day hidden, the hours and minutes crawling past with excruciating slowness as they waited, half expecting to be spotted by one of the bands of Southern soldiers prowling through the wide swathe of woodland.

Their caution had saved them from discovery, but they had covered little ground before the sun set and they could no longer see the way ahead. This night there was no barn to shelter them, but Jack had slung a blanket over the bough of a pine tree that bent low to the ground, creating a rudimentary shelter. Not that they needed it. The night was warm to the point of being stifling, the humidity in the air as unpleasant as the tiny insects that came out in their thousands to torment and bother them the moment they stopped.

'You hungry?'

Jack did not reply, but his stomach growled, answering the question for him.

'We need to find food.' Rose lay on her side, her head propped on her elbow. She watched him closely.

'We need to find somewhere that's safe first.' Jack's reply was waspish. His back was hurting like the devil. It was the legacy of a childhood of humping barrels of liquor in a back-street gin palace in the rookeries of east London, and a decade of being a soldier. The ache never left him, but at times it was worse, and at that moment, fiery lances of pain were searing up and down his legs.

'There's no need for that tone, mister.' She paused and waited for a reaction. When she didn't get one, she changed tack. 'You know which direction we're going to take in the morning?'

'No.' Jack had heard the pepper in her rebuke and had wisely remained silent. But the second question was a fair one. She had every right to be worried.

He looked across at his companion. In the moonlight, he could see the scars half hidden under her jawline on the lower left side of her face. He knew how she had got them, the marks the gift of an overseer's whip. It was one of the few things he knew about this girl who had been born a slave. She had been a servant when he had first met her, her place as maid to Elizabeth Kearney the reason she was now in his life.

She smiled as he met her gaze. 'You ain't much of a woodsman.'

'Never said I was.' Jack grunted at the mockery in her tone.

'You'll have to learn.'

'I will.' Jack agreed readily enough. He had been a soldier on campaign many times, so he knew how to live without comforts. But he had always been supplied by whichever army he was with. He did not know how to be self-sufficient, how to provide for himself.

'You've had it too easy.' Rose reached out and poked his side. 'You've got fat and lazy.'

Jack gasped as her finger jabbed hard into his flesh. She was being harsh. Granted, he was not as lean as in his younger days, but he had been with the Union army for just under six months and was as fit and strong as he had ever been.

'You'll have to get used to hard work too, now. Proper work. Not just parading around shouting at people.' Rose jabbed him again, harder this time.

'Yes, ma'am.' Jack was in no mood to fight.

'That's better.' Rose's hand came forward again, but this time it rested on his thigh. 'I like it when you stop complaining and do as you're told.'

'Complaining? Is that what I do?' He shook his head at the barb.

'Come on, let's get moving.' Rose barely managed to complete the sentence. She had put on a deep voice in what she clearly thought was an English accent but which sounded more like she had a heavy cold.

'I see.' Jack could not help chuckling at her impression. 'So I sound like a proper grouch?'

'You sound like an old man forced to leave his seat by the fire.' Rose began another attempt, but dissolved into giggles before she could manage it.

'Will you always abuse me so piteously?' Jack made a play of sighing in exasperation.

'Always.' Rose inched closer, then laid her head on his arm. 'Do you not like it when I tease you, then? Would you prefer it if I were a little mouse who did exactly what you told me?' She squeaked, then wrinkled her nose.

'So you can imitate rodents too. Is there no end to your talents?' Jack laughed, then moved his arm and pulled her closer so that her head rested on his chest.

'In time I'll show you all I can do, Jack Lark.' Rose stretched her arm across his belly, holding him close. 'If you stop them from taking me.'

Her words changed the tone of the conversation. They were

a reminder of the fate she faced if she were captured. He looked into her eyes. The fear was half hidden, but he found it there all the same.

'They'll kill me.' Rose offered the statement in as bland a voice as she could manage. 'For what I did to the man who gave me these.' Her fingers traced over the fretwork of scars on her jaw.

'They'll have to capture you first. I won't let that happen.' Jack made the vow without hesitation. He meant it. He would die rather than see Rose be taken.

'You promise?'

'I promise.'

Neither of them spoke for some time. It was Rose who finally broke the spell. 'We can go west. Find a place where we can start a new life. One where I don't have to be a servant and an ex-slave, and where you don't have to be a soldier.'

'What's out west?'

'Everything. Mountains. Plains. Forests. Rivers. It's all there.'

'And it's ours for the taking?' Jack could not help the glib remark. He had fought for everything he had ever owned. He could not imagine a future where fate could be so beneficent.

Rose lifted her head so that she could look at him properly. 'There's free land for anyone who wants to stake a claim. We can find a wagon, then head someplace where no one will ever bother us again.' She smiled and looked him dead in the eye. 'We can be pioneers.'

Jack considered the notion. It seemed a fair one. There was the small matter of money, but he was a boy from Whitechapel. He had been born poor, had found wealth, and now was poor again. He would find a way to get the money they would need. There was always a way. 'Well, that sounds a fine plan to me.'

Rose still watched him carefully. 'You don't want to be a soldier no more?'

'No. I'm done.'

'Will you be happy?'

The question caught him off guard. His life had been a struggle to make something of himself and then to understand quite what he had made. He had never pursued happiness.

'Will you be happy with a farm?' Rose spoke lightly, but there was a seriousness to her tone that had not been there before.

'I could live with it.' Jack snorted as he considered the notion. He knew nothing of farming, or of working the land. Yet here he was agreeing to Rose's plan without hesitation. It made him want to laugh.

They lay together in silence. Rose's ideas began to settle in Jack's mind. A part of him still wanted to scorn such naive dreams, but despite himself he started to conjure images of the future that Rose had inspired. He could see them, far off in the distance. They were hazy and ill defined, but he knew he could make them reality. He could learn the skills he would need to become this new man, this pioneer. He had come a long way from the streets of Whitechapel. He reckoned he could go further still.

'Of course, you have to get used to doing what I tell you.' Rose broke the spell. 'I'll keep you busy.' She smiled as she saw him grimace. 'As will the children.'

'The children!'

Rose chuckled at the reaction. 'We keep doing what we've been doing, mister, and there'll be children all right.' She shook her head at his naivety.

Jack stayed silent. They were too much, these thoughts of a

new future. There were too many new notions, ones he had never considered before.

'Have I scared you?' Rose understood his lack of reply.

'A little.'

'I thought soldiers were never scared.'

'No. That's not true. Soldiers know fear better than anyone, I reckon.' Coldness crept into his reply.

'And I'm scaring you with this talk of what we could be?'

'A little.' He repeated his first answer.

Rose smiled, then laid her head back down on his chest. 'Then let's not talk of it for tonight. Let's just see what happens.'

Jack felt her settle. He lifted his hand and ran it across her temple, his fingers moving as gently as he could make them.

He knew they made an odd couple, an escaped slave and a scarred Englishman who had once been a soldier. But he had a feeling they could create a future together, one far removed from both of their former lives.

He closed his eyes and concentrated on the sensation of Rose's skin under his fingertips. He let the ideas she had stirred settle in his mind. They might have been alien concepts, yet somehow he knew they were the right ones. It was time to stop wandering. It was time to be someone else.

# Chapter Five

---

J ack woke with a start. Rose was crouched at his side, her hand on his chest. It was early, the sky still dark grey and with only the very first fiery tendrils of dawn warning of the approach of another day.

'What is it?' He wiped a hand across his face and sat up.

'Hush.' She silenced him with a hiss.

Jack stopped moving and listened, his senses firing into life. He heard it almost immediately. Somewhere not far from where they were, someone was singing.

'We need to move.' He did not wait for her reaction. Instead he pulled on his boots, then retrieved his weapons from where he had left them.

'We could stay here. They might not see us.' Rose was on her feet at his side.

'No, we have to go. Shit on a brick.' Jack hissed the oath as his fingers fumbled with the buckle on his revolver's holster. It took him two attempts to undo it. The weapon inside was primed and loaded. It had been the last thing he had done before he had let himself rest.

'Are you ready?' He twisted, scanning the ground, a last

check that nothing was left behind.

'Yes.'

'Then let's go.' There was no discussion. He grabbed her hand and hauled her after him, leading her away from the singing, plunging them into a dense patch of woodland where the ground was smothered with twisted and interwoven undergrowth. He kicked his way through as quickly as he could, careless of making noise. His only thought was to get them away.

'Look! Over there!'

The first whoops and catcalls cut through the wood. Jack barely heard them over the roar of his own breath in his ears. He felt Rose slow and pulled her after him, not caring that he might hurt her.

'No!' Rose tugged back, hauling him around. 'This way!'

'Shit!' Jack spat out the word. A moment's anger flared at her lack of obedience. 'Go on then!' He bit down the anger and urged her to move. Direction did not matter. Speed was all.

They ploughed on, Rose now in the lead, crashing through the brush, stumbling and thrashing as they fought their way forward.

'Faster!' Jack could only urge her to speed up. Every few paces he glanced over his shoulder, looking for a glimpse of their pursuers. He could hear them, the sound of their progress coming between his own gasps for breath, but he could not see them.

The ground passed with stubborn slowness under his boots. Rose was trying hard, forcing her way ahead, yet still the yards crawled past.

'Go around!' Jack shouted at her as she paused, a fallen branch blocking their way. Frustration was building. The wood was fighting them, as much their enemy as the men who would surely delight in capturing a Union officer and an escaped slave.

He saw a flash of grey behind. Their pursuers were close now.

'Stop! Shit!' The words came out as little more than sobs. 'This way now.' He pulled Rose back, half yanking her arm out of its socket as he forced her to turn, and changed direction, moving off at a right angle to their current path. It was a desperate gamble, yet he was certain it was their only hope.

He plunged into a dense thicket of greenery, tearing at the jumble of scrub, ignoring the stabs of pain as thorns and splinters ripped his hands.

'There they are!'

He heard the cries behind them. The pursuit was close now. Still he kicked on, his actions ever more frantic as he fought to get them away. Ahead he could see that the wood was less dense, the tangled undergrowth giving way to clearer ground. He redoubled his efforts, battling on, face streaked with sweat, hands running with blood.

'Fucking hell.' He swore as he kicked away a branch that blocked their way. He stumbled forward into clearer ground. And that was when he saw them.

There were dozens of men waiting in the open woodland to their front.

He staggered to a halt, hauling the breath into his lungs. The sun was higher in the sky, the first light of a new day forcing away the last inky shadows of night. He could see his pursuers clearly now. And there were too many for him to count.

He did not pause for long. The idea of giving in never once entered his mind.

'This way.'

He turned them in a new direction. He felt Rose stumble, yet still he tugged her forward, cruel in his mastery. Any pain he inflicted would be as nothing against her fate should the Confederates take them. Now that they were out in the open, he tried to get them moving faster. Yet still the ground passed beneath his boots with spiteful sluggishness. No matter how hard he strove to force the pace, it felt as if they were wading through the deepest swamp.

Shouts came from all around them. Jack saw blurs of movement in the wood behind him; shadows in grey clattering through the trees in relentless pursuit. They were almost surrounded now. Only the way ahead appeared to be clear.

He ploughed on, straining every sinew to get them away. Rose stuck with him, silent and brave even as he dragged her forward without mercy. She did not cry out, or beg him to slow. Yet he knew they were failing. No matter how hard he tried, the sound of the pursuit was getting louder with every step. There was to be no escape.

He slowed, summoning the strength for what lay ahead. It was time to change the plan.

'You have to keep going.' The instruction left Jack's lips in between gasps for air. He held Rose by both arms, making her look at him. He could see her struggling to breathe.

'What . . .' Rose tried to reply, but she was fighting for air and the rest of her words would not come.

'Shut up and listen.' Jack mastered his body and forced the words out. 'I'll create a diversion. Keep going and don't stop for anything, you hear me?'

'The hell I will.' Rose blurted the words, then sucked down a couple of breaths. 'I ain't leaving you.'

'We have no choice.' Jack had no time for a debate. He turned her around, placing her ahead of him, then pushed her hard in the back, forcing her to take the first steps away. 'Go on! Move! Now!' He bellowed the orders just as he would in battle.

'I ain't—'

'You know what they'll do to you.' Jack shouted her down, cutting off the protest and revealing his fear. 'You need to go!'

She shook her head, stubborn to the last. 'Together. We go together.'

'No!'

'If you fight, they'll kill you.' Rose fired out the words.

Jack almost hated her then. The emotion surged through him, fear for her life making him desperate. 'I don't care.' He pushed her again. 'Go!'

There was no time for more.

A Confederate soldier crashed out of the tangled greenery just a few yards away from where they stood. He staggered to a halt, his mouth opening to trumpet his discovery.

Jack's head whipped around as he heard the man arrive. There was time to stare at the unfamiliar face, to see the sweat running down the man's skin in wide streams to darken a thick, bushy beard.

'I got 'em!' The triumphant shout was loud. 'They're—'

The sentence was never finished. Jack had drawn his revolver in one smooth, practised movement. He had it levelled and covering the Confederate's face in the time it took for the man to call out his final words. Then he fired.

The bullet took the man plumb in the centre of his forehead.

Jack did not look to see the Confederate fall. He grabbed at Rose with his free hand and dragged her after him. There would be no diversion. There would be no forlorn hope to give Rose time to get away. There would just be one last desperate attempt to escape.

The pair ran like the very hounds of hell were chasing after them. There was no thought to direction, just to speed.

Jack tried to watch the men in grey who came after them. He saw little more than shadows and fleeting shapes that dogged their every step. He fought down the rage, and a building sense of frustration. He had dared to think of finding a new future. Now fate had intervened to make a mockery of such foolish thoughts.

They ran hard, twisting and dodging through the trees. Rose led them. She was quick, darting ahead, her body snaking through the gaps between the trunks. Jack followed as best he could. There was nothing left to be done save to run for their lives.

# Chapter Six

The chase ended as suddenly as it had begun.

Jack had not seen one of the Confederate soldiers cut ahead. There was no shriek of success like the first pursuer had given. Instead the man simply stepped out from behind a tree trunk, his arms wrapping around Rose and half lifting her from the ground. Rose screamed and lashed out, fighting to get free, her legs kicking at the man who held her.

Jack did not alter his pace. He ran into the struggling pair without breaking stride, knocking them from their feet. They all fell together in a jumble of thrashing arms and legs, the Confederate at the bottom of the pile. Rose landed on his chest then rolled on, her lighter frame thrown forward by the impact with Jack's heavier body.

Jack alone had been ready for the collision. Pain flared as his body thumped into the ground, and his revolver fell from his hand as his elbow connected with someone's leg, then he was up on his knees and punching at the man who had grabbed at Rose. They were wild, uncontrolled blows, but the first half-dozen all landed true. The Confederate cried out and tried to punch back, but Jack was kneeling over him, and he knocked the flailing fists aside then lashed out, smashing his own fists into the man's face.

'Get up!' he roared, urging Rose to her feet. He continued to punch down even as he shouted the order.

Rose obeyed, though she was clearly hurting. Her dress was torn, and blood snaked from one nostril, but from somewhere deep inside she found the strength to stand. As soon as she regained her balance, she clawed at Jack, pulling him upwards, dragging him off the body of the man who had grabbed her. Jack twisted, his eyes running over the ground until they found his revolver. He snatched it up and forced it into its holster.

They started to run again, stumbling on with stubborn defiance. Their breath came in great gasps and their chests heaved with exertion. They made it no more than twenty yards before they saw other men in grey waiting for them.

'Hold there!'

The command was shouted and the pair staggered to a halt, obedient in the face of the levelled weapons that pointed their way.

The trees had thinned. They were no more than a hundred yards from open grassland that might have offered them some chance of salvation. Yet it might as well have been a thousand. Grey-clad figures now stood in their path, each armed with a carbine, a shorter version of the muskets that the infantrymen used. Every weapon was aimed at either Jack or Rose.

'That's right, you Yankee whoreson. Stay right where we can see you.'

Jack tried to pick out who was shouting the commands. He failed, the sweat running down into his eyes, blurring his vision. He sucked air into his lungs, ignoring the pain in his chest, swallowing down the fear at having been caught. It was not over. Not yet.

He felt the burn of frustration. He had dared to think of a different future, one where new skills would replace the ones he had learnt on the killing fields of battle. Yet he had just been pissing into the wind. Fate would not be denied. He was not destined to become a pioneer, a farmer, a father or even a husband. He was what he had always been: an impostor in a world that did not want him to succeed.

He wanted to howl as the anger built inside him. Ahead the men moved forward slowly, covering the pair with their weapons. He watched them come, his eyes taking it all in as he started to plan. He would not get the new future he had begun to crave. But that did not mean he would accept his fate meekly.

He would do the only thing he knew how to do; the only thing that he had ever found a talent for.

He would fight.

'Don't you move a goddam muscle.' The command was shouted from somewhere to Jack's left. The voice demanded obedience.

Jack finally picked out the man giving the orders. He was a tall fellow, heavily bearded, with a wild, unkempt shock of grey-white hair, and he wore a grey jacket with heavily braided sleeves. Jack knew who it was almost immediately. It was the same Confederate officer he had seen gun down the Union prisoner the previous day.

'That's right. I'm talking to you, whoreson.'

The man walked ahead of his men. His expression showed nothing but annoyance as he stalked forward until he stood half a dozen paces in front of Jack.

'You led us a merry goddam dance there.' He turned his head and spat, as if to admit as such soured his gullet.

Jack said nothing. He glanced across at Rose, who stood to his left. She pressed against him, the closeness the only indication of her fear.

'But we got you all the same. Ain't no way you could get away from me and my boys.'

Jack ignored the gloating. He kept his eyes moving, watching the Confederate soldiers. There were at least a dozen, perhaps more, and they had spread into a wide chain, the flanks of the line pressed forward so that Jack and Rose were close to being encircled. He saw no way through. No way out. No escape.

'Ain't no way you're getting away.' The Confederate officer followed the movement of Jack's eyes and barked a short laugh laced with scorn. 'Ain't no escaping what we got planned for you.' He laughed again, his head rocking back and forth.

Jack stopped his search for a way out and stared back at the man facing him. The white-haired Confederate officer was older than he had first thought, his face lined and weathered. He was tall and lean, but it was not his frame that interested Jack most. It was his eyes. They were of such a dark brown that there was no knowing were the pupil ended and the iris began. Despite their darkness, some force lit them from within so that they glinted as they stared balefully back at Jack.

'You want to fuck me, whoreson? The last person who looked at me like that ended up on her back five minutes later screaming for all she was worth.' The Confederate officer barked his short laugh once again.

Jack ignored the filth and turned his head so that he looked at Rose. It was deliberately done, his rejection of the man's question absolute.

'Just run.' He whispered the words. They were for Rose alone.

For a moment she stared back at him, not understanding what it was he was saying. He held her gaze until he saw comprehension dawn in her eyes. Her throat moved as she swallowed down her fear. He could only wonder at her courage and admire her for it.

He summoned a thin smile of his own, then carefully eased Rose away from his side, giving himself room. Only then did he turn back to face the tall Confederate officer. He could taste the madness, feel it moving deep inside him. He welcomed it, even closing his eyes for a moment as he savoured the sensation. It would soon be time to let it have its head.

He opened his eyes. He was no fool. He knew what was surely about to happen. After all, he had witnessed the fate of the Union soldiers captured by these men. He knew them to be killers, quite without mercy. He understood that he would die here, in this forgotten wood far from his homeland. It would be a meaningless death. It would not happen in a grand battle, his life one of thousands spent to achieve some grand aim. It would arrive in a tawdry, insignificant fashion, his passing likely to be forgotten even by the men who would bring it about.

The fact did not bother him. He had always known death would come. He had stared at the great piles of bodies after Solferino and been convinced that one day it would be his twisted corpse that would be gazed on with horror by some unknown passer-by. There was no regret, no sadness that this was to be his fate. There was only the shame at not having led Rose to safety. He would go to his death thinking only of what more he could have done to save her life.

The Confederate officer had been watching him closely.

There was no expression on his face; just the stony, deadpan look of a man waiting with growing impatience.

'You done fucking around now?' The question was delivered with a sneer.

Jack said nothing. He would not accept his fate meekly, not when there was still breath in his body. He summoned the fury that he would need if he were to try to fight a way free.

'Are you dumb, is that it?' The man stepped forward, coming closer. 'You going to say something back to me, whore-son, or will that only come when I string up that bitch of yours?'

Jack bit back the words that sprang to his tongue. He concentrated on one thing and one thing alone.

'You got yourself a fine piece there. Oh yes, I can see that. You want to watch as she kicks her heels one last time?'

Still Jack said nothing. He focused everything on his right hand, which was creeping closer to the revolver on his hip. He moved it slowly, hiding the action as best he could.

'How about you, missy? You going to speak to me seeing as that dumb fucker ain't saying a goddam thing?' The Confederate officer turned his gaze to Rose. 'Where you from?'

Rose lifted her chin. 'I'm from Boston, sir. I'm a free woman.' She sensed that Jack needed her to distract the Confederate.

'Free woman!' The officer spat the words out. 'I see the mark of the whip on you, so I reckon I know just what the hell you are, and you ain't no free woman. Did this whoreson rescue you? Did he promise you your freedom if you tickled that little prick of his?'

'I work for Mr Samuel Kearney of Beacon Hill, Boston.' Rose ignored the Confederate officer's vile invective, but her voice wavered.

'Well, you're a long way from fucking Boston now, missy,' the Confederate's face twisted as he leered at Rose, 'and I don't give a fuck who you say you are. You know what happens to dumb-ass bitches like you? Dumb-ass slave bitches who run?' He gave Rose a look of complete disgust before he glanced at Jack. 'I reckon we're done talking here, don't you?'

Jack said nothing. His hand was in place. He just had to wait for his moment.

The man who would decide their fate turned his back on them.

'Hey!' Jack spoke for the first time. It felt good to say something, to take control.

'You finally found your tongue, whoreson?' The Confederate turned back, a sly sneer creeping across his face.

'What's your name?' Jack did not dwell on the number of guns pointing at him. He did not think of what would happen the moment he put his idiotic plan into motion. He just concentrated his attention on the man standing in front of him. The man he would kill.

'You're English.' For the first time the sneer was replaced by another expression on the Confederate's face.

'And you're a dead man walking.'

This time the laughter was louder. The Confederate officer's head rocked back and forth as he guffawed at Jack's belligerence. It stopped abruptly. 'My name is Major Nathan Lyle. Mark it well. It's the name you'll take with you to your fucking grave.'

Lyle turned his back on his two captives. 'Tie that fucker up, boys. Then string up the lying bitch. Whoreson here can watch her die before I put a bullet between his eyes.'

'Lyle!' Jack called the Confederate back.

The man stopped and turned, his hands resting on his hips. 'Fuck you.'

Jack said the words quietly, as if remarking on something as ordinary as the weather.

Then he drew his revolver.

# Chapter Seven

───────◆───────

Jack fired an instant after having snatched the revolver from its holster. He was quick, the weapon drawn and shot in the blink of an eye. But Lyle was quicker.

Maybe he had spotted in Jack's eyes something of what he planned. Perhaps he just saw the movement of the weapon as Jack brought it up. Whatever it was, he threw himself to one side the moment the revolver fired.

The bullet hit him as he dived, tearing into the flesh above his hip with enough force to spin him around. Blood flew, bright against the greenery of the foliage, then he hit the ground with all the grace of a sack of horseshit.

'Run!' Jack shouted at Rose, then fired again. He did not aim; he just fired and then fired once more, his only thought to create confusion with a storm of violence.

The men surrounding them reacted instantly. A few dived for cover, just as Jack had hoped. Yet enough stayed on their feet, their carbines aimed at the foolish Union officer who clearly wanted to die.

There was time for Jack to see Rose dart away, running at a gap in the line of men surrounding them, her instincts showing her the way to go. Then the first bullet hit him.

It caught him in the thigh, the impact like a mule kick. The pain came immediately, fierce and hot. Still he fired, emptying the final chambers of his revolver even as he started to fall.

He heard a man scream, at least one of his bullets striking home. A second bullet seared across his scalp, the fast-moving projectile parting his flesh like a surgeon's cutting knife. He felt blood begin to run as other bullets zipped past him, the air punched repeatedly as Lyle's men returned fire.

He tossed the empty revolver away and turned to look for Rose. He caught a glimpse of her as she darted away into the woods. Already he saw men chasing after her, but he had given her a chance. It was enough.

'Shoot him down!'

Jack twisted back around as he heard Lyle shout the command. The Confederate officer was scrabbling on the ground, one hand clasped to the rent in his side. Blood flowed freely from the wound, covering his hand and running down the side of his leg. Yet it did not look to be fatal, and already Lyle was pulling himself to his feet, his hand moving for the heavy revolver on his hip.

His men obeyed. Those still with loaded carbines blasted away at the lone figure in the blue uniform of the Union. Jack had no idea how many times he was hit. The pain came in one great wave, every fibre of his being screaming out as it lanced through him. He hit the ground hard.

The shooting stopped the moment he went down.

His vision greyed as he lay there, yet he refused to give in. Even with the agony cutting through him, he moved, forcing his body to obey. Somehow he rolled onto his side. He pulled at his sword, but his hands were covered in blood and they slipped from its hilt. He tried again. This time he drew the blade, the steel rasping out of its scabbard.

He cried out then. He could not help it. The pain was beating him.

He forced himself to his knees, the effort taking everything he had. His head lifted. He saw Lyle standing over him. The Confederate officer's face was twisted, lips pulled tight and teeth bared so that he looked more like an animal than a man.

Lyle lashed out with his boot. Jack saw it coming, but his reactions were buried beneath the mountain of agony and he could do nothing to prevent his sword from being kicked from his hand. The impact threw him down, his body unable to hold him up a moment longer.

Yet he would not lie in the dirt. Acting on little more than animal instinct, he crawled forward, his mind already failing as the agony won the battle for his soul. He heard Lyle's laughter then, the scorn washing over him as he moved one inch at a time, leaving a snail-like trail behind him, the blood that poured from him marking his path.

He could hear the sounds of weapons being loaded, the familiar noise of ramrods grating on barrels as fresh cartridges were rammed home. He knew what was to come, yet he could think of nothing else to do, so he continued to crawl, head bowed and sobs coming from him without pause.

The Confederates hooted at him, laughing and goading him like a crowd at a dog fight urging a bleeding bitch to one last effort. He let it wash over him as a single thought crystallised in his mind. Rose was running. Rose was safe.

'That's enough.' Lyle's voice cut through the storm of noise. 'Finish him.'

The laughter stopped. The men were nothing if not obedient.

Jack heard the sudden silence. He stopped, his strength failing him at last. His head hung, yet he did not fall, a final moment's defiance keeping him from lying in the dirt.

He focused everything he had left on the thought that was repeating itself over and over in his mind. He had given Rose a chance. She was running. She was still free. Then everything stopped, and there was nothing more.

Jack came out of the darkness. He cried out like a baby torn from its mother's embrace, willing the dark to take him back. Then the pain came.

It took him completely. It left no room for anything else.

He knew nothing.

He remembered nothing.

He existed only in the white-hot horror of the agony. There he stayed, his world reduced to this one torment, this living hell.

The pain faded. White became grey. Somehow he forced an eye to open. He saw nothing more than shadows. He blinked, forcing his body to obey. His sight returned. Shapes formed out of the murk. Men moved around him, boots and ankles close to his head. He fought then, forcing away the torture that pierced his soul, desperate in the face of a single thought that clawed its way free from the searing pain: Rose.

Then he saw her.

Lyle dragged her past him. He heard her cry out in fear, a sound he had never heard before. He saw her fight. She kicked out, struggling with every ounce of her strength. Yet she was powerless, Lyle simply too strong.

Jack tried to turn his head to follow her progress, but his body refused to obey. As he lay there, a wave of sickening despair washed through him. He had failed, completely and utterly.

Shouts and hoots of triumph echoed around him as Lyle's men brayed at their victory. He could make out their threats; the disgusting, vile promises of what would be done to the slave girl before she was killed. His fear and grief were echoed in the deep, guttural roars of men become beasts.

The noise subsided. He closed his eyes, shutting off his view of the world. He gave in and willed the blackness to take him. He had nothing left.

He saw faces then, his mind conjuring the images as a final torment. Rose came first, her teasing smile haunting him for a fleeting second. Then the others; the faces of the dead. Molly, the first woman he had loved, whose death had set him on his path. Tommy Smith, a redcoat who had helped him in his charade; Captain Sloames, the man whose name and life he had taken for his own. Then came Fenris and Fetherstone, two men he had come to know and despise before he had killed them. More followed. The dead crowded into his mind, jostling and pushing for the right to be seen. Knightly and Nicolson, Kearney and Rowell. Men he had come to like and admire. Men he had watched die. Finally came the faces of the others, the nameless ones. Men he had never known, but whom he had cut down in the heat of battle. They taunted him then, this army of the dead, beckoning for him to join them.

The blackness came. He felt a moment of relief.

And then nothing else.

# Chapter Eight

———◆———

'Wake up, you damn Yankee son of a bitch.'

Jack obeyed. He did not want to. He wanted the oblivion of the darkness. Yet his eyes opened without his say-so.

Noise attacked him; a storm of unintelligible words that bombarded his overwhelmed mind. Then there was light, blinding and painful.

'Come on now. Ah, there you go. That's a sight to warm a man's heart.'

The words came at Jack. They hurt him. They spoke of a life he did not want. Yet his body responded, unwilling to answer his plea to return to the nothingness.

'See, that ain't so bad, now is it.'

He felt hands on him then. They lifted his head, their touch gentle. Something hard and metallic was forced against his lips, then came water. Despite himself, he opened his mouth, savouring the rush of sensations as he felt the liquid on his tongue and in his mouth. He swallowed it down, then pushed his lips forward for more, instinct demanding that he act. He took in another mouthful, gulping it down.

'That'll do you for now.' The voice came again. 'Can't risk you puking up. Could be the death of you.' A soft peal of laughter followed.

The metallic object was pulled away. Jack whimpered then, the sound escaping him. He craved more, but the hand lowered his head, the man's mastery over him complete and cruel.

'You rest easy now. Save your strength whilst we work on you. We'll have you fixed up in no time, Yankee son of a bitch or not.'

Jack felt the hands leave him. He almost cried out, the loss of their touch more than he could bear. Instead he closed his eyes, screwing them shut. His only emotion was sadness. Sadness that he was not yet dead, that somehow his pain-racked body was clinging to a life he no longer wanted.

More than one pair of strong hands worked on him. He could not figure out what they were doing, or even what part of his flesh they touched. He felt himself pummelled and then bound. He was surrounded by many voices that blended together into a single sound, one that was constantly underscored by the cries and shrieks of others. Somewhere there was laughter, the noise wholly foreign amidst a thousand screams.

Then the pain came, a single bright lance of agony that pierced the very centre of his being. The darkness rushed back and wrapped around him like the arms of a forgotten lover. He let it take him, comfortable in its presence and grateful for its return.

Jack opened his eyes. He knew it was not the first time he had done so, yet he could not say how many times he had come out of the darkness for a moment or two before retreating gratefully back into its embrace. This time, though, was different. This time his mind came back to him. He did not welcome its return.

'Ah, there you are. I must say, it is nice to see you at long last!'

It was a different voice to the one he remembered. He sensed he was somewhere new, somewhere quieter than before, a place that did not resound to the screams of the soon-to-be-dead. He turned his head no more than a fraction of an inch. The motion set off a pounding in his skull the like of which he had never known. Yet it allowed him to see the owner of the voice.

A large black man sat on a straight-backed wooden chair not far from the end of the bed in which Jack was lying. He was powerfully built, with a wide chest, huge shoulders and a bald head shaped like a cannonball. He got to his feet as he saw Jack looking at him, and came closer.

'I was beginning to believe you weren't ever coming back to us. I prayed for you to live, I tell you that without pride. I prayed for the good Lord to give back your soul. Seems like he heard me.' His voice was soft, the tone at odds with the formidable body. 'Maybe the good Lord didn't want you just yet.' The man smiled at the notion. 'You must be thirsty.'

He turned away, moving slowly. Jack followed his progress as he walked to an iron pail near his chair. He used a wooden ladle to scoop out some water, then returned to the bed.

The ladle came close to Jack's lips. The water tasted bitter, but he gulped it down. It was gone in a moment and he lapped at the ladle, desperate for more.

'You can have more in a while. Why, I've seen a man in a state just like you drink and drink till he was fit to burst. That fellow was dead within the hour.' The man widened his eyes as he delivered the story, as if it still astonished him. 'So we'll take it easy with you.'

Jack said nothing. The water was sliding down his throat, scouring away the crud that he could feel choking him. He laid his head back, exhausted by the simple effort of drinking.

'That's it. You rest now. There's plenty of time. Ain't no use rushing, no sir, no sense at all. I ain't going nowhere. I'll be here. Sitting with you fine gentlemen and praying for you all.'

Jack let the words pass him by. He lay back, breathing slowly, taking the pain that wormed its way through every part of him. He focused on it, letting it fill his mind and using it to drive away the thoughts that he could feel simmering just beneath the surface. He dared not think. Not yet. Not until the barriers were built and the memories were locked away tight in the darkness.

He kept his eyes closed and willed the blackness to take him back.

The room was filled with sunlight. Jack had been awake many times now. Each waking had brought the man who watched over him. Each of these visits had been accompanied by another ladleful of the brackish water.

'There you are. Praise the Lord,' the now-familiar voice called out.

Jack did not move. He kept his gaze focused on the ceiling, his eyes drinking in the sight. It was unremarkable, little more than wooden joists and the floorboards of a room above, yet he picked out the details with relish. The knots and twists in the wood, the grain and patina of the planks themselves, the bent nail driven deep and the one hanging by its tip, its head rusted.

'You take it nice and easy now.'

Jack heard the soft scuff of footsteps. Then the ladle came, just as he had known it would. This time he drank slowly, letting the sips linger in his mouth before he swallowed them. He let each one slide down his gullet, feeling it all the way, the sensation sending a delicious shiver through his veins.

'Look at you, as quiet as a mouse now. Why I tell you, you're the noisiest one I've known. Every night the same, regular as clockwork.' The large man shuffled closer, then peered down at Jack.

Jack felt a stab of annoyance. The man was blocking his view of the ceiling.

'Hollering at the moon, you've been. Night after night. Not a sound during the day, no sir, not even a whisper. But at night . . .' the man paused and shook his head at the memory, 'why, mister, you make more noise than a newborn babe.'

'He kept us awake, didn't he, Samuel?' a new voice – louder, more strident – sang out. 'Kept us awake half the goddam night.'

'Yes sir, oh Lord, didn't you cry out. They musta been real bad, those nightmares of yours, real bad. You had us both kinda worried. Mr Thorne there, why he said to me, Samuel, you've got to do something for him. But there weren't nothing I could do for you, mister. There ain't nothing anyone can do for a man fighting with the devil. So we agreed to let you be. Let you sort it out for yourself. And now here you are, wide awake and looking like you ain't got a care in the world.'

Jack heard the words, yet they barely registered. He cared nothing for these men in the room with him. He cared only for the pain, for the distraction it gave him. Yet he sensed it was fading. It no longer consumed him. There was space for something infinitely worse than agony.

Rose.

He no longer looked at solid pine and rusted scraps of iron. Instead he saw her face before him with utmost clarity. She was looking directly at him, her expression blank. There was no trace of emotion on her face, no light in her eyes. It was the face of the newly dead. A mask that showed what a person had been, not what they were.

The image remained there, frozen in his mind's eye. Tormenting him.

Jack awoke to darkness. There was little light in the room save for the pale, watery glow from the moon filtering in through the single small window on the wall opposite his bed. The silence wrapped around him, perfect and calm.

He did not know how long he lay there in the dark. Time passed, he knew that, but it no longer mattered. In the quiet, still hours, he let the memories out, allowing them to fill his mind. They took him swiftly and completely, these horrors that he had stored away in the darkest recesses of his mind. He heard cries, the sobs and whimpers of a man in torment. He knew they came from his own mouth, yet he could no more control them than a half-suffocated man could hold back his gasps for air. He did not care. He was consumed by the images filling his mind's eye, the memories of all that he had lost filling his soul.

One featured above all. Rose dominated his thoughts, her face always pushing through the memories, even the foulest horrors making way for her to step forward to torment him. Over and over he replayed the memory of their last moments together. He tried to piece together the interrupted images to make sense of the fleeting shadows of memory, searching them for anything he could cling to and so ease the torture. Not knowing her fate was more than he could bear. A part of him knew she must be dead, but somewhere deep in the shadows was the faintest flicker of hope that she was still alive.

He felt the shame of allowing her to be captured. He had vowed to keep her safe and he had failed. That failure tortured him, the burden of guilt so heavy that he was sure it would never allow him to live again. Yet there was just a single thought that did not torment him; one that lit a fire strong enough to force away the blackest darkness and ignite a desire that would give him the strength to go on.

He nurtured the need for revenge and cradled it close.

'You're awake.' It was a statement, not a question.

The memories fled, returning to their cages like beasts whipped by their master. He locked them away, binding them tight in the darkness.

'How do you feel?'

For the first time, he turned his head. A man was sitting up to his right in a bed parallel to his own. Jack ignored the question, allowing his eyes to rove around the room, his mind taking in the rush of details that had thus far been of no importance. There were two identical beds opposite him. Both were empty. There was a single slit window and a closed door. A chair waited by the window, a bucket nearby in the corner, and an empty fireplace stood guard on one wall.

'I apologise, that was a foolish question.'

Jack moved his head slowly so that he could inspect the room's only other occupant. It was hard to see much in the meagre light, but he got the impression of a neatly bearded face, the man in the bed next to his well-groomed and hand-some. He was sitting straight, his back resting against a pillow turned vertical, but both arms were covered with the sheet that he had pulled up high on his chest.

'It's good to see you awake. Well, to almost see you.' The man spoke in an urbane tone, the words delivered smoothly and confidently. 'Samuel and I had begun to believe you wouldn't make it.'

Jack eased his head back and let it rest. The pain was growing the longer he stayed awake. It came from all over his body. He did not know how badly he was hurt. He had done his best to reach out through his own flesh, checking that everything was in place. As far as he could tell, he was still whole.

'I think you may just be the luckiest man I've ever met.' The man continued to fill the silence. 'I was here when they brought you in. I wasn't at my best, I know that, not with this,' he twitched his right shoulder, but kept it hidden under the sheet, 'but I saw enough to know you were nearly dead.'

He turned to look at Jack. 'Yet here you are. Still with us after all this time.' He shook his head. 'It is an astonishing thing, is it not, the human form. I saw men die with barely a scratch on them, whilst others were ripped apart, their very limbs torn away from their bodies, and yet they lived on. I wonder what sustained them. What force could be taken from some so easily, whilst in others it keeps them alive when such a thing would seem impossible. I do wonder what that is . . .' His voice trailed off, and he looked away.

They sat in silence then, each alone with their thoughts, both waiting for another day.

# Chapter Nine

---

The door to the barren room was opened shortly after the first fingers of daylight began to probe through the gloom.

'Well, bless the Lord. Look at you two. Sitting up there like a fine pair of princes.' The man who had ladled water into Jack's mouth bustled into the room. He carried an iron pail, the water inside sloshing back and forth noisily as he placed it next to the single wooden chair near the window.

'Good morning, Samuel.' Jack's companion gave a friendly greeting. He was still sitting up, his arms hidden under his sheet. He had not moved since the one-sided conversation in the night.

'Good morning, Mr Thorne, and what a joyous day this is.' Samuel looked around the room as if making an inventory of its meagre contents, then turned to Jack. 'And good morning to you, sir. I cannot tell you how long I have waited to say that to your face.'

Jack said nothing.

His silence did not deter Samuel. 'We were not sure this day would ever come, were we, Mr Thorne? I said to myself,

Samuel, maybe that man there ain't ever waking hisself up. Not ever!' He paused and moved slowly towards the bucket in the corner, his nose wrinkling ever so slightly as he contemplated its contents. 'Why, we thought you might be like poor Mr Adams, God rest his soul.' He bent down and picked up the bucket, then turned towards the door. 'He was a sweet man, wasn't he, Mr Thorne?'

'He was indeed, Samuel.' Thorne seemed content enough to listen to Samuel and give him the necessary encouragement to continue.

'He never cried out, not once, not even at the end.' Samuel smiled at the memory. He kept moving towards the door, but he was in no hurry to leave and take the contents of the bucket outside. 'Course, he was hurt real bad, worse than even the both of you. You could hear the breath a-coming and a-going out that hole in his chest, couldn't you just, Mr Thorne? It was a miracle the Lord let him live as long as he did.'

'It was indeed, Samuel.' Thorne turned to look at Jack. 'Adams had been hit in the chest. I never saw it up close, but even I knew it was a mess. Yet he shared this room with us for over a week. Can you credit that? A whole week.'

'He was a brave man.' Samuel spoke sombrely. 'At least he is with the Lord now. He'll be at peace.'

Thorne glanced at Jack, a wry look on his face, then nodded at Samuel. 'Amen.'

Samuel stopped moving, his eyes clenched tight, his free hand clasped across his breast.

Jack cared nothing for the conversation that was going on around him. Instead he focused his energy on trying to shift up the bed a little. He succeeded in moving perhaps an inch before the pain got too much and he had to stop.

'You rest easy there.' Samuel had opened his eyes and spied Jack's sly movement. 'The orderly will be around soon enough to change your dressings. Might as well stay where you are till then.'

Jack heard the sense in the words and lay still.

'There, that's better now, isn't it just?' Samuel smiled. 'You've been in the wars and no mistaking. I don't think I ever saw a man with as many scars as you have, and I tell you, I've seen some sights in my time.' His eyes widened. 'My first master, why he were a whipping man. I think that devil whipped us bloody just for the fun of it, but I still don't think any of us had as many scars on us as you do. Now, I expect you fine gentlemen will be wanting something to drink. Let me get rid of this here waste and I'll be back directly.'

Neither man said a word as Samuel left the room. He was back almost immediately, shuffling across to deposit the now emptied bucket back in its place in the corner. Noisome task complete, he walked slowly to the iron pail he had brought in earlier, scooped up a ladleful of water and brought it to Jack.

Jack drank gratefully, sucking down the cool liquid and swilling it around his mouth before swallowing. Samuel smiled widely as he saw his patient's enjoyment, revealing a fine set of tombstone teeth.

'You can drink your fill now,' he said. 'There's plenty here and I can always get more.'

Jack drank as much as he could bear. When done, he rested his head back as Samuel moved over to Thorne. He could feel the water seeping through his body, bringing it to life.

'Where am I?' His voice cracked as he asked the question;

he cleared his throat as best he could and tried again. 'Where am I?'

Samuel and Thorne shared a smile as they heard him utter his first words.

'You're English,' Samuel said. 'I told you, Mr Thorne, didn't I say he was English?'

'You did indeed, Samuel.'

Jack paid no attention to the by-play between the two, and waited in silence for his question to be answered.

'You're in Gainesville,' Thorne said. 'They brought you here a few days after the battle. I was here first, then came Adams, and then another fellow whose name I never knew. The poor man only lasted a single night. At first you were more dead than alive. You just lay there. The orderlies thought about leaving you to die, but Samuel there, he wouldn't have it. We both owe him a great debt. We were put in this room to die, you and me. He refused to let us.'

'Hush now, Mr Thorne.' Samuel was clearly embarrassed by such fulsome praise. 'I was just doing my Christian duty. It ain't right that men are left to pass like that. It just ain't right.'

'No, it's not. But I think it is how things are after a battle. Not everyone can be saved. Would you not agree, Mr . . .' Thorne's voice tailed off. He looked at Jack with a rueful smile on his face. 'Why, we have gotten ahead of ourselves. We have lain next to one another all this time, yet I do not know your name.' He leaned across towards Jack, still careful to keep the sheet pulled high up his chest. 'My name is James Thorne. I have the pleasure of being a captain in the 8th New York State Militia.'

Jack did not answer. He was not interested in polite

pleasantries. Such things were beyond him.

'And what should we call you?' Thorne pressed the matter.

Jack continued to ignore him. He was assessing his body, wondering what he could move. The worst of the pain came from his left arm and from the lower part of his ribs. As far as he could tell, the rest of him was whole.

'I would offer to shake your hand.' Thorne had not moved, but his expression had changed as Jack snubbed him. 'But such things are beyond me now.'

The odd remark made Jack turn to look at him. Thorne had pulled back the covers with his left arm. There was little left of his right. The amputation had been done just below the shoulder. The stump was wrapped in bandages.

'It hurts. Every minute of every day. I can still feel my fingers; do you not find that ever so peculiar? They've been gone all these weeks now and yet I still feel as if they are there.' Thorne watched Jack closely as he revealed the hideous wound.

'Lark. My name is Jack Lark.' Jack did not shirk from the man's gaze as he spoke. He felt no shame at seeing Thorne's wound; he had witnessed more men with shattered limbs than he could ever hope to count. Yet he still felt compelled to give his name.

'That's better, is it not, Samuel? Well, it is a pleasure to meet you, Mr Lark, a pleasure indeed.' But there was little sign of that pleasure on Thorne's face.

Jack studied the man lying to his right. Thorne spoke politely enough, but there was a shadow in his expression. As much as he tried to project an urbane facade, there were cracks in his dignified exterior. Jack knew what it was to hide one's true self away, and he was sure Thorne was doing the same.

The notion did not interest him in the slightest. Thorne had his own concerns. Jack had just one.

He lay back, conserving his strength. It was time to force his body to heal so that it could stand up to the rigours of the challenge he would set it.

## Chapter Ten

---

Jack stood at the small window and stared outside as he caught his breath. He was growing heartily sick of the view. The room looked out onto the wall of the neighbouring building, and he gazed at its white-painted cladding, picking out the patches of peeling paint that were now as familiar to him as the mould-streaked ceiling had once been in his childhood garret back in London. Sunlight played across his face, but there was no sense of savouring or enjoying its touch. Instead he turned around and began another painful, slow shuffle to the far side of the room.

'You're moving better today.'

He ignored the comment and hobbled on.

Thorne was perched on the corner of his bed. He had got dressed, a habit he had only taken to the previous week. Until then, he had spent most of his time in bed, at first fighting a fever and then just lying there, unable or unwilling to rise. Occasionally he had tried to engage Jack in conversation. The rest of the time he lay in sombre silence. Jack knew his roommate was mourning the loss of his arm, the grief etched into every pore of his face. Yet not once had he spoken of it again, his comments to Jack rooted firmly in the trivial.

Jack had dressed the first day he could stand. It still hurt to do so, his wounds paining him from the moment he awoke to the moment he finally fell asleep. Yet he refused to listen to them, and pushed himself to the bounds of his endurance, only quitting when his body failed him.

It was happening far too slowly for his liking, but he was healing. Lyle's men had been armed with percussion carbines. Had they been carrying weapons that fired Minié balls, then he would likely be dead. He had taken at least a dozen wounds, but none of the musket balls had hit with fatal force, or worse, damaged a limb so badly that he had been forced to endure the horror of amputation.

Samuel and Thorne often spoke of his good fortune. Jack had heard the talk and it had taken all of his self-control not to kill them both for the crass remarks. He was not fortunate. He was cursed with life when death would have been a blessing. That life had quickly become intolerable, so he had set himself an impossible task. He would discover Rose's fate and he would find the man who had condemned him to this living hell. He would find Major Nathan Lyle and kill him. That death would be slow and Jack would thrill with every second of it. The notion sustained him, the bitter ambition fuelling his push to return to health.

He turned and began to retrace his steps across the room.

'I simply do not understand why you are refusing to give them your parole.'

'It's not for you to understand.'

'But you're being a fool.'

Jack turned sharply at the insult. Thorne was sitting on his bed doing up the buttons of his grey uniform jacket. The process was laborious, but he refused aid, insisting that he do it one-handed or not at all. He was dressing for a reason. Samuel had told them both that a Confederate officer from General Beauregard's staff would be coming that day to speak to them about their parole. With over a thousand Union prisoners to deal with, the Confederate army was allowing the fifty or so captive officers to return home if they gave an oath that they would not bear arms until formally exchanged for an officer of equal rank. The wounded officers were to go first.

'Be careful who you call fool,' Jack snarled.

'But why, Jack? Answer me at least. Why will you not give your parole?' Thorne had his back to Jack. Perhaps that was why he continued; had he seen the expression on the Englishman's face, he would surely have fallen silent. 'Are you that desperate to fight on?'

'That's enough.' Jack's tone was glacial.

'But we can go home. Does that mean nothing to you?' Thorne paused. 'Get in there, goddam you,' he hissed at the button that stubbornly refused to slide into its hole. His voice wavered, his distress building as he failed at the simple task.

'I have no home,' Jack replied. He walked across the room until he stood in front of Thorne. He slapped the man's hand away, then deftly buttoned his jacket. His expression did not change even as he reached for the uniform's empty right sleeve, which he rolled up until it was neat and square against the stump of Thorne's arm.

'You have no one?' Thorne looked at the floor rather than at Jack's hands.

'No.'

'How about back in England?'

'No.'

'What about the lady in the photograph?'

Jack grunted by way of reply. He had suspected for a while that Samuel and Thorne had gone through his clothing. He refused to wear his uniform, instead dressing in what cast-off garments the attendant had been able to scrounge for him, and it hung from a peg near the door, the jacket cleaned and the rents in the fabric sewn up with wide, rough stitches. He did not care that they had found the image of him and Elizabeth Kearney, a woman who had once infatuated him like no other. It was a reminder of another time. Of another Jack Lark.

The moment Thorne's jacket was buttoned, Jack turned away and returned to his own side of the room. He was walking more easily now, but every step still hurt like the very devil. His chest remained bandaged, the wrapping tight enough to make breathing almost impossible. Yet he did not allow it to stop him.

'I wish I knew why you won't tell us who she is.' Thorne continued to quiz his roommate.

'I wish you would stop asking.'

'I won't,' Thorne answered with surprising force. 'There are no secrets in this room.'

'What do you mean by that?'

Thorne searched out Jack's gaze. When he found it, he held it. 'How can there be secrets between us? Every night I listen to your screams. I have heard you cry out in terror. I have listened as you have wept. Every day I see what it is costing you to carry on. You stomp back and forth like a caged animal. I see how much that hurts you.' He did not flinch from the anger that shimmered in his companion's gaze. 'You can talk if you like. I'll listen.'

Jack felt a moment's pity then. Thorne was reaching out to him. There could be friendship there, the kind only shared suffering could create. Yet he did not want it. He wanted nothing and no one.

'Block your ears if I disturb you.' His voice was cruel when he answered. 'Just as I do when you weep for your fucking arm.' He turned away, hiding his face. 'And stop asking your damn fool questions.'

Thorne looked away and did not reply. Jack had said enough.

The Confederate officer came into the room carrying a thick leather-bound ledger. He was smartly dressed in a well-cut light grey tunic with two rows of buttons down the front, paired with pale blue trousers. He wore a yellow sash around his middle underneath a thick brown belt on which there hung a holstered revolver and a small pocket knife. Three gold stripes were on his collar and an elaborate gold braid Austrian knot decorated his sleeve. The jacket's facings at cuff and collar were also yellow.

Samuel trailed dutifully in the officer's wake like an enormous shadow. Two soldiers took up station in the doorway. Both looked thoroughly bored. The pair were charged with guarding the wounded Union officer prisoners in the building and spent most of their time in the room adjoining the prisoners' meagre sitting room. Their faces had become as familiar as the view outside the bedroom window.

'Good afternoon, gentlemen. My name is Captain Pinter. I think you know why I am here. I require some details so we can prepare your paroles.' The officer spoke brusquely, as if already heartily sick of the process he had just begun. 'I'll start with you.' He walked to stand in front of Thorne, who had risen to his feet the moment the party entered the room.

'Very well.' Thorne's own reply was clipped. 'Captain James Thorne, 8th New York State Militia.'

Pinter scratched down the name. 'And you understand the terms of your parole?'

'I do.'

Pinter nodded, satisfied with the answer. 'Now you.' He frowned as he looked at Jack, then turned to Samuel. 'I take it he is an officer?' he snapped.

'Yes, sir.' The big man bowed his head. He was a good foot taller than the Confederate officer, yet he was as subservient as a whipped dog.

'So what is your name?' Pinter turned to fire the question at Jack.

'You don't need my name.' Jack straightened his spine as he answered.

Pinter looked back at him with obvious disdain. 'You're English.' He chuckled as he recognised Jack's accent. 'You sure picked the wrong side, didn't you? We got a few Englishmen with us, but I ain't never seen one fighting as a Yankee.' He shook his head at Jack's foolishness. 'So are you refusing to give your parole?'

'Yes.'

Pinter smiled at the reply, the first sign of pleasure he had shown since he entered the room. 'Well, that's just fine with me. You'll be taken from here to a detention camp. There you will be held until the war is over and you Yankees have been well and truly whipped and sent on your way.'

'Very well.' Jack stared straight back at the Confederate officer. 'I refuse to give my parole.'

Pinter laid his pencil on the open ledger he still held. 'Well, it's your decision.' He paused, looking at Jack quizzically. 'I know you.'

'You do?' Jack studied the face looking back at him. 'I don't know you.'

'You were running, isn't that right?' A wide smile spread across Pinter's face. 'You were with that black bitch. We caught you two days after the battle.'

Jack's heart stopped. 'You were there?' The words came out wrapped in iron.

'I was. Of course, you wouldn't have seen me. Why, you and the major were chatting away like old friends. Until you shot him, that is. Now that was as dumb a goddam idea as there ever was.' Pinter smirked at the memory. 'We reckoned you were dead, there being so much blood and all. But one of the boys checked and there you were, still breathing away. We were going to finish you right there and then, but the major wouldn't have it. I think he wanted you to die real slow. Looks like someone else must have found you and brought you here. The major will not be happy when I tell him. Not happy at all. Not after what that black bitch of yours did.'

'What's that you say?' Jack took a step forward. The foul words Pinter had used to describe Rose seemed at odds with his educated manner.

Pinter's face creased into a scowl. 'You want to change your tone?'

'Just tell me what fucking happened.' Jack's world had shrunk to encompass the man standing in front of him and nothing more. He took another step forward, his hands clenched into fists.

Pinter took a pace forward himself. The two men were no

more than a foot apart. 'Don't speak back to me like that, you hear me?'

'Tell me what happened to her.' Jack's voice vibrated with barely controlled emotion. The anger was there, the rage burning, but it was underscored by something else. He felt a tantalising tremble of hope. There was something in Pinter's choice of words that hinted that Rose had not been killed outright as he had feared.

Pinter searched Jack's face. He would have had to be made of stone not to see the need in Jack's eyes, the desperate hunger for an answer to a question that had been asked a thousand times. He shook his head, disgusted at whatever he found there.

'You want to know what that bitch did?' He paused, a sly smile spreading across his face. 'She died. That's what she did. She died hollering and screaming. She shrieked so goddam much she pissed herself. Went right over the major too. I tell you, he was not best pleased about that, not pleased at all.'

'You killed her?' Jack could not hold the question back. The flickering light of hope deep inside him died, leaving nothing but blackness.

'What the hell else would we do to a runaway like that?' Pinter smiled. 'The major had her strung up right there in the woods. He did a fine job of it too. It took her a while to die. A long while.' He smirked as he delivered the news, relishing the distress he saw in Jack's expression. 'God alone knows what happened to her body after that. Could still be rotting there for all I know.'

Jack's world had collapsed. For a moment, all he saw was darkness, and he closed his eyes, feeling the grief surge through him. Confirmation of Rose's fate killed any hope he had dared to nurture. He was left with just a single emotion; one as cold and hard as stone.

He opened his eyes. 'Where is he? Where's Lyle?' he demanded.

'You might want to change your tone.' Pinter slipped the ledger under his arm, leaving his hands free. He was clearly pleased with the effect his words had had.

'Just fucking tell me,' Jack snarled. His hands rose of their own accord, forming the shape they would take if they were to wrap around Pinter's throat.

Pinter saw the movement. He reacted by shoving Jack hard in the chest. 'Shut your filthy goddam mouth.'

Jack staggered backwards, his vision greying, and sat back heavily on his bed.

Pinter laughed. 'You pathetic son of a bitch.' He stepped forward. 'You should learn to curb that tongue of yours. It'll get you into a whole heap of trouble down at the detention camp. I hear they don't take kindly to Yankee scum at the best of times. A mouthy one like you, well, I reckon you'll be lucky to get out of there alive.'

Jack did not care that Pinter was mocking him. Despite the pain, he could not think of anything save the single thought that hammered away in his head. Rose was dead and he was alone.

He nurtured the desire for revenge, holding it tight as the pain took him away. It was all he had left.

## Chapter Eleven

---

Thorne stood by the window, his neck bent at an awkward angle as he tried to look past the building opposite.

'Do you think that's them?' he asked without turning away.

Jack did not answer. He was sitting in Samuel's chair, rubbing at thigh muscles that were hurting after his morning exercise. It was a week since Pinter had started the process of dealing with Thorne's parole. The Confederate powers were surprisingly efficient, and the Union officer had been told the previous evening to be ready to move the following morning.

'I think it must be.' Thorne tore himself away from the window and walked to his bed. His belongings, such as they were, had been wrapped in a sheet, and now he picked up the bundle and held it awkwardly under his left arm.

He looked across at Jack. 'Will you say goodbye at least?'

Jack glanced at the man he had shared the room with for so many weeks. 'Goodbye.'

Thorne smiled ruefully at the Englishman's emotionless tone. 'You're a cold man, Jack. As cold as stone.' He sighed. 'I hope you find what you're looking for.'

'I will.' Jack's words were matter-of-fact. 'Have you got it?'

'Yes.' The stump that was all that was left of Thorne's right arm twitched, the missing limb moving out of habit as if to pat the jacket pocket that contained Jack's letter. 'I'll see that it gets there.'

Jack nodded. He had written to Samuel Kearney, Elizabeth's father and the man who had given him his place in the Union army. There was a sum of money owed, and Jack had asked for it to be placed in his name at the Massachusetts Bank. He did not know if Kearney would act on the letter, or when he would find a way to retrieve the funds. But the boy from the rookeries of east London knew the value of money, and he would not leave a debt uncollected.

He got to his feet before the thought to move had formed and faced Thorne. 'Thank you.'

Thorne did not reply. He just looked at Jack. Then he nodded.

'Mr Thorne?'

Neither of them had noticed Samuel arrive in the doorway. Despite his size, he moved quietly. 'They're here.'

The announcement brought a half-smile to Thorne's face. 'So this is it.' He looked at the big man. 'I owe you a great debt, Samuel.'

Samuel shuffled and gazed at his feet, his discomfort obvious. 'I was just doing the Lord's work, Mr Thorne. That's all.'

'No.' Thorne spoke with authority. 'You did much more than that. I shall not forget you. When this madness is spent and the Union is restored, I shall find you and repay this debt.' He took a breath, then turned to Jack. 'I wish you well, Jack.'

Jack did not reply. He felt nothing. He stayed on his feet

and watched as Thorne turned and walked slowly from the room.

'You should be going with him, Mr Jack.' Samuel spoke in a sombre tone. Jack walked to the doorway. The room where they slept was towards the rear of the house. They were allowed only into the adjoining room, a small sitting room with one narrow window that gave even less of a view than the one from the room in which they slept. Samuel had told him that they were not the only wounded Union officers in the building. At one stage it had housed nine more. Two had died and now the other seven were joining Thorne for their long journey to an exchange. Only Jack remained.

'They told me that you'll be moved tomorrow, Mr Jack.' The big man had not shifted from his place at the door.

'Then that means I have to go tonight. Have you found out where he is yet?'

'Yes, sir.' Samuel stood tall as Jack moved away.

'Well then.' Jack turned on his heel, wincing as pain lanced down his back at the sharp movement. 'Tell me.'

'I shouldn't. I didn't keep you alive just to see you get yourself killed as soon as you could stand.'

Jack offered a tight smile. 'So long as I stay alive long enough to kill the bastard, then I'm happy.' He looked quizzically at Samuel as he noted the reaction to his grim remark. 'You really care what happens to me?'

'I do.'

'Why?'

'Because you are a good man.'

'A good man?' Jack scoffed at the description. 'I am most certainly not one of those.'

Samuel spoke in a different tone. 'I've known men with

blacker hearts than Lucifer himself. But you, you're a good man, Jack Lark, as much as you try and hide it, and the Lord needs more good men in his world if some of its wrongs are going to be put right.'

Jack could not help staring at him. 'You think that is what I'll do? Put right a wrong?'

'Maybe. Maybe you'll just die. No, most likely you'll just die,' Samuel corrected himself. 'But at least you'll try to do something to make this world a better place.'

'You don't think I am up to it?'

'I know you're not. You'll no get more than half a mile before they catch up with you.'

Jack was watching Samuel carefully. It was as if a mask had slipped aside. 'So why bother to help me?'

'Because sometimes the good Lord tells you that you have to do what you know is right, no matter that you think you're a fool for doing it.' Samuel sighed, then took a moment to compose himself before he spoke again. 'The man you are after, Major Nathan Lyle, commands a unit of cavalry that folk call Lyle's Raiders. They went out west to Tennessee. There's another army forming out there or some such thing. You'll find them around Nashville.'

'Thank you.' Jack absorbed the information. It was all he needed.

'You know you ain't fit?' Samuel forced himself to look into Jack's eyes. 'You ain't strong enough for a journey like that. It's over five hundred miles.'

'But you'll still help me?' The distance was not a concern. He did not have much, but he did have time.

'What if I say no?' Samuel disagreed with obvious difficulty. 'You shouldn't do it, Mr Jack. You ain't right.'

Jack saw that the big man's mask was firmly back in place, the earlier candid tone now hidden. He ignored the comment and moved back to the doorway, glancing into the next room. One of the two guards stood in plain sight. He had a thin, horsey face and he stared back at Jack blankly. After several long moments, Jack looked away.

'Hey, Samuel!' the guard shouted. 'Get your hulking goddam black ass outside. There ain't no need for you to be in here no more. You can go back to the barn with the rest of the damn savages. That Yankee son of a bitch can fend for himself now.'

Samuel dipped his head and shuffled towards the door, but not fast enough for the guard's liking.

'Do as I say now,' the man barked, 'before I take a whip to you.'

Jack watched as Samuel scurried away, his eyes kept low, his head bowed. He could not imagine what it would cost to be so subservient in the face of abuse from a man not fit to shovel shit from a latrine. He knew he did not have it in him to act so meekly.

He consoled himself by thinking of what was to come. His plan was simple. That night he would dress and walk out of his room. From there he would find a way outside, then make for the livery, where he would steal a horse. Samuel had told him the layout of the two buildings and the quickest way from where they now stood to where the animals were to be found.

There was no great subtlety to the escape plan. He knew it would likely involve killing. He would have to pass through the guardroom, and there were sure to be more men stationed at the livery. The idea did not bother him. He had just looked one of the men he would most likely have to kill straight in the eye, and not even that had raised a flutter of emotion.

Nothing mattered. No one mattered. Save for Major Nathan Lyle, the man who had killed Rose.

Jack waited until it had been dark for several hours. He had no pocket watch, but he sensed that enough time had passed for the night to reach the dog hours when sentries thought only of sleep.

The room was lit with a faint pale moonlight when he got to his feet and dressed swiftly in his hand-me-down civilian clothes. He barely registered the pain. He thought only on what was to be done.

The urge to cough came on suddenly. He stifled it as best he could, burying his head in the crook of his arm, fearful of the noise he was making. A rattle deep in his chest followed the cough. It had been brewing for days. Like everything else, it had to be ignored.

He scanned the room once, then moved to the doorway. He thought about taking the sheets from the bed, but he did not want to be encumbered and so left them behind. He would start his journey with nothing save his battered uniform, which he had bundled into a small canvas haversack that Samuel had liberated from one of the dead prisoners.

The sitting room was empty and he crossed it without hesitation. The door to the room where the guards lived was wide open, and he could hear the sound of at least one man snoring. He did not stop even as he slipped inside.

It was exactly as Samuel had described. A scarred pine table was pushed against one wall with a mismatched collection of spindle-backed chairs tucked underneath. There was a wide wing-backed armchair in one corner. It was old, the fabric covered with rents and gaps through which wiry strands of coarse stuffing poked. A single gas lamp stood on the table, but it had long been extinguished. The only illumination in the room came from the watery moonlight filtering in through a wide bay window.

There was one guard in the room. He was asleep in the armchair, his head thrown back so that he looked up at the ceiling, his mouth open. He snored gently, the sound rhythmic.

Jack looked at the familiar horsey face. It was the man he had stared at that afternoon. He presumed the second guard had been moved elsewhere. There was, after all, only a single Union officer to be guarded. It was a pragmatic and sensible decision, but it would cost the sleeping guard his life.

The snores stopped. The guard woke gradually, his hand lifting to wipe away the drool that had run from the corner of his mouth. It was only when he straightened his neck and saw Jack that the first alarm showed in his eyes.

Jack was on him in an instant. There was no thought, just action. The guard had done nothing more urgent than sit upright before Jack had his hands wrapped around his throat. The man fought then, arching his back, his only thought to push Jack away. But Jack was ready. He brought his knee up sharply and pushed it into the guard's lap, forcing him back into the chair, his fingers locked like claws around the man's pulsating, trembling throat.

The guard fought for his life, his fists flailing and battering at Jack without pause. Jack kept his arms locked straight and ignored the blows, which grew steadily weaker as he throttled the life out of the man. At last the guard's arms fell to his sides. Still Jack held on, long past the point of death. There could be no mistakes, not when he was one man amidst an entire enemy army.

He felt no trace of compassion as he looked into the guard's bulging, staring eyes. He had held their gaze the whole time. He had seen the shock and the fear reflected deep within them; the rush of terror as the guard finally realised that death was coming to claim him. And he had seen the last light of life wither and die.

He gasped as he finally let go, the breath escaping him involuntarily. A strange groan followed as he pushed himself away from the body, a final rush of air escaping the open mouth of the man he had throttled. Then Jack was moving, his hands flexing as he eased the pain from his aching fingers. He scanned the room, expecting to find a musket or some other weapon. Yet he could see nothing more dangerous than a small pocket knife. Clearly the guard had not anticipated the danger in his task and had not bothered to arm himself.

It did not matter. Jack moved to the door that Samuel had told him led towards the livery, just a few minutes' walk away. It was a simple enough task to unbolt it then slip outside. He did so without so much as a glance back at the man he had just killed.

# Chapter Twelve

---

The night air was chill. After so long held prisoner, it felt strange to be outside, and for a moment Jack could do nothing but stand there as he tried to adjust to the change. There was a sharp breeze and he felt the touch of its icy fingers on his skin.

For the second time, the urge to cough came over him. He held his breath and choked it down, yet still he spluttered, flinging scraps of spittle from his lips. He could feel the sheen of sweat on skin that felt too hot.

He moved away quietly. The town was near silent at this dark hour, and he walked as briskly as he could through the quiet streets. He would not skulk in the shadows. Only thieves and ne'er-do-wells tried to hide in the night, and although he was both of those things, he had learned long ago that it was better to appear to be about a less illicit purpose.

He had no idea how many Confederate soldiers were stationed in the town. Samuel had told him that most bivouacked in the fields around about, but that many officers had found lodging in the houses of Gainesville. It was their horses he was after, their mounts likely to be of a superior quality to those from any of the cavalry units in the vicinity.

He paused, another cough struggling to be free. The air rasped in his chest as he sucked down a deep breath and used it to stifle the urge. It hurt to do so, his chest protesting as he stretched it then held it tight, the pain enough to bring tears to his eyes. A single one fell from his eye, carving a path through the sweat, cool against the heat emanating from his skin.

There was nothing for it but to carry on. He could feel his senses closing in around him; he heard little save for the rasp of his own breath and the thump of his heart.

The hand that reached out from the darkness to close around his mouth took him completely by surprise. A strong arm hauled him backwards. He could do nothing but back-pedal awkwardly as he was dragged into an alley that led down the side of a sorry-looking clapboard house. His assailant said nothing as he handled Jack as easily as a father might manoeuvre a difficult toddler.

As suddenly as the hand had appeared, it left Jack's face and he was pushed back so that his spine rested against the side of the building. His first reaction was to fight, and he bunched his hands into fists and searched the darkness for his assailant's face.

'Easy there.' The familiar voice spoke softly and soothingly. 'You take it nice and easy, Jack, I ain't going to hurt you.'

'You!' Jack did not have the breath to say more. A cough burst from his lungs before he could suppress it, spewing out whilst his eyes screwed shut against the pain the spasms sent shuddering through him.

'What are you doing here, Samuel?' He finally got the question out. He took as deep a breath as he could manage and peered into the darkness.

'Helping you,' Samuel replied with a soft chuckle. 'Looks like you need it.'

'I'm fine.' Jack wiped the traces of phlegm from his lips.

'Uh huh.' There was gentle mockery in Samuel's voice. 'You're barely on your feet.'

'I'm fine.' Jack forced firmness into his voice. In truth he felt appalling. He was sweating freely and his chest felt as if it had been bound with iron bars.

'You're burning up.' Samuel reached out with the back of his hand, pressing it against Jack's forehead. There was familiarity in the touch, a reminder of the care that had been given. 'You should go back.'

Jack swallowed and shook his head. 'No.'

'You ain't up to this.'

'I'll be fine.' His breathing was settling. 'What the hell are you doing out here? Won't they punish you if they find you wandering about the damn place?'

'A lot happens after dark around these parts.' Samuel's reply was calm and even. He was clearly not concerned. 'You ever heard of the underground railroad?'

'Yes. A little.' Jack knew something of the way slaves were smuggled out of the South and into the free North and it had been the underground railroad that had helped Rose on her own journey to freedom.

'Then you'll know that plenty goes on in this part of the world that the white folks don't know about.'

Jack was aware of the change in manner that had come over the slave. There was none of the subservience he had displayed when with his white masters. He was a different man to the one Jack had become used to being around.

'You're a part of it?'

Samuel grinned, revealing his bright white teeth. 'I do what the good Lord tells me to do.'

'And he tells you to smuggle slaves to the North?' Jack stifled another cough.

'He tells me to help others.'

'Even if you have to risk your life to do it?' Jack could not hold back the question.

'If that's what it takes.' Samuel's smile disappeared. 'If you'd seen what I've seen, Jack, you'd do the same. So I help where I can. It's not much. By the time they get here, they've already come so far. I just help move them on, get them one step closer to being free. Not helping, turning a blind eye to everything that goes on, well, that's just the same as being one of them.'

'Aren't I one of them?' Jack whispered the question. He had slowed his breathing to try to avoid bringing on another bout of coughing.

'No. This ain't about white folk and black folk. It's never that simple.' Samuel spoke with obvious passion. 'The colour of a man's skin, that don't mean anything. It's what's inside that matters. A man's heart, that's what's good or evil.'

'How do you know which is which?'

'I trust what the good Lord tells me.'

'He speaks to you?' Jack could not hide his scorn.

'Not like you mean.' Samuel flashed his bright smile once more. 'I ain't no crazy man, listening to voices in my head. But I know what he wants me to do.'

'And that includes helping me?'

'It includes telling you to go back to your damn bed and forget this.'

'I can't go back.'

'Why?'

'Because this is something I have to do.'

Samuel's smile widened. 'It's the Lord. He's guiding you.'

'No.' Jack's denial was immediate. The force of the reply made him cough, and he had to bury his head in the crook of his elbow to stifle the sound.

'Call it what you will.' Samuel waited for the fit to pass before he spoke again. 'But I tell you this. I think you're doing the Lord's work.'

Jack shook his head, but he had no breath for a reply. He could see the passion burning in the larger man's eyes. He could not hope to understand it. He had been born in the shittiest rookeries of London, where life was cheap and an unmitigated struggle from the cradle to the grave. Yet even such hardship as he had experienced could not have taught him what it would be like to be a slave. He did understand one thing, though. He knew what it was to fight against fate. He saw the same desire in Samuel's eyes. The two of them could not have been more different, and yet they shared that same obsessive, hopeless desire.

'It must be hard . . .' He could feel his chest tightening again, so he paused, sipping the air until the threat of another spasm ended. 'It must be hard to play that part of yours. To be so meek. So servile.'

'It kills me.' Samuel stared at him. 'It kills me a little bit more every day, but we do what we have to do, don't we? We play the part and hide our true selves away.'

'Do we?'

'Come on, Jack. You ain't said much more than three words straight since you woke up, yet I reckon I know you as well as I know any man. I see that you hide yourself. Keep everything close.' Samuel's eyes bored into Jack's own. 'You still sure you want to go ahead with this foolishness?' He edged closer.

'Yes.' Jack forced out the word.

'Then you'll need this.' Samuel handed over a leather satchel. 'It ain't much, they don't feed us too well, but it'll see you free of hereabouts. After that, you'll have to forage for yourself.'

Jack took the satchel and pulled the strap over his head, settling the bag on his hip.

'And you can have this.'

He took the second item, a bowie knife with a blade the length of his forearm. He had seen many of the soldiers on both sides armed with knives like this. It was a popular weapon and one that he was sure he would need.

He glanced at the sky. Already the fringes were starting to lighten. It was closer to dawn than he had thought. 'I need to go.'

Samuel nodded slowly in agreement. 'Head west. Don't stop, not unless you fall out of the damn saddle.'

'I have to get a horse first.'

'It's waiting for you. Follow this alley. It's hitched at the far end.'

'You did that for me?'

'I've got to keep you alive, even if you're intent on getting yourself killed. Anyways, you didn't have a hope in hell of getting out of here by yourself.' Samuel's opinion of Jack's plan was scathing. 'You can barely stand, let alone fight.'

'You'd be surprised.' Jack's defiant reply lost its power when he was forced to stifle another bout of coughing. He thought about the guard he had throttled. Samuel was underestimating him.

'This is your last chance, Jack. The horse is waiting for you, but I can take it back as easy as I brought it here. You can still turn from this path.'

'No.' Jack wheezed as he tried to speak. He would not submit so meekly. 'I cannot go back.' He paused and met Samuel's steady gaze. 'I killed one of them.'

Samuel greeted the news with a wide smile. 'Which one?'

'Does it matter?'

'The weasel-looking one, or the one with the pox scars?'

'The weasel.' Jack made the identification as best he could.

'Then you really are doing the Lord's work, for he was an evil son of a bitch and we are well rid of his blackened soul.' Samuel's expression turned grave. 'They'll chase you for it, send men out in every direction until they find you. They won't let you ride away. Not if you killed one of their own.'

'So be it.'

'You think you've got enough strength to outride them?'

'Maybe.'

Samuel chuckled. 'I reckon you might make it. So go. And don't get caught. I don't ever want to see you again, you hear me?'

Jack nodded. 'Thank you, Samuel. I owe you.'

'You owe me nothing.' Samuel reached out and clasped Jack's shoulder. 'One day you'll have to stop running, Jack Lark. One day you'll have to stop all this and be something else. Something better. Something good.'

'But not yet.' Jack sucked down a breath and forced a grim smile onto his face. Then he lifted the heavy arm from his shoulder and began to follow the alleyway to its end.

# Chapter Thirteen

'Alarm! Alarm!'

Jack had no sooner hauled himself into the saddle than the cry went up. He had no notion of what had given him away and there was no time to ponder on it. He could only assume that the dead guard had been discovered, and now the chase was on.

He raked back his heels, kicking into motion the chestnut mare that Samuel had saddled and bridled. The animal tossed its head, fighting his unfamiliar control, and forcing him to pull hard on the reins until it did as he commanded. He gave no thought to direction and just rode, letting the animal build up speed as it powered past the clapboard houses lining the main street of the small town.

Shouts followed him. Angry voices bellowed orders as the Confederate soldiers awoke to the confusion of a prisoner making a break for freedom. Jack paid them no heed and bent low over the saddle, willing his stolen horse to gallop faster. The sound of its hooves drumming on the ground drowned out the orders to begin a pursuit, the noise settling into a regular, mesmerising rhythm.

Within the span of a few minutes they were on the outskirts of town. Jack had no real notion of where he was, so he rode west as Samuel had suggested. The mare picked up speed as it hit the smoother going of the turnpike, but Jack still kicked back his heels, forcing the animal to even greater effort. Every second counted now. The Confederates would not let him go so easily.

Forcing his body to stay in the saddle, he clattered through the first mile even as his head pounded, his skin burned and his tongue tasted metal. It took all his strength just to cling on as the horse pounded along. But it would be a long time until he could rest, and so the fever, the pain and the exhaustion would have to be ignored.

Thanks to Samuel, he had a head start. It was not much of one, but he would just have to hope that it would be enough.

Jack spotted his pursuers shortly after sunrise. He was on high ground when he saw them. The turnpike twisted this way and that as it climbed the hillside. As he rode one turn, he caught sight of the small group of riders pushing their horses hard as they chased after him.

He rode on, not once glancing behind him. He knew he could not outrun the chase, not in the condition he was in. He faced a simple decision. He could try to continue until his body failed and he fell from the saddle, or he could make a stand.

He delayed the inevitable and pushed on. Yet he knew that the fever would surely take him before the day was out. He could not afford to waste what little strength he had left in a futile attempt to flee. If he did, and his pursuers caught him, as they surely would, he would be spent. He would no longer be able to fight.

It made the decision to stop and make some sort of stand an easy one, even though he had no weapon save for the bowie knife Samuel had given him. But there was something else; a thought that had formed the moment he had seen the dust cloud on his trail. Even as he went through the thought process of what to do for the best, he knew what he would decide; had known it from the minute he left Gainesville.

He wanted to fight. He wanted the confrontation.

He needed the chance to kill.

He spurred his horse on. Samuel had picked well and Jack forced the pace, the anticipation of what was to come lending him strength. He galloped for what he guessed was two or three miles more before he found what he had been looking for.

The farmhouse was abandoned. He had seen a couple of others like it from the turnpike. He could only suppose that the men who had toiled in its fields had gone to join the war and that the lack of manpower in the local area meant that such farmsteads were left untended. Whatever the reason, he turned his horse's head, curbing its speed and letting it pick its way off the raised turnpike and down the sloping ground that led to the farm.

It was a simple enough building. The lower level was wrapped in a veranda that was overlooked by the dormer windows of the upper storey. It had once been painted white, but now the weatherboarding was grey and dulled with age.

Jack approached it, his mind already planning what was to come. He made no effort to hide his trail, simply riding through the grassy field that surrounded the house before dismounting in the dusty bare earth near the front door.

His knees nearly buckled as he hit the ground. For a

moment, all he could do was lean his head against the saddle, hoping his legs would hold him upright and that his head would stop swimming. The weakness passed and some vestige of strength returned to his limbs.

It did not take him long to remove his horse's saddle and bridle, but it needed all of his strength to haul them to the veranda, where he dumped them unceremoniously in a heap before hitching his mount to the rail. The animal needed to be brushed down and then watered before being fed, but all of that would have to be done by whoever survived the fight that was to come.

The door was bolted shut. He did not have the strength to kick it down, so he followed the veranda, his boots loud on the wooden deck. He tested the windows as he moved. He had learned much on the streets of Whitechapel and was familiar with the art of burglary. He was no Jack Sheppard, but his knowledge of the pannie had secured him funds when he had needed them most.

He found what he was looking for on the side of the house furthest from the road. The window was loose in its frame and it took no time at all to jemmy it open with the bowie knife. He took his time clambering through.

There was little of note inside. The downstairs consisted of a single great room. A large wooden fireplace dominated one flank and a stove stood in a corner, a forgotten coffee pot still on its top. The place smelled of dust and old woodsmoke.

Jack crossed the room slowly. He moved gingerly, feeling the ache deep in his bones. He did not choose a path, but instead prowled around randomly, scuffing his boots so as to disturb the dirt on the floor. He kept at it, going back and forth until there was no discernible pattern to the marks he had made on the dusty floorboards. As he walked, he found another room tucked into one corner. It was not much, just a store for possessions or produce, but he made sure to open its door a few times, then left it ajar. He wanted to make sure that the men, when they came, would see it. He wanted them searching for the threat, their attention diverted by many possible hiding places.

The stairs creaked as he went up them, the house protesting at the interloper who thumped his way upstairs. His tired, slow tread was loud in the silence of the empty building. He made sure to kick his boots around as he went up like a toddler, one step at a time. He needed to make sure that he left multiple sets of footprints in the layer of dust, obscuring his trail so that even the keenest eye would not know if he remained upstairs. His aim was to plant seeds of doubt in the minds of the men who would come seeking his death.

The landing, such as it was, ran for no more than five yards. There were three doors, all shut. He chose the middle one.

It groaned as he opened it. The room was empty save for a single iron bedstead. He dumped his knapsack and the satchel that Samuel had given him on the floor, then took up position behind the door, which he closed. It clicked shut and then there was silence.

There was nothing more to be done. There was not much to his plan. The men chasing him would see where he had stopped. They were certain to search the abandoned farmhouse.

His only advantage lay in surprise. He was sure that his pursuers would be careful and that their advance would be cautious. If he were armed, it would be dangerous for them. If he had a rifle, he might lay an ambush and shoot one or more of them down before they even reached the building. But he had nothing more dangerous than his bowie knife, so he would have to wait, biding his time and hoping that he would be lucky, and that they would split up to search the farmhouse. One man, or perhaps two, would be sent upstairs to check the upper rooms. He would take down the first man to enter the room he had chosen. His plan did not go further than that.

He waited. The house was utterly silent save for the rasp of his own breathing. The exhaustion held him tight and he leaned back against the wood of the wall, letting it support him. He could feel the heat of his skin beneath the sheen of sweat. His head felt ridiculously heavy and it was all he could do to hold it up. He leant it back, resting it against the wall.

His eyes closed and he stood in silence. He let his breathing slow, keeping it shallow so as not to stress his tortured lungs. And he waited.

Jack came around with a start. There were voices outside, loud enough to have woken him. He had not meant to sleep, but his strength was failing and his body had betrayed him. But now the wait was over and he forced his aching limbs to move as he braced himself for what was to come.

He drew the bowie knife from its sheath and listened. The men sent after him were still outside. They were noisy, their voices full of confidence. They did not care if he waited for them. They did not fear a single half-broken Yankee.

He could feel sweat on his palm as he clenched and un-clenched his fingers. The bowie knife was ridiculously light, a pathetic weapon against men surely armed with muzzle-loading rifle carbines and revolvers. Yet it was all he had. It would have to suffice.

Thumps came from the lower level as heavy boots hammered

against the solid timbers of the locked door. It opened with a crash and his pursuers rushed in. Jack could picture their movements, conjuring the scene from the noises that reached his hiding place. The men sent after him came in fast, with no subtlety in their approach. There was no need for it. They were in pursuit of a single sick man. That knowledge made them complacent.

He listened to them as they searched the ground floor. Their confident voices called to one another and he heard a peal of laughter. Boots thudded on the stairs. More than one man was coming to search the upper floor. He could not discern if there were more than two.

'Check the front room.'

The voice came clearly. It was overly loud, the sound dominating the empty spaces. Jack tensed, holding himself ready.

He heard footsteps on the wooden floorboards of the small landing. A door creaked as a room was checked.

'Nothing here.'

Then the door to the room where he waited opened a fraction of an inch.

'He's not here. We're wasting our goddam time.'

The second voice was close enough to make him flinch. The door opened fully. There was a single step, a moment's scrutiny, time for Jack to see a shadow cast into the room. Then he struck.

He whirled around the opened door, every ounce of strength driving the knife hard and fast. The man in the doorway held a carbine, but he could do nothing to defend himself. His eyes opened in shock, then the blade took him in the throat.

It was a wicked blow, cruel and precise. Jack drove the knife deep, ripping through gristle and bone with such force that the tip erupted from the back of the man's neck. His left hand rose as soon as the blade was driven home, grabbing the front of the man's jacket, tugging him forward then twisting him around so that when he fell he would land on his back.

The weight came as a shock. Jack's left arm buckled as he tried to spin the man around. He could not hold his grip and the man fell away, tumbling to the floor face down. The knife was ripped from Jack's hand, the blade trapped deep in his victim's throat.

'What the devil?'

The confused shout came from the small landing. Jack paid it no heed. He bent low, his hands moving frantically to free the carbine from beneath the dying man's chest.

Boots pounded along the landing. Jack pulled the weapon free at the same moment as a second man filled the doorway.

'Jesus Christ!'

As the new arrival took in the bloody scene, Jack aimed the carbine. His finger curled around the trigger, the action instinctive, and he fired as soon as the end of the barrel covered the face of the man now staring into the room in shock.

The bullet took the man in the mouth. At such close range it ripped through his flesh, a bright spray of blood marking its passage before it buried itself deep in the wall above the stairs.

The man tried to cry out, but his mouth filled with blood. He fell to his knees, hands scrabbling frantically at the ruin of his face. Gore smothered his fingers, shards of bone and tooth caught in the flood. He stared at Jack, eyes bright with terror.

Jack met his stare, then reversed the carbine and slammed the butt forward, smashing it into the centre of the man's face and bludgeoning him to the ground.

'What the hell is happening up there?'

The question was bellowed from the lower floor. Jack paid it no heed. He dropped the carbine, then pulled a matching weapon from the hands of his second victim. He cared nothing for the men he had attacked. The one shot in the mouth lay face down, his ruined features hidden from sight, the blow from the carbine's butt either killing him outright or rendering him unconscious. The one with the knife buried in his throat was squeaking like a hungry piglet, the noise made obscene by the gurgle of blood.

Jack ignored the sickening sounds and squatted down, the unfamiliar carbine held ready to fire.

Two men had been sent upstairs to find him. Two men were now lying in pools of their own blood. That left whoever was downstairs.

Jack hid in the shadows and waited for their next move.

# Chapter Fourteen

———◆———

'What the hell is going on up there?' the voice from downstairs repeated.

'They're dead. Both of them,' Jack barked back. He had not made a conscious decision to reply, but the words came anyway.

'Shit.' There was a pause. 'Is that you, Lark?'

Jack tried to place the voice. It was familiar.

'Who else would it be?' He fired back the sarcastic reply, then inched forward, keeping low, until he was in a position to cover the stairwell. He forced his breathing to slow, saving his strength. His chest was tight and he could feel the phlegm rattling deep in his lungs.

'Did you kill both my boys, Lark?'

Jack glanced at the two bodies, one silent, the other choking softly to death. 'I don't think they're both dead yet. You want to come up and check?'

He coughed as soon as he finished speaking. It hurt, and he felt something shift in his chest. A thick wedge of phlegm gurgled in his throat, so he coughed again and then again, freeing it and spitting it to one side.

'You're a sick man, Lark. I reckon we can just sit down here and wait you out.'

Jack had no breath for a reply. His world was shrinking around him. Sounds were harder to pick up, whilst the light was duller than before. Even remaining still was difficult. His body was shutting down. Soon he would be able to do nothing.

'You still there, Lark?' The voice came again. It was followed by the scuffle of movement.

Jack blinked away the mist that covered his eyes, fighting to stay alert. The carbine felt extraordinarily heavy and he let it rest on his knees. He could just about make out voices murmuring from the floor below. They would be plotting his death now, their plan sure to be put into action in the coming minutes.

'You want to give up, Lark? Save us the bother of killing you?'

The voice was hectoring and loud enough to cut through the pounding in his head. Finally he realised who it was: Pinter, the officer who had been so pleased to discover that Jack had refused his parole. The identification sent a frisson of something akin to pleasure surging through Jack's abused body. Pinter was one of Lyle's men. One of the murderers he had vowed to kill. The knowledge lent strength to his failing flesh and he stood up, the carbine held ready.

'What say you, Lark?' Pinter called up again. 'We can end this easy, or we can end it hard. You want to choose which one of those it is?'

Jack braced himself. He understood Pinter's game. The questions were a distraction, nothing more. There would be no easy finish.

He raised the carbine, aiming it at the stairs. He was ready. Then Pinter opened fire and all hell was let loose.

* * *

The storm of bullets came without pause. They smashed violently into the walls of the landing, one after the other, humming and zipping through the air. Jack could not help flinching away as shot after shot ripped into the walls around him.

The sound of boots scuffing on wooden floors underscored the tempest, the impact of every footfall loud and heavy as another of Pinter's men stormed up the stairs behind the covering fire. Jack moved, thinking to fire back, but a bullet ripped into the door frame near his head, showering him with splinters and forcing him back.

Still the bullets came. He could do nothing but hide away, the rate of fire forcing him back. He heard the sound of boots on the landing, but there was no chance for him to look out, the volume of covering fire simply too great.

In moments, he knew, the man rushing across the landing would attack him. It would be a desperate struggle, one that he would likely lose. He was in no state to fight hand to hand. His only hope lay in shooting before the man spotted him, but in the almost empty room there was nowhere to hide. If he remained where he was, he was doomed.

He did the only thing he could think of. Even as he heard heavy boots thumping across the landing, he threw himself to the floor, dragging the man he had bludgeoned unconscious halfway across the front of his body, hiding himself from view. He kept his arms free and aimed the carbine at the doorway.

There was a moment's pause. The firing stopped, the storm of bullets cut off abruptly. Jack heard a whimper from the man with the knife buried in his throat. Then a body loomed into the doorway, carbine held out ready to gun down anyone foolish enough to be waiting for him.

Jack spotted the flash of surprise in the man's expression as he saw no one there. There was time for him to look down at the bodies lying on the floor before Jack shot him.

The bullet took the man between the eyes. He crumpled instantly, his body collapsing. There was a final soft sigh, then he was silent.

Jack forced himself up. His head swam as he found his feet and he staggered forward like a drunk. Yet there was no time to waste. He dropped the now empty carbine and with clumsy hands grabbed at the weapon dropped by his latest attacker, scooping it up at the second attempt then stepping around the body of the man who had brought it to him.

This time he did not pause at the doorway. Instead he lurched onto the landing, moving as quickly as he could. His shoulder thumped into the wall as he turned at the head of the stairs. Then he was rushing downwards, his legs like jelly and threatening to give way at any moment.

He cried out then. It was no war cry; more the whimper of a desperate man fighting for his life.

Pinter was waiting for him, and he rushed at Jack the moment his feet left the last step. Jack saw him coming. He raised the carbine, but he was slow, his movements clumsy, and Pinter was on him before he could fire, a strange-looking rifle lashing out the moment he was close enough. The sweeping blow smashed into the barrel of Jack's carbine, knocking it from his hands.

Pinter's lips were pulled back from his teeth and he snarled like an animal. He lashed out again, using his rifle as a club. Jack saw the blow coming, but he could do nothing to get out of its way. The rifle hit him hard, the force of the blow knocking him sideways so that he staggered across the room, his feet dancing on the floorboards as they fought to keep him upright.

Pinter came at him again without pause, hammering the rifle butt at him for a third time, catching him a glancing blow on the arm and knocking him to the floor. He hit the floorboards hard, his teeth snapping together. The world turned to grey and shadows rushed forward to take him into the darkness.

Pinter was on him before he could do anything more than twist onto his back. Even as his vision faded he saw the Confederate officer loom above him. He tried to twist away, but his body was not responding. Pinter thumped down, straddling his body and crushing his chest.

Jack fought back. He could barely see, but he lashed out, battering his fists at the man beating him with such ease. Pinter sneered and swatted his arms away. He still held his rifle, and now he pressed it down, forcing it across Jack's throat.

Jack managed to get a single hand under the barrel before Pinter could stop him. He pushed up with the last of his strength, but still his throat was half crushed, and he couldn't breathe. He flailed away at Pinter with his free hand, but his fist bounced harmlessly off the man's flesh.

Frantically he scrabbled at Pinter's clothing, a final, desperate notion surging through him. Even as everything started to fade to black, the fingers on his right hand searched for the small pocket knife he vaguely remembered seeing attached to Pinter's belt.

'Time to die, you dirty son of a bitch.' Pinter leaned down with his full weight. Jack's left hand was pushing back with all his strength, but still the Confederate was choking him to death.

Jack's fingers locked on the small knife. The air was gone from his lungs and his actions were awkward, but he managed to free the weapon, and as the darkness rushed to claim him, he punched the small blade into Pinter's side.

The Confederate officer howled. Some of the pressure released from Jack's throat and he stabbed again, thrashing his body wildly as he rammed the blade home with as much force as he could muster. He kept going, the blows coming one after the other, gouging at Pinter's side.

Pinter twisted away. The rifle lifted from Jack's throat and air rushed into his tortured lungs. He gasped down a breath, fighting to stay alive, then bucked his body. It was enough to shift Pinter's weight, and so he bucked again, throwing to one side the man who had come so close to killing him.

He lurched upwards, gasping and choking down air as he moved. Pinter fell, his left side smothered in blood from the dozen or more puncture wounds. Jack went after him, sobbing and wheezing as he hauled air into his lungs.

Pinter hit the floor on his back and Jack was on him in a heartbeat. It was his turn to be on top, and he pushed his knees forward, trapping Pinter's arms. The officer's eyes widened in terror as Jack rammed the blade into his chest.

'No!'

The dreadful wail came again as Jack clasped both hands to the knife's hilt, then leaned his full weight behind it, driving it deep, twisting the blade as he thrust it home.

Pinter was babbling and whimpering now, a series of pathetic mewling noises that finished with a final drawn-out sob as the knife tore through the muscles of his heart.

Jack rolled off his corpse. He was utterly spent. He could not move, so he simply lay next to the body of the man he had just killed. He did not think on what he had done. There was no notion of triumph. No roar of victory. There was just pain.

# Chapter Fifteen

———◆———

$\mathcal{J}$ack did not know how long he lay there next to Pinter's corpse, but it was already getting dark when he finally summoned the will to rise from the bloodstained floorboards. He moved gingerly, letting his body adjust to each new position before moving to the next.

Everything hurt. Every breath burned, and his chest rattled and wheezed with each lungful of air he drew in. He knew pain. He had been wounded more times than he could recall. Yet never had he felt so bad.

The agony nearly drove him to his knees when he finally got to his feet. His legs buckled and he came close to falling. Somehow he found his balance and stood there swaying, sipping at the air and wondering how he could find the strength to move on.

He looked down at Pinter. There was enough light filtering in through the building's windows for him to see the man's staring eyes. He tried to summon an emotion at the sight. Four men had been sent after him. He had killed them all. All had been from the same Confederate unit that had hanged Rose from a tree. He tasted a morsel of revenge. It was sweet and he wanted more.

Moving like some monster from a nightmare, he crossed the room then went up the stairs, his hand pressed hard against the wall to help him balance. It took him several long minutes to reach the landing, but time no longer meant much to him and he did not try to move any quicker. He was grateful to be able to move at all.

Still in no hurry, he searched the three bodies carefully. He took a single carbine, the weapon so heavy that he had to drag its butt across the floorboards. The three corpses had little else of use save for a wooden block of lucifers and another small pocket knife. He stopped long enough to retrieve his knapsack and satchel of supplies before he started work on freeing his bowie knife. It took a while, but finally he managed to wrench it from the Confederate's throat. The man had died at some point after Jack had left the room, but he still emitted a strange groan when the knife came out of the dreadful rent in his flesh.

Jack went back downstairs with the same care and speed as he had ascended. He could not breathe well and his whole body was sheeted in sweat, even though he felt as cold as ice.

He stayed in the downstairs room only long enough to find the odd-looking rifle that Pinter had used to create the storm of covering fire. He did not bother to look at it, his mind too fuddled to contemplate the workings of the unfamiliar weapon. But despite his state, he knew he had to take it. He would need it.

Outside, the five horses hitched to the rail at the front of the house greeted him noisily. He knew they needed attention, but like everything else, it would have to wait. They would have to endure, just as he was.

He worked carefully, making sure he searched every saddlebag for anything of use. Each saddle had a canteen of water strapped to it, and he took them all, pausing long enough to drain one half dry, the warm, brackish water it contained drunk with relish. The saddlebags yielded little in the way of food; just a handful of hardtack biscuits and a pouch of dried peas. They carried more in the way of ammunition, and he took a dozen packets of cartridges for the carbine and every box of rounds he could find for Pinter's rifle, stashing it all in a single set of saddlebags.

He knew he needed to plan his next move, but his mind was empty of every thought and it took all his willpower just to stay on his feet. He did not have the strength to re-saddle his horse, so he slung the saddlebags on the back of one of the animals left by the men he had killed. He was about to unhitch it when he paused, a single thought penetrating the murk that shrouded his thinking.

Even in his befuddled state he knew this new notion made sense, yet still he baulked at it. It would take all his failing strength just to put distance between himself and the farmhouse. Yet the idea refused to die. He looked down at the bloodstained clothing he still wore. It was poor quality and fitted him badly. But it was not its shabby appearance that had given him the notion to find an alternative. He knew he would need something more if he were to succeed, something that would allow him to move around the Confederate army with freedom.

He sighed, his hands dropping the reins he had been about to untie, then turned and tottered back inside, boots dragging in the dirt, arms and legs jerking in strange, juddering movements.

The house smelt of death. He plodded his way to where Pinter lay staring at the wooden ceiling. Blood still oozed from the wide tear in his flesh, but it did not stop Jack from stooping low and beginning to strip the corpse of its uniform.

It took a while, but eventually he freed the officer's jacket. He did not try to remove the blood that stained it; that could wait. The boots and trousers took longer to liberate, but he stuck to the task.

He took his time going outside for a second time. Every step was a trial now, his body begging him to stop. When he finally reached the horse he had chosen to take, he was swaying on his feet. Clumsy fingers took an age to unhitch the animal, and he nearly fell when the beast, finally freed, tossed its head.

He turned and began to trudge away from the farmhouse, leading the horse, Pinter's uniform bundled awkwardly under one arm. A bloodied grey jacket was not much of a disguise, but he knew the power of the insignia of rank. It would not be the first time he had masqueraded as an officer, and the idea of doing so again pleased him far more than it should. He was going back to a role he knew well, one that would help him on his self-imposed mission.

As he ground out the painful steps, he thought only of the moment when he would find Lyle and kill him. It was a good image, the kind that could sustain a man when he was fit to drop. He pictured Lyle at his mercy, the moment of the man's death at hand. His lips moved as he trudged on, repeating a single word over and over. Lyle would die with Rose's name in his ears. It would be the last thing he heard in this life, and Jack could only hope it would be the first he heard when he descended into the next.

The fire caught and Jack finally lay back, a soft groan escaping his lips as he let his head rest on the warm earth. He had no idea how long he had travelled that particular day. Time had passed, he knew that much, but he had barely any sense of it.

After the fight with Pinter, he had paid little attention to anything much at all, his faculties shutting down as the sickness held him in its remorseless grip.

He did know he had headed west. The days had blurred together so that he could no longer tally how long it had been since he had left behind the bodies of the four men sent to capture him. For much of the time he had been going steadily uphill, his days spent moving up slopes covered with thick swathes of woodland. He had passed well clear of the few remote farmsteads he had seen along the way, skirting away from the people who lived there. He had ridden on, barely aware of his surroundings, a single, fleeting glimpse of a white-tailed deer his only connection to another living being. He had paused to let his horse take a short rest or to allow them both to drink from the creeks that flowed downhill. Otherwise he kept moving, stopping only when it became too dark to see a way ahead.

That day he had halted when he had found himself in a clearing. It was no more than a dozen yards wide, but it offered enough room for him to build a simple fire that he could lie beside, and that was good enough.

It had taken an age to start the fire. A torn cartridge had finally got the meagre scraps of wood to burn, but he knew they would not last very long. His care of his stolen mount was as cursory as his fire-building. He had managed to remove the saddle and the tackle, but anything more was beyond him. The horse would suffer, but at that moment Jack could do nothing more than lie down and finally let his tormented body rest.

Yet even in his sickened state, he could not find the oblivion he craved. For a reason he did not understand, he could not close his eyes. Instead he stared up at the canopy of trees as if in some sort of trance, his eyes wide open yet not really seeing anything at all.

He coughed, the spasm feeling like it was tearing something important deep in his lungs. He sipped at the air when the bout had passed, pulling it in carefully lest it cause another painful attack. He knew that he had a fever. His skin tingled, and he was cold yet somehow still layered in sweat. He shivered, despite the heat generated by the fast-burning fire at his side.

He wondered if he would die should his eyes close. The notion bothered him. He did not fear death; it was too familiar to alarm him. In many ways he would welcome its arrival. It would, at the very least, release him from the torment of his abused and battered flesh.

Yet the idea of dying irked him. He was not ready to go. There was too much still to be done. The thought of death brought Lyle's face into his mind's eye. He could see the man with utmost clarity despite the short nature of their bitter acquaintance. Every detail was clear and Jack was certain he would recognise him no matter how long it took to track him down.

The thought settled. He would find Lyle. The man would be brought to account for killing Rose.

He tried to conjure a picture of Rose to replace that of the Confederate officer, but no matter how hard he tried, he could not form anything more than a fleeting image of her, the detail of her features somehow lost to him in the weeks since her death. He focused on her eyes, trying to recreate the fire that burned deep inside them and which had captivated him from the start. He failed, her face shrouded in a mist that he could not burn away no matter how hard he tried.

He hated himself then. Perhaps this was fate's way of telling him that his quest was destined to fail. He had not known Rose for long. Perhaps it was idiotic to feel such attachment to her. He could hear fate mocking him for the choices he was making, the laughter as clear as the crackle of burning wood. And he knew why he was being treated so piteously.

For underneath it all was a single uncomfortable and bitter truth. He was not searching for Lyle to avenge Rose, or to bring justice to a world that would never care. He was hunting him down simply for the purpose it gave to his own life. For without that, he had nothing. Without Rose, he had no one.

Frustrated and angry, he forced his thoughts towards forming some sort of a plan for the days ahead. The little food he had left would not last long. He had some vague idea of dressing in the Confederate officer's uniform that he had stashed deep in his saddlebags and attempting to buy supplies with the money he had found in one of Pinter's pockets. Yet to do that, he would need some kind of plausible cover story, and he had failed to conjure even a single coherent notion of what that could be, his mind unable to maintain any sort of concentration. So he just lay there and stared at nothing, refusing to acknowledge the images that flooded into his mind, until, finally, his eyes closed.

# Chapter Sixteen

———◆———

*J*ack awoke with a start.

'Whoa, lie easy there, boy. Don't you move a single goddam muscle.'

He blinked hard, forcing his eyes to focus. It took several long moments for him to recognise what was in front of him. The barrel of a gun was no more than an inch from his nose.

'So who the hell might you be, boy? And what in the name of all that is goddam holy are you doing on my land?'

Jack could see little of the man behind the gun. He got the impression of a thin patch of grey hair above a scruffy beard. The man's jaw worked from side to side like a cow chewing the cud, juddering and jerking as it moved.

'Are you deaf, boy?' The barrel of the gun jerked. 'Answer my goddam question, or so help me God, I'll put a bullet right between your goddam eyes.'

'No.'

Jack's lips were gummed together and his mouth was dry, and the word came out as a croak. It did little to appease the gun-wielding greybeard, who turned his head and spat out a great jet of dark liquid.

'Shit.'

The word was followed by another copious spurt from the mouth. Jack could smell the man, tobacco and gun oil underscored by the earthy odour of sweat.

'Well, I reckon I found myself a goddam shit-weasel.' The man contemplated Jack as what few teeth he had left worked on whatever was in his mouth. He seemed to be considering whether he was worth a bullet. 'Is that what you are, son? A goddam shit-weasel?'

Jack closed his eyes. The world was shimmering and turning grey, and he could feel his heart thumping in time with the pounding in his head. Talking was too much of an effort, so he stayed silent. Part of him willed the grubby greybeard to shoot him where he lay and so end the agony.

'Come on then, weasel. You get yourself up on your feet and let's see what you're about.'

The man eased up from his haunches, still covering Jack with his musket. Jack opened a single eye. He did not know if he could obey.

'Come on now.' The command was punctuated with another stream of spittle. 'Get yourself on up.'

Jack summoned the strength. The pain had sunk deep into his bones, but he began to lever himself upright. Standing took nigh on a full minute, and the greybeard watched him the whole time, his only comment another couple of mouthfuls of black juice that he expelled with casual ease.

'You're as sorry a son of a bitch as ever I saw.' The man contemplated Jack as he finally found his feet. Jack was a good foot taller, but if the greybeard felt a single ounce of concern, then no trace of it showed in the expression on his ancient, weathered face.

Jack found he could not stand still. He tottered from side to side, as if swaying in the breeze. The wood around him had taken on an unearthly quality. Nothing felt real. Not even the shudders that racked his body or the white-hot pinches that rippled up and down his skin.

'You got yourself a fine horse there, weasel.' The old man nodded his head at Jack's mount, which whinnied on cue. 'It looks like an army beast to me. Only those sons of bitches have saddles as fine as that one.' He watched Jack the whole time. 'Well, you know, I reckon I got me a deserter here. Is that what you are, weasel, a goddam yellow-bellied runner? Why, I reckon if you are, then I'll get myself a fine reward if I turn you in. Even if it is paid in those rat-shit Confederate dollars of theirs.'

Jack heard the danger in the old man's words. He knew nothing of the Confederate army, but he was sure they would not tolerate desertion. No army did. Getting himself hauled back to the nearest Confederate outpost would do him no good at all, not with the posse of cavalry that had been sent after him lying dead in a forgotten farmhouse.

The old man watched him for several long moments before he spoke again. 'Does that worry you, weasel? I reckon it does, seeing as how you just looked like you took a great big shit in your goddam pants.' Another thick spurt of juice was ejected from the old man's mouth. Something had clearly unsettled him, however, as for the first time, he voided the foul liquid poorly, and a thick stream of it ran down his chin. He lifted a hand from his gun to wipe the excess juice away.

And that was when Jack struck.

The notion to fight back had not fully formed in his mind before he lunged forward. Even in his sickened state he could see that the gun in the old man's hands was an ancient flintlock musket that was likely to be as reliable as a priest in a whorehouse. He grabbed the barrel and pulled it hard, thinking to rip it away from the man, yet his hands slipped and his fingers were powerless to maintain their grip.

The old man laughed, and tugged the musket out of Jack's clutches. 'You sorry son of a bitch,' he mocked, then guffawed at the sight of Jack lurching forward as if he were about to try again. 'So be it, shit-weasel.' He twisted the weapon, bringing the butt around so that it faced Jack. 'You want to do it this way, then who am I to say no?'

Jack knew what was coming, but he could do nothing as the rifle butt was hammered forward. Pain flared, as hard as nails and brutal in its ferocity, as the butt slammed into the centre of his chest.

He was unconscious before he hit the ground.

For the second time that day, Jack opened his eyes to see the barrel of a gun hovering menacingly in front of his face.

'Well, that sure took you long enough.' The old man was sitting on the ground, the musket held out with the butt resting on the ground. 'Now we can do this two ways, boy. You do as I say and I'll go easy on you. Try anything fancy again and so help me I'll beat your sorry ass black and blue. Now,' he looked at Jack with hard pale blue eyes, 'you want to choose which one of those it's going to be?'

Jack hauled a breath into his lungs, wincing at the pain it caused. He was as weak as a kitten and he knew the old man could beat him without breaking sweat. As much as it stung his pride, he could not fight. He was powerless.

'All right.' He forced the words out. 'You'll have to help me.'

'Now, boy, that ain't how this goes. Either you get yourself up onto your own two goddam feet, or I'll let you lie right where you are and leave you there to rot. You're a sick man, in case you hadn't noticed, and I ain't going to get any closer to you than I have to.'

The greybeard lumbered to his feet. 'Let me tell you what's going to happen. You're going to stand nice and still whilst I bind your arms. Then we are going to head over thataways. The nearest soldiers are a couple of dozen miles from here, and I know for sure that you ain't fit enough to walk even one of those goddam miles. So we're going to go someplace where you can rest up awhiles until you're well enough for me to turn you in.'

Jack listened to the instructions in silence. There was a moment's relief that he was not going to be handed over right there and then. The old man was a fool. He was gifting Jack the one thing he needed more than anything else. Time.

'All right.' The words rasped as he uttered them.

'Glad to hear you're seeing sense, weasel. But I warn you. You try to grab this here musket one more time and I'll ram it right down your goddam throat. You get me, boy?'

'Yes.' Jack hauled another painful breath deep into his tortured lungs, then gingerly started to rise. Once he was on his feet, he stood docile and compliant as his arms were bound behind his back.

Only when the old man was finished did he speak again.

'Now then, boy. It's time for me and you to take a little walk. You give me any shit and I swear I'll knock you down. You get me?'

Jack felt the burn of the rope on the skin of his wrists. He was bound tight. 'Yes. I get you.'

'Good.' The word was followed by a mouthful of the black liquid. 'Perhaps you ain't quite as dumb as you look.'

Jack heard the greybeard moving behind him. His horse snorted as the old man untied its reins from where Jack had lashed them around a tree trunk.

'Go on then, weasel. Start walking. Take it nice and easy and go where I tell you. Do anything else and you get a musket ball up your ass. You got that?'

'Yes.' Jack sucked down a breath and lumbered into motion. He had no strength to do anything but what he was told.

# Chapter Seventeen

---

The homestead was a mean, higgledy-piggledy sort of place. Not that Jack cared. Every step was a trial. He had no idea how long he had laboured along, or how he had done so for so long. He existed in a world shrouded in fog, his senses dulled to the extent that he no longer knew where he was. There was just the misery of existing, his fever-racked body in a state of constant torment.

His eyes took in the main cabin as he staggered out from the trees and into the level clearing in which it was situated. It was made from rough-hewn logs, with a single tiny window hacked clumsily into each flank. The two short sides of the building supported haphazard lean-tos that looked just about ready to fall over. All manner of things littered the ground around it, from a broken-down cart with spokeless wheels, to a number of splintered and cracked wooden barrels, most of which were filled with dark, scummy water. A hundred tree stumps surrounded the building, the evidence of the area being widened and reclaimed from the wood around it, and an enormous pile of logs had been dumped into one jumbled heap no more than four or five paces from what looked to be the cabin's only entrance. There were two further buildings, both as ramshackle as the main one. As far as Jack could tell, one was a stable, the other some sort of food store.

'Whoa there, weasel.' The grey-bearded man called Jack to a halt, the first words either of them had spoken in a long while.

Jack did his best. His body still moved, his feet making small shuffling steps on the ground as if his legs had not comprehended the command to stop walking. His head spun and he felt his muscles trembling. He did not know how much longer he could stand.

'What you caught yourself there, Pa?'

A new voice entered Jack's small world. It was a woman's voice, a reminder that there was life outside his own personal hell.

'I found him near the ferry road. I reckon I got me a deserter.'

'You think that's a soldier, Pa?' The voice came closer. 'I don't see how we think we can whip them Yankees if our boys are all like that. Why, he looks fit to drop.'

'He's sick.' The greybeard spat onto the ground. 'And he's your responsibility now, girl. I can't turn him in like that.'

'What am I supposed to do with him?'

'How the hell should I know?' Another stream of juice splattered onto the ground. 'Just keep the shit-weasel alive. Soon as he can walk, I'll take him in.'

'It's a shit-weasel, is it, Pa? I ain't seen one of those before.' The woman's voice mocked her father's words. 'You going to skin it, then?'

'Mind your tongue, girl. But I'll skin him if I have to. I reckon there'll be folk as say I should. Man like that should be fighting them Yankees just like your John is, not running around the woods. Now you do as you're damn well told, girl. I don't want none of your back-chatting, you hear me?'

'Yes, Pa.' The reply came obediently.

Jack barely listened to the exchange. He did not care about what was said. He thought only of how long it would be before he could lie down. He had nothing left.

A woman's face came into view. She was much shorter than he was, shorter even than her father. Jack got the impression of a narrow, pinched face with hair scraped back into a purposeful ponytail. She wore a homespun dress made from heavy grey cloth pulled tight around the waist, with long sleeves and a skirt that dragged along the ground. She was old enough to have fine lines around her blue eyes, but she had a slim, lithe figure that might have sparked a flare of interest in his mind were he not struggling to stay on his feet.

'What's wrong with him, Pa?'

'How the hell should I know, girl?'

'Is he shot?'

'Not by me.'

The woman stood in front of Jack and peered at him. 'You got a tongue in that there head of yours, mister?'

'He don't say much.' Her father answered for Jack.

'Hush a minute, I'm talking to him.'

'Don't you go feeling pity for the boy, Martha. I plan to get rid of the son of a bitch just as soon as he can walk.'

'Looks to me like that might be a whiles.' Martha was looking Jack directly in the eye. 'You caught yourself a sorry-looking creature there, Pa. Why, he's more scarred than our old table.'

Jack held her gaze. He could feel the world closing in around him. She was close enough for him to smell her. There was the hint of soap under woodsmoke. It was a good smell, clean and wholesome.

'Why, you're as broken-down and sorry a son of a gun as I ever saw, mister.' Martha put her hands on her hips and shook her head as she looked Jack over.

Jack felt the blackness rushing towards him. The last thing he saw was a pair of blue eyes, then oblivion claimed him and he fell face down into the dirt.

Jack awoke in almost perfect comfort. The bed he was in was soft and smelt of soap powder. He lay on his back, his head nestled into pillows, though his right arm was held at an awkward angle above his head. He was naked – the brush of the sheets against his skin told him that – but he felt better than he had for a long time. Although his body still ached, it was a dull, distant pain, one that could almost be ignored. He was hot, but his skin no longer burned as it had when he had walked through the wood with a musket barrel at his back. The change in his fortune was enough to give him hope.

He tried to move, but his right arm prevented him from doing so. It took a moment for him to realise that his wrist was bound to the bedstead with a thick wrap of rough old rope. He took a deep breath and wriggled up the bed as best he could, until he was sitting upright.

The room he was in was not large. The walls were made of rough planks of pine, devoid of all decoration. There was a stove in one corner and a table with four chairs tucked neatly underneath. Two moth-eaten brown armchairs faced the open wood fire, with a fat log placed in front of each. A simple dresser completed the mismatched collection of furniture, its shelves crowded with household objects from stacked plates to pans and dishes. The room was simple, clean and tidy.

There were two doors. One led outside, the other to what he supposed had to be a second, inner room that encompassed the far end of the cabin. Light filtered in through two small rectangular windows, but it was not enough to brighten the dull interior.

The outer door opened and the woman he remembered from his arrival walked in, her arms laden with wood cut ready for burning in the stove.

'You're awake,' she observed as she kicked the door shut behind her.

Jack said nothing. He studied her as she walked, her quick, purposeful bustle taking her across the room at a rapid pace. There was not a lot to see, her figure well hidden underneath a heavy brown shawl.

'You back with us now, mister?' The question was fired at him even though she faced the other way as she stacked the wood into a basket near the stove. She only paused when there was no reply to her question.

'You don't say much, do you now? You've been lying in that there bed for two whole days now. Most of that time we couldn't stop you from hollering and crying. Now you're finally awake and you ain't got a thing to say to the world.'

Jack absorbed the news, accepting it and storing it away. Later, he would try to make sense of all that had happened.

Wood deposited, the woman turned and walked towards him, her arms wrapping the shawl tighter around her, as if it were some form of protection from the stranger in her home. Yet wary or not, she still came to perch on the side of the bed, her hand reaching out to touch his forehead.

'You're still damn hot.' She shook her head as if disappointed with the discovery. 'Though not as bad as you were, mind. Why, when you first arrived, I could've fried an egg on your forehead.' She smiled at the idea. 'You thirsty?'

Jack nodded but said nothing. He too felt wary. He was powerless as he was, naked and bound. He found the notion almost amusing. He was also weak as a newborn. The woman could beat him with her hair comb.

She sat looking at him for a long moment before getting back to her feet and going to the table, where a large enamel jug stood. The sound of water being poured was overly loud in the silent room.

Jack watched her. Her shawl had slipped, revealing a lean body clad in the same dress he recalled her wearing when he arrived. There was little meat on her bones, but he could make out enough to know that there was an attractive woman hidden beneath the simple clothing. His scrutiny stopped as she turned and came back towards him, but she had seen him watching her and her expression was guarded as she approached.

'This ain't your first time in a sickbed, is it?' she asked as she sat on the edge of the bed again, then offered him the mug of water, holding it out handle first so that he could take it in his free left hand. 'I seen all those scars of yours,' she added in a conspiratorial tone, then smiled at something she read in his expression. 'Don't you worry none. You ain't the first man I've seen.'

Jack did his best not to squirm. Her remarks made him uncomfortable, so he drained the mug of water, savouring the sweetness as it unglued his mouth.

'I'm an old married woman. You ain't got nothing that I ain't seen before. Except all those scars of yours. Why, I sure ain't seen nothing like them. Not ever.'

She was looking him dead in the eye, and her gaze unsettled him. Her pale blue eyes showed no trace of anxiety as she sat next to a man her father believed to be a deserter. She wasn't a great beauty, her face too narrow and her eyes too close together for that. Yet she was capable and clearly able to look after herself. Something in her competent manner and her simple, clean appearance was appealing.

'So you ain't going to say nothing to me at all, mister? I've waited a long time for you to wake up. Least you can do is pass the time of day with me.' Her eyes narrowed as she rebuked him, but there was a hint of a smile on her lips.

'What would you have me say?' The words felt odd as he spoke them. It had been a while since he had said anything much at all.

She smiled as he finally broke his silence. It sat well on her face. 'Well, that's better. Let's start at the beginning. What's your name?'

'Jack.'

Her smile broadened. 'That's a fine name. It suits you. So let's do this proper. My name is Martha Joseph, and that grumbling son of a gun you sometimes see around the place is Garrison Garnet, my father.' She paused to stifle a giggle. 'How odd this is. You've been lying there all this time and we never knew your given name.'

'I'm sorry.'

'There ain't nothing to apologise for. You're sick and it's our Christian duty to take care of you, seeing as how it was that father of mine that found you. That's just how it's meant to be.' Her brow furrowed. 'But where are you from, Jack? You don't sound like anyone I ever spoke to before.'

'London.'

'London! London, as in England?' Martha's eyes widened. Jack nodded.

'Well, I never be. I ain't never met someone from England before. Then again, truth is, I ain't never really met that many people from anywhere before.' Her hand lifted to tuck a few errant hairs behind her ear. Her brown hair was still pulled back behind her head, yet enough had escaped the tie holding it there to whisper around her face. 'So what in the name of the devil are you doing fighting for them Yankees?'

Jack frowned. He remembered that Martha's father had believed him to be a deserter from the Confederate army. Clearly that opinion had changed.

'Why do you think I'm a Yankee?'

'We found that photograph of yours. Of you in a Yankee uniform with a girl at your side.' Martha looked away, a slight shadow of crimson appearing on her cheeks. 'Oh, don't you worry none. We didn't go through your things or nothing. But that picture, well, it just kinda slipped out.' She paused and glanced over at Jack. 'She sure is pretty. Is she your girl?'

'No.'

'But I bet you want her to be. She's one of the most beautiful people I ever saw.'

'Yes. She is.' Jack sighed. 'She isn't mine.'

Martha's smile widened at the news. 'You sound sad. She turn you down?'

'No.'

'Uh huh.' She shook her head at the firm denial. She clearly understood that he was not telling her the whole truth. 'Well, I can't sit here lollygagging with you all day. I got work to do and Pa will create if I don't get everything done just the way he likes it.' She paused, then reached out to pat Jack's arm, the one bound to the bedpost. 'I'll ask him to untie you. You ain't about to kill us in our beds, are you now, Jack?'

She smiled, then got to her feet before bustling back over to the far corner. Jack said nothing. Yet her words lingered. He would recover his strength and then he would run. He wondered if that would mean fighting the two people who had brought him back to health. Martha saw no danger in him, but he knew she was wrong to trust him so easily. He would let nothing stand in his way. As soon as he was strong enough, he would leave. And he would kill anyone who tried to stop him.

He felt the coldness creep into his being. It was a reminder of who he was now, and of the task he had set himself.

# Chapter Eighteen

---

Morning sunlight streamed through the window behind Jack's bed. It was cold in the cabin, but warm enough under the blankets piled on top of him, so he stayed still, enjoying the play of the sunlight as it wandered across his face. He forced his mind not to think, but to savour the moment, to try to seek pleasure in his world of darkness.

He was recovering. It was a slow process and he chafed at his incarceration. At least he was no longer bound to the bed. Martha had been true to her word and her father had untied him the very same day. It had been an unnecessary precaution. He had been weak from the sickness, and that sickness had lingered, stealing his strength so that he was able to do little more than eat and drink, and even those two simple tasks exhausted him. The short stagger to a chamber pot took all he had, and so, even now, several weeks after he had been brought to the cabin in the woods, he still could not make it across the room.

A cloud shut off the beam of sunlight. Jack became aware of someone else's presence in the room.

He opened his eyes to see Martha's father, Garrison,

sprawled in one of the armchairs, his musket across his lap. He was dressed in dark blue overalls and a checked shirt that gaped open at the neck. On his feet were heavy boots, the kind that would last a man a lifetime if they were looked after right.

Jack had seen little of the man since he had arrived. There had been short intervals when Martha and her father had eaten at the table, and even shorter ones when Garrison had stomped across the room before disappearing into the cabin's bedroom, where he and Martha slept. Otherwise he spent his time outside. Sometimes Jack heard him at work, the never-ending need for fuel keeping the old man chopping wood for hours at a time. At other times he left the farmstead completely. Jack did not know where he went, or what he did.

Now the old man had chosen to come inside. He sat opposite Jack, his eyes riveted on him. Jack pushed himself up the bed until he was sitting, and the two men stared at one another, neither keen to be the first to break the silence. Garrison chewed incessantly, his mouth working back and forth in the same odd, juddering motion Jack remembered from the very first moment the pair had met.

Time passed, the silence growing ever more uncomfortable with each passing minute. It was only broken when the old man sat forward and aimed a stream of brown juice at a spittoon placed near his chair. Some missed, the grim liquid splattering noisily across the pine floorboards.

'Hellfire.' The comment was growled softly as he pushed himself to his feet, shuffled to the spillage and mopped it up with a grubby handkerchief produced from a pocket in his overalls.

'She creates,' he spoke whilst moving back to his chair, 'if I make a mess in here.' He sat down with a huff. 'Her mother was the same, God rest her soul. Women like things tidy, don't they just.' He looked across at Jack, a moment's embarrassment on his face. 'You comfy in there?' The question was delivered in a gruff tone.

Jack nodded. 'Yes.' He sensed disapproval.

'I figured. You've been lying there long enough.'

'You want me out?' Jack saw no point in beating around the bush.

'You fit?'

'Maybe.'

'Then you can get up.' The old man's eyes wandered to a deep set of gouges on the pine floorboards. They led from the door of the bedroom to the feet of Jack's bed frame. 'Then we can put that there thing back where it belongs and I'll have someplace to sleep at night.'

'This is your bed?'

'Whose did you think it was?' The reply was snapped. 'You think we're sitting here with a dozen spare goddam bed frames around the place?' He shook his head. 'Damn fool Yankees.'

The last comment was delivered under the old man's breath, but Jack heard it well enough, just as he figured he was meant to.

'I didn't know.'

'Well, you know now.' The old man stared at him belligerently, chewing all the time. 'So are you malingering, weasel? Lying in my goddam bed whilst my daughter fusses over you like a mother hen?'

'No.' Jack denied the accusation, but it stung. He worried that there was an element of truth in it. He had never been idle for so long. Perhaps he had been hiding by lying there when he could have forced himself into activity.

'She's a good girl, my Martha. It's easy to take advantage of a girl like that, one with a good Christian heart in her and all. Her husband,' the old man's mouth twisted as he used the title, 'he sits there like some kind of goddam emperor or something whilst she fetches and carries for him. I reckon you young 'uns are all the same now. Wouldn't know an honest day's work if it jumped up and bit you in the goddam ball sack.'

The old man considered Jack for a long moment, then shook his head. 'Oh, don't get me wrong. Martha married well. John Joseph is a good man. Good enough anyways to be off fighting you Yankee sons of bitches.'

'You think I'm a Yankee?' Jack recalled Martha telling him the same. They had not spoken of it again, their conversations since solely concerned with his health.

'I know so. We found that fancy-ass photograph or whatever it's damn well called. You standing there in your goddam Yankee uniform with some New York filly at your side.'

Jack nodded. 'It's true. I fought for the Union.'

'At the battle over Manassas way?'

Jack nodded.

'Our boys sure whipped your butts that day, didn't they, weasel?' For the first time, a tone of something other than disapproval left the old man's mouth. 'Bet you thought they would run at the sight of you all. You didn't think we'd fight like that, no sir; I bet you thought it'd be easy.' He paused, then looked at Jack knowingly. 'That when you ran, weasel?'

Jack held the man's gaze. The Union army had been broken. He could have left the field of battle with his regiment, battered and bloodied though it was. He had chosen instead to take a different path, one that had ultimately led to a quiet wood and the hanging of a runaway slave. Just a touch of that bitter memory was enough to ignite a flame of anger.

'You want me up?' He fired the words out. 'You want to turn me in?'

'If you're fit.' The old man did not flinch from the anger in Jack's voice. He stared back without a qualm. 'Winter's coming. If I don't take you in soon, you'll be stuck here all winter, eating my food and likely sleeping in my goddam bed whilst I'm in nothing more than a child's truckle. I reckon it's high time I earned myself a few of those Confederate dollars to pay me back for all the chow you've been shovelling down your goddam neck.'

'Fine.' Jack tasted the fury then. He started to move, his hands clawing away the blankets in one angry sweep.

'You think you can jump me, weasel?' The old man sat up straighter, the musket now held ready to use. 'You think you can take me down?' He laughed at the notion. 'Well, you're a big fellow and all, been in the wars a fair bit too judging by all them scars, but you still won't get me, though you're welcome to try.'

Jack ignored the abuse. He had his feet on the floorboards, the wood cold on the soles of his feet. He stood straight up, forcing his body to obey. The moment he was upright, his head spun and he retched, the spasm uncontrollable and violent, then sat back down heavily.

'Hellfire, don't you spew your goddam guts up on my bed.' His threats forgotten, the old man jumped to his feet, pausing only long enough to prop his musket against his chair before rushing over carrying his spittoon, the liquid inside sloshing noisily. 'Do it in here if you have to.'

Jack caught a glimpse of foul black liquid before its smell

hit him. A moment later, he puked, a great rush spewing out of him. It went on for some time. Most went in the spittoon.

He was shaking by the time he had finished.

'Pa, what in the name of the devil are you doing to poor Jack?'

Jack heard Martha's voice as he flopped back onto the bed. It was as if she spoke from some great distance.

'You should know better at your age. I don't know what you said to him, but I can see the good it did.' Her words came quickly.

'Mind your tongue, girl.' Garrison fired the command at his daughter, his anger all the swifter for being brought on by shame. 'Know your damn place.'

'Yes, Pa.' The fire left Martha's voice, and she stopped in her tracks, head bowed.

'Now you tend to your chores and get this man well. Then get the son of a gun out of my goddam bed. You hear me, girl?'

'Yes, Pa.' Martha's voice was small.

'Well, don't just stand there. Get on with it.' Garrison growled the last of his instructions before marching out of the room.

Jack closed his eyes, trying to stop himself from shaking, the tremors racing up and down his body and leaving him cold. He felt a hand on his forehead, the touch now familiar.

'You lie back, Jack, take it easy. We'll look after you. My pa, he might cuss and moan some, but any fool can see you're still sick, and no Christian could stand back and see you taken away to who knows what fate whilst you're like that. So you sleep now. You're safe here.'

'Thank you,' Jack muttered.

'There's no need to thank me.' Martha tutted away his

gratitude. 'We'll get you well then you can be on your way. You must have someplace to go.' She spoke softly, as if worried her father would overhear her make the promise.

'I do.' Jack kept his eyes closed as he replied.

'Well, that's good. We all need someplace to call home.'

'No.' Jack was lulled by her touch. His tongue was speaking without thought. 'I don't have a home.'

'Then where are you going to go?' Martha did not understand his remark.

'There is something I need to do. Someone I must find.'

'A girl? The one from that photograph?'

'No. A man.' For a reason he did not fully understand, he felt able to speak the truth.

'A friend?'

'No.' He opened his eyes and saw Martha staring directly at him. She flinched as his gaze found hers, but did not look away. He held her stare. 'It's a man I am going to kill.' He paused, waiting for the reaction.

Martha's eyes flickered back and forth as she considered his words. 'You must really hate that man.'

'Yes.' Jack felt his stomach churn. Whether it was just nausea or a reaction to his own words, he did not know.

'Then we need to get you fit.' Martha's tone was brisk. 'And I reckon that might take a while.' She offered a tight smile. 'There's no future in hate, Jack.'

'There is for me.'

'The good Lord would say different.'

'The good Lord would understand.' Jack's voice was tight.

Martha's eyes widened at the blasphemy, but she did not stand or back away. Instead she leaned closer, tucking the sheet over Jack's body. 'Well, you've got a home here as long as you need it, no matter what old grumbling Garrison might say.' She sat back and smiled. 'You get some rest, Jack. We got plenty of time and you're safe here. We can worry about that future of yours another day.'

Jack did as he was told. He was grateful to Martha, both for her care and for her protection. He sensed she had more to say on the matter of his plan to find the man he wanted to kill. But she was right: for the moment that could wait. Yet in another regard, he knew she was wrong. He would never be safe. He would never be home. And his future had only one thing in it.

Revenge.

## Chapter Nineteen

---

$\mathcal{S}$now smothered the ground. It was ball-achingly cold and had been for over a month. The new year had been ushered in with a blizzard, the snow driven so hard by the wind that the three of them had been incarcerated in the cabin for the best part of a week. Martha's father had grumbled every hour of every day, and most especially after he was forced to spend hours fighting to clear a path to the wood store near the cabin's front door. He had spent the rest of his time whittling a collection of small woodland animals that he lined up around his armchair in pairs like a modern-day Noah, before burning every last one the day the blizzard stopped and they could finally force their way outside.

Jack had spent the time recovering. Martha had cared for him. She did not fuss, no matter what her father might mumble under his breath when he thought she could not hear him. By the end of the week of the great blizzard, Jack was able to move around the cabin without feeling faint, and the first signs of strength were returning to muscles wasted by so long confined to a sickbed.

As much as he admired Martha for her good spirit and

charitable care, he was heartily sick of being an invalid. The
first day Garrison had ventured outside after the blizzard, Jack
had followed. The next day he had dragged the heavy bed
frame back into the cabin's single bedroom, replacing it with
the truckle bed he had found in there.

The following day he had started chopping wood. He had
worked all morning, stopping only when he could no longer lift
the axe. The afternoon he had spent with Pinter's rifle, learning
how it worked and how to strip and clean it. On just the one
occasion had he allowed himself to fire a full magazine load of
sixteen shots to get a feel for the weapon. He would have shot
more, but he was aware that he had only the ammunition he
had taken from Pinter's saddlebags. The cartridges came in
boxes of one hundred, produced by a company called the New
Haven Arms Company. He had one full box and one nearly
half used, and he had no idea when he would get more. He
would have to husband it carefully.

He had found a broadside tucked into one of the boxes of
ammunition. The advertisement claimed the rifle to be the most
effective weapon in the world, with a penetration of eight
inches at one hundred yards and five inches at four hundred.
Having fired it, Jack was dubious of the claims, especially the
one that stated that the rounds shot by the rifle could still kill at
one thousand yards. But even if he judged it to be less powerful
and to have less of an effective range than the bold claims on
the broadside, the rapid rate of fire certainly made up for it.

The rifle was quite unlike any other he had seen. It took
copper cartridges that were much smaller than the Minié balls
he was used to. It had taken him a while to figure out how they
were fired, the lack of a nipple for a percussion cap under the
weapon's hammer leaving him bewildered. He had only been

sure that the cartridges themselves contained the firing charge when he had used the weapon for the first time.

Up to sixteen of the cartridges could be fed through an opening at the front of the weapon into a magazine that ran along the underside of the barrel, where they were held in place by a spring. When the odd-shaped handle around the trigger was cranked forward, the fired cartridge was ejected and a fresh one forced under the rifle's hammer. The same mechanism moved back a heavy bolt, which pushed the rifle's hammer into position ready to fire again and closed the breach around the fresh cartridge. Now that he had practised with the weapon, Jack could understand how Pinter had been able to keep up such a rapid rate of fire.

Such a rate would give a man an advantage in a fight even against a rifled musket. Jack knew that a good soldier armed with a rifled musket like the Springfield the 1st Boston had used could fire three shots a minute, yet this new rifle could fire sixteen in a much shorter span of time. The broadside he had found with the ammunition claimed that as many as sixty shots could be fired in a single minute. That might take some doing, but nonetheless, any regiment armed with the weapons would have a devastating advantage on the field of battle. The only drawback he could find was that the weapon felt lighter and less sturdy than the rifle muskets he was used to. The groove in the underside of the magazine would also be prone to collect dirt, and he could only imagine that in the filth and chaos of battle, the weapon would surely get blocked or even broken.

He bent down and picked up another log that he placed on the stump where Garrison had been chopping wood for decades. Something about the rifle unsettled him. It spoke of a different way of making war, one that he could not fully begin to comprehend. He had the feeling that he was standing on the precipice of a new age, one where men could be killed with even greater efficiency. He shivered as he pictured the effect a rapid-fire weapon like Pinter's rifle could have on the tightly packed ranks of an advancing infantry column. The carnage would be like nothing seen before: men gutted and cut down like wheat before one of the new-fangled mechanical threshing machines.

He sucked down a breath of freezing air, forcing thoughts of war from his mind, then swung the axe. It hummed as it slipped through the air, smacking into the log with a great thump, splitting the wood into two neat halves. It was an action he had repeated a hundred times that day already. It was his fifth morning of chopping wood. He worked slowly, taking his time and feeling the strength returning to his limbs. His arms and back ached abominably. Yet there was pleasure in the simple work, and satisfaction to be found in the strain in muscles that were still weaker than he could ever remember.

Garrison walked past every once in a while, greeting Jack's slow efforts with a grunt that might have been approval but which was more likely a remark on his lack of productivity. Jack did not care. He was sweating hard, the heat of his body a wonderful contrast to the chill on his skin from the cold winter air. The sky above his head was bright and clear, and for the first time in as long as he could remember, he felt something other than the blackness of grief and despair.

He swung the axe again, his breath condensing around his face, but missed, the axe taking the corner off the log rather than splitting it into two equal pieces. The sight displeased him far more than it should have, and he paused, taking a moment to stand the log back upright then leaning on the axe, sipping down breaths of the glacial air.

All was still. Snow shrouded the mountain woodland, smothering any sounds and leaving it unnaturally quiet. Only the occasional roar of snow falling from a tree broke the eerie silence. It was a time for animals to burrow deep and wait out the cold. And for humans to chop wood.

Jack took a bigger breath, forcing the cold air deep into his lungs. The action still caused a moment's flare of pain, his ribs protesting as he stretched them. He was feeling better, yet his situation still pricked at his conscience. He was wearing clothes that were not his, Martha raiding her husband's chest for items that almost fitted him. He was eating food that was not his, in a cabin that belonged to a man who had once hoped to trade him in for a handful of Confederate dollars. He was living on charity. He did not need Martha's father to chivvy him along and force him to his feet. The day he would leave could not come quickly enough.

'You call that chopping wood, boy?'

Jack looked up sharply. He had not heard Garrison approach. The old woodsman could move so quietly that he made not a single sound.

'What do *you* call it then, old man?' He swung the axe again, harder this time. The wood split in two, the axe hitting it with such force that both halves jumped off the tree stump.

'Old man indeed.' Garrison huffed, then came closer. 'I whipped your skinny behind easily enough the first time I tried, boy. Don't make me do it again.'

'I was sick then.' Jack bent down to toss the two halves of log into the heap he had been building that morning. The week sheltering from the blizzard had depleted their stocks. If they wanted to be warm, then many more logs would have to be split.

'Sick or not, I still put you on your goddam ass,' Garrison growled. He was leaning on his musket as he watched Jack at work. He was a man comfortable in his place in the world and confident of his ability to stay there.

'What's all this talk of fighting?' Martha interrupted the bravado. She was wearing a simple black dress with a white collar. Its hem was damp and lined with snow and her sleeves had been rolled up to reveal a pair of lean, muscled forearms. She was carrying a pail of water in each hand and both arms showed the strain of the load. Yet she marched across the snow-slicked ground easily enough and even had a moment to smile at Jack. 'You feeling good there, Jack?'

Jack nodded. Martha was a hard worker who was as tough as her surroundings. He had never once heard her complain, no matter how cold and dark it had become, or how much her father bawled her out. He liked her for it.

'Thank you.' He stopped what he was doing and spoke clearly. It was overdue. 'Thank you both.'

'For what?' The words came out in between breaths as Martha ploughed on with her load.

'For keeping me alive.'

Martha stopped. She was breathing hard and her breath hung in a cloud in front of her face. 'It was our pleasure, Jack.'

Jack turned to look at Garrison. The old man had not moved and showed no sign of doing so. He stared at Jack, holding his gaze. He did not say a word in acknowledgement of Jack's thanks.

Jack shivered, whether from the cold or from something

else, he did not know. Deep in the old man's eyes he saw something shift.

'Well, boy.' A thin smile played across Garrison's face. 'You've been about as much use as a blunt goddam axe around here, but I never did expect much from a shit-weasel Yankee.'

Jack ignored the abuse. He kept his eyes locked on the old man. His expression was saying something different to his mouth.

'You still planning on leaving us, Jack?' Martha put down the pails of water and looked across at him. The frigid air did not bother her.

'Soon as you tell me I won't die of the cold,' Jack answered seriously. There had been no more talk of a bounty. The idea had faded away like snow from boots placed near a stove. Nor had there been any talk of the war between the states. It was winter. Survival was all. Everything else could wait until the land had thawed and life began again.

'Hell, it'd be high summer if we wait for that.' Garrison chuckled at the idea. 'You'd be like a child in these mountains, boy. Got about as much chance as surviving in them too.'

Martha smiled at the teasing. She knew her father. 'It'll be another month, Jack, maybe two, before you're ready and all. Specially if you're set on heading all the way over to Nashville. You ain't got your strength back yet. Not properly.'

Jack heard the truth in the words. He could feel the cold sinking into his bones now that he had stopped working. Aches were becoming pains and his body was already weakening. The thought of raising the axe again did not fill him with joy.

'You still going to find that man, the one who killed Rose?' Martha asked bluntly. There were few secrets left between them. The week of the blizzard had taken care of that.

Jack nodded. 'I'll find him.'

'And you'll kill him for what he did?' There was no trace of censure in Martha's voice. She was very different from her father in so many ways, yet she had inherited a fair measure of his toughness.

Jack nodded again.

'Why?'

To Jack's surprise, it was Garrison who asked the question. He had said little when Jack had told them his long and sorry tale. He had been interested in Jack's stories of faraway wars in the Crimea and Persia, and he had listened intently when he talked of the bitter struggle at Delhi. But he had offered nothing when Jack had spoken of his determination to find Rose's killer.

'Revenge,' Jack answered truthfully. There was no dissembling with the people who had saved him. In truth, he found the blunt, simple nature of his current life a relief. He had nothing left to hide and no secrets to protect. He had told them everything.

'That it?'

'That's all I have, old man.'

'Well, it's as stupid a goddam notion as I ever heard. You ain't got a chance in hell of finding that man. You'll just find yourself an empty grave.'

Jack had no easy reply. The words were an echo from the past. He remembered his mother saying something similar. Yet here he was, still standing. Just.

'You sound like you're going to miss me,' he teased.

'I'll miss you like a man misses a dose of the shits. You know they're gone, but you sure as hell don't want them back.'

'You'll have to chop your own wood.'

'Amount you're getting done, I could do it before I take my morning piss.' Garrison could not help chuckling at his abuse. He paused, then became more serious again. 'This is a big old country, boy. You really think you can find one man?'

'Maybe,' Jack replied honestly. 'Maybe not.' He shrugged. 'I'm still going to try.'

'And then?'

'Then what?'

'What you going to do after?' Garrison shifted, easing his weight from one foot to the other. 'If you find this man, and kill him, then what're you going to do?'

'I have no idea.'

Garrison shook his head slowly. 'There ain't no future in this, boy. No future at all. A man needs more than chasing and killing.'

'I don't have anything else.'

'Then find something. Find it whilst you still can.'

Garrison spoke with more passion than Jack had ever seen in the old man. The cold and the quiet, still air only served to emphasise the heat in the words.

'I will. When he's dead.' Jack held onto the iron in his soul. It was the only thing binding him together.

'Might be too late then, boy.'

Jack smiled. He did not like being called boy, but it beat being called a shit-weasel. 'You'd better be careful, old man. Sounds like you're beginning to care about me.'

Garrison's mouth twisted, then he turned his head and spat. When he looked back at Jack, he was smiling. 'Then we'd better get you on your way as soon as we can. I'm too old for all this shit.'

Martha and Jack laughed at the look on the old man's face,

but their laughter stopped abruptly when a different sort of sound came from the woods to the south of the cabin.

It was the sound of men on the move.

Jack saw them first. They were little more than shadows, but there was no doubt they were coming their way.

'Get inside, girl.' Garrison spoke first. He stood up straighter, his musket held across his front. 'Go on now.' He added the extra command as he saw his daughter hesitate.

Jack hefted the axe. All thoughts of the cold and the ache deep in his bones were forgotten.

A motley collection of men came into sight. All four were on foot. A tall, beefy man with lank hair led them. He was unkempt and dirty, and his body was buried beneath a great brown blanket, but there was no hiding his size. The three others were shorter, and lean as whippets. They were all swathed in layers of drab-coloured blankets, their boots wrapped in rags and their heads covered with hats and sheets so that little of their bearded faces could be seen.

'Martha.' Garrison stopped his daughter as she reached the cabin door. 'Get Jack's fancy rifle.' Then he turned to face the four men who had no business being there.

Jack would have had to be a fool not to feel the tension that rippled through the icy air. The arrival of the four men could only mean one thing.

Trouble.

# Chapter Twenty

———◆———

'How can I help you boys?' Garrison called out to the group the moment they stepped out from the treeline. He held his musket ready.

Jack balanced the axe in both hands, then walked to stand at the older man's shoulder. He could sense that violence was only a short way off. The four men would want something. Whatever that might be, he was sure Garrison could not afford to give it away. He would have to fight to hold on to what was his.

The big man stepped forward whilst his companions hung back. He was carrying a black pistol in his great maw of a right hand.

'What you got here, old man?'

Jack watched carefully. The pistol was half covered by the end of the blanket that swathed the big man's right arm. He held it with practised ease.

'Just my home, son, there's nothing much here. Just enough for us.' Garrison spoke slowly and clearly, making sure nothing was misunderstood.

The big man smiled. He had few teeth. 'And who's that ugly son of a gun holding that there axe?'

Garrison turned to look at Jack, his expression neutral. 'Why, that's young Jack. He's my boy.' He looked back at the big man. 'He can't speak or hear nothing. He's just one big dumb son of a bitch who don't know what day of the goddam week it is.' He glanced back at Jack then slowly shook his head. 'Disappointment to a man, his only son standing there with the brain of a fucking two-year-old.'

The big man looked Jack over. 'That right? He don't understand us?'

'Not a goddam thing.' Garrison glanced at Jack again. 'Ain't that right, you shit-for-brains son of a bitch?'

Jack kept his expression neutral, playing his part as he stared back at the men who had brought danger to this remote corner of the woods. He did his best to look like a fool, even as he ran his eyes over the group. The big man was the most dangerous, his size and bearing marking him out as the leader. The rest looked worn out. Two were old, their faces half covered with unkempt and matted beards and what little skin was left bared to the bitter winter air blackened with grime. One was much younger, barely more than a boy to Jack's eyes, his face coated with soft downy fuzz rather than a full beard. Their blankets were crusted with dirt, and what clothing he could see was filthy. There was no hint of a uniform in their worn, raggedy appearance and only the muskets they carried gave any hint that they might once have been soldiers. But even from a distance Jack could see the rust on the ironwork, and he doubted they would fire. He grinned like a fool. The last time he had been faced with four men he had been alone. They had all died at his hand.

'Now then, boys, I reckon it's best for us all if you go on your way. Ain't nothing here for you except maybe some water, if that's what you need.' Garrison sounded anything but welcoming. He took a few paces forward, placing himself in front of the group's leader.

Jack's arms were protesting at holding the axe. Yet he forced them still, not willing to show even a moment's weakness. Garrison was the same. He stood no more than ten yards in front of the big man, yet it was as if he had not a care in the world. To Jack's eyes the old man seemed small, frail even, when compared to the much bigger and younger man. It was as brave a display as any he had seen.

The big man stared back at Garrison for several long moments before he removed his hat, which he held awkwardly in front of him.

'No sir, we can't do that. We need someplace to stay so we can get out of this damned cold for a bit, and we need to find ourselves something to eat.' He sounded almost apologetic. 'We're sure starving.'

'Ain't nothing here for you boys except some water.' Garrison repeated his earlier answer, his tone even and calm. 'Best for us all if you just move along now.'

The big man nodded, as if he agreed with everything Garrison said. But he did not move so much as a single inch. 'Who's that girl we saw?'

Jack forgot his aches and pains. He saw a different kind of hunger in the man's eyes and it sent fire fizzing through every vein in his body.

'She ain't nothing to concern you.' Garrison's tone had changed, the words growled and the warning clear.

The big man's meaty fingers toyed with his hat. He looked once at Jack, his tongue flicking out to lick his lips. Then he nodded and put his hat back on his head before turning to glance back at his companions.

There was a pause, lasting no more than the span of one or two heartbeats. Then the man turned on a sixpence, moving with a speed that belied his bulk, his revolver aimed at Garrison, the muzzle held stock still.

Garrison did not move, but Jack saw the old man straighten his spine as he faced the threat. He had been given no chance to fight back.

'We need food, we need shelter and we need a little comfort. I'm right sorry, old man, but I reckon we just found ourselves all three.'

He fired twice in quick succession.

Jack saw Garrison's clothing twitch as both bullets hit him squarely in the centre of his chest. Then he fell without a cry.

He was dead before his body hit the ground.

Jack moved fast, acting on instinct as a bullet smacked into the snow-covered ground no more than a yard from his feet. Another shot followed, and he felt the snap in the air as the bullet seared past.

He dived behind the woodpile, then scrabbled across the ground, working his way to the far side. He could feel his body coming to life, the feeling of being shot at just as he remembered.

He paused at the edge of the woodpile, sucking down a breath of air. He could hear the sound of boots scuffing through snow, but now was not the time to hesitate and try to place his new enemy. It was time to act.

He dragged down another breath, then broke from cover. A bullet came for him immediately. It gouged a great splinter from a log that spat upwards and caught him on the cheek. But it did not slow him and he darted forward, bursting through the cabin door.

'Martha!' he yelled even as he turned and dropped the locking bar across the door. A bullet smacked into the stout timber with a loud thump, but for the moment he was safe.

'Here!' Martha rushed forward. She had not been idle and she threw him his rifle.

Jack snatched the weapon from the air. He could hear shouts outside, the four men on the move. He was certain they would try to mount some sort of attack. Rifle in hand, he strode across the room, taking up a position with a clear shot of the door.

'You got me some cartridges?' He snapped the question.

'Here.' She tossed him a box.

Jack caught it, then tore it open.

'Where's Pa?'

'They shot him down. Now get out of sight.' Jack had no time for niceties. He held the rifle upside down in his left hand whilst his right pushed the brass tab underneath the barrel to the top until it pivoted to the left, opening the chamber that ran along under the barrel. Then he started to drop cartridges down into the tubular magazine.

'He's dead?' Martha had not moved.

'I don't know. Fuck it.' His clumsy cold fingers dropped a cartridge. A great hammering started up as the men outside tried to batter a way in. The bar he had dropped was there to hold the door shut against the wind. It would not last long against men determined to force a way in.

'Oh my Lord.' Martha stood there, her hands covering her mouth.

'Shit.' Jack was loading as fast as he could. Behind him he heard wood splintering. 'Get out of fucking sight!' He snapped the order, then dropped another cartridge and rammed the box into his pocket.

The door splintered, then slammed open, smacking against the wall and letting in a great blast of cold air.

Jack pivoted the brass tab so that the opening closed, then cranked the rifle's action. He lifted it in one smooth motion, settling it against his shoulder.

A man rushed into the open doorway.

Jack saw a pair of pale eyes above cheeks covered with a boyish beard. He heard the lad yell, a war cry that turned to a shriek of terror as he saw what awaited him.

Jack fired. The bullet tore through beard and bone. Momentum made the younger man stagger forward before he fell face first at Jack's feet.

Jack kept the rifle pulled tight into his shoulder. He fired a second round into the body writhing at his feet, then cranked the handle and fired a third. The lad jerked like a floundering fish, but Jack was already swinging the rifle back up, the butt never once moving from his shoulder.

One of the older men rushed the door. He was slower than the young lad. Jack shot at him but missed, the bullet close enough to make the man's clothing twitch. It was enough to turn him around and have him diving for cover outside. Jack cranked the rifle's mechanism, then fired again. This time the bullet struck, hitting the man deep in the gut with enough force to spin him around so that he hit the snow on his back.

Jack had seen enough. He lowered the rifle, darted forward to kick the man's legs out of the way then slammed the door shut. This time there was no bar to hold it shut, the wood splintered and broken.

Martha had not moved, despite his order, so he grabbed her by the elbow and frogmarched her to the cabin's bedroom. He could see the tears on her face, a silent stream that ran down both cheeks. She said nothing as he led her away. She did not rave or scream. Instead she was silent, her jaw clenched tight.

'Stay here.' Jack pushed her towards the far side of the room. 'Get down on the floor and don't bloody move.' The commands came out one after the other, staccato and without emotion.

He turned away. Outside he could hear two men shouting and another voice crying for aid. He was still outnumbered. He was still trapped.

'Jack.' Martha called to him as he stalked back into the main room.

He turned.

'What can I do?'

'Stay here.' Jack's tone was glacial. Deeply buried emotions were raging through him now. The arrival of the four men had awakened the part of him that had been hibernating. The fight was his spring and he was coming alive.

Martha opened her mouth to say something more. Whatever she saw reflected in his gaze was enough to make her think better of it, and she closed her mouth and slunk down, hiding behind the bed in which Jack had spent so long recovering.

The voices outside had fallen silent. Whatever plan they had formulated was now ready.

Jack did not care to think what it might be. It was time to reawaken the part of him that thrilled to the smell of blood and powder smoke.

It was time to fight.

# Chapter Twenty-one

---◆◆◆---

The young lad lying inside the cabin was still alive despite the bullets Jack had pumped into him. He looked up as Jack marched back through the room. His hands were smothered with blood from clawing at the great tears in his own flesh; still more was in his mouth and dribbling out from his lips like red wine from a drunk. He tried to speak as Jack came close, but he choked on the blood, the words drowned and lost for ever.

Jack ignored the pathetic sobs and gurgles. There was no room for pity or for mercy. Not when the fight was on.

He crouched, then moved forward, taking up position behind the door. There he paused to fish out the packet of ammunition he had crammed into his pocket and reload the rifle, replacing the rounds he had fired. He would need every single one.

The boy bleeding to a slow death scrabbled at Jack's leg with bloodied fingers. They left marks on his borrowed trousers before he reached down and knocked the hand away.

He stood, then sucked down one long, deep breath. He had no plan save to charge out and start shooting.

He reached out with his left hand and grabbed hold of the door. This time he glanced down at the dying lad. Two wide eyes stared back at him. There was no disguising the boy's fear. Jack looked away in disgust.

There was time for one last calming breath, then he tightened his grip on the door, ready to throw it open and rush outside.

He had moved it no more than a fraction of an inch before there was a shout, then a single shot, the bullet burying itself deep in the door and making it shudder.

'Shit.' Jack could not help flinching as the bullet struck. He held the door still, reluctant to move it another inch.

'Come out with your hands up,' the voice of the big man called. 'We'll let you and the woman go. Just come on out, boy. Nice and easy.'

Jack winced. The voice came from close by, and it was clear that the leader and his one surviving companion had the door well covered. He paid the man's claim no heed. There would be no easy escape from this squalid fight in the snow. He was utterly certain that if he stepped outside, even with his hands up, he would be shot down. Yet the cabin had only one door, and the windows were cut small in the sides and offered no way out to anyone other than a small child. He and Martha were trapped like eels in a barrel.

'Shit.' He swore again, and crouched down, his mind whirring.

'Come on out, boy. We ain't going to hurt you. Let us look after our friends. They'll die if we leave 'em much longer, and that ain't Christian.'

Jack ignored the voice, just as he ignored the plea in the eyes of the lad lying at his feet.

'I'll give you another minute.' The voice came again. 'I won't have it said that I didn't give you a choice. You do what's right, boy, 'cause this is your last chance. If you want that woman in there to get away with her hide intact, then you'll do as I goddam say.'

Jack heard the growing anger in the big man's voice as he was ignored. He was pleased. Anger clouded a man's judgement. It would help him when he put his desperate plan into action.

He looked down at the lad lying in a pool of his own blood. The younger man was still alive, but Jack knew he could not last much longer.

He leant forward. 'Sorry, chum.' He whispered the apology into the lad's ear. 'I need you.'

'Are you ready?'

Jack smiled at Martha in reassurance. He had not wanted to summon her from her hiding place, but there was no other way for him to open the door. Not now that his arms were full.

'Throw it open, then get out of sight.' He gave his last instructions. They were followed by a gasp as he struggled to hold the weight of the lad's body.

'You sure about this, Jack?' Martha was looking at him as if he were mad.

'No.' Jack gave the single-word answer, then grappled with the burden that twitched and squirmed in his grip. He had his left arm wrapped firmly around the dying boy's chest to hold their two bodies close. He could feel the heat of the lad's blood on his front, soaking into his clothes. His right hand held the rifle. It was an awkward embrace and he was struggling to keep them bound together.

'Go on now,' he hissed. 'Before I drop the bastard.'

Martha hesitated only for a second, then reached forward, her body already half turned away. She snatched at the door and threw it open. At once, Jack thrust the dying man in front of him and stormed outside.

Both men left outside fired. Bullets immediately hit the body screening Jack, the wet, slapping sound they made as they ripped into the lad like a butcher slamming hunks of meat on a granite counter. The body jerked as it was hit with enough force to tear it from Jack's grasp. Yet it had served its purpose.

The rifle was pulled tight into Jack's shoulder even as the dying boy fell face down in the snow. He fired immediately, snapping off a shot at the first shadowy form he saw. He strode forward, past the body of the other man he had shot down, cranking the rifle's mechanism then firing again. He caught glimpses of both men left fighting. They were lying in the snow behind tree stumps no more than twenty-five yards from the cabin. He shot fast, cranking and firing, thinking only to cow the two men with violence. He saw spurts of snow thrown into the air as his bullets created a storm around his targets, then he ran, dashing for the pile of logs.

As soon as he reached them, he crouched down, the cold air rasping in his lungs as he hauled it in. He reloaded, fingers nimble, the act more familiar. This time he did not drop a single cartridge.

He heard sounds of movement, both men rushing through the snow now that the bullets had stopped zipping past their ears. A heartbeat later and bullets lashed against the woodpile, splinters showering over him.

He dropped the last cartridge into the magazine, the rifle now fully loaded. This was the moment of truth. To move now was to risk death. Every instinct begged him to stay where he was. To stay safe. To keep out of the line of fire. Yet he had to move if he were to fight, if he were to beat the men who had killed Garrison. It was the moment when some men cowered and hid, while others stood up and did what had to be done.

More bullets tore into the stacked logs. He had heard enough now to place the direction of the shots. Both men were firing revolvers, the distinctive sound telling Jack what he would face. He took one more breath, holding it deep in his lungs.

Then he moved.

He burst from behind the logs, legs powerful and strong; sickness forgotten. He ran hard, ignoring the shots that flayed the air around him. He covered the ground in great loping strides that took him away from the entrance to the cabin. More bullets came for him, the air punched repeatedly as they seared past. He kept moving, determined to draw the men away from Martha's hiding place.

The shots stopped. He heard the men moving, forced to chase after him if they were to keep him in range of their handguns. He darted past the broken-down cart, then broke right and ran for another dozen yards. His boots scrabbled for purchase on the snow-slick ground, then he slid down onto his side and skidded to a breathless halt behind one of the barrels that littered the ground around the cabin. Like the others it was filled with scum-covered black water topped with ice. It was foul-smelling and streaked with mould, but it would be enough to stop a bullet.

As soon as he reached cover, he was up on his knees, rifle aimed back the way he had come. He fired the instant the weapon was level, hammering bullets at the two figures he could see chasing after him, driving both men into cover. He took a breath, then fired three more shots, all counted with care, all aimed, and all sending up fountains of snow near where he had seen one of the men go to ground.

Then he paused. Revolvers typically fired six bullets. If they believed that that was what he was armed with, they would be expecting him to be reloading now.

One of the men stood. It was not the big man, the leader, but one of the grey-haired pack dogs. He emerged from behind a fallen tree trunk, thirty yards from where Jack waited, running hard, his arms pumping. The snow was deep near the fallen tree and undisturbed since the week of the great blizzard, and it began to slow him.

Jack adjusted his aim. The rifle in his arms tracked the runner, the end of the barrel held still. Then he fired.

The first bullet struck the snow six inches in front of the running man. He tried to alter his path, but he had taken no more than a single step before Jack fired again.

The second bullet hit him in the side of the neck. Blood erupted from the gruesome wound, bright red against the virgin snow. The man stopped, dropped his revolver, then clamped both hands around the dreadful tear in his flesh.

The third bullet arrived a moment later, striking him in the chest. The fourth hit as he crumpled to the ground, driving deep into his gut. He landed on the snow and lay still. He had not cried out as the bullets ripped through him. Now he died in silence as the snow-shrouded wood absorbed the retort of the final bullet.

Jack ducked down behind the barrel, his left hand already digging for the ammunition in his pocket. He snuffled the air as he reloaded, the familiar taint of spent powder lingering. Around him the silence pressed in. There was no sound, save the rasp of his own breathing.

He dropped fresh cartridges into the magazine, burning his fingers on the red-hot barrel. They were the last, the box now empty. Rifle reloaded, he paused, straining his hearing. He heard nothing. He stayed in his cover, every sense reaching out as he tried to place the big man. Yet there was nothing except an uneasy silence.

He risked a glance around the barrel.

Four men had brought death and violence to the remote cabin. Three were now dead.

But the fourth had disappeared.

# Chapter Twenty-two

---

*J*ack counted off ten more seconds, then forced himself to move.

He flinched as he scrambled to his feet, expecting to be shot at any moment. He broke from cover, dashing back the way he had come, heading for the broken-down wagon. No bullets came for him.

He slid to a halt. His heart hammered deep in his chest and his breath came in little more than shallow gasps that caused great clouds of condensed air to form around his face. Still nothing. No sounds of movement, no shots, just the eerie silence of the snow-smothered woodland.

'Shit.' He hissed the word, then risked a quick glance around the front of the wagon. He saw nothing and no one.

His eyes lingered on the body of the old man that he could see a few dozen yards in front of the cabin. Garrison lay where he had fallen. The snow around him was stained black with his blood.

'Jack!'

He froze. Martha was shouting for him.

'Jack!'

The call came again.

He risked another glance around the wagon. This time he heard the sound of movement, but still he could see nothing.

'You there, retard?' The big man's voice rang out loud and clear in the chill air. 'You come on out. You hear me?'

Jack peered around the wagon once more. The big man was stepping out of the cabin's shadow. He had Martha clamped to his front, a knife held to her neck.

'Leave your rifle and come out!' he shouted again, voice pitched higher, the strain obvious.

Jack's mind raced. The big man was a fool. He should have come out shooting, using Martha as a shield just as Jack himself had used the dying man. Instead he had chosen to take a hostage. Jack's mind stilled. The man had made the wrong choice.

He forced the coldness into his being. He could not allow Martha's fate to matter, just as he had to convince himself that her father's death meant nothing to him. He held his emotions tight, refusing to let them sway him. He told himself he was a soldier; a killer; a man with nothing but the desire for revenge filling his soul. That revenge was all that mattered. No one and nothing could be allowed to get in its way. If the moment came, he knew he would have to act without compassion. If need be, he would make himself kill them both.

Yet there was something he could do. He could offer a distraction. He rose to his feet, numb from more than just the cold. He still held the rifle.

The big man saw him immediately.

'Put that down, or so help me I'll slit her open.' He jerked the knife, pressing it closer to Martha's neck.

Jack did not obey. He found his balance, feet a shoulder-width apart. The big man and his captive were no more than thirty yards away. He had a clear shot.

He looked at Martha. There was no fear in her eyes, even with a blade at her throat. There was just simmering anger. And hate.

Her hand was moving. It crept across her belly with infinite caution. Jack caught the flash of a blade. He saw what she intended and could only admire her for it. If the big man noticed what she was doing, Jack did not doubt that he would kill her without a qualm. Yet he could not allow himself to intervene. He had to be prepared for however the scene played out, so he pushed his fear for her away and held himself ready to start shooting.

'Let her go.' He held the rifle vertically, his fingers clearly well away from the trigger. But he could swing it down and be firing in the span of a single heartbeat.

The big man laughed at the demand. 'No. That's not how this goes. If you'd seen what we've seen, if you'd been through what we've been through, then you'd know we're way past doing what an ugly son of a bitch like you tells us.' He paused and looked around him 'And you killed my boys.' His voice vibrated. He shook his head slowly from side to side. 'I ain't about to let that go.'

Jack watched the progress of Martha's knife. He forced himself to feel detached from what was to come. Martha was not his kin. She was not his concern. If she fought, her fate was in her own hands. His fingers tensed. He was ready, no matter what.

'You know what you've done?' The big man pushed Martha forward, almost dislodging the knife from her hand. 'You know what those boys suffered before today?' Great tears began to stream down his face. 'They fought for this land. They stood against those Yankee sons of bitches, and they fought, you hear me, retard, they fought for people like you.' He took another step, cruel in his mastery of the woman in his arms. 'And now you've killed them, you dirty son of a bitch. You killed my boys.'

Jack cared nothing for the passion in the words. He had been through more than the big man and his dead companions could ever know. He had lived in darkness, and he knew the evil shadows that lurked there better than any. These men's suffering meant nothing.

'You think you're special?' He spat out the words. He would try to give Martha her chance. 'You think you're the only one who ever suffered?'

'Shut your goddam mouth.' The big man hurled the words back. He forced Martha forward. 'You know nothing.' Spit and snot smothered his face now, dripping into his beard, clinging to the already matted fibres.

'I know everything.' Jack watched Martha's eyes. She was ready.

'You know shit. None of you does. You ain't seen your mates butchered, your own brother ripped apart by Yankee bullets.' The words spewed out of the man now, like vomit from a drunk. 'You don't know shit.'

Martha struck. She had turned the knife in her hand and now she rammed it behind her, driving it deep into the big man's groin, slicing the blade back and forth, tearing it through his flesh until it was buried to the hilt.

The man screamed, the sound feral and full of agony. His hands clawed at the wound, frantically trying to hold himself together. Then the blood came. It rushed out, past the groping fingers and the buried blade. It sprayed out in a great rush, smothering the snow and turning it black.

Jack walked forward. He did not rush. There was no need. It was already over.

The big man's scream died away. He fell to his knees, hands still clutched to the great tear underneath his belly. He looked at Jack then, eyes full of dumb surprise and terror. Martha's strike had severed something crucial deep in his body, and the blood came without pause.

'You all right, love?' Jack asked, turning away from the dying man.

'What do you want to do with him?' She asked the question as if he were dead already.

Jack looked the man over. He was writhing in agony, his body shaking and juddering whilst blood poured out to stain the snow.

'Leave him to bleed out,' he said.

Martha nodded. She did not ask Jack to offer mercy; she simply walked away. In that moment she was as cold and hard as the frigid world around them.

Jack did not have to watch her to know she was heading towards Garrison's body. He kept his eyes on the man grinding a blood angel into the snow, giving Martha a moment alone with her father.

He could choose to administer a clean death to the man who had tried to kill him. He had done it before. Then it had been out of mercy, a final gift to a friend. It was a part of the soldier's creed. Brothers in arms should not be left to suffer. At the end, every man hoped to be spared the torment of an agonising wound, and trusted his comrades to do what had to be done to ease his passing.

He locked his gaze onto the big man's eyes. They stared back at him, crazed with agony and terror. He was a stranger who had violated the place that had given Jack back his life. And he had killed a man Jack had come to think of as a friend. He deserved no mercy.

Yet his claims resonated in Jack's soul. Unless he had been lying, the man had fought at the battle over the Bull Run river. No matter his crime, no matter his brutality, he was still a soldier.

Jack lifted the rifle to his hip. He held it there, letting the big man see the muzzle that now pointed directly at him. He waited for understanding to arrive in the man's eyes, then he pulled the trigger.

The bullet hit true, shattering the big man's skull and ending his torment. The sound of the single shot reverberated around the forest, then all was quiet and still once again.

Jack bent low and scooped up the man's fallen revolver, then turned his back on the corpse and went to mourn a friend.

# Chapter Twenty-three

There was only a simple wooden cross to mark the grave. It would not stand the test of time. In a few years, or perhaps less, a passing animal would knock down the cross, and the grave would be forgotten. Except by the two people standing over the freshly turned earth.

Jack looked down at the patch of grey-brown soil. He could smell it clearly, the warm aroma easy to detect in the frozen, ice-clad world. The dark loam stood out against the snow, the low mound visible from yards away. Yet already fresh snow had started to cover it. In a few hours it would be hidden completely.

The cold was buried deep in his veins now. There had been heat pumping through him, the task of digging the frozen ground taking him several hours. He had been forced to halt half a dozen times, his strength failing him. When he had stopped, Martha had continued. It had not taken long for the shame of seeing her striking the ground to revive him and send him out into the cold once more. Together they had dug a hole deep enough to take the body that seemed so very small now that the life force had been stolen from it.

The four men had been treated with less ceremony, consigned to a single shallow, unmarked grave in the woods. Each had been searched for anything of value or use, the act done not out of greed but out of practicality. Jack had made sure to take every last round of ammunition from the bodies, even keeping their battered muskets for the time being. There had been precious few rounds for the revolvers the gang had used. Jack wondered if they had stashed their backpacks before walking towards the cabin.

'There should be a preacher here.'

Martha had wrapped herself in furs. She stood next to Jack, contemplating the ground where the body of her father had been incarcerated for all eternity. A cloud of condensed air billowed around her mouth as she spoke for the first time in several hours.

'Was he a godly man?' Jack asked. He was reminded how little he knew of the friend he now mourned. Martha's father had not struck him as being close to his God; more a man bound to the unforgiving world in which he had lived.

'No.' Martha's eyes did not leave the mound of earth. She did not speak again for some time. When she did, her voice wavered. 'I don't like the idea of him lying down there in the cold.'

'He's not there.' Jack almost felt the need to reach out to her. But Martha was not that sort of woman. He had not seen her embrace or kiss her father once in all the months he had shared their cabin. 'He's gone now. What's left . . .' he paused, trying to find the right words, 'well, that's not him. That's just the bit left behind.' For a moment he saw again the great heaps of the dead after Solferino. There had been so many bodies. The mauled, mutilated carcasses had been piled into corpse mountains, all notion of humanity lost.

The sight of those corpses had been a reminder to Jack of the fate he faced. All that he was and all that he could be would be forgotten, and his bloated, stinking carcass would be left to rot wherever he happened to die. There would be no mourners at his graveside, no one to tend his grave or to think on his life. For he had lost everyone who had ever touched him. He was quite alone in the world.

'He'd be angry at me if he saw this.' Martha broke the silence. She sniffed as she spoke, then wiped a gloved hand across her face. The fur came away damp. 'He'd say we'd done a poor job of digging his grave.'

Jack grunted in acknowledgement of the wry remark. 'He would.'

'He liked you, you know.' For the first time, Martha turned to look at Jack. 'I ain't ever seen him with anyone like he was with you. Not even with my John.'

'He told me your John is a good man.' Jack was uncomfortable and sought to divert the conversation.

'He is.' Martha's answer came quickly. 'He is a good man.' The words were repeated, but there was little conviction in them.

'You must miss him.' Jack watched Martha's face closely. Her eyes were puffy and moist, and there were trails of half-frozen tears on her cheeks. A crust of snot was smeared under each nostril, and a thin tendril of it streaked across one blotchy cheek. She did not care that she looked a mess.

'I miss a lot of things.' Her lips moved as if about to form a smile, but it never came. She glanced at Jack and saw him looking directly at her. Her chin lifted, a hint of defiance in her gaze. 'But missing something never solved nothing. It's what you do that matters. There ain't no use pining like a damn dog over what might have been. You got to get on with your

damned life and find a way to fill it until it's your turn to lay
down and die.'

Jack acknowledged the hard wisdom with a grunt. Martha
glared at him, almost daring him to challenge her. He knew she
was talking of him, of his quest to find Rose's killer.

'You think that's what I've been doing?'

'What you going to do now?' Martha dodged the question
and fired her own back at him.

'Go inside and try to get warm.'

Martha's eyes narrowed. 'You still going to kill that Lyle
man?'

'Yes.' Jack did not evade her question.

'Then it's time you left. Snow will thaw soon enough. You'll
be all right.'

Jack nodded. 'Very well.'

'You know it won't fix nothing?' Martha sniffed hard, then
cuffed her face to wipe away the tears.

'No. No, I don't know that.'

'Then you're a fool.'

'Maybe.' Jack was too cold to feel anger. 'Maybe not. But
I'm still going to do it.'

Martha said nothing more. She looked him in the eye for
several long moments before she turned away to face her
father's grave once again.

'The Lord is my shepherd; I shall not want. He maketh me
to lie down in green pastures; he leadeth me beside the still
waters. He restoreth my soul; he leadeth me in the paths of
righteousness for his name's sake.' She spoke softly, her eyes
screwed tight shut. 'Yea, though I walk through the valley of
the shadow of death, I will fear no evil; for thou art with me;
thy rod and staff they comfort me.'

Jack had heard enough. He knew what it was to walk in the valley of the shadow of death, and he had done so alone, with no God to comfort or guide him. He took one last look at the mound of soil, already half covered by fresh snow. Then he turned away.

'Thou preparest a table before me in the presence of mine enemies; thou anointest my head with oil; my cup runneth over.' Martha opened her eyes and looked at Jack's back as he left her. 'Surely goodness and mercy shall follow me all the days of my life and I will dwell in the house of the Lord for ever.'

She finished speaking. There was no sound other than the soft patter of falling snow.

Jack sat at the table in the cabin. Pinter's rifle lay in front of him. He had thought to strip it down and clean it, but he was too numb with cold and too tired.

The door to the cabin opened, a burst of cold air streaming inside for the span of a few heartbeats before the door was barred shut against the elements.

Martha stood at the threshold. Her boot scuffed at the dark stains in the planks near the door that told of the desperate struggle they had fought to stay alive. Then she walked straight to where Jack sat.

'I want to come with you.' She made the statement in a voice as cold as the air she had let in.

Jack studied her face. Her eyes were red raw. 'Where do you want to go?'

'I'm going to find my John.'

Jack did not reply immediately. It was a time for carefully chosen words. 'You know where he is?'

'Fort Donelson.' Martha was standing as still as a statue.

'And where is that exactly?'

'Way west of here. It's near enough to Nashville. Ain't that where you're headed?'

Jack watched her closely. 'What'll happen to this place if you leave it?'

'Nothing. It'll sit quiet. People round here know whose it is. They'll leave it be. It ain't going no place.'

'What if another group like the one that came by this morning find it?'

'You've suddenly got a whole lot of questions.' Martha's voice was as hard as the ground that now shrouded her father. 'How about we make this nice and simple? We're both headed in the same direction, so we can go together. Way I see it, that doubles our chances of finding the people we're looking for.'

'Just like that?'

'Just like that.'

'You make it sound easy.' Jack tried to find the right words to dissuade her. He did not want company. He wanted to be alone. The stay in the cabin had been a mistake. He should have taken his chances and left the moment he was strong enough to stand. He had allowed himself to get involved with other people. People he neither wanted nor needed. Life was simpler if he were alone.

'I don't care that it won't be easy.' Martha had still not moved. 'I don't care what happens to this place. I don't care about nothing no more. I'm going to find my John. You and me can go together, or we can go separately, I don't mind. 'Cept without me, you ain't going to get out these woods.'

'What would the old man say? About his daughter leaving this place.' Jack changed tack.

Martha did not so much as blink. 'This was his place. Never mine. And like you said, he ain't here no more.'

Jack moved his hands. They closed over the rifle. 'No.'

'No?'

'I travel alone.' His voice was like granite.

Martha held his gaze. 'I gave you your life. You would have died if I hadn't kept you alive. You owe me.'

'So I have to risk my life to repay you for saving it. That seems a little ironic, don't you think?'

'You owe me.' Martha was unconcerned by his refusal. 'And you need me.'

'I need you?'

'To show you the way. You ain't from round here. You leave this here cabin and you could wander in these woods for the next month without ever seeing sight of the turnpike.'

Jack laughed then. He did not mean to, but the sound escaped him nonetheless. He was not laughing at Martha. There was nothing funny in her grief. He laughed because fate had him in its grasp and would not let him go. No matter how hard he tried, he was not to be left to his own devices. For a reason he could not fathom, fate had a habit of attaching him to all manner of waifs and strays.

'You laughing at me?'

'No.' Jack looked at her then, as if seeing her for the first time. He had thought her meek, her blind obedience to her father revealing a weak character with little spirit or fight. He had been wrong. She had killed the man who had threatened her. She was tough and deserved better than the hand life had dealt her.

'So that's what you want?' His hand left the rifle and he stood up so that he faced her. 'You want to ride off not knowing where the hell we're going or what we'll find when we get there?'

'Yes.'

Jack nodded. He had tried to fight fate and he had failed.

'So be it.' He said nothing more.

Jack stood next to his horse and looked back at the cabin. The windows were boarded up, and he had nailed the door shut with stout planks of wood across its front. The place was as secure as he could be bothered to make it. It would have to do. He had plenty of concerns. The fate of the cabin was not one of them.

'Are you done?' Martha's tone was waspish. She was keen to get away.

Jack sighed, then looked up at her. She was already mounted on her father's grey mare. Garrison had looked after the animals well through the winter. Both horses appeared fit and ready for the journey ahead. He wished he could say the same for their riders.

'You not going to say a goodbye?' He summoned his strength, then hauled himself into the saddle. The fight, and the digging of the graves that had followed, had drained what little reserves he had. But it was time to leave, no matter what the state of his health. He had delayed too long already.

'I've said all I'm going to say.' Martha glanced once at the mound where her father lay buried, then gathered her reins. When she spoke again, there was no trace of emotion in her voice. 'If you're done lollygagging, we can be on our way.'

'Yes, ma'am.' Jack gave the reply through gritted teeth, then gathered in his own reins. He was beginning to miss the meek Martha who did what she was told.

He had done all he could do to prepare for the journey ahead. Both horses carried saddlebags full of rations, and behind their saddles he had tied as many blankets as he could find. Into his own knapsack he had packed every ounce of ammunition he possessed and as few items of clothing as he thought he could get away with. He had taken the time to search the woods for any backpacks the men who had attacked the cabin might have hidden. He had found nothing.

'You'd better lead.' He gave the instruction without looking at Martha. 'Make yourself useful.'

There was a short tut of disapproval, then Martha geed her horse up and walked it forward. They would take their time, saving the animals' strength.

Jack watched Martha as she rode away. She was dressed for the journey, her bony frame wrapped in a thick layer of furs. For his part he wore a liberal swathe of Martha's husband's furs. Both of them were armed. He had Pinter's rifle in a sheath attached to the saddle next to his leg, and the revolver he had taken from the man who had killed Garrison, a battered but serviceable Navy Colt, sat in a holster on his hip. Martha had a single carbine taken from the Confederate soldiers Jack had killed and a revolver from one of the men who had attacked the cabin. The rest of the weapons had been left behind.

They were as prepared as he could make them. Only time would tell if they had what they needed to find the two men they were looking for.

# Chapter Twenty-four

'Hold yourselves there.'

The instruction came from the picket who had emerged from a cabin close to the turnpike. It was one of a dozen like it. The rudimentary structures had likely been built just to last the one season, the soldiers ordered to make their winter quarters across the turnpike making themselves as comfortable as the situation would allow.

It had been early one morning when they had finally left the trees behind. After so long lost amidst the dense, confined spaces of the mountain woodland, the sight of the rolling, snow-free hills of the Virginian countryside flowing all the way to the distant horizon had quite taken Jack's breath away. The patchwork of fields and woods with their warm mix of greens and browns spoke of life and comfort, something he had half forgotten existed.

They had taken their time, riding slowly or leading the horses, as they left the mountains behind and made their way towards civilisation, or at least what meagre civilisation they could find as they steered clear of any major towns or cities.

They had passed small farms surrounded by split-rail fences, the wooden houses and barns nestled comfortably into their surroundings. Before they had come across the military checkpoint, they had seen little evidence of life, the winter confining the farmers and their families indoors, wisps of smoke trailing from chimneys the only evidence of their existence.

'You got yourself a pass there, mister?' The picket had come to stand close to Jack's saddle. He was swathed in blankets, with one wrapped over his head, so that Jack could see nothing more than the clouds of air that escaped his mouth. If he was armed, Jack could not see the weapon.

'No.' There was no snow on the ground here, but Jack could still feel the cold seeping into his body now that they had stopped. 'I need one?'

'By rights you do. You a serving man?'

'Yes.'

'What regiment?'

'Lyle's Raiders.' Jack gave the name just as he had planned should he ever be challenged. He hoped it would help him track Lyle's command down. He spoke in a clipped tone, his eyes riveted on the picket the whole time. The revolver on his hip was loose in its holster, a preparation he had made as soon as he had seen the Confederate unit camped across the turnpike.

'Uh huh.' The picket gave a long sniff. 'Figures. You boys don't tend to care much about bits of paper. So where you headed?'

'Nashville.'

'Nashville! Sheet, you got yourselves a long way to go. Take you a whiles, and that's for sure.' He frowned. 'If you got that far to go, what you doing out in this weather?'

'My job.'

The picket contemplated the answer for several long

moments. 'I hope your job includes killing them damn Yankees. Say, are you English?'

'Yes.'

'Figures. I thought you sounded different.' The sentry shifted under his wrappings. 'So what's your name, mister? My captain will want it. He'll write it in the log.'

'Captain Pinter.' Jack gave the lie smoothly, taking the dead man's name without a qualm.

The sentry was unconcerned to discover that he addressed an officer. 'And that your woman?'

Jack twisted in the saddle and looked back at Martha. There was little of her to be seen under her covering of voluminous furs.

'Yes.' He faced the picket once more. 'She's mine.'

'Uh huh.' The sentry sniffed again, liquid gurgling deep in his throat. He looked at Martha for a long time before he spoke again. 'You want to stay a while? Warm yourselves by our fire? We got it right cosy in there.'

Jack had no intention of taking up the offer, kindly meant or not. 'We'll be on our way. I got a report I need to give Major Lyle. He won't stand any delay.'

'Uh huh.' The refusal was greeted with another snort and gurgle. 'Well, you take care out there, sir. There's lots of wild men on the roads these days. Been a few Yankees too, since we whipped their butt over Manassas way. You watch out, specially with a woman and all.'

'I'll be careful.' Jack's tone was as cold as the air he breathed. 'You done asking questions now?'

The sentry looked at him for several long moments, then turned and shuffled away, heading back to the sanctuary of his hut.

Jack watched him go, his hand moving to his holster to refasten the buckle only when he was sure the man was not about to turn back around. The talk of a pass bothered him. They could not rely on every sentry to let them go so easily. Sooner or later they would run into an officer or a sergeant who was more intent on doing his job. If nothing else, they would need a better story and a damn good reason for being on the road.

But what bothered him more was the sentry's reaction to Martha. He sighed. Her presence complicated matters. If he were alone, his journey would be easier. He turned in the saddle to look back at her again, and saw she was staring right back at him, as if able to read his thoughts.

'We sit here much longer, these poor horses will freeze to death. Us too.' Her admonishment was given with a snap in her tone. 'We moving on or what?'

Jack took a deep breath, then tapped his heels and walked his horse on. He would have plenty of time to think on the long road ahead. If Martha became a burden, then it would be easy enough to ditch her. Her hopes of finding her husband did not matter to him. He was no knight in shining armour, and he had no interest in reuniting husband and wife. He cared only for revenge, and for the moment when he would find Nathan Lyle.

The campfire roared into life, the flames bursting up from the scattering of powder Jack had sprinkled liberally over the damp wood. He hoped they would last long enough for the wood to catch rather than just scorch.

'What you going to do when you run out of that there powder?'

Jack looked across at Martha. She had a habit of staring at him that was beginning to grate on his nerves. 'I won't run out.'

Martha pulled away the blanket that she had wrapped over her head. Her hands started to work on her hair, just as they did every night. She pulled it from the band that held it behind her head, then began combing her fingers through it. Jack found himself watching her. There was something very feminine about the way she was trying to do something to the lank and greasy strands.

'You catching flies?' Martha spotted his scrutiny. She paused for a moment, then continued, clearly unconcerned that he was watching her.

'It needs a wash.'

'All of me needs a wash. I ain't had more than a lick and a spit since we left.'

'We'll have to find somewhere to stop soon. The horses need some good fodder or else they won't last the journey, and there are a hundred things we will need.' Jack turned his attention back to the fire. The flames were dying back and he peered closer at the wood to see if it had caught. 'Then we need to find out how to get where we're going.' He scowled. He had embarked on the journey with little idea of how to reach his destination. 'There must a railroad or something.'

'How we going to pay for it?' Martha grimaced as her fingers worked on a particularly stubborn knot.

'You got any money?'

'A little.'

'Then we'll add it to what I've got and use that.'

Martha's hands paused. 'You're quick to want to spend my money.'

Jack shrugged. 'You wanted to come with me. Anyway, we can always find more.'

'And how will we do that exactly?'

'There are ways.' Jack might have been born without a brass farthing to his name, but he had always known how to find money.

'You a thief?' Martha scowled as she used the word.

'Among other things.' Jack could not help smiling as he thought of the back-street hotel he had robbed in India. It was one of the good memories. One of the few.

'I don't hold with thieving.'

'I don't hold with starving.' Jack looked across and caught her eye. 'Look, Martha, I'll do whatever it takes. If you don't like how I go about it, then turn a blind eye or go your own way. I'll thieve if I have to. Kill too if someone gets in my way.'

Martha held his gaze. Her hands had stilled. 'You mean that, don't you?'

'I do.' Jack did not look away.

'Killing this one man means that much to you?'

'Yes.' Jack's tone was carved from granite.

'She must have been one hell of a girl, your Rose.'

'She was.'

'You want to talk about her?'

'No.'

Martha smiled at the abrupt reply. 'How long you been like this, Jack?'

'Like what?'

'Like you're made of stone or something.'

Jack grunted by way of reply. His fears were becoming fact. If he were alone, there would be no one to pose difficult questions. If he were alone, he would not have to think of anything save the journey, and the moment of Lyle's death. Instead, here he was, sitting with a woman he barely knew, being forced into a conversation he did not want to have, being asked questions he did not want to hear. He said nothing and instead poked the fire, nearly extinguishing the few flames he had coaxed into life in the process.

Martha broke the silence. 'You don't want to talk.'

Jack's only answer was a brief glance in her direction before he went back to staring at the fire.

'My John's the same. Sometime I bother him something awful.' Martha's tone changed, the words coming out flat. 'I know I shouldn't, but you know, I want to know what he's thinking, what he wants, what he hopes for. After Joshua died, well, he just didn't want to talk no more.'

'Joshua?' Jack could not help the question. A large flame burst into life from one of the mouldy logs. Martha's face was hidden in the shadows, but there was enough light thrown to allow him to see her lips pressed tight together.

'He was our boy.' Martha moved her head slowly from side to side as she replied. 'He died. Weren't more than a month after I birthed him.'

'I'm sorry.'

'God wanted him back.' Martha's reply was instant. 'He was too perfect for this world so the Lord took him on to the next.' She tipped her head back and looked up at the sky. 'Sometime I think I can almost see him up there.'

Jack glanced up too. The stars looked down, untroubled and serene. 'I like the stars.' He made the admission freely. 'They don't give a shit about us. They just sit there without a care in the whole bloody world. That's what I like about them.'

He immediately felt foolish. He was a hardened soldier, yet he was spouting on like some street-corner poet.

'You think your Rose is up there too? With my Joshua?'

Jack shook his head. 'I've no idea, love.'

'I think she is.' Martha inched closer to the fire. 'You knew her a long time?'

Jack heard the need in her voice. She didn't just want to talk; she had to. Like a soldier on the eve of battle, she needed the distraction.

'No.' He found a thin smile. 'I hardly knew her at all.'

'That the truth?' Martha gave a smile of her own. 'You hardly knew her at all, yet now here you are, hell bent on chasing down the man you think killed her, no matter that you're killing yourself in the process. I reckon that makes you a fool, Jack Lark.'

'Perhaps.' Jack could not help laughing a little at Martha's verdict. He'd been called a fool a lot in his life. Yet here he was. Still breathing. Still fighting.

'You told us she was a slave.'

'She was. She escaped.'

'Then she must be something special. It ain't easy being a slave and it's even harder getting away. Those poor people. Why the Lord put them on this good earth just to let them be treated like that, I don't know.'

Jack was intrigued. 'You're from the South and your husband is in the Confederate army. Don't you believe in slavery? Isn't that what you're fighting for?'

'No.' Martha's reply was firm. 'We never had slaves; that's for rich folk. All we care about is getting enough to eat, our family, doing God's will and staying alive. We leave the politicking to them that wants to do it. It ain't for the likes of us.'

'But your husband went to fight,' Jack pressed her. 'He's fighting so those rich folk get to keep their slaves.'

'Lordy, my John ain't fighting for them slaves. He's fighting for our rights! We just want to be free.'

'The North want you to be free too.' Jack had heard a dozen arguments supporting the Union's position during his time in the North. This was the first time he had heard the view of someone from the South.

'The hell they do. They want to make us just like them, when all we want is to be left alone and to live as we see fit. I don't need some know-nothing sitting up there in Washington telling me how to live my life. Soon as we broke away from the Union, why, them Yankees thought they'd invade our homes and fight us till they brought us to heel like some damn dog that needs a whipping to know who's master. We ain't fighting to let them rich folk get to keep their slaves. We're fighting for our liberty, just like the founding fathers said we should.'

Jack shook his head. The argument sounded dreadfully similar to the one he had heard in the North. The Union was not just fighting to free slaves. They were fighting to preserve the very idea of the United States. They wanted America to be one great united nation. To achieve that aim, they could not allow the Confederate states to break away and form their own version of the founding fathers' vision.

'And what if the North are fighting for the same things?'

Martha was watching him closely. 'Maybe they are. Maybe they're not. Maybe they're just fighting because that was a whole lot easier than sitting around a table and working it all out. All I know is those Yankees want to stop us doing what we want. That's why my John went to fight.' She offered a wan smile. 'So are you still a Billy Yankee at heart, Jack?'

'No,' Jack answered honestly. 'I never was.'

'Why'd you fight for them then?'

'Because someone asked me to.'

'That it?'

'He paid me.'

'So you fight just for money?'

'No.'

'That don't make a whole lot of sense.' Martha chuckled at the conflicting answers.

'No, I know.' Jack laughed too. 'I don't understand it either. I hope your John is a less complicated man.'

Martha's laughter stopped. 'No one ever called my John complicated.'

'But he's a good man?'

'I known him my whole life.' Martha evaded the question. 'Pa didn't like him.'

'Why doesn't that surprise me?' Jack tried to lighten the tone. 'Did the old man like anyone?'

'He liked you. Well, after a while he did.' Martha tried to smile, but the expression evaded her. 'He is a good man, my John. I don't blame him for that temper of his, or for what he does when I make him angry. When we were first married, I doubt there was anyone happier than the pair of us.' She finally managed to find a half-smile at some old memory. 'A lot of things changed when Joshua passed.' She paused, staring off into the distance. 'But John's not a fighter, not really.' Her voice hardened. 'It frightens me to think that he has to fight men like you.'

Jack was wondering at Martha's choice of words. 'Does he hit you?' He did not shirk from the question. He had been brought up in the rookeries, a hard place where people had to struggle to survive. He had known enough men who beat their wives to recognise the hidden meaning.

'Sometimes. If I deserve it. Sometimes even if I don't.' He caught a flash of defiance in her reply, and her chin lifted a fraction.

'Maybe he'll be different when he comes home. War changes a man.'

'Maybe he will. He weren't always like he is now, but I ain't counting on him coming home like he was before. I ain't that lucky.' Martha avoided Jack's gaze. 'So what were you like before you became a soldier who fights, or maybe doesn't fight, for money?'

Jack heard the mockery in her tone and was pleased. The Martha sitting opposite him had proved herself to be as tough a character as he had ever met, and he could only admire her for it. Yet there were clearly other sides to her character. He could not imagine this Martha submitting meekly to her husband and taking a beating from him. Perhaps the time alone with her father had changed her. Or perhaps she was a different person when she was with her husband. Whichever it might be, he could see the change that had come into her expression as the conversation had turned towards her marriage, and so he decided to steer it in a different direction.

'I've always been fighting one way or the other, and I've been a soldier a long time now. It's who I am. What I think I've always been deep inside.'

He paused for a moment, wondering if he should continue. It was rare for him to speak with such candour, yet Martha had been open, and he could sense that he could talk to her without fear of recrimination.

'I like it. I like being a soldier. I like what I can do. Something happens to me when I'm fighting. It's like I become the person I was meant to be. Everything else, well, that's just so much bullshit.'

Martha did not reply. She was looking at him, her brow furrowed as if she had finally awoken to the fact that she had tied herself to a dangerous man she hardly knew.

'We need to do something different,' Jack did not give her time to dwell, 'if we're going to get where we want to go.' He was thinking back to the sentry and his half-hearted attempt to get Jack and Martha to stay. The next time they might not get away so easily.

'Different?'

'It's too dangerous to travel as we are.' He smiled as the idea formed in his mind, stirring the memories of his first time as an impostor. 'You'll need to change. You won't like it, I know that, but it is what it is, and you'll just have to get used to it.' He watched Martha's expression. It was clear she was wary of whatever it was he had planned. 'It's time you became someone else.'

# Chapter Twenty-five

'You sure 'bout this, Jack?'

'You look fine.' Jack did not bother to turn around in the saddle. It was not the first time Martha had asked the question. It was mid morning and they had been riding since first light. This was the fourth or fifth time she had interrupted the quiet ride.

'I don't sound like a man.'

'Then don't say anything.' This time Jack reined his horse in and brought it to a stand, then turned to glare at her. 'Look. I don't want to have to say this again. You look fine.'

Martha stopped her own horse. 'I look like a bushwhacker.'

'Yes, you do, and that's the point.' He offered something that he hoped was close to a reassuring smile. 'Even your old man wouldn't recognise you.'

Martha scowled, then lifted her hat. Her hands clawed at the remains of her hair. 'I look stupid.'

Jack smiled at her expression. He had been many things in his time, but it was the first time he had tried his hand at being a barber on anyone else's hair except his own. He had done a fair job, at least to his mind. He had not chopped her hair close to her scalp; he had left a fair amount so that it reached almost down to her neck. The clumps, and the few odd parts that stood upright, would settle with time. 'Least you don't have to worry about washing it any more.'

Martha's scowl deepened. 'I look stupid. No one will think I look like a man.'

'Who said anything about a man?' Jack could not resist teasing her. 'But when we get you the right clothes, you'll look like a scrawny little shite well enough.' He laughed then, the sound coming easily.

'What will my John say when we find him?'

'I imagine he'll be so pleased to see you that he'll not even notice your damn hair.' Jack bit his tongue and said nothing more. He had been about to say that Martha's husband would likely be too busy getting her into bed to worry about the state of her. Martha was no great beauty, not like some women he had known. But she was attractive. He was not sure if it was her competent, ordered manner that was appealing, or if there was something in her lean, work-hardened body. But he would not remark on it, or make a coarse comment. He knew she would not approve if he did.

'I still don't see why I couldn't just hide it.'

'Because that would be a risk.' Jack repeated the conversation they had had before. 'This journey isn't safe, especially not for you. There'll be more men like those back at your cabin; hell, even those damn soldiers were lusting after you as soon as they clapped eyes on you.'

'Lordy! Lusting!' Martha gave a shocked laugh at the idea. 'Ain't been no one lusted after me ever.'

Jack saw the flush of crimson on her cheeks as she used a word she had likely never said before. 'There's no accounting for taste.' He chuckled as he saw the flush spread. She looked younger with the colour on her cheeks. 'Some blokes like their bints skinny.'

Martha laughed harder this time. 'Jack Lark, you say the most terrible things.' She stopped, and looked at him with a more serious expression on her face. 'But I still don't know why you think chopping my hair off and sticking me in a pair of long pants will make anyone believe I'm a man.'

'It will work.' Jack was pulling on his horse's reins the moment its head dropped, the action instinctive. 'I know how it's done.'

'You pretended to be a woman?' Martha's eyebrows lifted.

'No, not yet anyways.' Jack could not help grinning at the notion. 'But I've pretended to be someone else half my damn life. It's all about confidence. If you don't doubt yourself, then no one else will. Believe you are what you are pretending to be and you'll be fine. Besides, I've known men with less muscle on them than you. Folk will take one look at us and see an officer and his orderly. With you dressed as a woman it would be different. They'd likely see me as a threat and you . . . well, you'd be something they'd want.'

'You have a low opinion of people.' Martha was no longer smiling.

'Maybe. But it's what I've seen. Men like the ones back at your cabin, men who have been in battle, and especially those who've run, they've turned their backs on who they were. They've seen and done things that came straight from hell. That means they're capable of anything.' Jack looked away, unable to meet her gaze.

'You need to be more careful, Jack.' Martha called for his attention.

'What do you mean?'

'Sounds like you're starting to care 'bout me.'

'Shit.' Jack looked at her and saw she was smiling. 'Shit.' He repeated the single word, then kicked his heels and forced his horse back into motion.

For Martha was quite correct. His simple hunt for revenge was getting complicated. And in his experience, complications increased the risk of something going wrong. He had the dreadful feeling that one day he would be forced to choose between Martha and his mission. Before, that decision would have been an easy one and he would have dropped Martha no matter the circumstances. That was no longer the case. He had not meant for it to happen, yet somehow he had let her fate become intertwined with his. He could no longer cut and run. To his dismay, he realised that he was stuck with her.

Jack did his best to put his misgivings aside as they rode into the small town that straddled the turnpike. Thus far they had avoided populated areas, buying supplies along the way from the farmsteads that dotted the countryside. Yet they needed more things than they could get from a farmer, and so they had to risk venturing into a town.

A fine grey rain had begun at dawn and showed no sign of stopping. It did little to improve the look of the place, which appeared to huddle down in the mist and the murk. He had no idea what it was called. He did know that it was not much to look at. The turnpike ploughed a straight line through the centre. It was lined with split-rail fencing and a collection of no more than a dozen mismatched buildings. A few boasted porches, or signs that proclaimed their type of business, but most were anonymous, their purpose known only to the people who lived there. However, he was pleased to spot a livery for the horses, and there was also a small general store. He had a long list of items he wanted to purchase, and the horses needed some good-quality forage to prepare them for the journey ahead. It would mean spending more of the little money he and Martha had between them, but the idea did not trouble him. He would just have to find them some more.

'I've got two spare rooms, sir, but those are the last two I have, and I ain't got no choice but to ask you to pay a little over the full rate if you want them both.'

Jack stared back at the man who ran the only hotel in the small town. He was short and almost perfectly round, with beady little eyes that were never still. There was not a hair on his head, but he still managed to maintain a thin, pointed goatee beard that he had dyed an incongruous shade of red. At least he was dressed well, in a long black frock coat with matching trousers and waistcoat, but any elegant effect was ruined by half a dozen obvious stains and a thick wedge of padding that played peek-a-boo through a tear in the seam at the jacket's right shoulder.

'We'll take them.' Jack did not look back at Martha for permission.

'Yes, sir.' The hotelier turned quickly, then stood on tiptoe so that he could pull two keys from the uppermost level of a rack attached to the wall behind him. 'You'll find them at the top of the stairs on the right. We serve dinner in the dining hall from six till eight. Breakfast in the morning too. I got some fresh bacon in just last Tuesday.' He handed over the pair of heavy iron keys with a sickly smile.

Jack did his best not to snort at the hotel manager's choice of the word 'fresh' for meat over a week old. He had seen the dining hall on the way in and had read the prices on the large chalkboard perched on top of the mantelpiece. They were steep, even for a place with few choices.

The hotelier had finished speaking and now stood looking at Jack, wringing his hands. 'Is there anything I can supply you with, sir?' His eyes darted to Martha, who had hung back and kept out of the conversation. 'Perhaps your,' he paused and scowled as he tried to find a word to describe her, 'companion . . . um, servant . . . perhaps one of you would like a bath?'

Jack stared back at the manager, his expression unaltered. 'Yes, we would.'

'Very well, sir, I'll have my man get to it right away. He'll be with you toot-de-sweet as them Frenchies say.' The fat little man nodded vigorously in response to Jack's agreement, the motion setting his many chins in motion.

Jack nodded but did not offer thanks. He found the hotelier's ingratiating tone irksome.

'Is there anything else—'

'No.' Jack cut the man off. 'That's all for now. Have the bath brought up. Make sure the water is hot.'

'Yes, sir, my man will be on that directly.' The hotelier bobbed up and down, as if offering one tiny bow after another.

Jack turned and handed one of the keys to Martha, then picked up the jumbled heap of saddlebags he had dumped on the floor.

'You can't keep me in here.'

'Yes, I can.'

'You ain't my husband, Jack. You don't get to tell me what to do.'

Jack sucked in a breath, holding onto his temper only with great difficulty. Not for the first time, he wished for the more subservient Martha who did as she was told. Her father's death had changed her. Jack did not know if that had been for the better.

The two of them were in her room. It was not much to look at. The walls were made of panelled wood and the floorboards were scuffed and stained from long use. The only furnishing was an iron bedstead with bedding that looked like it was from the previous century, and a battered pine trunk under the window.

The bath had been duly delivered, although it had taken the best part of half an hour for the decrepit servant to fill it with hot water. Jack had let Martha have it first, spending his time kicking his heels in his own room until she had finished and come to fetch him. She had waited in his room whilst he bathed, though by the time he had got in, the water was barely tepid.

Still, it felt good to be clean and in fresh clothes, though whatever pleasure he had felt was disappearing quickly as Martha refused to obey his instruction to stay in the room whilst he went out.

'Jesus wept,' he hissed through gritted teeth. 'You think this place is safe? We don't even know where we are, for God's sake. It's safer for you to stay here whilst I take a look around.'

'Don't take the Lord's name in vain, and don't you shout at me.' Martha stood near the room's single window, her hands on her hips. She was dressed in her husband's trousers and a grey plaid shirt, clothes she had lent Jack but which he had given her back.

'You think you can go out looking like that.' Jack waved a hand in her direction. 'You look ridiculous.'

'And whose fault is that!' Martha coloured at the jibe. She

plucked at the shirt, which was massive on her thin frame. 'This is your idea, or had you forgotten?'

'You need to stay here. I'll get you some smaller clothes. Then you'll be able to come and go as you damn well please.'

'And where are you going to get those clothes, Jack? I didn't see no place selling outfits, did you? And we ain't got a dime left even if there were.'

'Don't you worry about that.'

'Don't patronise me.'

'Then don't ask bloody stupid questions.'

'Don't take that tone with me, Jack Lark.'

'Then don't bleat on like a bloody sheep. Jesus Christ.' Jack winced and ground his teeth in frustration as he waited for the inevitable rebuke.

'Do not take the Lord's name in vain.'

'All right.' Jack lifted his hands as if to ward her away, even though she had yet to take a single step in his direction. 'I get it. You don't want me to tell you what to do. Fine. I won't. But for the love of God, think about it. We don't know this place. We don't know if we're safe, or if even now some bastards are planning to steal everything we have. I'm just saying we should be cautious.'

'So I stay here whilst you go out and drink our last few cents away. I know what you menfolk are like. One sip of whiskey and your brains fly out of your head. Then you're as wild as a bobcat and woe betide any woman that dares stand in your way.'

'I'm not like that. I'm not about to get corned. Stay here, stay safe, and I'll sort out some clothes and try to find out just where the hell we are, and where we should be going. Is that all right with you?'

Martha still glared back at him. But his words had made some sort of sense and finally she nodded. 'All right. You go. But I tell you this. You come back drunk, and so help me you'll wake up missing something you kind of like, you hear me?'

Jack did not doubt she was more than capable of making good on the threat. 'Yes, ma'am, I hear you.'

He had won the battle of wits. Now it was time for him to find what they needed.

# Chapter Twenty-six

---

'This way, sir, it's not far now.'

Jack did his best not to grimace. The hotel manager had insisted on escorting him to a tavern further down the turnpike. The little man, eager to please, fluttered around him like a hungry pigeon hoping for crumbs. He had also maintained a running commentary that had begun to grate after the first dozen paces.

'I know the owner. It'll be my pleasure to introduce you.'

Jack strode on, the little man half running to keep up. When Jack had asked where he could get a drink, the manager had produced a battered black top hat, the offer of an escort made before he could refuse it. The hat was several sizes too large, and the man had to hold it in place lest it fall to smother his face.

For his part, Jack had dressed in Pinter's uniform. The jacked fitted passably well, and he had done his best to scrape away the marks of old blood and repair the rents in the fabric. He knew he still appeared rather unkempt, but at least the uniform made the revolver on his hip look less out of place than it would have done had he been in civilian attire.

Jack moved around a deep pool of water that had formed in a rut in the turnpike, nearly knocking the hotel manager from his feet in the process.

'I beg your pardon.' The apology for the contact was instant, even though it had been Jack's fault. 'Now, here we are, sir.' The hotelier plucked at Jack's sleeve and turned him towards a single-storey building. 'The Beehive Tavern. The finest establishment in the entire county.'

Calling the place a tavern would have taken a leap of faith Jack did not have. The building did not boast a sign, and there was little indication of life behind the shuttered windows. For a moment he thought he was being played false, and that he was in the midst of a bait and hook, but then the door opened and he caught a glimpse of a bar running across the far side of the main room.

'Evening, Chester.' The man leaving the bar nodded a greeting, then belched softly. If he noticed Jack's presence, he made no note of it and ambled on his way.

'Evening, Bill.' The hotelier, Chester, hopped from foot to foot at Jack's side. 'Why, that's Billy Brown.' He spoke quietly to Jack. 'You know him?'

'No.' Jack did not bother to hide his frustration at the ridiculous question.

'He's a friend of mine.' Chester puffed out his tiny chest. 'Owns a transportation company. Comes to me for advice on matters of business.' He spoke in a confiding tone and was careful to pitch his voice low so that the man could not hear him. 'You have a good night now, Bill. I expect I'll be seeing you tomorrow.' His voice was suddenly overly loud as he called after the man.

Jack could not help noticing that Billy Brown acknowledged

the shout with nothing more than a shake of the head.

'Now, sir, before we go in . . .' Chester, emboldened, reached out and put an arm in front of Jack, as if frightened he would bolt indoors. 'You signed in at my establishment as Captain Pinter. Is that the name you would like to be known by when I introduce you to my good friend Albert?'

'Yes.' Jack was losing patience.

'So be it. Some fellas, why they're right particular 'bout this type of thing. A man can't be too careful. Now,' he paused and fixed Jack with a sickly smile, 'it would sound better if I knew your given name. Then I can make the introduction proper and just like it should be.'

'Jack. My name is Jack.'

'Well, thank you, Captain Jack Pinter it is. Do you mind if I call you Jack?'

'Yes.'

Chester's odd smile widened. 'And you can call me Chester.' He paused as he only then understood Jack's answer, and the smile faded.

Jack shook his head and opened the door, tired of standing in the chill early-evening air. Chester recovered quickly and rushed past so that he still entered first.

'Ah! Here we are then. And here is Albert.' The hotelier waved towards the bar at the far end of the large room.

Jack glanced around. There was little to look at inside the Beehive. Benches lined the walls, and there were two large, roughly hewn tables. The bar was made from more of the same wood; behind it were a stack of barrels and a number of deep shelves lined with whiskey bottles and glasses of various sizes. There were just three other customers. Two men sat at one table sharing a bottle of whiskey, and a third, who wore a grey army uniform, waited patiently outside a door on one side of the room.

Jack was thousands of miles from his former home, but there was something about the hint of debauchery in the air. The Beehive smelt of raw spirits, ale, sweat and woodsmoke. It was familiar enough to awaken memories he had tried hard to forget.

'Albert!' Chester strode across the room, his arms stretched wide. 'How good it is to see you this fine evening. I have brought you a new customer. I have the pleasure of introducing Captain Jack Pinter, who is doing me the honour of residing at my humble hotel. I think you'll be interested in making his acquaintance.'

Jack paid the windy and theatrical introduction little attention. Instead he focused on the man he was being introduced to. The owner of the tavern was a heavyset fellow with slicked-down dark hair and a fine pair of mutton-chop whiskers. He was not tall, but he looked powerfully built, with heavily muscled arms that were on display below shirtsleeves that had been rolled almost to the shoulder. Jack would have guessed him to be in his early forties, but the lack of even a single grey strand in either his whiskers or his hair made it possible he was younger. He was dressed in black pinstripe trousers with a bright green and blue paisley waistcoat over a white shirt and a thick gold watch chain stretched across his belly. He looked thoroughly unimpressed with the jester at Jack's side.

'Jack.' Chester gave an awkward half-bow as he ignored Jack's refusal to allow the use of his given name. 'May I present my good friend Albert Lawrence, the owner of the Beehive Tavern.'

Jack nodded a greeting to the man behind the slab of wood.

'What'll it be?'

The simple question was delivered without emotion and in an accent that came straight from Jack's home town. Jack suddenly understood Chester's interest in the introduction. It was likely the first time he had seen two Englishmen in the same place.

'I'll take a glass of ale.' He did his best to hide his surprise. He was in some forgotten town in the wilds of God alone knew where, but he had found a fellow Englishman.

The man swept a tankard from under the counter, then turned to snap open the tap on the beer barrel behind him. If he was startled by Jack's accent, then not a trace showed on his face.

As he poured, Jack noticed movement elsewhere in the tavern. A thin woman wearing a tight-fitting dress of dark reds and black had summoned the man waiting patiently by the side door. Jack had been in enough drinking dens to spot a whore at a dozen paces.

'You'll have to wait if you want to take a turn with the girls, chum. There's only two working tonight.' The comment was made in the flat, dry tone of a man barely interested in the conversation.

Jack turned back to see Lawrence watching him, his tankard of ale placed on the bar in front of him.

'Captain Pinter is not that sort of man.' Chester answered for his guest, then turned to look at Jack with an uneasy smile. 'He has a companion back at my hotel.'

Jack's expression did not alter, even as he realised that Chester had made his own conclusion about the arrangement between Jack and his supposed orderly. He did not care what the fat little man thought.

'Don't see how that matters. A fellow can tup a whore if it suits him. Now then,' Lawrence fixed Chester with a stare, 'why don't you walk your chalk like a good fellow.'

'Walk your chalk indeed.' Chester smirked at the phrase, his chins wobbling as he began to chortle. But he must have spotted something in Lawrence's gaze that stopped the laughter and had him backing away. 'Very well, I shall leave you two fine English gentlemen to your discourse. I am sure you have much to converse about, seeing as how you are citizens of the same shores and all.' He took a few steps backwards before sweeping his ridiculous top hat back onto his head. 'Jack, may I wish you a pleasant evening. Albert, I'll see you on the morrow.' Goodbyes made, he walked to the door with a swaggering gait that might have worked had he been a foot taller and a few stone lighter.

'Nice man.' Jack made the observation wryly, then took up his tankard. 'How much for the ale?'

'On the house, chum.' Lawrence had reached for a cloth and he now wiped the bar clean. His tone had changed. 'You can pay for it by telling me how the fuck you ended up in this godforsaken shithole.'

Jack grinned at the turn of phrase. He had found a corner of London in the southern states of America. 'I'm just passing through.'

'But you've been on these shores for a while, I take it. What with that uniform you're wearing.'

'It's a long story.'

'I've got all night.' Lawrence smiled as he replied. 'Unless there's somewhere else you'd rather be.'

'I've got time.' Jack sipped at his drink, relishing the taste. It had been a long time since he had drunk freshly poured cask ale.

'You lonely, mister?'

The question came from a dark-haired girl he had not noticed approach. She was pretty, her skin pale against the black of her hair. The bodice of her dress was half open; what she had, she was putting on display for all the world to see. But Jack had seen too many whores in his time to be even remotely interested. This one had the glazed, listless gaze of a girl who had worked too long. One glance at the bloodshot whites of her eyes and the dilated pupils told him she was on opium, or whatever the poor, unfortunate souls in this part of the world took to dull the pain of their miserable lives.

'Leave him be, love,' Lawrence said. 'Go back to your room.' He dismissed the girl in a kindly tone. 'Poor cow.' He spoke softly when she had wandered away.

Jack watched the girl as she walked back to the side door. He felt something close to pity. He had a fair idea that her life would be wretched, a fate shared by whores the world over. Yet some escaped that bitter destiny. The sight of the girl had reminded him of Mary, who had once plied the same trade in his mother's gin palace and whom he had worshipped. She had been one of the few girls to come across a way out of her situation, finding herself a rich man who was prepared to take her and her son and give them both a better life. He wondered where she was now. When their beauty faded, most girls would have to leave the place where they plied their trade and go to work on the streets, the price they could charge for their services getting steadily lower until they were either dead or destitute, whichever happened to come first.

'I can call her back if you want her, chum. No skin off my nose either way.' Lawrence had spotted Jack staring after the girl.

'No, you're all right.' Jack drained a fair slug of his ale. 'So how the hell did *you* end up here? Where are you from exactly?'

'Southwark.'

'Figures. You southern bastards never did have much sense.' Jack grinned as he made the old joke.

'Southern, is it?' Lawrence matched Jack's smile with one of his own. 'Where you from then, chum?'

'Whitechapel.'

'Oh, there you go. Best I turf you out now then, otherwise you'll probably pinch something soon as I turn my back.'

Jack laughed. It was good to talk to someone who knew his London.

'So why you wearing grey?' Lawrence took up another tankard and poured himself a glass of ale. 'This ain't our fight last time I checked.'

'No, it's not. But like I said, it's a long bloody story.'

Lawrence shrugged. 'Well, I ain't one to pry and I won't poke my beak in where it ain't wanted.'

Jack liked the answer. 'There any soldiers around here?'

'A few. Some lads are waiting for orders to join these new units they're putting together. A fair few went west a few weeks ago. Near killed off my trade.'

'Where were they headed?' Jack sipped at his ale.

'I'm not rightly sure I can remember. You looking for your mob?'

Jack nodded. 'I was wounded. Time I was right, they'd moved on.' It was an easy enough lie. 'I heard they were headed to Nashville.'

'Well, that's a fair way away. I'm sure some of the bods that came through here were going that way, but I don't recall much of what they said, to be honest.'

'Fair enough. What's the best way to get there?'

'There's a railroad line south of here that'll take you all the way to Chattanooga. From there you can make your way to Nashville easily enough, I reckon.'

'Where do we need to go?'

'I reckon your best bet is to head to Lynchburg. From there, the railroad works its way to a pass through the Blue Mountains, then down the Great Valley until you're way down in the arse end of Tennessee. I expect there's connecting lines up to Nashville and beyond down there, but I've never been that way myself.'

'I'll figure something out.' Jack made a mental note of the names. After days wandering without much notion of where they were going, it felt good to have a destination to aim for. He would ask Chester for directions to Lynchburg before they left.

His attention was taken by the sound of the side door opening. As he watched, the man he had seen enter a short while before staggered out, a contented smile plastered across his face and his hands busy tucking his shirt back into his trousers. But it was not the fact that his clothing was in disarray that interested Jack. It was his stature. The lad was a good six inches shorter than he was, and the grey uniform he wore revealed a wiry, lean physique.

'Who's that lad over there?' he asked over the rim of his tankard as he took another draught.

'That?' Lawrence barely glanced at the young man, who was now walking slowly back to his spot at one of the tables, where he had left a half-empty bottle of whiskey. 'That's Billy Brown's boy.'

'The same Billy Brown that owns a transport operation?'

'That's the one.' Lawrence's brow furrowed. 'You know him?'

'We've not been introduced, no.' Jack hid his face behind his tankard. 'Is he a friend of yours?' An idea was forming in his mind. It was not a friendly one.

'He drinks in here. He's all right, I suppose. Wouldn't trust him with a brass farthing of my own rhino, mind.'

'And his lad?'

'Now he's a prize pillock.' Lawrence looked over at the young lad. 'Spends his pa's money well enough, and a lot of that comes to me or the girls.' He looked at Jack, a knowing expression on his face. 'But he'll be away soon enough. He joined up, so the army can worry about him now.'

Jack watched Lawrence carefully. The owner of the tavern had probably worked out what he had planned. 'What time would you reckon he'll leave here?'

'Late. He'll finish that bottle before he's done.'

'And he walks from here?'

'He lives on the far side of town. Fifteen-minute walk if you're sober. It'll take him thirty tonight, that's if he makes it at all.'

Jack watched Lawrence's eyes, searching them for a hint of censure. There was nothing. 'How long will it take him to finish that bottle?'

'An hour, maybe longer if he goes back for another ride.'

'Then I'd better have another ale,' Jack pushed the tankard towards Lawrence, 'and you can tell me how a lad from Southwark ended up here.' He was a patient man when he had to be. He could wait.

Jack drained the last of his ale, then paused, the tankard still close to his lips, as he listened for the sound of the tavern's door closing. Only when he heard it did he lower the tankard for the last time.

'You on your way now, Jack?' Lawrence did not bother to hide the smirk that crept across his face.

'Maybe I'll take a little stroll.' Jack grinned back. The ale had warmed his belly and he had enjoyed his time in the Beehive Tavern. Lawrence had been a good companion, and it had been an interesting distraction to swap tales of childhoods spent in London's less salubrious neighbourhoods. But the time for talking was done.

'You think you'll pass back this way?'

'I have no idea.' Jack gave the honest answer.

'Stop by if you do. I should still be here.' Lawrence grinned, then reached over the bar and offered his hand. 'Well met, Jack.'

Jack shook the hand. 'I reckon I'll see you again.'

'Not if I see you first.' Lawrence guffawed at his own joke, then nodded at Jack. 'Take care of yourself. And if you get into any mischief, well, just don't kill the lad, all right.'

'I won't.' Jack turned on his heel and headed for the door. The evening had been pleasant, and useful. Lawrence had given him a good steer on how to start the journey to Nashville. Now it was time to secure some of the other things he would need to get there.

The chill of the air hit Jack as soon as he stepped outside. He had drunk enough ale to feel the ground give a lurch as the cold smacked him around the chops, and he was forced to reach out and hold onto a hitching post near the tavern's entrance to steady himself.

It was dark, but the moon was out and it cast enough light for him to be able to pick out the shape of a man staggering his way up the turnpike. Billy Brown's son had not gone far.

Jack sucked down a breath of the wintry air, then shivered as it rasped into his lungs. It was unpleasant, but it was sobering, and so he stood where he was, letting the chill take away the heat of the ale.

Only when he was sure he was ready did he move. He walked briskly, his breath forming a cloud around his face.

'Hey!' he called. He pitched his voice so that his words would carry, but not so loud that he would wake anyone sleeping in any of the buildings nearby. 'Hey, you there!'

He quickened his pace. The wandering figure had come to a halt. The lad in the grey uniform turned around with difficulty and peered into the darkness as he tried to locate the voice calling after him.

'You forgot something,' Jack called again.

'You talking to me?' The words came out slurred.

'Yes!' Jack headed directly for the lad. 'You left this in the tavern.' He slipped his right hand into a pocket as if searching for the forgotten item and increased his pace so that he would arrive at something like double time.

'I left what?' The lad was struggling to stand still. He shuffled from foot to foot, then lurched to the right, as if the ground suddenly sloped beneath his feet.

'This.' Jack's fist shot out of his pocket. The blow landed exactly as he had planned, cracking into the point of the lad's chin. He held back some of his strength, but the punch still had enough force to knock the lad's head back, his teeth snapping together with an audible click before he fell, hitting the ground flat on his back, his arms spread wide.

Jack was on him in a heartbeat. But there was no need for a second blow. The lad was out cold.

'Sorry, chum.' Jack bent down to grab his jacket, then hauled him off the main road and into the shadow of one of the buildings just down from the tavern.

Once safely out of sight, he rummaged through the lad's pockets, finding what he was looking for almost immediately. Billy Brown clearly took care of his son, and even a night's drinking and whoring had made little dent in the wedge of folded banknotes, some plain, some grey in colour, held in place with a fine silver money clip. Alongside the notes were a few gold and silver coins. It was no fortune by any means, but it would be enough to tide over two frugal travellers.

'Right, chum. Let's be having you.' Jack stuffed the money deep into a pocket, then started to unbutton the lad's overcoat. He had directions and now he had some ready cash. He just needed some clothes that would fit Martha's skinny frame.

Billy Brown's son's evening had not finished well. But Jack's had worked out really rather nicely.

# Chapter Twenty-seven

———◆———

*J*ack relished the feeling of being outside and in the saddle. He and Martha had spent days incarcerated in railroad cars, with the two horses travelling in trucks put by for animals. The long period of enforced inactivity had stretched all their nerves, and he could sense that the horses were enjoying the freedom as much as he was. The price for securing the right passes to allow them to use the Virginia and Tennessee Railroad had been steep, not least because they had no proper documentation. That lack had cost them a pretty penny, the prices coming with a substantial surcharge that paid the railroad officials to turn a blind eye.

The first railroad had taken them from Lynchburg in Virginia as far as Chattanooga in Tennessee. More money had changed hands to secure them places on a locomotive heading north to Nashville. That journey had been shorter, but no less painful, and Jack had chafed at sitting on his backside doing nothing.

Unwilling to spend any more of his stolen dollars on a hotel, he had led them out into the countryside the moment they had arrived in Nashville. The horses, as tired of travelling as Jack was, had needed the exercise, and it would give them all a well-deserved break before they embarked on the last leg of their journey, up the Cumberland river to the town of Dover and Fort Donelson, the location, they hoped, of both Martha's husband and Lyle and his raiders.

They had been in the saddle at dawn. Jack could not remember a time when he had enjoyed exercise so much. The morning had been beautifully clear as they rode through the gentle hills and open farmland that came right up to the fringes of the town of Nashville, which was set on a bluff near the Cumberland river.

For once, the sky was clear of heavy grey rainclouds. Jack's body still ached from the wounds he had taken, and he often wondered if he would ever be free of pain. But it was not enough to spoil the pleasure of the early-morning ride, and he let his mind empty as he kicked back his heels and urged his horse into a canter.

A single pistol shot snapped him from his reverie.

'What was that?' Martha pulled her horse to a halt.

'No idea.' Jack kept riding. 'But I know what it's not.'

'What's that?'

'Our concern.'

He rode on. Despite his glib answer, he still listened carefully.

'There!' Martha called out.

It was enough for Jack to bring his own horse to a halt. He turned in the saddle and saw Martha pointing behind them. It was immediately clear what had caught her attention.

Two riders were riding hell for leather directly towards them. Even as he spotted them, they turned off the track and tore up a slope towards a wooded ridge.

'What they doing?'

'How the hell should I know?' Jack gave the waspish reply, then turned his horse around and rode back until he was next to Martha.

He squinted as he tried to make out what was happening. He could see a second group of cavalry thundering along the track as they gave chase. There were more riders in this second group, but he could not count their number. He wished he had a pair of field glasses so that he could see what was what as the group turned off the track and followed the two men up the slope.

'Come on.' He kicked his heels, then turned his horse around and rode back along the track, trying to keep the two groups in sight.

'What you doing?'

'I want to see what's going on.' He turned to flash Martha a smile. 'Don't worry. We'll keep our distance. I meant what I said. This isn't our concern.'

He kept his eyes on the two groups. The men being chased had turned across the slope so that they now rode parallel to the track. He walked his horse slowly, knowing Martha would follow. It was a foolish thing to do, he knew that, but it would be a break from the tedium.

One of the two riders being chased broke from a patch of woodland, closely followed by his companion. They were high on the sloping ground three or perhaps four hundred yards above the track. As Jack and Martha watched, the lead rider twisted in the saddle whilst still at full gallop. He held a black object in his hand. A moment later, the crack of a revolver firing reached their ears.

The rider fired again and again, the short flurry of shots coming so fast that the sound blurred together. They heard a shout of pain as at least one of them hit a target.

Shots came back then. None hit, but they were enough of a warning for the man shooting to turn back around and kick his horse hard.

The pursuers burst out from behind a small group of trees. This time Jack was closer and he counted eight men in the group. All wore grey uniforms.

'Come on.' He urged his horse into a trot and took a path parallel to the two groups. They were much lower down the slope, and he was pretty sure that the fast-moving riders would ignore the two spectators.

He was forced to kick his horse to a faster pace almost immediately. The two groups were charging across the open ground on the upper slope. More shots came as the pursuers tried to bring down their targets. One man broke from the chasing pack. Even from a fair distance, Jack could hear his yips and yells as he encouraged his animal on.

The men being chased changed direction. With bullets snapping past their ears, they turned southwards and careered down the slope, their horses plunging on even as the ground fell away. It was bravely done. On such a steep slope, either animal could twist or even break a leg at any moment. Yet the two riders being pursued did not care. They rode fast, gambling their lives in the hope that the men chasing them would not be prepared to risk such folly.

Their pursuers turned to follow. But only their leader increased speed to match the two men risking everything on the sloping ground. The rest slowed, the men unwilling to put their own animals in danger.

The pair being chased turned as they hit the track Jack and Martha were following. They were no more than two hundred yards away, close enough for Jack to see that both wore blue uniforms. It was by no means certain, as many regiments on both sides followed their own ideas about what sort of uniform they should wear, but he assumed they were from the Union army. As he watched, the pair pulled hard on their reins, bringing their mounts to a halt. Both drew sabres.

He understood their plan immediately. The leader of the chasing pack had got far ahead of the rest of his men. He was alone.

Yet the lone rider did not hesitate. Jack caught the flash of sunlight as the man drew his own sabre. He kicked his horse hard, even as the two men he chased forced their own mounts back into motion and pointed them at the single horseman coming against them.

The distance between the three closed with mesmerising speed. The lone rider ducked low in the saddle as the three men came together. Jack heard the war cries of the blue-clad pair, then a scream as one was cut across the chest. The single rider burst through, hauling hard on the reins of his horse. He turned fast, then kicked with his heels, forcing the animal back up the slope. One of the men he had chased down was still in the saddle. The other was on the ground, clutching at his torn chest.

Jack could only applaud the skill. He was still riding forward, the fight drawing him in. He could hear the hooves of Martha's horse on the track just behind him.

The two men left in the saddle threw themselves into a second round of combat. Neither had much momentum now and both halted as they came together. Jack was close enough to hear the sound of metal on metal as they exchanged blows with their sabres. Both men knew their trade and they fought hard and fast, thrust, cut and parry coming one after the other with a bewildering speed.

The rest of the chasing pack was close now. The surviving Union rider saw them, and he cut hard, then broke from combat, his heels working to force his tiring horse back into a desperate gallop. Jack heard his cries as he urged his mount away, seeking to prevent the inevitable for a while longer.

The leader of the pursuers did not ride after him immediately. Instead he waited for his men to catch up, then barked orders. 'Two of you pick up that there whoreson. The rest of you follow me. Let's go get that son of a bitch before he skedaddles.'

As he turned to give chase once more, his hat fell back to reveal a shock of grey hair so pale that it was almost white. The sight brought Jack up short, and he pulled on his reins, bringing his mount to a halt, and peered at the grey-haired man with the bloodied sabre. There was something familiar about him that he had not noticed before.

Even as Jack squinted, the man sheathed his sabre and drew a revolver. At once, Jack knew who he was looking at. The weapon was beautiful, with carved ivory grips and metal that had been polished so that it gleamed like silver. It was Jack's own gun, which he had lost when he had been shot down and left to die. He knew of only one man who could have taken it.

The man with the revolver glanced in Jack's direction before turning back and forcing his horse into a wild gallop. It had only been for a second, but it had been enough time for Jack to get a proper look at his face. It was one that had become as familiar to him as his own, so many times had he seen it in his mind's eye.

He had found Rose's killer. He had found Major Nathan Lyle.

# Chapter Twenty-eight

*J*ack kicked hard, forcing his mount to find the speed he would need. Every thought fled from his mind save for one. The moment he had longed for had arrived.

'Lyle!' He howled the man's name, then kicked his horse again and again. The two men who had dismounted to deal with the fallen Union rider heard him coming. Both looked up as he thundered past, but he was moving too quickly for either to even contemplate intervening.

He rode like a madman, forcing his horse to even greater speed, focusing everything on the men ahead. He had lost sight of the Union rider, but he could see Lyle riding just in front of his men. They broke off the track, plunging into the fields on the southern side of the road. The going was good, the ground firm from the winter weather, and they raced along as they pursued their one remaining target.

The ground flashed by under Jack's horse's hooves at breakneck speed. He heard shots as he rode off the track, but paid them no heed as he followed the group of riders ahead, kicking his horse furiously, not caring for the risk.

He caught a glimpse of the last Union rider. The man was

going fast, but Lyle was in hot pursuit. As he rode, Jack smelt a whiff of powder smoke. It was fuel to the fire burning deep inside him, and he urged his horse to even greater speed, forcing the animal to stretch every sinew as he chased down the man he wanted to kill.

He lost sight of the men as they disappeared behind a wood. They were still a fair distance away, but he knew he was gaining. He had only the simplest plan: he would ride until he caught up with them, then he would draw his revolver and shoot Lyle down. If anyone tried to intervene, he would shoot them too. Nothing mattered save this moment of revenge.

He raced around the wood, forcing his horse to maintain its speed. The ground was worse here, the going littered with hummocks and divots. He did not care and he willed the animal on, his eyes fixed on the grey-haired rider chasing so hard after the Union fugitive.

He did not see the hole in the ground. His horse's leg disappeared into it and there was a crack as loud as a gunshot. Jack was thrown immediately, his world spinning around him for one long-drawn-out moment before he hit the ground.

The impact was brutal. Every ounce of breath was driven from his body in the second before his head hit the ground and everything went black.

Jack came back into the world to the screams of an animal in agony. He sat up only with difficulty. The pain came then, surging through him in waves that started in his skull and seared down his body with enough force to leave him shaking.

With an effort he forced himself onto all fours. He stopped moving, his head hanging low, the pain as bad as any he had ever felt. Then he puked, the vomit rushing out of him, burning and foul in his gullet. He vomited twice more, slathering the ground in the rank mixture.

He did not want to move, but his horse was screaming in agony. It lay on the ground, kicking its legs as it tried to get to its feet. It lurched half upright, then fell back before trying again, its screams coming without pause. Its front left leg was bent at an impossible angle, the limb shattered.

Jack pushed himself up, staggering like a drunk. He did not bother to wipe the traces of vomit from his face. Instead he drew his revolver. His arm shook as he raised it, the weapon impossibly heavy. He took a step forward, then another, forcing the strength into his legs, moving until the revolver's muzzle was no more than a few inches from his horse's head. He did not hesitate. Pulling the trigger, he ended the animal's agony with a single gunshot.

Then he stood still, eyes focused on the dirt beneath his boots.

He did not know how much time passed before he lifted his gaze and thrust the revolver back into its holster. The opportunity he had longed for was lost.

Jack trudged towards Martha in silence. He carried his saddlebags and they were growing heavier with every step. He was in a foul mood. His failure to catch Lyle rankled. It was worse even than the pain in his body, or the pounding in his head.

'Where have you been?' Martha had tethered her horse to a section of split-rail fencing that ran along one side of the turnpike and had been rubbing it down as he approached. There was no anger or recrimination in her question.

Jack did not bother to reply. He was tired and in pain. It had taken him a long time to retrace his steps and find her.

'Where's your horse?'

'Dead.' He growled the single word, then walked to the small pile of their kit that she had made next to the saddle she had taken off her own horse. He dumped the saddlebags without ceremony before shrugging the rifle off his shoulder and dumping that too.

'You want to tell me what happened?' Martha stopped tending to her horse and came towards him.

'No.' Jack pulled the strap of his canteen over his head, then started to undo the belt around his waist. He dropped the belt and its holstered revolver on the ground, then started to remove his jacket.

'You hurt?' Martha had the sense to keep the questions short.

Jack did not answer. He pulled off his shirt and grunted as he saw the blood caked around one elbow and more splattered across the back. The undershirt he wore was worse, and he had to pull it hard to get it over his head.

As he inspected his wounds, Martha retrieved his canteen and a spare undershirt she had pulled from his saddlebags. 'Stand still.'

He was too tired to argue and obeyed without a word as she wetted the undershirt then used it to wipe away the worst of the blood. There was something intimate and familiar in her touch that he did not want to dwell on.

'You're more scarred than our old table,' she muttered under her breath as she worked on him.

When the worst of the blood was cleaned away, she stood back to admire her handiwork. 'You'll do. They'll bleed some more, but I reckon you'll be all right.' She wiped a hand across her forehead, leaving a streak of blood on her skin. 'Was that him?'

Jack took a deep breath, then nodded. He could not meet her gaze.

'Uh huh. I figured. You went off like a bat leaving hell.' She paused, only speaking again when he looked up at her. 'Did you get him?'

Jack shook his head.

'You were going to ride off and kill him just like that? With his men all around him and all?'

'Yes.' Jack was starting to feel the cold on his bare skin. Yet he welcomed it. It matched the coldness in his soul.

'They'd have killed you.'

Jack answered with a glare.

'You don't care? You don't care that you'd be dead? You'd leave me here all alone?'

'You're a big girl.' Jack's tone was like ice.

Martha held his gaze, then shook her head. 'It won't wash, you know. Not with me.'

'What won't?' Jack shivered for the first time. The cold had him.

'This act of yours. Like you don't care if you live or die. You want to live, Jack. You just don't like to admit it, because then you'd have to think about what you're going to do next. And I reckon that frightens you. I reckon that frightens you a whole lot.'

'What do you know about it?' Jack stared at her, daring her to speak on.

'Oh, I know plenty.' Martha took a step towards him. 'When my Joshua died, I just wanted to lay down and join him. That pain, why, it was so bad, I didn't know how to go on. John was the same. He never talked about it, not once, but I know it hurt him just as bad as it hurt me. It changed him.

Changed us both, I guess. Maybe he thought it was my fault that our boy died. I wouldn't blame him if he did. I mean, I was Joshua's mother. I was meant to look after him. Meant to keep him safe.' Tears rolled out of her eyes, and she made no effort to wipe them away. 'It was different afterwards. John had changed. When I didn't obey him, he beat me. He beat me so hard I thought he was going to grant me my wish. And I didn't lift a finger to stop him. It wasn't his fault, none of it. I gave him the boy he had always wanted and I watched that boy die. So when he beat me, I wanted him to kill me. I wanted to die so that the pain would just go away.' She took another step so that she was within an arm's reach. 'I didn't die, Jack. So I had to find a way to keep living. You need to do the same.'

Jack felt the weight of her words. He lifted a hand and licked a finger, then reached out to wipe the streak of blood from her forehead. Her skin was warm under his touch. It was a reminder that there was life in the world. He repeated the gesture, his touch gossamer light.

He dropped his hand. The warm of the touch was threatening to spread through his frozen husk of a soul, and he could not allow that to happen. He forced the coldness into his being and held it close. He would need it.

He turned his back on Martha and went to pull on his bloodstained clothing.

# Chapter Twenty-nine

'Hey! You there. Stop right where you are.'

An old man shouted the challenge at Jack and Martha as they walked up a rough track that led to a small farmstead. Martha was leading her horse. The animal now carried all their kit and they needed to husband its strength. With only the one mount between them, they would be walking from here on.

Jack's hand dropped to the holstered revolver on his hip. He had no intention of stopping.

The farmstead was small, but it was clearly well looked after. There was a fine Dutch barn with a scattering of small outbuildings, and a handsome two-storey clapboard farmhouse with a wide veranda and neat dormer windows across its upper floor. A pair of locals they had spoken to had told them of its whereabouts. The two men had been quick to relate the tale of the Confederate cavalry chase and the two captives who had been left at the farmstead. The news that the Union riders captured by Lyle's men were being held in the area had drawn Jack here in the hope of finding the man himself.

'I ain't telling you again.' The old man sounded angry. He

was armed with a pitchfork and he now pointed this at the pair coming towards him.

'Shut the fuck up.' Jack was in no mood to argue. The old man had grey in his beard and there was more in what little hair clung precariously to the dome of his head. He was no threat.

'You be off with yourselves now.' The words were delivered with less venom. 'I've got two goddam Yankees in my house and I've been told to guard the place well and see off any strangers that come to take them away.'

'What do you mean?' Jack's hand rested on the hilt of his revolver. He had not slowed his pace, but changed his direction slightly so that he walked straight at the man.

'Well, for all I know, you could be another one.'

Jack walked closer. 'Do I look like a bloody Yankee?' He was surprised. He was wearing Pinter's uniform. Clearly the old man didn't have a clue.

'You could be anything. You talk funny and I want you off my land.' The old man held out his pitchfork again, pointing the prongs at Jack's chest.

'Oh, shut your muzzle.' Jack knocked the pitchfork to one side and strode past the old fool without giving him another look. 'Martha, ask chummy here for a place to stable the horse and get him to give it some fodder. If he doesn't do what you say, then you have my permission to shoot the stupid old sod.'

'Where are you going?' Martha had followed in his wake. Now she stood next to the man with the pitchfork, who had lowered his makeshift weapon and was looking at the ground.

'I'm going to find out what the hell is going on,' Jack said. 'If you hear shooting, then start digging me a hole.' He carried on towards the farmhouse. The gallows humour sat well in his mind. If Lyle were inside, he knew that only one of them would come out.

Jack opened the farmhouse's front door and walked inside. The place was warm to the point of being fuggy. It smelt of woodsmoke and blood.

'Who are you?' A man dressed in a grey uniform rose from an armchair placed near the stove that was warming the room.

'Captain Sloames, 3rd Virginia Cavalry.' Jack had been an impostor a long time and he gave the lie without hesitation. The name was a nod to the officer who had picked him from the ranks to make him an orderly. The real Sloames had died suddenly, giving Jack his first opportunity to become someone else. The name of the regiment he had picked out of the air. It sounded reasonable to him. 'Now tell me what the hell is going on here.' He gave the instruction in the clipped tones of an officer who was used to being obeyed.

The soldier scowled, yet still stiffened as if about to stand to attention. 'Not sure it's rightly any business of yours, Captain.'

'Don't be so damned impertinent, soldier.' Jack snapped the reply as he strode into the room. 'What unit are you?'

'Lyle's Raiders.'

'I know Lyle. He's a good fellow.' Jack tried not to choke on the words. 'What are your lot doing here?' He glanced quickly around the room, then returned his scrutiny to the man in front of him, looking for a flicker of recognition. There was none.

The man looked uncomfortable. 'I reckon you'd best ask the lieutenant.'

'Fine.' Jack's answer was immediate. 'Well, don't just stand there gawping. Go fetch your lieutenant, goddammit.'

'He's with the prisoners.'

'What prisoners?' Jack came to stand directly in front of the man.

'We caught ourselves two Yankee officers, Captain.'

'And where are they?'

'In the back room. One's hurt pretty bad. The other not so much.'

'And your lieutenant is with them?'

'He is.'

'Fine. I'll go to him.' Jack made to move away, but stopped almost immediately. 'My man is outside with my horse. If you see him, tell him to wait there.'

'Yes, Captain.'

Jack nodded, then walked towards a door at the back of the parlour. He felt a fluttering of hope. The chances of finding Lyle were growing with every moment.

He did not stand on ceremony, opening the door and walking straight into the rear room. The smell hit him again the moment the door was open, but stronger this time. It was the smell of mangled flesh and open wounds.

A man dressed in the blue uniform of the Union sat in a wing-backed armchair. As far as Jack could tell, he was not wounded, but from his glazed expression it was clear the shock of capture had left its mark. The second prisoner had been laid on a dining table. Jack could only assume this man was the one who had been cut out of the saddle by Lyle. He was bleeding heavily from a deep wound across the chest. A woman – Jack had no idea who she was – was trying to staunch the bleeding with what looked to be torn sheets, whilst a fresh-faced young man with the twin gold bars of a lieutenant on his collar, and the yellow facings and golden Austrian knot of a cavalry officer on his sleeves, looked on in obvious horror.

'You. Where's Lyle?' Jack fired the question at the officer.

'Who the devil are you?' The officer scowled as he looked at Jack.

'Sloames, 3rd Virginia Cavalry.' Jack repeated the lie, then came to stand at the dining table and peered down at the man, whose chest had been laid open to the bone. Mercifully he was unconscious.

'3rd Virginia Cavalry?' The lieutenant's face creased into a frown.

'Who are these men, Lieutenant?' Jack gave him no chance to dwell. He would return to the question of Lyle's whereabouts, but in the meantime he wanted to keep the man on the back foot.

'Prisoners, sir.'

'You think that one will live?' Jack looked across to the woman working on the wounded man. She was old, with grey hair bound tight. She glanced up at him for no more than a moment before returning to her gory task.

'I don't rightly know.' The lieutenant came to Jack's side and joined him looking at the man on the table.

'I think he'll die.' Jack allowed no pause in the conversation. But he was not dissembling. He had seen enough wounds to know which would kill and which gave a chance of survival.

'You do?' The lieutenant sounded appalled at the idea.

'I do. What's your name?'

'Lieutenant Taylorson, sir.'

'How long have you been with Lyle, Taylorson?' Jack fired off the question.

'A month,' Taylorson replied.

Jack nodded. The answer had saved the young officer's life.

Had he been serving with Lyle when Jack had been captured, he would have killed him on the spot.

'I'd like to meet Major Lyle and shake his hand. Is he here?'

'No. He rode on with the rest of the men. Say, are you English, Captain?'

'I am. I came a long way to join our cause.'

'I sure wish a few more of your countrymen felt the same.'

'Me too, Lieutenant.' Jack shook his head as if rueful at his country's reluctance to join the war. 'So what are you doing here?'

'Catching spies.' Taylorson was young enough to puff his chest out at the bold statement.

Jack glanced across at the uninjured Union officer. The man seemed happy to play no part in the conversation, but was watching intently.

'That what they are?'

'What else could they be down here?' The lieutenant looked at Jack quizzically.

'You tell me.' Jack took a step closer to the table and peered at the bloodied chest of the Union soldier.

'Why, they're spies for sure. Major Lyle is certain of it. Ever since them Yankees pushed General Crittenden back at Fishing Creek near Mill Springs, there's been goddam spies all over the place, reconnoitring our lines and trying to get up to Fort Henry and Fort Donelson. We caught sight of these two Yankees and Major Lyle wanted them taken.'

Jack hid a smile. Martha had said her husband was stationed at Fort Donelson. 'You were with him when they were captured?'

'I was.'

'Was it you who cut him down?' Jack nodded at the bleeding man.

'No, sir, but I was right there with Major Lyle when he defended himself.'

Jack noted that Taylorson did not have the decency to blush at the claim. Yet he would not tell the lieutenant that he had seen Lyle take the two men on single-handed. He had been an impostor for too long to reveal more than was necessary.

'Where's the major now?'

'He's riding for Fort Donelson on the orders of General Forrest himself.'

The wounded Union officer on the table gave a soft splutter. Blood frothed from his lips and dribbled from the corner of his mouth.

'See those bubbles?' Jack needed to keep Taylorson distracted. He pointed at the blood. 'That's air. It means his lungs are gone.' He looked across at the woman wadding fresh linen into the man's ruined chest. 'You're wasting your time, love.'

'You a physician, sir?' The reply was sharp and delivered with a scowl.

Jack had the sense not to press. He turned back to the lieutenant, who was staring at the blood creeping down the Union officer's cheek. From his grey pallor, it appeared the young officer was just about ready to puke.

'What's at Fort Henry and Fort Donelson?' Jack asked the only question he wanted an answer to. He spoke softly, trying not to break the spell that had fallen over Lyle's lieutenant. 'I'm not familiar with either.' He held his breath, waiting to see if Taylorson would bite at his lure.

'Fort Henry protects access to the lower Tennessee river and Fort Donelson does the same for the Cumberland.' Taylorson swallowed with difficulty. 'The Yankees will have to capture them both if they want to control the rivers, and if that happens they can split our defensive line right across the north of Tennessee. They'll be able to push further south and these rivers will be their supply lines.'

'So we need to stop them before they take the forts,' Jack replied smoothly. He was quietly impressed. The lieutenant was proving to be a useful source of information.

'That we do, sir.' Taylorson rallied, colour returning to his cheeks. 'If we hold the forts, we control the rivers. And those forts of ours won't give in easy.'

Jack nodded. 'They won't, not with men like us to defend them.' He looked hard at Taylorson, but saw nothing in the younger man's expression to alarm him. 'How do I get there?'

'You can ride, but it's a fair long way. There are paddle steamers ferrying supplies and reinforcements that way. You could try to get a berth on one of those, I guess. It might not be easy.'

Jack shrugged. He would find a way. The lieutenant was still staring at the blood that flowed steadily out of the Union officer's mouth.

'You guard these men well, Lieutenant. If I see Lyle, I'll tell him of your diligence.'

'Thank you kindly, Captain.'

Jack turned on his heel and left Lyle's officer and the two Union men to it. He had learned enough. He had missed Lyle this time, but now he knew where the man he sought could be found. It appeared fate was being kind to him in placing Martha's husband and Lyle at the same spot. It meant he could now kill two birds with one stone. Or at the very least, kill one of them.

* * *

Jack walked a few paces ahead of Martha, who was leading the horse. They had stayed at the farmstead for another hour, giving the animal time to be fed and watered. Jack had not spoken to Lyle's lieutenant again, but he had been there to witness the Union officer's body being brought out of the farmstead. He felt no satisfaction at having predicted the man's death. It was a reminder of the fate he himself faced when he found Lyle. The Confederate officer had demonstrated his skill in the fight with the Union officers. It had been no small thing for him to take on both men and win. Jack had learned much that day, not least that his foe was a dangerous man.

'You daydreaming there, Jack?' Martha broke the silence.

Jack sighed. He might have guessed she would want to talk. 'Yes.'

'What you thinking?'

'That I like peace and quiet.' He turned to fire a warning look in her direction.

'You sure do.' Martha did not meet his gaze, but instead looked at the ground.

They walked on. They had covered a good half-mile before she tried again.

'You see them Yankees?'

'I did.'

'Then you saw that our boys were doing their best for them. Especially the one that got hurt.'

'They were.' Jack knew he would not be left alone until Martha had said what she wanted to say. 'What of it?'

'You don't think it's kind of queer?'

'No.'

'You sure about that? You said these men killed your Rose without a thought, and shot you down too.' Martha paused, as if summoning the courage to continue. 'I ain't doubting you or nothing, but if they're such devils and all, why did they take those two Yankees to that there farm? Why didn't they just kill them out of hand?'

Jack didn't care for the question. 'How the hell should I know?'

'It's just . . .' She didn't finish the thought.

'Spit it out.' Jack wanted the conversation done.

'Well, don't you think they might not be the devils you think they are? They sure didn't look like monsters to me, Jack. They just looked kinda ordinary. And they did the charitable thing looking after those Yankees.'

'It doesn't change a thing.' There was iron in Jack's reply. He remembered the wood where he had been taken, and where he had had his last glimpse of Rose. There had been no mercy that day. There had been just pain and blood and death. 'Now you save your breath for walking. I reckon you'll need it. We've a long way to go.'

He shut down the conversation. Yet as he walked, he could not help thinking on what Martha had said. He refused to acknowledge the truth in her words. He knew nothing was clear-cut. To his way of thinking, men were made up of a mixture of traits. Good and bad. Honest and deceitful. Love and hate. No one was just one thing or the other.

The same would likely be true of both Lyle and his men. But he had spoken the truth to Martha. It didn't change a thing. For if it did, it would mean he would have to change his path, and he could not face that. He would find Lyle, and he knew he would kill him. If he turned from that path, the one that he had walked for all these months, he did not know where he would go or what he would do.

Revenge was all he had, he knew that, just as he knew the darkness in his own soul. He did not live in a world of colour, but in one where there were just shades of grey. Those greys were getting steadily darker and he knew that one day they would turn black.

And then darkness would rule his soul.

# Chapter Thirty

_J_ ack studied the paddle steamer tied up against the dock. It was called the _Rowena_, the name picked out in proud red paint on the side of the wheelhouse that was perched all alone on the very upper deck. The steamer was made from wood painted white. It was propelled by a great stern-mounted paddle wheel powered by a steam engine. Two tall smoke stacks belched thick plumes of grey-black smoke into the late-evening sky, where they were quickly lost amongst the dark clouds that hung low over the river.

He was no great lover of boats, or ships, or whatever the crew insisted the paddle steamer was called. He had spent much of his life on long voyages, first to the Crimea and then back to London from India. Still more time had been wasted on the Atlantic crossing from Liverpool to Boston. Most of these periods of enforced incarceration had been spent either bored out of his mind or puking up his guts. He was not looking forward to the next few days.

They had been forced to sell Martha's horse. The animal was exhausted and there was no way of getting it aboard the small paddle steamer. It had fetched a good price, the demand for horses high as the Confederate army bought up every one in the area. He was not sorry to see it go. Life would be simpler and cheaper without animals to care for.

It would also be simpler now they were so close to their destination. The *Rowena* would take them up the Cumberland river to a town called Dover and the nearby Fort Donelson. There they would hopefully find Martha's husband, and if Taylorson had been telling the truth, they would also discover Lyle and his raiders.

'This way, sir.' The young crewman assigned to the *Rowena*'s passengers turned to look anxiously back at Jack, who had hesitated to step onto the wooden pontoon dock that led out to the steamer.

Jack nodded, then took a deep breath before following the lad. The *Rowena* was carrying a dozen officers and twice as many other ranks, along with a large amount of supplies. Jack had been fortunate to secure the berth for the two of them, although his willingness to spend his stolen money had certainly encouraged the army clerk who issued passes for travel by river to find a way to accommodate them. He had only been able to get them a single cabin, though, something he had not yet told Martha. She would find out soon enough.

The two of them were the last to go aboard, and he could sense the crewman was in a hurry to get them installed in their cabin. He led them at a fine pace, his body reacting without thought to the shifts in the dock beneath them. Jack followed more circumspectly, with Martha trailing behind him. At the rear of the short procession, a second crewman carried their baggage, such as it was, the stained and battered saddlebags balanced easily in his arms. Jack's failed pursuit of Lyle had cost them more than the life of his horse. He had managed to break or mangle most of their cooking equipment, and he knew that at some point he would have to find them more if they were to continue on their journey.

It did not take them long to cross the pontoon and then the simple wooden gangplank that led on board the paddle steamer.

'Your cabin is on the Texas deck, sir.' The young crewman turned and made his farewell brusquely. 'Able there will show you the way.'

Jack nodded his thanks, then stood back to let the man carrying the saddlebags take the lead. The steamer was already crowded. The deck they were on was smothered with soldiers' kit, and he could see that the troops being shipped upriver had already started to make themselves comfortable on the lower deck. The passenger cabins were on the next level up, so he followed their baggage up a wide and surprisingly elegant stairway. The crew clearly took pride in their ship's appearance. The brasswork gleamed, the decks were clean, and the wood was well polished and for the most part in good condition.

The crewman carrying the bags opened a door midway along the length of the upper deck and plunged inside, leaving Jack and Martha to follow him. The cabin was dark and smelt of an unpleasant mix of damp, wax and sweat. It boasted a single narrow bed, covered in a heavy counterpane of dark reds and blues. There was a steamer trunk at the foot of the bed and a dressing table pushed into one corner.

The crewman laid the saddlebags down on the lower part of the bed with exaggerated care, then nodded a farewell and left without another word. Jack went straight to the far side of the room, where he opened the first of two small square windows.

'You expect us to share that there bed?' Martha crossed the cabin and began to undo the buckles on their saddlebags.

'It was all I could get.' Jack glanced over his shoulder. His companion did not seem overly upset, which was a good thing. He had not been sure how she would react.

Martha pulled out a bundle of clothes from the uppermost saddlebag. She had dumped her own clothes back at the hotel. Now all she had were some of the things she had lent Jack from her husband's wardrobe, and the uniform Jack had taken from the lad he had beaten. She shook out a shirt. 'And where are you expecting to sleep tonight?'

'I'll kip on the floor.' Jack was struggling with the second window. The catch was rusted shut.

'Uh huh.' Martha's tone had changed.

'What does that mean? Oh fuck it.' Jack swore as he tore a fingernail on the catch.

'Nothing.' Martha folded the shirt, then pulled out her one spare pair of oversized trousers.

'I know you by now, love.' Jack turned, his finger in his mouth. 'You don't approve?'

'I'm a married woman. It ain't right that you and me are sharing a room.'

'We don't have a choice. I can hardly doss down with the blokes downstairs; I'm an officer after all. You'll just have to grin and bear it.'

'Will I now?'

'Yes. Look, I'm not going to jump on you or anything.' Jack gave what he hoped was a reassuring grin – enough, he hoped, to hide the fact that he had thought about exactly that the moment he had seen the single bed. He was most certainly no saint. The thought of being with Martha had crossed his mind.

Martha looked at him for a long moment, then sighed. 'I

stink. I want to change out of these clothes. So you can just turn around and give me a bit of privacy.'

'Yes, ma'am.' Jack could feel her awkwardness. They had travelled together for weeks, yet something had changed now they were in the cramped cabin. The small space was too intimate for comfort.

He did as he was told and turned his attention back to the reluctant catch on the second window. He heard the rustle of clothing behind him as Martha undressed. He had no intention of trying to steal a look, but he could not help seeing her reflection in the glass. There was something in her work-hardened body that was most certainly attractive. He stood taking in the image for longer than he knew he should, only stopping when she dropped the shirt over her head.

Nothing good could come of this desire. Martha was married to a man she was prepared to cross hundreds of miles to find. It was a decision that he did not fully understand, not with what she had told him of her husband's quickness to use his fists. But she clearly had enough love for the man to risk her life to go to him, and he knew he should respect her choice and not make the man a cuckold. There were enough black marks on his soul already.

'I'm going to get some air.' He moved towards the door, making sure not to look at Martha as he moved past her. She knew him well enough by now. He was certain she would be able to read his expression.

He stepped outside with relief. It was cool to the point of being cold, but he welcomed the chill after the stuffiness of the cabin. He walked to the rail, taking a firm grip with both hands to steady himself against the movement of the steamer, and gazed out over the river. It looked almost enchanting in the last of the day's light, and he stood there savouring a moment's peace and giving thanks that it was too cold for any of the biting insects that would have made even a moment outside a misery.

Around him the steamer was noisy. On the lower deck he could hear the voices of the soldiers left to sleep outside. He listened to their laughter and imagined their faces as they swapped tall tales, or listened to a familiar story told by one of their number. A few men near the front of the boat were singing. He did not recognise the song, but he could hear the enjoyment in their voices. He had an inkling that he could be at home in the company of those soldiers. They might belong to an army he had once fought against, but he suspected that sitting amongst them would feel little different from the evenings he had spent with the men of the 1st Boston.

The thought brought to mind the aspect of this war that he found most difficult to come to terms with. These were not two foreign powers wrestling for control of some distant, strategic land, the opponents separated by language, heritage or perhaps the colour of their skin. These two sides were made up of brothers, cousins and compatriots. He was pretty sure that such men would be happy to share a campfire with one another and swap stories without rancour. Yet here they were, tearing their country and each other apart.

He shook his head at his own foolishness. Men would always fight, and generals and politicians would always want them to. It was the way of the world; always had been and always would be. Soldiers never had a say in the matter. They went where they were told to go, then fought whomsoever they were told to fight. They would die to satisfy the whim of a politician, and there was not a damned thing they could do about it. Unless they were like Jack. Unless they tore up the unwritten rulebook and broke free of the shackles of the society into which they had been born. It was not easy. Just a few would do it and even fewer would live long to tell the tale. Yet here he still was, taking a path of his own choosing and fighting to be free of the life he had been allotted.

It was not often he contemplated what he was doing. He had come a long way since he had first taken an officer's scarlet coat for his own. He had fought more times than he could count, and finally become the soldier he had always wanted to be. It defined him, his talent for battle the one thing that he had held close through every trial. Yet his desire to be a soldier had led him to what he was now: a mercenary; a man with nothing in his heart but a cold, remorseless desire for revenge.

For a moment, the notion shamed him. As he looked across the river in the fast-fading light, he wondered quite how it had happened. He had not set out to become this man, this hardened, lonely killer. Somewhere he had lost what he wanted to be. He could blame fate. He could console himself that it had not been his choices that had brought him to this point. It would be easier that way. Yet he had never chosen the easy path, and he knew that he stood here today solely because of decisions he himself had made. It was no one's fault but his own.

He tried to conjure an image of Rose in his mind's eye. He'd told himself that she was the reason he had embarked on this soul-destroying mission. Her loss still burned deep inside him. Yet no matter how hard he tried, he could no longer fully see her face in his mind. Somehow it had faded until it was little more than a lifeless portrait. Somewhere along the way he had lost her too. He was hunting for a man he would try to kill; yet he would do so for the memory of a woman he was already starting to forget.

The door behind him opened, breaking his chain of thought, bringing him back to the here and now. Life carried on. A man could dwell on his fate and wonder at the decisions that had brought him to where he was. Yet no amount of soul-searching could change the past, and there was damn all a man could do to change his future. That just left the present.

'Come back inside, before you catch your death.'

He smiled at Martha's tone. There was a challenge there, as if she was daring him to obey. A part of him had known this moment was coming. He already knew what he would do. He had known since the moment he had glimpsed her in the glass of the cabin window.

He turned to face her. She had removed most of her clothes so that she stood there dressed in just an oversized shirt. There was no beguiling smile on her face or teasing glint in her eye. Martha was no shy virgin. She knew what she was asking him to do, just as he knew what he wanted.

It was time to live in the present, to take what comfort he could find and cast his future, and his past, to one side.

Jack lay in the bed, his arms crossed beneath his head. Martha slept beside him, or at least lay still as if she were sleeping. She had stayed close, but had rolled over so that she faced away from him. Her back rested against his side and he could feel the bones of her spine pressed against his skin. Her warmth seeped into his flesh and he was grateful for it.

The steamer rocked gently, creaking and groaning as it moved on the swell of the river. He should have felt at peace. There was something comforting in Martha's presence, in the feel of her flesh against his. Yet he felt nothing but guilt. It was not for making Martha's husband a cuckold. Martha had been a willing partner, who had not been coerced or persuaded into bed. What had happened had happened between two people who had needed, who had wanted, the other. There was no shame in that, at least not in his mind.

But there was shame in forgetting Rose.

As he lay there, he tried again to summon her face in his mind. Once again he failed, the image remaining stubbornly out of his reach. He tried to torment himself, replaying the moment when he had been gunned down like a sick dog. But try as he might, he could not do it. The memories were there, but they were like an old wound. No matter how hard you poked the scar, you could not recreate the pain of its taking. The scar remained, but over time it faded until it became just another part of you, a link to a past that would never disappear, but which no longer had the power to torment.

Yet there was another face, one that he could recall in perfect clarity. He tried to think of Rose, but the only face he could see was that of Nathan Lyle, the man who had killed her. The glimpse he had caught of the man the other day had done little to refresh the image he carried. For it had already been perfect in every detail.

He was coming to realise that he was better at hating than he was at loving. He lay in the darkness and held the image of the man he would kill in his mind's eye. He had got close once, and the next time he would get closer. Then Nathan Lyle would die, and Jack would finally be free.

# Chapter Thirty-one

It was late afternoon when the *Rowena* docked at Dover. The rain had started at dawn, and it was still coming down with no sign of easing off. It shrouded the town, hiding much of it from the view of the soldiers who lined the rails as their journey came to an end.

Jack stood outside the cabin he had shared with Martha, sheltering from the rain in the covered walkway that led around the deck. The Cumberland river was wide here, its low banks mainly covered in trees. Its cold waters raged around the little paddle steamer as it came into the dock, the fierce flow making the ship buck and lurch so that he was forced to hold onto the rail.

It was bitterly cold as the rain lashed down. It was a miserable evening, a time for staying indoors and curling up by a fire. Instead, Jack looked out in the rain and stared at a town he could barely see, wondering if his foe was tucked away in one of its many buildings.

* * *

Jack and Martha disembarked last. They walked away from the *Rowena* and into the midst of an army. The streets of Dover were crowded with Confederate troops. Most were hauling supplies, the soldiers pressed into service as pack mules as the officers charged with dealing with the supplies coming upriver did their best to organise the chaos. A rare few were at ease, and these fortunate souls scurried through the deluge, hats pulled low and shoulders hunched as they weathered the storm.

Ahead, a miserable-looking column of infantry marched away from the river. To Jack's eye they looked a motley crew, even allowing for the rain. They wore little in the way of uniform, with no two dressed alike, and moved with no discernible order. He tried to pick out the officers, but in the rain they all looked as dishevelled and scruffy as each other. It was a unit of scarecrows and vagrants that looked nothing like a body of formed military men.

He pressed on, leaving Martha to follow with their saddle-bags, just as an orderly should. There was little weight to them, their possessions now reduced to a few spare clothes. Jack still wore his knapsack, which contained all his ammunition and a spare revolver. The Navy Colt he had taken from the man who had killed Martha's father was in a holster on his right hip, and he carried Pinter's rifle. For her part, Martha carried a single carbine, the shorter weapon still far too big for her tiny frame.

Jack was not unduly concerned at their lack of supplies. The town of Dover had been converted into one great depot. There would be provision and ordnance stores aplenty. He was dressed in the uniform of a Confederate officer, which meant that unless this army was wholly dissimilar to any other he had served in, he could simply requisition anything he needed, his signature on a scrap of paper likely to be all the authority required.

Even as he trudged through the mud and the rain, he felt a sense of returning to where he belonged. He was back amidst an army on campaign. It was not his army, and he wasn't meant to be there, but it was still familiar territory. He was a soldier amongst soldiers. He was home.

They were soaked to the skin by the time they reached the Dover Hotel. It was a handsome two-storey clapboard house with a veranda across the front and a balcony above. A tall brick chimney ran up one flank, the red of the bricks dark against the white-painted clapboard.

It came as something of a relief to walk up the steps and onto the veranda. The rain was lashing down. The soldiers encamped in and around Dover would be enduring the last hours of a miserable day that would surely be followed by an even more miserable night. The temperature was already starting to drop, and the soaked soldiers would likely freeze when night fell. It was cold enough for the rain to turn to snow, and Jack offered a silent prayer that by some miracle the hotel would have a room for them.

The reception area was cramped, the space barely big enough for both him and Martha to step inside. A clerk standing behind a counter greeted them. He was old enough for his bushy beard to be fully grey, and he peered at the two of them through tiny pince-nez spectacles perched on the very tip of his nose. Jack returned the greeting with a genuine smile. The reception room was delightfully warm and he could smell coffee. The idea of going back outside was abhorrent.

'You looking for a room, Captain?' The clerk had seen the

three gold bars on the collar of Jack's uniform and was clearly familiar enough with military men to know what rank it denoted.

'Yes. Do you have one for us?' Jack tried not to sound too eager.

'I haven't had one for the last three weeks or more,' the clerk replied with a slow shake of his head. 'Those generals and their staff took over the whole place.'

'Is there anywhere else we can stay?'

'Not here.'

Jack sighed. It had been a forlorn hope, and he had known this would be the likely answer. Dover was now a vast military camp. That meant there would surely be enough senior officers around the place for all the comfortable accommodation to have been taken.

'You have the general staying here?' He wanted to linger. He did not care that the two of them were forming a puddle of rainwater on the floor.

'Which one?' The grey-bearded clerk chuckled at his own answer. 'We got ourselves so goddam many. But in answer to your question, they're all here. Floyd, Pillow, Buckner – hell, we got them *and* their staff. There ain't room to swing a damn cat about the place.'

Jack did his best to smile. The clerk seemed happy to talk, and he was content enough to stand in the warm. 'Least that means they'll have a chance to plan. We sure need that if we're going to whip them Yankees.'

The clerk looked at Jack with an odd expression, as if he could tell that he was uncomfortable with the phrase. 'Would you be English, Captain?'

Jack nodded. There was no hiding his accent.

The clerk seemed pleased to have made the identification. 'There's a few of you fellows about these days. Seems some of you are keen to help even if your government don't want to. Still, we're grateful and all.'

Jack could not help smiling as the clerk gave him thanks on behalf of all the Confederate states. He wondered how the man would react if he realised he was faced with a couple of impostors. 'Just so long as we beat those Northern bastards.'

'Amen to that, Captain. But they'll sure take some whipping.' The clerk shook his head as he faced up to an unpleasant truth. 'They took Fort Henry and now they're just upriver and sure to be coming here.'

'When did that happen?'

'Five days ago now. I heard they pretty much flattened the place with those ironclad ships of theirs. Some of our boys managed to get away and come here. We're all that's left.'

'But we're making a stand here.' Jack made it sound like a statement when it was really a question.

'Oh, I'm sure we are, Captain. I never saw so many people in this town. And you've all been so busy. Digging rifle pits all around the place and bringing the guns up to Fort Donelson over yonder. Those goddam Yankees won't know what's hit 'em if they do come this way. We'll put a stop to their invasion, and send them running back the way they came.'

Jack had listened carefully to the clerk, gleaning what information he could. If the Confederate army was making a stand around Dover, it seemed likely that both he and Martha would find what they were looking for, either in the town itself or in Fort Donelson.

'Now, Captain, I'm right sorry to do this, but I need you and your boy there to step on outside.' The clerk grimaced as he made the demand, as if it truly pained him. 'But if you stop by here again, well, if I got anything then I'll let you have it.'

Jack nodded his thanks, then glanced outside. The wind had picked up and the rain now lashed against the side of the hotel. The light was fading and it would soon be dark. He needed to find them a place to wait out the night.

'You stay safe out there, Captain.' The clerk gave them a warm farewell as Jack prepared to step outside. 'Whip those Yankees good.'

'So where are we going to stay?' Martha followed Jack out and was forced to press her lips up against his ear so that her words were not lost in the storm.

'No idea, love.' Jack turned up the collar of his greatcoat. 'But that went well.'

'How do you figure that?'

'That bloke never doubted who you were. And you didn't say a word.' He flashed her a thin-lipped smile. 'You're learning to shut up.'

Martha shook her head at the mockery. But still she found something close to a smile. 'Go on then, Captain.' She addressed Jack with the same title the receptionist had used, although she laced it with a dollop of sarcasm. 'Find us someplace to stay.'

# Chapter Thirty-two

———◆———

Jack pushed away the blanket and forced his frozen body into motion. It hurt to move, the soreness in his back as bad as he had ever known it. As he lurched to his feet, a single white-hot lance of pain cut down into the pit of his spine with enough force to make him stagger.

'Jesus Christ.' He hissed the blasphemy through gritted teeth, his hands kneading his lower back as well as his stiff, frozen fingers could manage.

'Don't take the Lord's name in vain.' The rebuke was delivered from underneath the blanket he had shared with Martha.

'Don't you ever let up?' Jack snapped the waspish reply, then coughed, his lungs protesting at the chilled air he was hauling into them.

'Don't you ever learn?' Martha's retort was just as snappy.

He did not blame her. He had found them little in the way of shelter. They had trudged around the streets of Dover until night had fallen, every building and outbuilding already packed full with Confederate soldiers. Tired, fed up and chilled to the bone, he had given up. He had liberated half a dozen blankets from some soldiers' packs he had found bundled together under a tarpaulin in the back of a wagon, then made them a rudimentary shelter in the lee of a wood store on the fringe of town. It had been an uncomfortable night, and he doubted either of them had slept much as they huddled together under the purloined blankets.

The morning had dawned grey and cold. It had stopped raining, yet still everything he owned was damp, and he knew his weapons would need careful attention if they were not to rust. Such jobs, though, were for the future. For the moment, all he could think of was getting something hot to drink.

He coughed, forcing the phlegm from his throat, then looked down at the bundle of blankets. Martha had yet to move. He would let her lie there for a while longer. He ran his hands over his face, feeling the rasp of stubble across his chin and cheeks. He hated shaving, but unless he wanted to accept having a beard, it was something he would have to face soon. His hair was also longer than he liked. He added finding a barber to his ever-growing list of chores.

'I'm going to find us some coffee,' he said, bending down and picking up Pinter's rifle. Even in the midst of an army he would not go unarmed. He was making to leave when Martha called him back.

'You'll need to find a cup to drink it out of.' She pulled the blanket away from her face and peered up at him, her nose wrinkled in disgust. 'We'll need a pot too, and our own beans, and something to eat if you're planning on keeping us alive.'

'I'll find us something.' Jack looked at her. Her face was pale and her poorly cut hair sticking up at every possible angle, and in the morning light he could see the wrinkles around her eyes. She was as far away from an elegant lady as he could ever imagine finding, yet he was pleased she was there.

'Don't stand there lollygagging. Go on now, get on with your chores.' Martha had seen him staring, and she chided him for it.

'Yes, ma'am.' Jack gave her a salute, then did as he had been told and went to find them what they needed.

The encampment came right up to the edge of the town. The Confederate soldiers had built themselves more permanent shelters than the pathetic one Jack had made for himself and Martha, and small wooden huts stretched away in every direction. The first occupants were emerging as they prepared for another damp, cold day. Fires were being lit, and Jack could smell the first brews of coffee.

He kept moving, wanted to learn more of the place where he hoped to find Lyle. Walking also helped stave off the chill, for it was bitterly cold. He passed through lines of huts and cabins before reaching a long line of rifle pits. The soldiers had clearly been busy preparing the defences. He could only imagine that it would have been a brutal task to hack the entrenchments from the frozen ground.

The rifle pits nearest to Dover faced south, and had been strengthened with reinforcing walls of logs covered with thick yellow clay. Beyond the line of defences, the ground sloped downwards for what Jack judged to be close to one hundred feet before levelling out. The soldiers had not been content to simply dig the pits. They had cleared the ground that came up to the defences, creating a wide field of fire, a brutally difficult task in the conditions. Any trees that had been felled had been laid down with their crowns facing away from the line of rifle pits. From what he could make out, the Confederate soldiers had taken care to weave the tangled limbs and branches into an abatis that would seem impassable to men coming from the south.

'Mind yourself there, goddammit.' A burly corporal bustled past him carrying a large iron pot full of steaming water.

'Goddammit, mind yourself.' Jack saw an opportunity and snapped the rebuke at the corporal, who staggered to a halt as he realised that he had just made a dreadful error. 'Is that how you address officers in your outfit?'

'No, sir.' The corporal made an awkward turn to face Jack.

'That is a damn sloppy way to behave, soldier.' Jack stood tall as he berated the man. 'Now put that bloody pot down and stand to attention.'

'Yes, sir.' The corporal dumped the pot, some of the precious hot water slopping over the edge, and stood ramrod straight, his eyes staring into the space above Jack's head.

'What's your name?'

'Corporal Hightower, sir.'

'Well, Corporal Hightower, when you next go about your business, you keep a careful eye on where you are going.' Jack had to hide a smile as he bawled out the soldier. He was enjoying himself. 'Is that clear?'

'Yes, sir.' Hightower's eyes did not shift a single inch as he fired back the reply.

'Now then.' Jack changed his tone. 'Have you and your boys got some coffee going?'

'Yes, sir.'

'Then I would be obliged if you would share a cup with me.'

For the first time, the corporal's eyes lowered. The polite request had taken him off guard. 'Of course, sir.'

Jack nodded his thanks. 'Then you had better pick up that damn pot of yours and show me the way.'

'Yes, sir.' Hightower hurried to obey.

Jack followed him into the network of wooden huts. 'I would guess you've been a soldier a fair time, Corporal. Am I right?' He was hoping to start a conversation. He needed more than just coffee, and the corporal might be able to tell him something of what was going on.

Hightower glanced across, then gave a half-smile. 'Yes, sir. I've served in the regulars since I was nineteen years old. That's near enough ten years now, I suppose.' He did his best to read Jack's expression whilst still carrying the heavy pot. 'How could you tell?'

'The "yes, sir, no, sir" routine.' Jack tried to sound friendlier than he felt to try and make the man feel at ease.

'Yes, sir.' Hightower chuckled as he replied. 'Sometimes it's the best way to deal with an officer.' They walked on a few paces before he spoke again. 'I'm right sorry to barge into you like that, sir. It weren't right, officer or no officer.'

'No harm done,' Jack replied. 'So if you fought in the regulars, shouldn't you be up North?'

'Maybe.' Hightower shook his head. 'It weren't easy for those of us that left. But some things are more important.'

'More important than your mates?'

'Yes, sir.' Hightower pressed his lips tight together as he thought on his decision. 'There's nothing more important than family. My brothers, they're all down here. I knew they'd fight, my cousins too. Hell, even my father tried to enlist, and he's an old man. I couldn't fight against them.' He stopped walking and looked across at Jack. 'That wouldn't be right, sir. I couldn't do it.'

Jack looked the corporal in the eye. He had an idea what the man's decision had cost him. It would have been no easy thing to leave behind men he had served alongside. For his part, Jack still missed his messmates from his time as a redcoat. They had become his family. Walking away from them had been one of the hardest things he had ever made himself do.

'Well, I'm sure your regiment here is glad to have you.'

'I hope so, sir.' Hightower resumed walking. 'We'll find out soon enough if I know what I'm about. What with the Union army just up the road and all.'

'They'll want to take this place, that's for sure.' Jack drew on what scant knowledge he had.

'They will that. From what I hear, they took Fort Henry easily enough. They've got those fancy ironclad ships of theirs and they'll want to use them again, I reckon. Yes, they'll try to trap us in here then grind us into the dirt until we give up.'

'You think they want to trap us?'

'Hell, sir, I don't see what else they'd do.' Hightower shook his head at the foolish question. 'Way I see it, those Billy Yankees will try to corral us in here then pound us with those ships of theirs until we give in. And if *I* know that, then those generals of ours will surely know it. Way I hear it, they want us to skedaddle just as soon as we can.'

'Then what's the point of gathering the army here, if not to make a stand and fight the Union off?' Jack didn't understand and didn't bother to try to hide it.

'You tell me, sir, you being the officer and all.' Hightower looked across at him. It was clear he was unsure of the man who had berated him yet who now chatted away like an old friend.

'You'd be amazed at how little they tell us, Corporal. Although perhaps you've been in the army long enough to know just how little the damn generals tell anyone about their plans.' Jack mounted a fair defence, playing the old-soldier card as effectively as he could.

'They don't like to share their plans, as that would mean they would need to have a goddam plan in the first place.' Hightower glanced at Jack as he made the less than flattering comment. 'If you'll pardon me for saying so, sir.'

'You have that right, Corporal.' Jack gave as reassuring an answer as he could. In truth, he still did not understand the Confederate generals' plan. They had gathered a large force around Dover and Fort Donelson. The risk that the Union forces would encircle them was a real one, but to his mind surely that was what the Confederates would want. Only by making a stand could they defeat the Union army and force them to retreat back along their lines of communication. But if Hightower was correct, the Confederate commanders were more concerned with getting trapped than making a stand. If that was the case, he couldn't for the life of him work out why they had gathered such a large force there in the first place.

'Well, here we are, sir.' Hightower announced their arrival at his hut. He dumped the pot of water on the ground, then turned to face Jack. 'You still want that coffee?'

'That would be grand, Corporal.'

The men who shared the hut with Hightower pushed themselves to their feet as they realised an officer was amongst them. Like most of the army Jack had seen, they were a scruffy bunch, their uniform – if it could be called that – little more than a collection of similarly coloured grey jackets matched with any other clothing the men had. Yet he saw that the muskets that had been stacked together looked well cared for, and their camp was as tidy as the men could manage given that they were forced to live in what was little more than a sea of half-frozen mud.

'Coffee for the officer.' The snapped instruction had one of Hightower's men scurrying to the fire and the coffee pot. 'It's as weak as piss, sir, but we're nearly out of beans.'

'I'm sure it will be just fine.' Jack meant it. He sorely needed a hot drink. The cold had permeated deep into his bones and his gut felt like it was full of ice.

'Here you go, sir.' Hightower handed over a tin mug full of steaming black liquid, then made a play of looking at the weapon Jack carried. 'That's a fancy rifle you got there, sir.'

'You want to take a look?' Jack sipped his coffee, then held out the rifle.

'If you don't mind.' Hightower took it reverentially. 'I thought as much. It's one of those Henry repeaters. I ain't ever seen one this close before. One of the officers in my regular unit bought hisself one just before I quit, but down here they're as rare as gold in horseshit.' He ran his hands over the weapon, then raised it and pulled it into his shoulder before sighting down the barrel. He held the pose for a long moment before he lowered the rifle and offered it back to Jack. 'It's a fine weapon, sir. Why, you can load her on a Sunday and shoot her all week long. With a few hundred of these, we could whip those Yankees all by ourselves.'

Jack took the rifle back. 'Perhaps. But you'd have to find ammunition for the bloody thing.' He made the comment ruefully. He had used much of the ammunition he had taken from Pinter and knew he would need more. 'Any idea where I could find myself some?'

Hightower pulled a face. 'You can try the armourers, but I can't imagine they'll have the right ones for that beauty of yours. I ain't seen one anywhere since I came down south.'

Jack grunted at the bad news. It appeared that he would

have to husband his ammunition carefully. When it was gone, that would likely be it. Then the desirable rifle would be no more use than a simple cudgel.

'Now tell me, Corporal,' he changed the subject, 'do you know where I might find the 65th Virginia?' He asked the question not really expecting much in the way of an answer.

'Of course I do!' Hightower greeted the question with a guffaw. 'Hell, sir, you're looking at them!'

Jack had to hide his surprise at the answer. He had expected it would take days to locate the regiment in which Martha's husband served, if it was even there at all. It appeared that for once, fate was smiling down on him. One of them, at least, had just found what they were looking for.

'I know where he is.' Jack sang out the news the moment he reached the meagre shelter he had shared with Martha.

Martha had not been idle whilst he had been away. She had found enough wood to get a fire started, coercing the damp kindling into flame by using one of Jack's revolver cartridges, just as he had shown her. She had folded up the blankets he had stolen, and was busy sorting through their sparse collection of spare clothes to find them both something slightly drier to put on than the damp, mud-streaked things they were wearing.

'Lyle?' Martha looked up at him sharply. There was no hiding the concern in her expression.

'No. I found John.'

'John?' For a moment, Martha looked confused, as if unable to understand whom he was referring to. 'You mean my John?'

'Who else would I bloody mean?' Jack smiled. 'I found his regiment.' He turned and pointed away towards the lines of soldiers' huts. 'It's just across there.' He paused, uncertainty pushing its way past the happiness at his easy success. 'You've done it.'

Martha said nothing. She folded one of his shirts, then unfolded it and started again.

'You can go over there right now. The journey's over. For you, anyway,' Jack spoke slowly.

Martha looked up at him and held his gaze. 'I should go.'

'Yes, you should.' Jack searched her eyes. He knew her well enough to read her uncertainty. It surprised him. It was rare to see her so hesitant. 'I'll come with you if you like.'

'Yes.' Martha rose to her feet. 'If you don't mind, I sure would appreciate that.' She looked at the neatly folded shirt in her hand as if seeing it for the first time, then tossed it onto the blankets she had stacked on the ground. 'We can't just leave our things like this, though. Someone will take them. There's a lot of thieves around.' For a second there was a flash of something in her eyes. Then it was hidden.

'Leave them. If they get pinched, then so be it.' Jack walked past her, switching his rifle to his left hand, and picked up his knapsack, which he slung over his shoulder. It contained the only things he owned of value. If someone took the blankets and filthy clothes he would not be concerned. With Martha going to her husband, he would be able to shift for himself. His life was about to get a whole lot easier.

'Come on then. Look alive-o.' He geed her into motion. 'Anyone would think you don't want to go. I know I'm fabulous company, but this is what you came here for.'

Martha bent down and picked up the saddlebag with her things in it. 'You think I should go right now?'

'Yes,' Jack answered instantly. But he regretted his glib remark. Martha had been no simple travelling companion. He was being cruel, severing the tie with callous thoughtlessness. 'Look, you haven't seen the last of me. I don't think anyone here is going anywhere any time soon, least of all me. But you came all this way to find your husband, and there he is. You should go and see him.' He reached out and gripped her arm with his free hand. 'I'll be here if you need me. We've been through a lot, you and I. I won't forget all you did for me. I'll always be in your debt, so if you ever need me, well, just whistle and I'll be there.'

Martha reached across and held his hand for several long moments before pulling away. She nodded once, then hefted her saddlebag into her arms and started to walk.

'Hey, you boys the 65th Virginia?' Jack called out to a group of soldiers seated around a fire. It was barely alight, but the men were lingering beside it, savouring the last of its dying warmth.

'Yes, sir.' One of the men lumbered to his feet and swept his hat from his head.

'You know a John Joseph?' Jack had half forgotten Martha's married name.

'John Joseph? Sure I do.' The man turned and pointed at a group of huts close by. 'He's in K Company. Those boys are over there.' His eyes narrowed. 'He in some sort of trouble?'

'Not at all.' Jack took Martha by the elbow and began to lead her away. 'I've got a present for him.' He gave her what he hoped was a reassuring smile. He was rewarded with an expression carved from granite.

It did not take long to cover the ground to the huts the soldier had indicated. Jack was struggling to understand Martha's reluctance. They had both set off to find someone. When he had spotted Lyle, nothing else had mattered. All had been forgotten the moment he gave chase, Martha included. Now they had found the man she sought, and for a reason he could not understand, she was as reluctant as a bullock being led to the butcher's.

Martha stopped suddenly, staring ahead. Jack understood immediately. The man she was looking at was of middling height, with a good roll of fat around his belly. He was nearly bald, and wore what hair he had left long. It was paired with a thick moustache and a curly beard that smothered the whole of his lower face. He was nothing like the man Jack had pictured.

Martha moved forward slowly, as if wary of what was about to happen.

'John!' When she called out to him, her voice wavered.

The man turned. He looked at her for several long seconds, his face creased into an expression of annoyance. And then he truly saw her.

'Martha?' His cry turned heads. Dozens of his mates stared at him, then at Martha.

He walked quickly towards his wife and folded her into his arms, embracing her tightly, unconcerned at being the centre of attention. He held her for a long time. Eventually he pushed her away from him, gripping her around the arms as he got a proper look at her. There was no hiding the smile on his face.

'What the hell have you done to your hair? And what in all of God's heaven are you doing here?'

'Pa died. Some men came to the cabin and killed him.' Martha was holding herself stiffly. Her expression was carved from granite, any pleasure at the meeting hidden away. 'So I came to find you.'

'You shouldn't have come. This is no place for a woman.'

John's broad smile started to melt away. 'What were you thinking?'

'I was thinking that I wanted to be with my husband.'

'And how the hell did you get here?' John scowled as he ignored her answer. The pleasure and surprise at seeing his wife was fading as questions crowded into his mind. His hands tightened on her arms. 'It can't have been safe.'

Martha glanced over her shoulder. 'Jack brought me.'

Jack had been hanging back. There was much to see in this meeting of husband and wife. He knew he was incapable of understanding all of it, but he could tell that there was plenty that was not being said.

'And who the hell is Jack?' John pushed his wife to one side and came to stand foursquare in front of Jack.

'He was staying with us. Pa took him in. He was sick.' Martha gave Jack's story in a clipped tone. 'He saved my life when the men who killed Pa came.'

John was studying Jack carefully, measuring him up. 'You brought my wife all this way?'

'I did.' Jack saw anger flare in the man's eyes.

'All that way? Just the two of you?'

'All that way. Just the two of us,' Jack answered evenly. He could sense the violence in the man standing in front of him. He tried to understand it, to wonder what it would be like to have another man take care of your wife during a dangerous journey. He failed. Empathy was not one of his strongest skills.

'And why would you do that?' John's hands went to his hips. He had the build of a man who slept by the fire and ate most of the time he was awake. But his mates surrounded him, and their presence gave him the confidence to confront a stranger, one who had done him either the greatest service or the greatest wrong. It was clear that he was trying to figure out which one of those it was, and in the meantime he had defaulted to a defensive posture that clearly painted Jack as a villain.

'We were both heading in the same direction. I figured I was in her debt for her taking care of me when I was sick. So I repaid that debt by bringing her to you.'

'So I should be thanking you?' John shook his head at the notion.

'Yes, yes, you bloody should.' Jack tasted the first stirrings of anger. Martha's husband was clearly a prick.

'So you treated her right?'

'Yes.'

'All that way?'

'Yes.' Jack felt not even a shred of guilt as he lied. Perhaps he should act with more meekness, or even feel remorse at making this man a cuckold. But he couldn't do it. He just didn't have it in him.

'And I'm supposed to believe you?' John fired out questions that were more accusations than requests for answers.

'Yes.' Jack held onto his growing anger with difficulty. 'And now you get to take care of your wife.'

'You telling me what to do?' John's face turned sour. 'I don't need a goddam Englishman telling me what I should or shouldn't be doing.' He had clearly picked up on Jack's accent.

'Fine. Do whatever the fuck you want, chum. But your wife risked her life to find you. I would think you would cherish her for that. Instead here you are acting like a dog with a dick up its arse.'

John took a step forward. Martha moved quickly to come between them. 'We owe Jack our thanks, John. I wouldn't have made it here without him. He kept me safe and acted like a gentleman the whole time.' She placed her hands on her husband's chest and spoke firmly, even as she lied. 'Now,' she turned and faced Jack, keeping her back against her husband's chest, 'I think it's best if you go, Jack.'

Jack looked at her then, holding her gaze. Then he nodded and turned on his heel, walking away without another word. He had done as he had promised and delivered Martha to her husband. The moment should have brought him satisfaction at a job well done. He did not understand quite what he felt, but he knew there was not an ounce of pleasure as the ties that had bound him to her were cut away.

# Chapter Thirty-three

'The Yankees are here!'

Jack rose to his feet as the cry was shouted around the encampment. He had been eating, but the hardtack that was all he had managed to find was almost inedible. He tossed it into the mud without a second thought.

He had been sitting in the damp shelter he had shared with Martha, his mind dwelling on the encounter with her husband. There was no denying there was a sense of relief at having handed her into another man's care, but there was another emotion trying to force its way to the forefront of his mind, one that he refused to acknowledge. He did not want to admit, even to himself, that he missed her.

Around him, the Confederate lines were a hive of activity. Men streamed away from their huts, rushing to their allotted places in the rifle pits. Bugles and drums hastened them on, whilst sergeants and officers shouted orders at their men.

Jack had no place to be, and would play no part in whatever was ahead. Yet there was something in the cacophony that resonated deep in his gut. Feeling his heartbeat beginning to race, he grabbed his rifle and made sure his revolver was in its holster, then jogged after the nearest soldiers.

The rifle pits were built across a ridge of slightly higher ground, and he followed them to the west, keen to discover the rest of the Confederate position. They stretched away from him, tracing the contours of the ground, until they ended in a deep ravine with a fast-moving creek running along its bottom.

When he reached the ravine, he picked his way down and across, taking his time. He had no desire to twist an ankle on the treacherous ground. He had just crossed the creek when he heard the first rifle shots. They came individually. He did not have to see the Confederate lines to know that they had sent out sharpshooters to interfere with the progress of the Union troops. It told him the blue-coated army was close, so he increased his pace as he scrambled up the far side of the ravine, unwilling to miss whatever was going to happen next.

He emerged to see more entrenchments stretching away in front of him. Like the ones closer to Dover, they had been dug deep and reinforced with sturdy tree trunks and mounds of clay. Another long abatis covered the approach to these pits, the dense tangle of branches blocking much of his view of the ground to the south and west, the direction he expected the Union army to come from. The pits themselves were packed with Confederate troops, the men, like him, waiting for events to unfold.

He turned northwards, making his way up the sloping ground to where he guessed he would find the fort itself. He had been walking a while and he estimated he was a good mile from Dover. The area between the entrenchments and the higher ground was lined with more of the shacks and huts the soldiers had built to shelter from the winter weather, deserted now that the men were down in the rifle pits.

He paused near one of the larger huts, taking a moment to check that no one was there to watch him before ducking inside. As he had suspected, the hut belonged to some officers. The interior looked cosy, the men who lived there lucky enough to have found themselves a couple of cots to sleep in. Many of their belongings had been left behind, and he found what he was looking for no more than ten seconds after he went inside. A standard-pattern infantry officer's sabre was lying on a table in its scabbard, and a pair of field glasses in a leather case hung from a nail driven deep into one of the hut's supporting pillars. He felt a pang of guilt as he tucked the sabre under his arm, but it was not enough to stop him grabbing the leather strap of the glasses case and slinging it over his shoulder. They were a valuable pair of items, and he was sure their owner would feel their loss keenly. But he consoled himself with the notion that whoever owned the equipment was clearly a fool to leave it behind when faced with the enemy. And fools got what they deserved.

He scurried out of the hut, then pushed on, stretching his legs as he walked up the slope, only pausing long enough to fasten the scabbard's belt around his waist. When he reached the top, he opened the leather case and pulled out the field glasses. They looked new and smelled of the protective oil that their former owner had applied to prevent them from rusting.

It was something of a relief to stop. His chest heaved with the exertion of his walk, but at least he had a fine view of the surrounding terrain. He was standing on high ground surrounded by the trenches and buildings that he guessed constituted the fort itself. To the east, around two miles away, were the buildings of Dover. To the north of the town he could see the wide Cumberland river. The long line of rifle pits ran around the eastern and southern flanks of the town, stretching all the way from the river to the ravine he had crossed. They then continued around the south of the fort before turning northwards until they reached another, smaller river that flowed from south to north.

From what Jack could see, the Confederate generals had sited the fort and its surrounding entrenchments well. The wide Cumberland river protected the northern flank, and the second, smaller river he had just seen for the first time protected the fort from the west. The southern and eastern approaches were open to attack, but the long line of rifle pits and their protective abatis had been located to cover any attack from those directions. It was a strong position, but he could not help thinking back to what the Confederate corporal, Hightower, had said. There was indeed a feeling of being shut in, the same rivers that protected the place also trapping the soldiers there. The risk of the army being encircled was a real one.

He looked south. From where he stood, he could see over the rifle pits and the abatis, so he put the field glasses to his face and searched the ground beyond for a sighting of the Union army. He saw nothing.

Disappointed, he turned to the north and looked over the fort. It was nothing like he had imagined, being little more than an irregularly shaped fieldwork with ten-foot-high walls of earth and logs occupying the highest area of ground around one hundred feet above the Cumberland river. The line of rifle pits to its southern flank was interspersed with positions for field guns, while nearer to the river he could make out a line of three interlinked gun emplacements that had been hacked from the mud of the bluff high above the waterline, designed to protect both the heavy guns that had been dragged up to the fort and the men who served them. Each cannon stood in its own position, with its barrel aimed over a parapet. Both the parapets and the sides of the emplacements had been reinforced with stout wooden planks, which were topped with coffee sacks filled with sand. The cannon sat on barbette carriages rather than the two-wheeled gun carriages he was used to seeing on a battlefield. The barbette was made up of a stout wooden chassis with fixed iron rails running along its length, mounted on a level platform with a fixed iron pintle at the front and a pair of small traversing wheels at the rear. The gun barrel sat on a separate wooden carriage with iron rollers that rested on the chassis's fixed iron rails. When fired, the massive recoil would drive it back up the rails where it would be held in place with heavy wooden chocks to be reloaded before being levered back into position when ready to fire.

As he ran his eyes over the position, he realised very quickly that the cannon had been sited to cover an approach by river, being aimed out to the north and west, the direction any Union flotilla would take were it to sail down the Cumberland to launch an attack on the fort. There were three cannon sited in the first battery he saw: two 32-pounders alongside a much larger rifled cannon. Further to the west, and cut lower into the bluff, was a second battery housing another nine cannon: eight 32-pounders and a huge columbiad. He was no artilleryman, but it was clear that any Union ships seeking to steam down the Cumberland river would meet a devastating fire from the two gun batteries.

He studied the river through his field glasses, concentrating on the western approaches to the fort, and saw immediately that upstream, the river bent around to the north. Its natural path would screen any boats heading their way from sight until they were almost in range of the heavy cannon in the water batteries. He panned westwards until he could see where the second river, which ran along the western edge of the fort, flowed into the much wider Cumberland. From what he could make out, the backwater from the Cumberland was flooding back along the smaller river, making it a formidable obstacle. The fort was safe from attack from the west.

He had seen enough. There were gunners working around their precious cannon and he had no intention of getting any closer to them. He was satisfied with what he had seen, and he now carried a solid mental picture of the ground the Confederates had chosen to defend.

With the sound of gunfire increasing, he returned to his earlier vantage point on the southern flank of the fort. He studied the ground to the south and this time he was rewarded with his first glimpse of the Union army.

The sight of the blue uniforms brought him up short. They were advancing in column, the men moving slowly and carefully towards the Confederate position. The glimpse of the familiar uniform stirred emotions he had buried deep. Less than a year before, he had fought alongside men like the ones he now watched. The 1st Boston had been his home for several months, and he had come to care deeply about its men. Yet now he stood on the opposite side of the war, amidst ranks dressed in brown and grey instead of blue.

The Union army advanced with caution, but the Confederates did not send anything more than a few dozen sharpshooters to challenge their arrival. The main body of men stayed in their rifle pits, watching the enemy approach. They catcalled and hooted as the hated Northerners came into sight, but that was all. The Union army would be left without interference to take up the positions that would pin the Confederates in their defences. It smacked of weakness and timidity. As Jack watched the Union columns, he imagined what he would do if he were in charge. It would be simple enough to clear channels in the abatis and send forward men to contest the enemy's arrival. The Confederates could give the Union troops a bloody nose, and perhaps even force them to retreat, whilst knowing they themselves had a strong defensive position to fall back to.

In his mind's eye, he imagined the Confederate soldiers swarming forward, the men yipping and yelling like fiends. If they fought cohesively, they could form line and flense the Union columns with musket fire. The Union troops, in their denser formations, would be sure to take heavy casualties. Even if it did not force a retreat, it would make the Union generals more cautious whilst also boosting the morale of the Confederate soldiers defending Fort Donelson. Doing nothing handed the initiative to the Union, and Jack could only imagine what it was doing to the spirits of the men standing idle in the rifle pits, forced to watch as their doom approached.

He sighed. The Confederate generals clearly had their own ideas. As he watched the Union columns creep forward unopposed, he was forced to remind himself that this was not his war. He fought only for himself now, for his own aims and ambitions. The two sides in this bitter struggle could find their way to hell without his assistance.

He looked away from the main body of the Union army and panned east. Almost immediately he spotted a column of Confederate cavalry riding into the eastern approach to Dover. They looked little like the cavalry he had seen during his time with the British army. There was no pomp or splendour about these riders. They wore little that could be thought of as a uniform, and what they did wear was mud-splattered and filthy. Yet even from a distance he could sense their confidence. He could see it in the set of their shoulders and the busy, purposeful bustle as they dismounted.

He kept the field glasses pressed to his face and continued to scan the ranks, searching for the one face he wanted to see. He found it within the span of a single minute. He took a sharp intake of breath, then held the field glasses still as he studied the man he had come so far to kill.

Men surrounded Lyle. As Jack watched, the grey-haired Confederate officer strode through the dismounted ranks, clapping one man on the back, then stopping to bawl out another. Suddenly he stopped, staring into the half-distance, as if somehow aware of Jack's distant scrutiny. It allowed Jack to sharpen the image in the field glasses, bringing his enemy's face fully into focus. He held it there, committing it to memory, so that every pore, every wrinkle, every whisker became indelibly etched into his mind.

It was time to simplify matters. He was alone once more, beholden to no one but himself. He would no longer waste time dwelling on the war, on Martha, on states' rights or the fate of a million slaves. He would just do what he had come here to do.

He would try to remember Rose. And he would kill Lyle.

# Chapter Thirty-four

*Dover, Tennessee, 14 February 1862*

Jack sat in his meagre shelter as the dawn of another day arrived and shivered. He was not sure which was worse, the bitter icy wind that now cut through the air, or the previous night's blizzard. Snow now smothered the ground, and the encampment around Dover had been reduced to little more than a frozen wasteland through which the men moved like ghosts.

The Confederate army hid away in its huts and suffered. Like Jack himself, it had done precious little the previous day. The Union army had launched a single attack. There had been an exchange of artillery fire along with a long-range bombardment from a single Union ship, and Jack had heard of a body of Union infantry attempting an assault on a part of the Confederate line. Nothing had come of the isolated attack.

For his part, Jack had spent the day wandering the encampment. He had gathered a few supplies, securing himself some hardtack, salted meat and coffee beans that would sustain him for the next week or more. The gunners up at the fort had fed him, the men serving the huge guns happy to share their stew with the lone Englishman wandering through their lines. They had seemed pleased to have him visit, and he had spent an hour in their company, talking of London and making up answers to their questions as to how an English officer had found his way into the Confederate army. It had been a diversion, the conversation a fair price to pay for the hot meal. Yet the talk of his former home had been unsettling, and he had turned the conversation to the defence of the fort.

He had expected to be told of plans for a long, resolute defence of the strong position. Instead, he had heard about a breakout, the commanding officers already committed to abandoning the fort to the Union forces and forcing their way through towards Nashville.

To Jack's mind, such a plan made little sense. If the Confederate army had wanted to avoid a confrontation with the Union forces pushing deep into the South, they could have pulled back long before the Northerners had arrived. Instead they had waited, creating a strong defensive position around the fort and holding ground that governed access to part of the strategically important river network. To give that ground up without a fight had to be nothing short of folly.

But whilst nothing he had heard made much sense, none of it was his concern. He hunched down in his shelter, burying himself beneath the blankets he had stolen and gnawing on his hardtack. If the rumours were correct, the breakout would be attempted later that day. He would be ready for it. He did not care what the generals planned. He cared only for using the confusion that would ensue for his own means.

* * *

Jack emerged from his shelter like an animal leaving its burrow. It was not much protection, but it was better than setting foot into the world.

The night's snow storm had been replaced with persistent rain. It had washed away much of the snow, but had turned the ground into a quagmire. Mud coated every surface and the going was so bad that even a short journey took an age.

Jack slogged his way towards Dover. He was carrying everything he deemed useful. Two muddy, mildewed blankets had been rolled up and bound to his knapsack, which contained a few spare clothes and all his remaining ammunition. He wore the Navy Colt revolver on his right hip and his stolen sabre on his left. Pinter's rifle was slung over one shoulder, and the long bowie knife Samuel had given him was in a sheath that hung over his right buttock. He had all he needed.

But he had little by way of a plan. He had last seen the Confederate cavalry encamped in and around Dover, so that seemed as good a place to start his search as any. When the breakout was attempted – if it was attempted – he planned to find a horse and ride with the cavalry. In the confusion he would look for Lyle, and then, in the midst of the melee, he would strike.

He ploughed on, head down and shoulders hunched. He paid no attention to the column of infantry heading in the same direction, or to the courier forcing his horse through the quagmire as he tried to take an order from one senior officer to another. None of them mattered to him. He forced the coldness deep into his being. He would not lend a hand to help the breakout. He would fight only if threatened, and he would kill anyone from either side without a qualm. He was a man alone, a lone killer amongst two armies of killers. He cared only for his target, and for the long-overdue revenge that he would find in the bitter chill of a wintry fight.

'Halt! Halt!'

Jack barged past a sergeant and ploughed on even as the long column of infantry he paced alongside ground to a standstill.

'There's General Pillow!'

A few men in the column found the energy to call out as a group of officers rode past. Their animals were sloughed in mud up to the saddle and not one of them acknowledged the half-hearted cheers sent their way.

'Turn around, boys!' An officer came back along the column, forcing his way through the ankle-deep mud. 'It's all off. Back to your positions.' He repeated the instructions then floundered onwards.

Jack stopped where he was. He found himself standing next to a grey-bearded sergeant of infantry.

'You heard the man. Turn around, boys. Back to the lines.' The old sergeant repeated the order. He looked at Jack, a knowing, world-weary expression on his face, then turned away.

Jack could feel the anger beginning to boil deep in his gut. It would be easy to release it and howl his frustration at the world. But that would achieve nothing.

He turned round and began the long, weary slog back to his shelter. As he trudged through the muddy slurry, he forced himself to feel nothing. Frustration, anger, futility, none would serve him well. There would be another time, another opportunity. Lyle was not going anywhere, and that meant Jack would have to be patient. His time would come.

\* \* \*

It was mid afternoon when Jack heard the cannon in the fort open fire. They fired as one, the power of the great opening salvo making the very ground beneath him shudder.

He was on his feet within moments, pausing only long enough to grab his weapons and his knapsack. He did not know what the cannon fire meant, but anything could happen, and he would not be unprepared.

He walked as quickly as the filthy footing would allow. It had rained again in the hours after the breakout had been cancelled, the icy downpour only adding to the misery of the poor bloody infantrymen hunkered down in the entrenchments or in their paltry little huts. The deluge had only stopped in the last hour. Now a watery sun fought its way past the clouds to cast an eerie, pale light across the Confederate lines.

He arrived on the higher ground of the fort just in time to see the Union gunboat flotilla emerge from the distant bend in the Cumberland river. It was a fine sight, each of the leading ships belching out a thick plume of dirty black smoke that rose high into the grey-blue sky.

He found a vantage point, then pulled out his field glasses and brought the ships into sight. There were six in total. Four were the famous ironclads that he had heard about, the low-sided ships with hulls plated with iron that were said to be strong enough to be impervious to a direct hit from a cannonball fired from even the heaviest calibre of gun. The last two were wooden ships, the more traditionally built vessels hiding behind the stronger-hulled ironclads.

The guns in the fort fired. He was close enough to feel the thunder in the air as they spat their solid round shot at the flotilla. He watched for the fall of shot, wondering if the gunners who had fed him knew their trade. He was rewarded with half a dozen great geysers that erupted from the surface of the river. The early shots were missing their targets.

The Union ships returned fire, their heavy projectiles hurtling through the air then slamming violently into the bluff below the batteries, but the Confederate gunners stuck to their task, firing as soon as they were loaded. This time they had the range, and as Jack watched through his field glasses, heavy shot crashed into the leading ironclad. He peered at the Union ship, looking for signs of damage. He saw nothing.

The Union flotilla sailed on. They were firing back almost constantly now. Round shot and shell pounded into the fort. Some hit close to the two batteries, tearing up the parapets and almost burying the guns underneath great avalanches of earth. Others roared past overhead, sailing over the batteries to crash into the valleys and ridges behind the fort where the Confederate troops hunkered down in their rifle pits and entrenchments.

Jack could not help flinching as a solid round shot smashed into a tree not more than fifty yards away from where he was standing. The impact tore the tree from the ground as easily as a child might pull a dandelion from a patch of earth. Great shards of wood showered down, the tree reduced to so much kindling in the span of a single heartbeat.

The Confederate gunners continued to pound the Union ships, shell and shot smashing into the leading ironclads as they sailed ever closer to the fort. Jack could almost smell the gunners' desperation. If they failed in their task, the Union flotilla could take up an incontestable position in the river and shell the Confederate defences without interference. The entire area would become untenable, the infantrymen certain to be battered into submission without ever being able to fight back.

The gunners stuck to their drill, loading and firing their great cannon without pause. Infantrymen were summoned to the batteries, ordered to throw back the earth unsettled by the Union barrage. Others came without orders, drawn to the spectacle on which all their fates depended.

The Union flotilla sailed ever closer. Through his field glasses Jack could see the dreadful punishment the Confederate artillerymen were dishing out. Even the fabled ironclads were being damaged. One listed to the side, whilst another drifted in an odd direction, as if unable to correct its course.

Still the guns on the ships returned fire. They were killing men now, gunners and the infantrymen supporting them cut down by well-aimed shots that smashed into the batteries. Yet no matter how many men fell, the intrepid gunners stuck bravely to their task. With the direction of their officers, they concentrated their fire against the gunboats moving steadily downstream. Shot after shot smashed into the vessels, the sound of each vicious impact loud enough to reach the ears of the great crowd now watching the fight.

The two sides traded blows like a pair of stubborn prizefighters. Shot and shell thundered back and forth, the air full of the dreadful noise of their passage and the terrible crash of their impact. The Confederate gunners took their punishment, but their great cannon kept on firing, even as the men who served them bled and died. Slowly, inexorably, the gunners in the fort gained the upper hand. They began to fire faster than the Union flotilla, their shot hitting their targets with a greater frequency, their devastating power only growing as the ships sailed ever closer.

The Union flotilla knew when it was beaten. Three of the ships turned tail and fled upriver. The other three drifted past the fort, all damaged and unable to steer a course.

The Confederates cheered then. They knew the importance of this victory. The hillside echoed to the sound of the unearthly rebel yell, the same dreadful war cry Jack had heard for the first time on the slopes above the Bull Run river. The cry went on and on, echoing across the entrenchments and loud enough to be heard throughout the streets of Dover, only coming to an end as first one man, then dozens more fell to their knees to give thanks to the Lord for their deliverance.

Jack lowered his field glasses and walked away, picking his way through the men who shouted their prayers toward heaven. He did not look at them as they prayed. He did not share their faith. He did not believe in some faceless deity. He believed in the weapons he carried. He had faith only in himself and his ability to kill another man before he himself was killed.

# Chapter Thirty-five

It was still dark when Jack pushed back the blankets and ventured outside. It was bitterly cold. Snow once again smothered the ground. Where there was no snow, there was ice. Where there was no ice, there was half-frozen mud.

He entered this world of frost, ice and mud stamping his feet and blowing on hands and fingers that he could barely feel. Only when he could sense his body slowly starting to thaw did he bend down to pick up his kit.

There was to be a second breakout attempt. He had long given up trying to understand the minds of the Confederate generals who had allowed their army to be trapped in Fort Donelson. They had won a great victory, their gunners' heroic defence keeping the Union flotilla at bay. With the gunboats beaten back, there was no immediate reason to quit the fort and its surrounding defences. The Confederates were well supplied and had open access to the Cumberland river. The men were in good spirits, the victory over the flotilla and the lack of any sustained attack by the Union land forces sure to have boosted their morale. Yet there was no notion of a resolute, steadfast defence. In its place there were only whispers of retreat; of breaking through the Union lines then fleeing south.

Jack hoisted his knapsack onto his back and once again began the long slog towards the cavalry lines. It was still dark, but already the Confederate troops were on the move. This second breakout plan called for the infantry to mass on the left of the position, concentrating in and around Dover. They had quit the entrenchments during the small hours of the night, carrying with them everything they would need to fight and then to march, their knapsacks packed with rations and their pouches bulging with full loads of ammunition.

Jack trailed behind a regiment of infantry, staying close enough to hear the excited talk from the rearmost ranks. The men were bitterly cold and chilled to the bone after days enduring the worst of the winter weather, yet as far as he could tell, they were still in high spirits. All he heard were calls to whip the Yankees, along with the simple desires of men longing for nothing more luxurious than a solid roof over their heads and warm food for their bellies. Such delights, the men believed, would be waiting for them in Nashville.

For his part, Jack thought of nothing save killing Lyle. If this second breakout were not called off like the first, then the Confederates would have to bludgeon a way through the Union right flank. That fighting would likely be fierce. He would do his damnedest to make sure he worked his way into the battle. And he vowed he would track Lyle down.

Jack watched from a knot of higher ground on the very fringes of Dover as the Confederate army prepared for its breakout attempt. From where he stood, the small town looked more like a military depot than a place where ordinary people lived.

Tents filled every free space, and the streets were lined with wagons filled with military supplies. A large field hospital had been erected to the north of the town, near a small cemetery. He grunted as he saw the pragmatism behind that particular decision. At least the dead would have a short final trip.

He looked away from the town towards the dozen or more infantry regiments massed in columns on ground to the south of Dover. The Confederate soldiers were there in their thousands, and they made a lot of noise. The men were cold, but they reassured themselves that the same must be true of the enemy. On the far side of the infantry regiments were the cavalry. The men on big horses would lead the attack, then ride to protect the flanks of the attacking infantry columns and spread chaos and confusion amongst the Union lines.

It was a night for stacking fires and burying deep beneath blankets. It was not a night for preparing for a desperate fight. Yet fight they would. The men had been assembled for one task: to cut a way through the Union lines and abandon Fort Donelson. They would save the Confederate army to fight another day, and they would carry an impostor in their midst.

Jack huddled in his stolen grey uniform, pulling the collar up higher in a vain attempt to keep out the icy wind that whistled across the higher ground that provided him with his vantage point. He bided his time, patient in the face of another delay. Waiting for the moment when he could strike.

The first streaks of dawn lined the far horizon when the orders came for the lead infantry regiments to move out. Jack was near frozen by that time, the hours of inactivity turning the blood in his veins to so much ice. Yet as the first column started to move, he forced life back into stiff, aching limbs and turned to walk back into Dover.

The cavalry would lead the breakout. He had watched them go, wondering where Lyle was. He had not had a clear sight of Lyle's Raiders, but he was sure they would be in the van of the attack. Now he had to find a way to get there for himself. He waited for a column of infantry to clear his front, then headed into the streets of Dover. He walked briskly, to warm his frozen flesh as well as to look purposeful.

He found what he was looking for almost immediately.

'You there! I'm from General Pillow.' He began to shout whilst he was still a good six yards away from the sentry positioned near the entrance to the Dover Hotel, the establishment that had turned him away just a few days before. The man was charged with guarding the dozen or more saddled and bridled horses hitched to a rail outside the hotel.

'Sir?' The sentry, who looked barely in his teens, turned to face the officer who had emerged from the darkness.

'I'm with General Pillow,' Jack repeated with a snap of authority. 'I need a horse and I need it now.'

'Sir, I got orders to hold these animals here.' The young soldier winced as he gave the negative reply. Snot had crusted around his nose and he cuffed his sleeve across his face as if suddenly becoming aware of the muck.

'I don't care. *I* have orders for General Forrest and I need a horse right now.' Jack glared at the man, then stomped past him towards the nearest animal, a neat bay mare with a dark mane. 'This one will have to do.' He started to unhitch the horse from the rail.

'Sir?' The sentry pressed close. 'I'm right sorry and all, but I don't know who the hell you are. And I've got my orders.'

'And I've got mine.' Jack hissed the reply. 'The success of the breakout, hell, the fate of the whole goddam army depends on these orders reaching General Forrest.' He kept working on the knot, his frozen fingers struggling with the task. 'Are you going to stop me, soldier?'

'Sir . . .' the younger man paused, clearly uncertain, 'I don't know what I'm supposed to be doing.'

'Then make yourself useful and untie this damn knot. My fingers are fair frozen here.' Jack fired the command. The sentry needed to learn to obey him, and the simple instruction would be a start.

'But sir—'

'Do it, soldier. Every minute I delay increases the risk of failure.' Jack reached out and clasped the lad around the shoulder. 'Look, son, I know this isn't the proper way of doing things, but it is urgent, I give you my word on that. My name is Major Lyle and I serve with General Forrest. Your officers will know me. Now untie that knot and let me be on my way.'

'Sir, I ain't rightly sure 'bout this.' Despite his reservations, however, the sentry leaned his musket against the rail and started to untie the reins.

'You're a fine soldier, I can see that. Tell me your name so that I can give a good account of your actions.'

'Private Wyatt, sir.'

'And the name of your officer?'

'Lieutenant Meehan, sir.'

'Good, good.' Jack nodded as if making a mental note. 'I know Lieutenant Meehan, I shall let him know that you had the courage to do what was right.' He stepped forward and took the reins from Wyatt's hands the moment they were untied. 'Now stay at your post, Private. Do not let any Tom,

Dick or Harry come along and take these horses. You hear me?'

'Yes, sir.' The sentry stood back. A thick river of snot was now running from one nostril.

'Good man, Wyatt, you have done our cause a great service this morning.' Jack put a foot into the stirrup and pulled himself up into the saddle. He took a moment to adjust the slings on his scabbard so that it hung properly at his side, then nodded once to the sentry before kicking with his heels to urge the mare into a trot.

As Jack left the entrenchments behind and rode into the broken ground to the south of Dover, he could hear the distant sounds of infantry going into action. The rattle of musketry was soon underscored with the boom of enemy artillery opening fire. The sounds were familiar to him: the roar of a regiment firing a volley and the long-drawn-out reply of men firing by companies. The noise of battle was the clatter of his trade, and a part of him was thrilled to be back where he belonged.

Once past the cleared area on the far side of the abatis, the going was poor, the ground made slippery by a thick coating of ice. Jack rode as fast as he dared, urging the mare to pick up the pace. He caught fleeting glimpses of the fight, but the distance was too great for him to make out enough to know if the breakout was succeeding, or if the Confederate infantry were breaking themselves on the lines of Union infantry that surrounded the fort. He saw a Union regiment standing its ground, the men formed up in line of battle and pouring a single volley into an unseen Confederate force to their front. He heard the unearthly rebel yell as the Confederate troops pressed home an attack, the war cry punctuated with the screams of men being shot down. The Union poured on a final volley then broke, the line dissolving into a panicked mob, all sense of order and discipline lost the moment the men turned to run for their lives. The morning had barely dawned, but already men were dying.

He found a seam of open ground and forced his mare into a canter. He felt the first fluttering of fear. It was not fear for his safety; it was fear of missing out. If the Union troops did not hold their ground, then the breakout might succeed with a speed that would see the Confederate cavalry he sought push on without his ever being able to catch up with them.

He worked his way around the Union right, urging his stolen horse on as he followed the path the Confederate cavalry had taken. It was easy enough to do so. The hundreds of horses had cleared the ground of snow, their hooves churning the half-frozen dirt beneath to leave a clear trail that even a blind man could follow.

Ahead, the body of an eviscerated horse confirmed he was on the right path, the sight invigorating rather than disgusting. Lyle was close. Jack could sense his presence. This time he would not fail.

He kicked his heels, urging the mare to greater speed. He kept looking to his right, searching the broken ground and thickets for a sight of troops from either army. He saw nothing save a handful of wounded men making their way back to Confederate lines. There was no sign of the cavalry that he sought. The horsemen would surely have been working past the Union army's right, and he could only pray that they would have to change direction if they wanted to sweep into the enemy rear.

For once it appeared his prayers were to be answered. The path he followed swung west, the trail the cavalrymen had left bypassing a stand of tall trees then heading towards what he could only think to be an undefended flank on the Union right. He knew he was closer to the fight now. The sound of gunfire was intensifying, underscored by the undulating rebel yell, first quietening until barely audible, then increasing in volume so that it almost drowned out the sounds of volley fire. And then there were the screams, the dreadful, heart-rending noise a man made when his flesh was torn and his life force poured out of him. Together they were the musical score of a battle. He was back where he belonged, the battlefield the one place he truly understood, the place where he was master.

The going worsened. The ground broke up, swampy marsh interspersed with pockets of harder frozen soil. His pace slowed, his need to close with the Confederate cavalry tempered by the need not to break his horse's leg and thus deny him the chance of finding his target for a second time. The slower pace let him search the ground ahead more thoroughly, and he caught a glimpse of Union infantry retreating from the battlefield. They had fought hard, holding their ground and pouring out the volleys he had heard. But now they ran, their ranks broken, the red, white and blue of the Stars and Stripes bright in the gloom of the early morning.

That was when he saw the Confederate cavalry for the first time.

General Forrest, the commander of the cavalry, clearly knew his trade. He had held his men back, screening the hundreds of mounted soldiers from view behind a dense tangle of woodland. Now he released them.

The riders poured out of their concealment, their cries and yells capturing the attention of the fleeing infantry. The men in the broken ranks could do nothing save turn and run in the opposite direction. It was a futile attempt: on the boggy ground, they were no more able to outrun the horses than a toddler could outrun its mother. And so more men began to die.

Jack raked back his spurs. It was time to risk everything. If he hesitated now he would miss his chance.

Forrest's cavalry tore into the Union infantry. The men on foot stood little chance against the rampaging riders. They were cut down in swathes. Some of the riders had pulled swords from scabbards and rode through the melee hacking and cutting at any man in their path. Others rode with revolvers outstretched, gunning down man after man as they scythed through the broken ranks.

Jack bent low in the saddle and willed the mare to press on. He could do nothing now but trust to the animal's speed to get him into the fight before it was over.

Ahead, the cavalry cut through the fleeing Union soldiers then pressed on. They did not linger, or turn to gouge a second path through the survivors of their first charge. Forrest clearly knew that the fate of the Confederate breakout did not depend on the slaughter of a single Union regiment, and he urged his men onward.

Jack bit back a howl of frustration as he saw the cavalrymen ride on. He galloped past the bodies of the soldiers who had been cut down, drawing his own revolver as he did so in case any man left on his feet tried to stop him. He did not ride to fight, but he would not hesitate to kill should anyone stand in his path. He was there to find Lyle. The fight, the breakout and the lives of the men around him were meaningless. His revenge was all and it was close now. He could feel it. He could smell it in the stink of spilt blood that tainted the air. He could taste it in the acrid tang of the powder smoke.

The Union men still on their feet thought only of flight. Jack was left to trot through the field of broken bodies without interference, the closest surviving infantrymen running from his path. He did not look at the dead or the dying. He had seen the results of cavalry riding down a broken infantry regiment before, both from the saddle and from the blood-splattered ground. He had experienced the wild rush of delight at charging at a broken enemy, and he had known the bowel-wrenching fear of being pursued by victorious riders with sabres bloodied to the hilt. There was nothing new for him to see on this field of butchery.

He rode on, following the Confederate cavalry and leaving the slaughter behind, until he reached an open pasture. Union infantry streamed across it, the men in blue uniforms running as fast as they could. The broken ranks offered another inviting target for the hard-riding Confederate cavalry, and he expected to see the riders galloping into their midst to work a second slaughter.

Yet for a reason he could not fathom, the cavalry were barely moving. He was closer to them now, and he saw the hundreds of men and horses bunched together, any order to their formation lost after the killing spree. They still advanced, but they were slow. Finally he had his chance.

'What the hell is going on?' He roared the question as he forced his mare into the rear of the cavalry. 'Why are we stopping?'

'Marsh up ahead!' shouted a man. 'We can't get through.'

The answer made sense. The Union infantry were enjoying the most precious commodity to be found on the field of battle. Luck.

The great mass of cavalry laboured on, the men kicking and

urging their tiring animals through the marshy ground. In their midst, Jack worked harder than any man, pushing his mare onwards and forcing a path through the great press of riders and horses. He searched the men around him as he made his way through their ranks, his eyes running over every face as he looked for Lyle.

'Hold here!'

Orders were shouted. The men leading the cavalry were no fools. They could see they would not be in time to attack the Union infantry in the flank. Jack caught a glimpse of the blue-coated infantrymen. Most had cleared the pasture and now formed a line on its southern flank. He was close enough to hear the officers bawling at their men, and to see the soldiers turn around and begin to reload their muskets. Any chance of an easy victory was lost.

Yet the cavalry were not the only ones on the battlefield. Even as they began to re-form their ranks in the broken ground to the east of the open pasture, Confederate infantry regiments emerged on its northern edge.

They came on anyhow, their ranks disordered, advancing in one great mass, the lack of common uniform making them look more like a mob than an army. Yet their colours led them and they crossed into the open ground without pause.

The Union infantry on the southern edge of the field saw them coming. These men had broken once, but they still had fight left in them. At the commands of their officers, they re-loaded, then presented their weapons, aiming at the great mass of Confederate soldiers coming against them. A moment later, their volley roared out, the men in blue flinging a storm of shot into the Confederate ranks.

The volley ripped into the Confederate infantry. Dozens

fell, their bodies torn apart by the fast-moving projectiles. Yet the advance did not pause. Those men who fell were ignored, the Confederates callous and uncaring as they surged forward.

In the silence that followed the volley, the rebel yell emerged from deep in the mob, the dreadful keening washing over the line of Union men standing against them. The discordant sound was quite unlike anything Jack had heard before coming to these shores. It doubled in volume as the Confederates rushed across the field. A few men fired as they charged, their shots knocking down a man here and another there all along the Union line. Most just ran, their mouths wide open as they released their inhuman cry.

To their credit, the Union line held. It was bravely done, the men forcing ramrods down rifle barrels fouled with spent powder even as the great mass of enemy infantry charged towards them.

'Fire!'

This time Jack heard the Union commander roar the single command. The men obeyed, flinging a second defiant volley into the faces of the charging Confederates. It ripped through the leading ranks, tumbling men from their feet. But the charge was unstoppable now. The Confederates ignored their casualties and rushed onwards, the great rebel yell unaltered even by the loss of so many men.

For a second time, the Union line broke. One moment it was steady, then the men ran, their brave display forgotten as they fled.

Jack had forced his way to the front of the cavalry ranks in time to see the Confederate infantry tear into the slowest-moving Union troops. He turned away from the killing, his only thought to find Lyle. He allowed no emotion to trouble him as men died not far from where he sat in the saddle. It was as nothing to him. Nothing mattered. Not death. Not fear. Not glory. Not even victory or defeat.

There was just his need for revenge.

# Chapter Thirty-six

~~~~·•·~~~~

The sun had risen higher in the sky when Jack saw Lyle for the first time. The sight came suddenly. He had been searching the ranks as the cavalry manoeuvred away to the west and around the marshy ground that had prevented their charge on the broken Union ranks. They had not fought since their first charge. Quite simply, the Union troops were retreating faster than the Confederate army could advance. As far as he could tell, the whole right flank of the Union army had been pushed back. The Confederate general's plan had worked. His men had forced open the road from Dover to Nashville, and now the entrapped army could flee Fort Donelson.

But there was the sound of more fighting away to the west. Jack could only suppose that the Union general had ordered his men to attack the westernmost Confederate defences, matching the attack on his right flank with one of his own on the left. It was a sound plan. The Confederate right had been stripped of the men needed to launch the breakout attempt. Those that remained would be hard pressed to hold against a determined Union assault.

The glimpse of Lyle did not last long. Almost as soon as Jack clapped eyes on his target, the Confederate cavalry surged forward. They rode fast, pushing across grassland strewn with dead and wounded bodies. Confederate infantry milled at the field's far side, the men taking cover along a hedge line as a battery of Union guns forced them to go to ground.

In the midst of the cavalry, Jack began to feel the thrill of the attack. They were swinging around the flank of the battered infantry regiments, their pace increasing. There was excitement in the faster tempo. He could feel it humming in the air. The animals could sense it too. Many of the riders were forced to work hard to hold their mounts in check.

Hooves thumped into half-frozen ground. The drumming noise they made was mesmerising. There was something glorious in this moment. Jack had charged with cavalry before. He knew the thrill well and something of it once again resonated deep in his being. Yet the man who had ridden with the Bombay Lights at Khoosh-Ab was much changed, and even as the riders around him began to bawl and yell, he felt the excitement flutter and die in his breast. There was no joy to be had on that grey morning. There would just be death.

The Confederate cavalry charged into the open ground in front of them. Ahead, Union infantry formed two lines to either side of the battery of cannon that had pinned the Confederate advance in place. The guns themselves were lined up on a road, the artillerymen using the hard surface as a solid foundation for the wheels. They fired one after the other, great gouts of flame exploding from the barrels as they flung another devastating salvo at the infantrymen who were trying to hide behind the fragile hedge line. The sound deafened the men guarding the guns, and the blanket of foul-smelling grey smoke that smothered them meant they did not see the great mass of Southern cavalry charging at their flank.

The Confederate cavalry tore across the open ground, the men screaming as their animals powered forward. Jack went with them, revolver held ready.

The Union infantrymen saw them at the last moment. The men on the right flank of the line turned to stare in horror as hundreds of marauding cavalrymen burst out of the cloud of powder smoke. They broke instantly at the sight of death hurtling towards them.

Then the charge hit.

Men died in their dozens as the Confederate cavalry cut deep into the broken ranks. Some were simply hacked down, their faces and shoulders slashed by the swords of the rampaging cavalrymen. Others were bowled over, their bodies pulped beneath the heavy hooves of the Confederate horses.

Some Union soldiers stood their ground. Southern cavalry-men were shot from the saddle by the defiant few, their screams of pain adding to the chaos. Animals fell too, their inhuman shrieks of agony loud as bullets and bayonets found homes in their flesh.

Jack rode into the chaos without fear. He spurred his tiring mare on, yanking hard on the reins to steer the animal around a flailing horse that had been shot in the neck. The horse went down hard, throwing its rider and taking down another two mounts that were too close to avoid it.

He spotted Lyle, his bright shock of grey hair marking him out, and changed course, steering a path for his target. He did not fire even as he flashed past a Union infantryman standing stock still in the midst of the melee. It was not his fight. It was not his war.

A Union soldier darted across the front of Jack's mare. The man had dropped his rifle and now ran with hands held over his head as if protecting himself from a sudden downpour. A moment later, a Confederate rider half severed the man's head with a sweeping blow as he galloped past.

'The guns! Ride for the guns!'

Jack heard the cry amidst the roar of the fight. The men commanding the Confederate cavalry knew their job. The Union infantry regiment was as good as broken. The real prize still lay ahead.

Some riders heard the order and spurred on, forcing their animals back into the gallop. For his part, Jack paid it no heed. He would let nothing turn him away from his encounter with the man he had hunted down.

Lyle was in the van of the attack. He held a sword in his right hand, the blade dripping with gore. As Jack watched, he kicked his horse hard, forcing it into a lurching gallop. Jack did the same, cruel in his mastery of the flagging animal. He rode past a small huddle of Union infantrymen, then around the flank of the pair of Confederate riders aiming revolvers at them.

Lyle broke free of the press around him and changed direction, heading away from the men riding for the guns. Jack spotted his target alter course. He saw why immediately. Many of the men from the broken ranks of the Union regiment were fleeing across another field to the south. They ran hard, weapons and discipline forgotten. But they had not forgotten their colours.

The Union regiment's colour party ran as one, the two flags deep in their midst. Even as their ranks broke around them, the sergeants and corporals trusted with carrying the regiment's pride into battle stayed together, their duty tethering them to the colours.

Lyle had seen the opportunity. Taking the flags would make him famous. They were guarded by more than a dozen men, with still more men from the broken companies running nearby, yet they offered a rich target amidst the slaughter.

Six other men rode with Lyle. They had seen the officer change course and they went with him, the lure of taking the colours too strong to resist. Behind them all rode Jack. He was alone now, the rest of the men around him following other officers towards the battery of guns that still fired on the beleaguered infantrymen.

He was still far short of the group when Lyle charged home. Jack had to admire his style. He ploughed straight into the men surrounding the colours, his animal's momentum knocking three from their feet. He hacked down at those that still stood, cutting his sword across a man's face then backhanding the blade into the neck of another.

For a single heartbeat, it seemed that he would be overwhelmed. A sergeant armed with a rifle raised his weapon, aiming the muzzle straight at the Confederate officer, whilst at least three others twisted around and looked ready to strike him down with their bayonets. The man with the rifle held the muzzle of his weapon so close to Lyle that it appeared to almost touch his side.

Jack lost sight of the fight as the rest of the Confederate riders crashed into the melee. Two fell, the desperate men around the Union colours striking them from the saddle. Yet four remained, and they chopped down, swords hacking at the heads and shoulders of the men surrounding them.

Jack urged his mare on, aiming for the snarling, bleeding

huddle ahead of him. He spotted Lyle. The Confederate officer was still whole, and was flailing with his sword, his teeth bared in an animal snarl of anger.

A Union soldier saw Jack coming. Pale eyes amidst dark streaks of powder looked up at him in horror. The man braced his feet then raised his musket, thrusting the bayonet out so that it would rip into the breast of Jack's mare. Jack shot him down before he came close, firing on instinct, the bullet taking the soldier in the centre of the forehead. He crumpled without a sound.

Jack powered on into the melee. A Union soldier rammed a bayonet at him, but he saw the strike coming and kicked out, catching the blade and deflecting it away. The man who had tried to kill him died a moment later, one of Lyle's men chopping down with his sabre and cleaving the Union soldier's head nearly in two.

The struggle was breaking up. The two men carrying the colours broke away, their sergeant running with them. Lyle saw them go. Jack was close enough to hear his howl of frustration before Lyle kicked back his heels and forced his horse to race after the flags. Just one of his men followed, the rest too engaged with the Union infantrymen fighting for their lives.

Jack kicked a Union soldier out of his way, then went after the two cavalrymen. Ahead, the men with the colours ran fast, covering a dozen yards of open ground before scrambling down a slope that led into a shallow ravine. Lyle went after them, but the poor going at the entrance to the ravine forced him to slow. His horse picked its way down the slope, gifting the fleeing colour party precious time.

Jack raced on, his arm outstretched, revolver held steady. He had felt nothing as he gunned down the Union soldier. Now there was not even a flicker of emotion as he fired for a second time, aiming squarely at the spine of the rider who had followed Lyle out of the melee. The first bullet missed. Yet it came close enough for the Confederate to look back over his shoulder in shock.

Jack saw the sudden fear on the rider's face; confusion too that a man from his own side had fired at him. He fired again, and then again. Both bullets hit and the rider fell away, his body tumbling from the saddle. His horse ran on, the animal veering to one side so that it avoided the broken ground ahead.

Jack slowed his mare. He thought nothing of the fact that he had now killed soldiers from both armies. Instead he ground his teeth in frustration as his horse scrambled cautiously down the uneven and treacherous snow-covered slope that led down into the ravine, his only emotion a jolt of fear that Lyle would get away.

The ground levelled at the bottom of the slope. They were in a shallow gully, thick with snow and tangles of bush and thorn. Jack forced his horse on, kicking it again and again as it floundered on the soggy ground. The animal did its best. It wallowed through the worst of the drifts, then increased speed as its hooves found harder ground.

Gunshots came from ahead. The gully twisted to the right, hiding the fight from Jack's view. It took several long moments for his tiring horse to cover the ground. As he reached the bend, he saw Lyle shooting from the saddle, his horse stationary. He was using the revolver he had taken from Jack to blaze away at the men carrying the Union regiment's colours.

'Lyle!' The cry sprang from Jack's lips.

Lyle heard him. His head whipped around, taking in Jack's arrival, before he turned back to the three Union men straining every sinew to carry their colours to safety. His arm straightened, then the revolver fired, the bullet taking the Union sergeant in the neck. The man fell, his death scream cut off abruptly as he drowned in his own blood.

The two corporals carrying the flags saw their sergeant go down. Lesser men would have given up, but still these two pressed on, their passage slowed by the long staffs of the colours. Neither man carried a weapon, their hands full with the heavy flags.

Lyle paid Jack no heed. He holstered his now empty revolver, then drew a sabre before forcing his horse back into motion. He would catch the two corporals with the colours in a heartbeat, and the men knew it. They turned, bracing themselves for a final desperate fight. One that would likely see them left dead on the ground and their regiment's precious colours taken as a prize.

Jack saw what was to come. His horse lurched and stumbled as it covered the broken ground, but he opened fire regardless of the jolting, blasting the revolver's bullets at the man he had travelled so far to kill. His horse's stumbling gait made aiming impossible, yet he needed to draw his enemy to him, and so he fired the last bullet then rammed the Colt back into its holster.

Lyle's horse reared as one of Jack's bullets snickered past its ear. The Confederate officer kept his seat, but it was enough to halt him in his tracks. He turned to face Jack, his face contorted with anger.

'Run!' bellowed Jack as he covered the last yards that separated him from Lyle. The two Union corporals were staring in confusion as another Confederate rode to their aid. 'Run!' There was time for him to shout the order for a second time before he drew his own sabre and lashed his heels back, forcing his horse to find one final burst of speed.

The two corporals needed no further urging. They turned and scrambled up the side of the gully. Jack had bought them enough time to get away.

Lyle saw him coming. With his horse barely under control, he rammed his own heels back and came towards Jack, the sabre that he had meant to use to hammer the Union soldiers into the ground now held out ready to fight the unknown rider who had arrived to steal away his chance of glory.

# Chapter Thirty-seven

*J*ack cried out as he charged at Lyle. It was little more than an incoherent snarl, a release of months' worth of anger and frustration. The shout turned into a rebel yell of his own making as he gripped the sabre tight and braced himself for the fight he had sought for so long.

He watched Lyle's eyes in the moments before they came together. He saw the anger in them, an irrational hatred that simmered in the man's gaze as he was forced to fight for a reason he could not understand. Then the moment for thinking passed.

Lyle lunged the moment he came close. Jack saw the blow coming and hammered it to one side. He slashed back at Lyle's face only for his target to sway back in the saddle so that the blade whispered past a bare inch from his skin, then pulled his blade back in time to make the parry against Lyle's next strike.

The clash of metal on metal was loud in the gully. Sparks flew as the two men hacked at one another. Blow followed blow, neither man able to find a way past the other's defence. Both controlled their horses without thought. The animals stood shoulder to shoulder, each snapping and biting at the other at every opportunity.

Jack whipped his sabre away from yet another parry, then darted the tip at Lyle's eyes. The strike was deflected, yet Jack saw the opening and slammed his left hand forward, punching Lyle in the face. It was a good blow and it rocked Lyle backwards. His balance shifted and his horse stepped away, opening a gap between the two men for the first time.

Lyle's bloodied face snarled at Jack, then he kicked hard and cut at Jack's side. Jack beat the attack away, then back-handed his sabre so that the rear edge cut at Lyle's head. Again Lyle recovered in time to parry the blow.

'Over there!'

Jack barely heard the shouts at first. He slashed at Lyle, the blows flowing from him as he found his true speed. Lyle could do nothing but defend, his parries becoming more and more desperate as Jack attacked without pause.

'Shoot him!'

The order came from Lyle. Jack saw the men out of the corner of his eye. They were coming around the bend in the gully. There had to be a dozen or more of them. All wore Confederate grey.

'Shoot him down!' Lyle repeated the order, even as he parried yet another slashing blow. At once, more than one of the approaching riders straightened their arms, aiming their pistols at the man their officer fought.

Jack felt the rage then. It was building inside him, an unstoppable ball of fire that would soon take his mind completely. Nothing mattered save the need to kill, to strike down the man who had killed Rose.

'This is for Rose! You hear me, you bastard?' He spat the

words at Lyle, punctuating them with more hammer blows from his sabre. The madness was winning the battle for control of his soul. He would kill Lyle this day. He knew it; was certain of it. In moments, one blow would find a way past the other man's sword and Rose's death would be avenged.

The first shot rang out, the bullet cracking off a rock a yard from Jack's side. A second followed a moment later.

Jack let the fury have its head. He struck at Lyle, bellowing in frustration as his opponent just about managed to fend off the blow. Bullets came at him almost constantly now. One hit him, the missile cutting through the soft flesh at the top of his arm. He barely felt it. The madness had him. He could feel it swamping his soul. Lyle had to die. He slashed again. This time the parry came late and he roared in triumph as he saw the opening he had fought for finally arrive. The moment had come.

'For Rose!' He screamed the words and pulled back his sword, gathering every ounce of strength for the blow that would kill the man he had come so far to find. He saw Lyle's expression change. There was fear there as he too realised what was to come.

Jack rammed the blade forward. The tip was aimed squarely at Lyle's heart. The moment it was launched, he knew the strike was true and he yelled out in victory.

Then a bullet hit his blade.

The sword he had taken from the unknown Confederate officer was not cheap. Yet still it shattered as the bullet struck it an inch above the handle.

'No!' Jack nearly fell as his thrust of victory turned into an awkward lurch to stay in the saddle.

Lyle reacted first. He hauled on his reins and pulled away

from Jack. 'Shoot him down!' The order sprang from his lips the moment a gap opened between the two men.

Jack's fury was blinding and powerful. Lyle had to die, even if he had to kill him with his bare hands. Yet even with the madness simmering through every fibre of his being, one thought pierced the all-consuming rage. He could not fail. He could not let Rose down, not now, not after everything he had been through. And he would let her down if he died.

The bitterness surged through him. This chance was gone. If he wanted another, then he had to stay alive.

He threw the remains of the sword at Lyle, a wild despairing cry escaping his lips. Then he pulled his horse's head round and rode for his life.

He kicked his mare without remorse, forcing the animal to find its speed even on the rough going. Shots tore through the air around him. Yet the range was long for revolvers and his mount gamely picked up the pace, increasing the distance still further so that the final shots never came close.

He shouted at the heavens as he rode away, frustration, anger and rage spewing out of him. Lyle had been there for the taking, yet fate had intervened to cheat Jack of his revenge.

He had come so very close. Yet Lyle still lived.

# Chapter Thirty-eight

J ack walked amidst the ranks of a bloodied and mud-splattered Confederate regiment. It was almost dark, the day of futile struggle at an end. The men were silent, their dour faces reflecting their sombre mood. They had fought hard; had done what they had been ordered to do. They had pushed back the Union line's right flank and opened the road to Nashville. Yet now they retraced their steps, abandoning the ground they had paid for in blood. And they did not know why.

Jack led his exhausted horse, the animal utterly spent. He walked beside others as tired and as bitter as he was.

As they reached the outskirts of Dover, an officer pushed through the ranks offering the men some form of explanation. The Union right had folded, but its left had pushed the Confederates to breaking point. The Union troops had taken the outermost line of defences, but somehow the Confederates left behind had held on. With nearly half his force facing annihilation, the Confederate general had seen no other course of action but to pull the rest of his command back. Or at least that was the tale the officer told his cold and tired men as they trudged a weary path back to the frozen lines where they had started the day.

Jack broke away from the regiment as he came near his shelter. It still stood, the meagre collection of boxes and blankets that he had used to fabricate his rudimentary refuge just as he had left it. He hitched his stolen mare to the rail of the nearest house, then dumped his remaining weapons on the ground. All needed to be cleaned, yet at that moment he did not care for the task. He let the rest of his equipment fall, then slumped down beside it, too cold and miserable to do anything more.

A long, dispirited line of Confederate infantry trudged past, the men quiet now, their shoulders drooping like men defeated.

'You not even going to light yourself a fire?'

He started as the question broke him out of his trance. He had not noticed anyone approach. He looked up at the scrawny soldier in a grey uniform who had come to disturb his rest. It took him several long moments before he realised who it was.

'What are you doing here?'

'Paying you a visit.' Martha stood looking down at him, her face hidden in the shadows. She was carrying a coffee pot, a small hessian sack and two mugs, which she deposited on the ground. Then she busied herself moving kindling and wood from the pile Jack had made, tossing them down in the place where he had burned wood before.

'I've been waiting for you.' She spoke casually as she made the fire. 'I brought us coffee.'

She looked at him over her shoulder just the once. It was enough for him to see the bruises on her face and the swelling around one eye. Her upper lip was swollen too, with a crust of blood in one corner.

'I like what you did with the place.' She did not look at him as she made the glib remark.

'Did he do that to you?' Jack ignored her poor attempt at levity and asked the question even though he already knew the answer.

Martha said nothing as she arranged the wood. It took her a while before she held out a hand. She kept her face turned away. 'Cartridge.'

Jack fished out a cartridge from its pouch and handed it over. He watched her closely as she tore it open and sprinkled the damp wood with powder.

She held out her hand a second time. 'You got any lucifers left, or you expecting me to rub two sticks together here?'

Jack grunted, then twisted to fish out his last wooden block of matches from his knapsack. 'There's not many left.'

'Then you'll have to find us some more. Looks like we're staying here a whiles.'

Jack noted her choice of words. 'You're not going back?' He asked the probing question without changing his tone. He was past being gentle.

'Not this time.' Martha struck a match, held it for a second, then pushed it into the kindling. 'I'm done with all that.'

'You want me to sort him out?'

'No.' The answer was delivered quickly. 'This one ain't your fight, Jack.' She turned to face him as the first flames caught. In their light he saw the defiance in her eyes, just as he saw the full extent of her battered face. Her husband had not held back.

'Do you want to stay with me?' He made the offer freely. Once he had wanted her to go, seeing her as little more than a burden. Now he was oddly happy that she had come back to him. He was too tired to wonder why that might be.

Martha nodded. 'I'll help you find that man you want to kill.'

Jack snorted. 'I found him.'

'And?' Martha looked directly at him. She no longer bothered to hide her face.

'We fought.'

'Is he dead?'

'No.' Jack sighed. 'There were others with him. I had him . . .' he paused and shook his head slowly as he felt the regret, 'but I couldn't finish him.'

'So you'll just have to find him again.' Martha made it sound simple. 'Do it properly next time.'

'That won't be easy. He knows I'm after him now. He doesn't know why, or at least I don't think he does.' Jack vaguely remembered shouting Rose's name as he fought Lyle, but he thought it unlikely that it would have meant anything to the man fighting for his life. 'But he will know that someone in this army tried to kill him.'

He was watching Martha. She had the fire going now, and came to pick up the coffee pot. She moved around him with familiarity. That pleased him.

'Maybe he'll think you're one of them Yankees.'

'Maybe.' Jack doubted it. 'Maybe not.'

'So it won't be easy. But then nothing worthwhile ever is.' She offered the homespun advice as she pulled the stopper from the canteen of water that he had left on the ground with the rest of his kit. Then she paused. 'You sure it's worth it? Is finding this revenge of yours worth all the pain?'

'Yes.'

'It ain't bringing you anything but misery.'

'I don't care.' Jack dragged a breath of icy air deep into his lungs, holding it there before releasing it. 'I need this.' He watched her carefully as he made the confession.

'What'll it give you?'

'Peace.'

'Killing gives you peace?'

Jack did not answer immediately. He considered her question. He had fought for such a long time, first to prove himself, then to find himself, and then until he had finally become the soldier he had always wanted to be. He had killed more men than he could count to get to that point. He remembered many of their faces. They looked back at him in his mind, their eyes reflecting that moment of horror when they realised they were going to die. He was a killer of men and a true soldier. That thought brought him comfort. Killing one more man would make little difference to the tally on his soul, but he believed with every fibre of his being that it would be the one thing that would free him of the burden of guilt he had carried since he had awoken to find himself in a Confederate hospital with Rose nothing more than a fading memory.

'I think killing that man will bring me peace.' He gave the answer suddenly. He could feel something akin to anger stirring deep in his gut. 'People, well, they just come and go. I have nothing save what I am.' He glared at her then, daring her to contradict him. The anger built inside him. 'This is what I do and what I'm good at, what I am *bloody* good at it. So yes, killing gives me peace. It's the only thing I can do.'

'You sure about that, Jack?' She reached out to him, her hand tracing down the thick scar on his left cheek. 'I look at you and I don't see a man at peace.'

Jack shook off her fingers. The warmth of her touch repelled him. He held onto the coldness inside him. He needed it. There could be no doubts, no second thoughts. He had embarked on this path and he would not be distracted. If Lyle lived, the guilt would have to be carried until it was Jack's body laid in the cold earth. He did not have the strength for that. The burden would break him.

'Where's your man?' he asked.

'With his company.' Martha sat back, holding out her hands towards the flames to warm them.

Jack looked at her for a long time, then pushed himself to his feet.

'You going to hurt him?' Martha did not sound concerned.

'Yes.'

'For what he did to me, or for something else?'

Jack heard her tone change. It matched the coldness in his own voice. It was a sharp question, one that probed deep. She knew him well enough to sense his anger and frustration at being thwarted. 'For what he did to you.'

'So you're getting revenge for me now, is that it?'

'He deserves it.'

'He'll get his punishment. The Lord knows him. He will have seen what he has done.'

'The Lord.' Jack scoffed at the mention.

'Yes, the Lord.' There was fire in Martha's voice now. 'You think you have to take responsibility for everything? Ain't no one else except the mighty Jack Lark who knows what's right and what's wrong?' Her mouth twisted as she fired the words at him. 'Who made you the Lord's angel of death?'

Jack looked down at her. He could see her face clearly in the light of the fire. He saw her pain, and her fear. And he saw her guilt.

'I did.' He spoke softly and did not shirk from her accusation.

'I made myself into this. I'm not going to change now. And I don't care for this Lord of yours. Seems to me he doesn't give a shit about what goes on down here. But I do. That husband of yours, he beat you like a dog and now he's sitting over there feeling like the big man. Well, he isn't, and it's time he learned that.'

'And you're going to teach him.' Some of the fire had left Martha's voice. Her hand had strayed to her face, the fingers touching the puffy flesh around her eye.

'Someone has to.' He took a pace forward and rested his hand on the top of her head. 'None of this is your fault, Martha.'

'You don't have to do this. Violence doesn't solve anything.' She looked up at him.

Jack let his eyes take in her battered and bruised face. Blood lined the fine wrinkles around her swollen eye, which was bloodshot and sore. She looked older than he remembered. Hers was not the pretty face of a young girl. It was the face of a woman who had lived long enough to know what it was to suffer.

He offered her a thin-lipped smile, then reached out and traced a soothing pattern on her temple. He repeated the movement over and over, his touch gentle. Then his hand went still.

'You're wrong.'

'About what?'

'Violence.' He withdrew his hand. 'Violence solves everything.'

He held her gaze for several long moments, then walked into the darkness to find the man who had beaten his woman.

---

# Chapter Thirty-nine

*J*ack was too cold to rest. Even though dawn was still far away, he walked through the streets of Dover. Movement, even if painful, was preferable to lying on the frozen ground. He was not the only one. Since leaving his shelter, he had seen many men, both officers and soldiers, heading into town.

He had returned to the shelter in the small hours of the night. Martha had been sitting just as he had left her. She had not said a word as he settled down on a blanket. There had been no questions as to what had been done. Yet she had come to him and lain down next to him so that her back pressed into his front. She had held his hands, cradling the broken, bloodied knuckles against her lips. She had stayed in that position, motionless and silent, until he had got to his feet.

Even though it was still long before dawn, the streets of Dover were a hive of activity. Officers bustled this way and that, but most were gathering near the small cemetery just above the town. Jack followed them there, wondering what was causing such a commotion so early the day after the failed breakout attempt.

He soon saw what was drawing the crowd. A mounted officer was the centre of attention, the men pressed close around him as they listened to what he had to say. The officer was tall and muscular, with dark hair and a heavy moustache and beard. A nearby fire cast enough light for Jack to see his sun-browned skin. He had hard grey eyes that roved over the crowd to meet the gaze of any man bold enough to look back at him.

'Well, are you coming with us?' Jack heard the officer shout the question at another mounted man in the crowd.

'I'm sorry, General Forrest. I ought not to leave my command, but ought to share their fate.'

'All right. I admire your loyalty, but damn your judgement.'

Forrest's firm retort was met with mutters from the rest of the gathered officers.

For his part, Jack could only admire the reply. He now knew the man at the centre of the crowd to be the fabled General Bedford Forrest. Every man in the fort knew the commander of the Confederate cavalry. Now Jack saw him for the first time, and it was hard not to be impressed, by both his appearance and his attitude. The man was clearly not one to suffer anyone who disagreed with him.

'I'm going to cut my way out.' Forrest addressed the rest of the crowd. 'All of you who wish to leave can follow me. If you prefer to stay and take the consequences, then do so, but I will not sit here like a sheep waiting for the butcher's arrival.'

There was a growl of approval that rippled through those gathered around. The short, pithy speech was enough to catch Jack's interest. Forrest was proposing another breakout. If the leader of the Confederate cavalry was going, that would mean Lyle was going too.

'What about the others, General?' a voice from the throng sang out.

'Floyd and Pillow ain't got the fight in their bellies,' Forrest answered immediately. He sat easy in the saddle, as though proposing an escape through an enemy army was an everyday occurrence. 'General Buckner will be given command. He will surrender the fort and the whole force with it.'

Forrest's direct speech and call for action was impressive. For his part, Jack had no intention of being left behind. He had been taken prisoner by the South, and was not going to wait around to see if it would be any different being a prisoner of the Union.

'We leave within the hour. Gather your gear, and bring any man who wants to come with us. I can't promise you an easy ride, and we may have to cut our way through the Yankee line, but there's no way in hell I'm sitting here waiting to surrender.'

The gathering growled its approval then immediately started to break up. Jack left with them. He walked fast, ignoring the chatter of the men around him as they pondered their decisions. He had made his own the moment he heard Forrest propose cutting his way free.

'Look alive-o,' Jack called out to Martha the moment he approached their shelter.

'What's going on?' To her credit, Martha sensed his urgency immediately and got to her feet, her hands already reaching for his knapsack.

'We're getting out of here. Forrest and his men are planning to cut their way through the Union lines. They'll let anyone who wants to go with them.'

'And we're going?'

'You want to sit here and be taken prisoner? I have no idea what the Yankees will do to you if they find you here.' Jack fired back the reply.

'The Yankees, Jack?' Martha picked up on Jack's choice of words. 'Why, I do believe you are starting to sound like one of us.'

Jack paid the pithy comment no heed. He had never been a Yankee, just as he was now no Confederate. He was his own man; nothing more and nothing less.

He bent over and picked up the carbine he had taken from one of Pinter's men, a weapon Martha had carried before. 'You'd better take this. It's cleaned, but you'll have to load it. You remember how?'

Martha took it. 'I remember. You think it'll be that bad?'

Jack shook his head. 'I have no idea. I can't imagine the Yankees will just let us leave.' He offered a tight smile. 'We may have to fight our way through.'

Martha looked at the carbine in her hands. It looked too big for her, even though it was several inches shorter than a regular rifle.

'I ain't fought before.'

'It's easy, you just point the barrel and pull the trigger.' Jack gave a glib answer as he started to sort out his own weapons.

'And then you kill a man.'

Something in her tone stopped him. He turned to look at her. It was easy enough to see her fear. 'Look, just follow me. I won't abandon you.' He reached out and placed a heavy hand on her shoulder. 'You'll be fine, I promise.' He patted her once, then stood back and scrutinised her. 'At least you look the part now.'

'Well, I sure stink as bad as any of you men.' Martha's mouth twisted into something halfway between a smile and a grimace. She said nothing more as she went to Jack's knapsack and fished for the cartridge pouch.

It took a while, but working together they loaded their weapons, gathered their gear, then saddled the mare that Jack had stolen. It was dark and bitterly cold, but it was time to quit their shelter and ride with Forrest and his men. It was time to leave Dover, Fort Donelson and the Confederate army behind.

Jack and Martha rode in the midst of a motley crew. As far as Jack could judge, around five hundred men had followed Forrest that night. The four hundred cavalrymen of his own command had been joined by men from a number of different units, along with the remains of a single battery of artillery that had been badly mauled in the previous day's fighting. Jack and Martha were not the only ones to share a horse's back. With more men wanting to go with Forrest than there were mounts, a fair few had resorted to either sharing an animal or else finding a precarious perch on the cannons and their limbers.

The group left the Confederate lines with little fanfare and took the old Charlotte road that ran out of Dover. A few men stood and watched them leave. They rode in darkness, their way lit only by the light of the moon. They could see neither army. The troops on the front lines were forbidden from lighting fires to avoid giving their position away and so drawing fire from the dozens of cannon that now faced each other. It made for miserable conditions, and Jack was glad to be riding away from the doomed fort.

The column pressed on. It moved slowly, the pace dictated as much by the treacherous going as by the slower-moving caissons, limbers and carriages of the artillerymen. To Jack it felt odd to be moving so leisurely. It did not feel as if they were engaged on some wild breakout attempt.

Within the first hour, they reached a wide creek to the east of Dover. In the meagre light, it looked formidable. At least one hundred yards wide, with dozens of floating islands of ice across its surface, it was a daunting barrier. As Jack watched, Forrest rode directly into the surging waters. He pushed through the ice, forcing his horse through the fast-moving current, then, without stopping, urged the animal up the far bank before turning and waving to the lead ranks to follow.

The men at the head of the column needed no further urging. They followed the route their commander had taken, the air full of the noise of the horses splashing through the freezing creek. When it was his turn, Jack could not help gasping as he walked his mare into the water. It was deep enough to reach the horse's saddle, and frigid on his lower legs.

'That way.' An officer waiting on the far side of the river pointed to another road on the far side of the overflow. 'That leads to the Cumberland Ironworks. Follow it all the way to Cumberland City and don't stop for nothing.'

Forrest knew his trade, and the column proceeded slowly with men sent to scout the way ahead, whilst others took up the positions of advance and rear guard. Yet he need not have bothered. No Union picket challenged their progress and they passed through the enemy lines without a shot being fired. Many more men could have come with them. Forrest had saved his own regiment, along with a battery of guns and a few hundred other troops, but the rest of the Confederate force had stayed behind and now would be forced to surrender.

The Confederate government would lose a large portion of their army, but for the moment, Jack and Martha were safe.

# Chapter Forty

*J*ack stood in the open doorway of the farmhouse and looked outside at the rain that was coming down in torrents. There had been days of the relentless, frigid downpour, and the deluge had turned the roads around Nashville into so much slurry.

Jack and Martha had found the abandoned house on the outskirts of the city and had taken it for their own. The owners had clearly left in a hurry, and Jack could only suppose they had joined one of the long columns of refugees that were now leaving Nashville every day as the Union army pressed ever closer. It had been stripped of everything of value, but there was still enough furniture left behind for Jack and Martha to be comfortable enough.

Jack stood and listened to the rain as it lashed down, cradling the mug of coffee Martha had given him in his hands, relishing the heat on his skin. The bitter black brew was a poor substitute for a mug of good tarry soldier's tea so thick you could almost stand your spoon upright in it, but at least it was warm, and it helped to stave off the chill of another bitterly cold morning.

As he watched the rain, he wondered how much longer the Confederate army would remain in the city. It was a pitifully small force, and getting smaller every day. Nashville was the largest settlement he had been in since he had left Boston all those months before, and it was not a pretty place. The large state capitol that stood on a hill overlooking the city was as fine a building as he had seen in America, its design making it look like some sort of Greek temple, and the tall lantern in the centre of the roof allowed it to totally dominate its surroundings. But no other building came close to matching its splendour, with much of the centre of the city given over to industry.

Nashville's position on the banks of the Cumberland river provided good access to the rest of Tennessee and beyond, but it was the network of railroads that met in the city that gave it a much greater importance now that war had begun. Four lines converged here, representing a strategic hub that the Confederate army could ill afford to lose. But Jack saw no sign of a defence being prepared. Indeed, the only thing on the minds of both the citizens of Nashville and the exhausted and sickened soldiers was flight.

Every day he saw fewer soldiers on the streets. So many were sick. One officer of artillery he spoke to told of one third of the army's strength being ill. The force that was being assembled after the loss of the river forts was falling apart before it had even had the chance to face the enemy.

Jack still wore Pinter's uniform and so it was easy enough for him to walk through the city unimpeded. He had purchased himself a new sword to replace the one lost in the fight with Lyle. It was a standard officer's sabre, made at the Nashville Plow Works, and it looked just like ones he had seen in the North, although the maker's name and the initials CSA had been stamped on the underside of the guard to remind the owner which side they were on. Back at the farm, he had worked on the blade, oiling and polishing the steel and sharpening the edge with a whetstone. It was no maharajah's talwar, but it would do the job.

His stolen uniform also allowed him to ask questions that would likely have aroused suspicion were he dressed as a civilian. He now knew that Fort Donelson had surrendered the day after Forrest had led his men away. Nashville was full of talk of an unconditional surrender, the Union's General Grant refusing to give an inch to the beleaguered and surrounded Confederate forces. Close to twelve thousand men had been forced to lay down their arms, a horrendous blow to the Confederate cause.

The Union army now held the vital river arteries that could be used to strike further south. The Northern forces would be able to use the rivers to transport men and supplies without the need to march long distances across country. They had broken the back of the Confederate defensive line in northern Tennessee and Kentucky, and now the Southern generals were hastily assembling every man they could find to form an army that would have a fighting chance of stopping the inevitable Union push south.

'Are you going out in that?'

Jack drained the last of his coffee, then turned to smile at Martha, who had crept up behind him. 'Later, maybe. No one's going anywhere at the moment.'

'And when they do, you'll go with them.'

Jack sighed. He was in no mood to repeat the familiar argument. 'Yes.'

Martha shook her head at his answer. She was still dressed as a soldier, but her clothes were now clean. The stay in the farmhouse had given them more than just the time to tend to their clothing. Both had been able to rest, and so find the strength they would need when they embarked on the next leg of their journey.

'You don't think it's time to let this one lie, Jack? You found that man twice already. You even tried to kill him. Isn't that enough?'

'No.' Jack turned back to look at the rain, which if anything was coming down even harder.

'You're a pig-headed fool, you know that?' Martha had not moved as he turned away, and now stood facing his back, her hands on her hips.

'Maybe,' he sighed. 'I think I preferred you when you didn't say boo to a goose.'

'And I preferred you when you were sick. Least back then you showed a lick of gratitude.'

'Gratitude!' Jack scoffed. 'Seems that commodity is in short supply around here.'

'Like common sense.' Martha's tongue had sharpened in the months Jack had known her. 'You fought that man and you lost.'

'I didn't lose.' Jack snapped the reply but still did not turn to face her. The argument was a repeat of one they had had half a dozen times since they had quit Fort Donelson.

'Well, he's still alive, so you didn't exactly win.' Martha's exasperation was obvious. 'It ain't worth it.'

'What isn't?'

'Devoting your life to this. To fighting and killing. Don't you want to be more than that?'

'No.'

'Of course you don't,' Martha's reply was instant, 'because

then you'd have to face up to the fact that you haven't got any-thing else. If you're not fighting, then what you going to do?'

Jack whirled on the spot, his anger rising fast. 'Don't lecture me.'

'If I don't say it, I don't see anyone else round here that's going to.' Martha took a step closer, even in the face of his fury. 'You've got to stop this, Jack. You're not fighting this man. You're fighting yourself.'

'You can keep your homespun bloody advice to yourself. I don't need you to tell me what's what.'

'You sure do.' Martha did not retreat. 'You're going to get yourself killed.'

'You're not the first to say that. And look at me. See, here I am.'

'Oh, I can see you all right. How could I miss this great big fool who's going to kill himself just so he can avoid taking a good hard look at what he's about?'

'Perhaps I'm not the only one who should be doing that. Why are you still here, Martha? Why are you hanging onto my damn coat-tails?' He closed on her and gripped her by the arms. 'Isn't it the truth that you don't have anywhere else to go? Your bloody husband didn't want you, so you hooked yourself onto me. Well, you listen to me. I don't need you, you hear me? I'm taking care of you out of bloody pity.' He shook her then. 'You don't like what I'm doing, then why don't you walk your bloody chalk and leave me to it.'

Martha did not flinch as the words flowed out of him. 'I'm here because I care, Jack. I know that's not what you want to hear. You don't like people getting close to you because that forces you to think. And you don't like that, you don't like that at all, because then you have to face up to what you are. I reckon you don't like what you see.'

'I know what I am.' Jack pushed her away from him, making her stagger backwards. 'I don't need some bloody harpy like you to tell me.'

'Oh, but you do.' Martha came forward without fear. 'You whine on about your precious Rose, about avenging her and killing the man who murdered her. Truth is, you don't care all that much about her because you don't really care about anyone save yourself. You ain't fighting that man for her; you're fighting him for what he did to you, you just ain't got the guts to admit it.'

'Shut your damn mouth.' Jack spat the words out, refusing to acknowledge any truth in her damning verdict. 'You didn't know Rose. You don't know what I felt for her.'

'I know she ain't precious enough to you to stop you taking me to your bed.'

'I haven't heard you complaining,' Jack's fury was instant, 'and you a good God-fearing married woman and all.'

Martha's hand moved fast, cracking against Jack's cheek with a sound like a rifle shot. 'You son of a bitch.'

The slap did nothing to lessen his anger. 'You like telling truths? Well, now you listen to one. I don't want you here. Is that clear enough for you?'

Martha's eyes searched his face, flickering back and forth as she read his expression. Then she nodded.

'You remember the day my pa found you in the woods? You were as helpless as a newborn piglet, yet I told him it was our Christian duty to take you in. We cared for you, and fed you. Without us, you'd be dead.'

'I've paid my debt,' Jack hissed. 'I fought for you and your father.'

'And look what it got him.'

'And that's my fault?' Jack reached out once again, taking one of her arms and dragging her closer, not caring that his fingers dug deep into the sparse flesh. 'You ever think on what would've happened if I hadn't been there? Those men would still have come along. Your damned father would still be dead, and so would you. Except they wouldn't just have killed you, would they, Martha? I reckon you know what they would have done to you first. And that ain't a pretty picture to think about.' He pulled her forward so that her face was just an inch from his own. 'Go home.'

Martha stared back at him. There was no fear in her expression.

Jack met her gaze. He hated her in that moment; hatred so pure and simple that it made him feel sick. He pushed her from him with enough force to nearly send her crashing to the floor.

'Go home,' he repeated, then he turned on his heel and strode out into the rain.

Jack rode in the midst of an army, yet he was totally alone.

The Confederate force in Nashville had been ordered to withdraw, and he had gone with them. Those physically able to do so were told to march south-east towards a place call Murfreesboro. Those too sick to march – and there were many – were either crammed onto overcrowded trains headed for Chattanooga, or else left in Nashville to face an uncertain fate under the Union army that was approaching the city from the north.

The soldiers were not the only ones quitting the city. Refugees streamed out of Nashville, choking the roads and filling any spare space on the trains heading south and east. For those leaving on foot, it was a miserable journey. The rain gave them little respite, and the cold was an enemy every bit as deadly as the men in blue uniforms. The disheartened, bedraggled columns snaked south, the men, women and children united in their misery.

The soldiers around him might have been struggling to stay on their feet, but Jack had never felt stronger. He travelled light, his knapsack and saddlebags containing no more than the minimum he would need to survive. And he travelled alone.

He had not spoken to a soul for days. Martha had left by the time he came back to the farmhouse on the day of their fight. He did not know where she had gone. Now he rode without another person to fend for and he revelled in the freedom. There was no one to tell him what to do. No one to feed and care for except for himself. His life had been pared down to its essentials. He had his weapons. He had what he needed to survive. And he had purpose.

There was little chance of finding Lyle in the midst of the retreating army. The cavalry would be kept busy, the Confederate generals sure to order the mounted units to probe deep into the countryside around the army to gather intelligence and watch the Union forces as they headed south. But eventually the army would have to stop retreating. The Confederates could not allow the Union invasion to go unchecked. At some point they would gather their strength and they would fight.

When that happened, Jack would get his chance. Somewhere in the confusion of battle, he would find Lyle for a second time. This time he would make sure that he did not fail.

# Chapter Forty-one

Corinth, Mississippi, 2 April 1862

*J*ack brought his horse to a stand on the crest of a ridge of high ground, then dropped the reins as he fished his field glasses from their leather case. The metal was cold against the skin around his eyes as he brought the glasses up, and he caught the whiff of the protective oil he had applied the previous evening to keep the metal from rusting.

He saw the column of infantry immediately. The men did not look like much. There was little sense of a uniform, and as far as he could tell, the troops carried smoothbore muskets not vastly dissimilar from the weapons they would have used when fighting the British fifty years before, in the war of 1812.

They were not the first infantry column he had seen that day. The army's retreat had stopped, and now it was consolidating around the town of Corinth, just over the border from Tennessee in northern Mississippi. The choice of Corinth made sense. It was a strategic rail hub that straddled the vitally important Memphis and Charleston Railroad, the only east–

west line in Confederate territory, which had been completed a few years before and now connected the great Mississippi river to a harbour on the Atlantic Ocean. Corinth was also situated on the north–south Mobile and Ohio line, which linked it to the harbour at Mobile, Alabama, and to Columbus, Kentucky.

With the Union army using the rivers, the Confederate generals were relying on the railroads to bring in vital supplies and every last man it could find. Troops were coming from all over, as the officer commanding the Confederate army, General Johnston, scoured the entire theatre of war for any man who could hold a musket. Jack had heard that as many as forty thousand men were now in place in and around Corinth. He had not heard what Johnston planned to do, but he could not see how the Confederates could let the Union army proceed much further without making a stand.

Jack felt ready for whatever happened next, the rest he had had since leaving Fort Donelson allowing him to build up his strength. Even the horse he had stolen from outside the hotel in Dover was in fine fettle. He had spent the last of his money on the animal's care, and now he could sense that its vitality matched his own. His weapons were in perfect condition, and he had plenty of cartridges for his revolver courtesy of the Confederate army. He had not found any more of the special rounds he needed for the Henry repeater, but he still had enough left to fill the weapon at least twice. That would have to be enough. The lack of ammunition did not concern him. It would take just one bullet to kill Lyle. If he ran out, he had his new sabre. If all else failed, he had his bare hands. He had killed men with them before. Doing so again would give him nothing but pleasure.

He had begun his search for Lyle the previous week. He had

not entertained much chance of success, and thus far he had failed to find him. Johnston's cavalry units were either on outpost duty, or scouting far into the countryside around Corinth to keep a check on the Union advance. There had been no chance for Jack to locate his adversary, and he had ended up riding around aimlessly. But the long treks had helped build the strength of both horse and rider, and for his part, Jack felt nothing but calm. There would be another time, another fight. Then he could commit murder and find the salvation he needed.

'You there! Say, are you with General Withers?'

Jack lowered his field glasses. A Confederate officer dressed in a light grey uniform with elaborate gold braid Austrian knots on the sleeves was riding towards him. The officer's collar bore a single gold star, and the facings of his jacket were light blue. The contrast between his fine appearance and the attire of the men in the column behind him that Jack had been watching was stark.

'No.' Jack gave the short answer in the hope that the man would simply ride on. He was to be disappointed.

'Hellfire and damnation.' The officer rode closer. 'How the hell am I supposed to find the general and his headquarters when he keeps moving, yet tells no one where he is going?' He reined in close to Jack's mare. 'Major Andrew Denton.'

Jack could only suppose the name was given by way of an introduction. 'Captain Pinter,' he replied in a similarly curt fashion.

Denton rode easily and fitted his uniform well. He was not a big man, with sloping shoulders and a small pot belly that rested neatly on his saddle. His thin face was decorated with a neatly trimmed goatee and moustache.

'Well met, Captain Pinter.' He walked his horse around so that he faced the same direction as Jack. 'Hell, they don't look like much, do they now?' He smiled to take the sting out of the remark. 'I could see you were running your eye over my boys. They're good lads. Keen to fight, too. Those Yankees won't know what's hit them.'

Jack grunted by way of reply. He had not sought company since leaving Nashville, and felt no need to change that self-enforced policy. Denton was looking at him in expectation of a remark. Jack decided to disappoint.

'Is your outfit ready to fight?' The major pressed on regardless.

'Yes.'

Denton turned in the saddle, his hand resting easily on the pommel. 'Are you English?'

'Yes.' Jack did his best not to sigh.

'I thought so. Why, I have a fellow from your country in my own regiment. Now let me think, I'm sure I can remember where he's from if I just put my mind to it.' Denton paused, his free hand coming up to touch his mouth. 'Edin-borough! Yes, I'm sure that's the place. Is that close to where you're from, Captain Pinter?'

Jack tried to restrain a grimace. 'No, that's in Scotland.'

'But it must be nearby. It's all the same country, after all.'

'I'm sure the Scots would disagree.'

'I could introduce you to him if you like,' the major continued with enthusiasm.

'No. Thank you.'

Denton smiled. 'Well, anyway, I am right pleased to meet you, Captain Pinter, even if you don't know where that old hooplehead Withers is hiding.' He paused for a moment, then shook his head as if in disbelief. 'An Englishman, right here in Mississippi. Who would've thought it?'

'Well, if you'll excuse me.' Jack carefully returned his field glasses to their case, then gathered up his reins.

'Of course, Captain Pinter.' Denton's smile faded as he realised Jack was about to leave. 'I mustn't hold you from your duties. What regiment are you with?'

'Forrest's Cavalry.' He gave the lie easily.

'You're one of Bedford's men!' Denton exclaimed. 'Why, we came across some of your fellows just the other day.'

'Where was that?' Jack was suddenly more interested in the conversation.

'About ten miles east of here. They'd been up scouting the Union positions around Pittsburg Landing.'

Jack lowered his reins. 'They say where they were headed?'

'Indeed they did not.' Denton's eyes narrowed. 'Should I not be asking you that question?'

Jack flashed a smile. He had put Denton on his guard, and so tried to defuse the situation with charm. 'My fellows don't stay still for long. It makes it hard for chaps like me to catch up with them.'

'Well, I am sure that is true.' Denton matched Jack's smile with one of his own. 'You fellows are here, there and every-where, and that's a fact.'

'So did my boys tell you much about the Union positions at . . . where did you say it was? Pittsburg Crossing?' Jack knew exactly where Denton had said the Union force was encamped, but he thought it best to let the major tell his news. Then he could be on his way.

'Pittsburg Landing.' Denton preened as he corrected Jack. 'They told me a little, but I know the ground well enough myself. The Union army is encamped about twenty miles north-east of here. They've got the Tennessee river to the east of their position, whilst their left flank is anchored on Lick Creek. Their right, well, that's nestled nice and close against Owl Creek, and they got Snake Creek to the north. Leaves just one side open, facing towards us here in Corinth.' He used his hands to draw lines in the sky as he described the Union position.

'Now, the Tennessee river is not a friend to them.' Denton paused to glance across at his regiment. The column was nearly past, but the sight did not spur him to leave, and he carried on his explanation, clearly relishing the opportunity to show off his local knowledge to an officer from Bedford Forrest's famous unit. 'I've lived around these parts my whole life, and I can tell you, you need a big old boat to cross it. Those creeks, why, you can only get across those at the bridges, and believe me, there are not many of those. Those Union boys might feel nice and safe, but the truth is, they've gone and got themselves trapped.'

'Why would they do that?' Jack was interested. He wanted to know as much as he could. Anything he learned could only help him find Lyle.

'That General Grant, he's waiting for reinforcements. I heard it said that another Union army under General Buell is marching to link up with his men. Grant, he's the commander of the army at Pittsburg Landing,' Denton explained.

'What's the ground like?' Jack was warming to the major and so pushed for more information.

'Oh my, that ground is poor. There's underbrush every-where, and there's no way you can hope to move artillery around without one hell of an effort.' Denton was happy to continue, even though the rear-file markers of his regiment were now passing by. 'Nor is it flat. There are slopes, ravines and gullies all over the damn place, and a steep ridge near the Tennessee river. Why, I remember trying to get back up that thing when I was a boy. We'd been fishing on the river and we decided to try to land there.' He shook his head. 'We sure got ourselves in a pickle.' He grinned at the memory.

'Major!' A young officer from Denton's regiment had stopped and now called across. 'Are you coming?'

'I'll be there directly, Lieutenant.' Denton leaned across and held a hand out towards Jack. 'Well, it sure was a pleasure meeting you, Captain Pinter.'

Jack shook hands warmly. Denton had been helpful. 'Likewise. Let's hope we don't have to retreat again soon.'

'Retreat!' Denton's eyes widened in mock surprise. 'Why, Captain Pinter, has no one told you? The retreat is over!'

Jack felt a hint of colour rush to his cheeks. 'I've not been back with the army for long.'

'Well then, sir, I am pleased to be the one to tell you.'

'Tell me what?'

'We're going to counterattack! We're going to hit them Yankee sons of bitches right now, before their two armies can unite.' Denton grinned wolfishly as he revealed the Confederate plan. 'Grant's got himself stuck on bad ground and we're going to strike so hard, why, his whole army could be destroyed!'

Jack matched Denton's smile with one of his own. The Union army was trapped and the Confederates were going to launch a daring attack.

The battle he had hoped for was coming.

# Chapter Forty-two

---

*Ten miles north of Corinth, Mississippi, 3 April 1862*

The infantry column stopped for what seemed to Jack to be the hundredth time. It was grinding its way north, but the speed of the march was excruciatingly slow. It had been stop-start ever since they had left Corinth early that morning, and Jack doubted they had covered more than ten miles in as many hours.

But at least the army was finally moving in the right direction. Major Denton had been quite correct. The time for retreating was over. Johnston had gathered every man he could find, and now he was striking north, his target the Union army under General Grant encamped around Pittsburg Landing.

The poor conditions underfoot made no difference to the plan. Johnston had seen the opportunity, and now his army would have to slog its way north along rain-soaked roads. Mud was everywhere, the cloying ground sapping the strength of the men trudging through it, and leaving baggage trains and artillery regiments bogged down. The army's first objective was Monterey, Tennessee, halfway between Corinth and Pittsburg Landing, but as far as Jack could see, Johnston would be lucky to get even half his men there.

Jack walked in the gap between two infantry regiments, leading his horse to save the animal's strength. It was tough going, the mud so thick that he had to work hard just to pull his boots out of the gloop to take another step. He walked as an infantryman did, his world reduced to the filth beneath his boots and the backs of the men ahead.

He trudged on, stepping around a puddle of vomit left in a footprint. The men were suffering. Shit and puke mixed with the mud as the sick voided themselves before slogging onwards. More than a few bodies had been left to lie by the side of the road, those unable to take another step simply abandoned to their fate.

The rain began again. It came down hard, the wind driving it into the faces of the men. Jack was reminded of another march in the foulest conditions. Then he had been in India, serving with the fabled General Nicolson as part of a large British force ordered to attack a column of mutinous sepoys at Najafgarh. The monsoon rains had reduced the ground to so much slurry, the going even worse than it was today.

In India, Nicolson had been there to inspire his men. He had got down in the muck, helping to pull the guns along by hand, sharing every hardship faced by his men. No such example was being set on the road to Monterey. The Confederate commanders were nowhere to be seen. The officers of each regiment were doing their best, and Jack could hear the shouts of encouragement as the raw troops ground out the miles. But there was only so much these officers could do. There was little that could be done by anyone, save to endure, and take another step forward.

Jack kept himself to himself. It was not his place to lead or inspire. For once, he was beholden to no one save himself. So he walked alone.

The road narrowed as it passed through a thickly wooded area, so that there were still more delays as the column had to re-form to fit into the more constricted space. As soon as it stopped, men plonked themselves down in the mud, only dragging themselves to their feet when the ranks in front of them resumed the march.

For his part, Jack stayed on his feet, waiting through the endless delays with a newly found stoic patience. He no longer bothered to look for Forrest's regiment of cavalry. The army was advancing on three different roads and the cavalry would surely be working hard to protect the flanks of the exposed columns. But his time would come.

For the Confederate army marched to do battle. And in battle Jack would find his man.

The call of the fife and the beat of the drum sounded flat in the damp morning air. At least they did something to stir the miserable groups of men huddled deep under rain-soaked blankets, the soldiers forcing their tired, aching bodies to rise from the quagmire in which they had slept.

Jack stood and shook off the water that had collected on his blanket. It had been another wretched night, with little thought of sleep. The rain had started before dark had fallen, and had only eased when the first grey fingers of dawn had crept across the far horizon. He had made a camp beneath the boughs of a large tree, sheltering his horse as best he could underneath the thickest branches, which he had covered with most of his blankets. He had saved just one for himself, spending the night hunkered down under it, simply waiting for the night to be over.

He dumped the blanket onto his knapsack, then stretched his spine as far as he could, his hands kneading at the persistent ache deep in the pit of his back. He did not know when the column would be ordered to resume the march, or indeed if it would be able to resume it. The men were in a poor condition. This was no experienced army, its ranks full of men hardened to the rigours of a campaign. Instead, many of the regiments were filled with raw levies, their lack of discipline revealed in the haphazard nature of the lines.

'Men! Gather round!'

Jack heard an officer call for attention, his voice loud over the mumbles and muttered oaths of the men who had awoken to such a miserable morning.

'Listen up! I have here a letter from General Johnston.' The officer took a moment to move across to a tree stump that would allow him to stand higher and so be seen by more of his troops.

Jack did not bother to move as the men of the nearest regiment gathered around their officer. He could hear well enough where he was, and the promise of words from a general he didn't know held little attraction to him. He had long since lost his faith in such encouragement. It was what officers did that mattered, not what they said as they tried to imitate the great generals of the past.

'Soldiers of the Army of the Mississippi.' The officer read the opening line of his letter with gusto. The effect was spoiled as he broke off to cough. Only when he had hawked noisily did he continue. 'I have put in motion to offer battle to the invaders of your country. With the resolution, and discipline, and valour becoming men fighting, as you are, for all worth living or dying for, you can but march to a decisive victory over the agrarian mercenaries sent to subjugate and despoil you of your liberties, your property, your honour.'

The officer paused to draw breath. 'Remember the precious stake involved. Remember the dependence of your mothers, your wives, your sisters and your children on the result. Remember the fair, broad, abounding land, the happy homes, that will be desolated by your defeat. The eyes and hopes of eight million people rest upon you. You are expected to show yourselves worthy of your lineage, worthy of the women of the South, whose noble devotion in this war has never been exceeded in any time. With such incentives to brave deeds, and with the trust that God is with us, your generals will lead you confidently to the combat, assured of success.'

The speech was greeted with silence. Jack reckoned a fair few of the men had grasped little of the convoluted sentences. To his own ears, the words, so carefully crafted to inspire, fell flat.

He did note the differences to the talk he had heard in the North. There, the men ordering the soldiers to war had spoken of uniting the country and refusing to allow their great union to become broken and fractured. Here, he noticed that the tone was different, the Confederate general calling on his men to fight to defend their homes from Northern aggression.

Not for the first time, he wondered at the folly of this great civil war. The two sides were like brothers refusing to listen to one another before coming to blows, except here there was no parent to slap them apart and force a truce until hot tempers had cooled.

He turned away, shaking his head. There was nothing civil

about this war, yet he had already seen such courage from both sides. The battle at the Bull Run river had been fought by two armies full of men who believed absolutely in their cause. These men were not professional soldiers, trained armies doing a job their country paid them to do. They were citizen soldiers, men with lives and families who were willing to give up everything they had for their cause. Such a notion shamed him.

He began to gather the things he would need to prepare for another slog through the filthy countryside, trying to ignore the revulsion that he felt deep in his gut. Thousands of men would die in the battle that was to come, with countless more certain to perish in the war that would follow in its wake. He was no pacifist. He knew the need for war and understood it. Yet there was something dreadfully sad in this fight of brother against brother, cousin against cousin, and it left him sickened to the core.

# Chapter Forty-three

South of Pittsburg Landing, 6 April 1862

A heavy white mist hung low in the wooded valley as the army awoke to the call of the fife and drum. Jack was on his feet long before reveille. He had been too cold to sleep, and so he had passed the bitter dark hours of the night leaning against a tree, or just walking aimlessly through the encampment. He had not been alone, for he had released his memories from their cages deep in his mind.

In those dark, witching hours of the night, he had been in the company of the men with whom he had fought before. He had remembered the soldiers in red coats who had marched up the slope towards the Great Redoubt at the Alma, and recalled the single company of defenders who had stood resolute and defiant at his side behind the barricades at Bhundapur. In his mind's eye, he had ridden again with the Bombay Lights as they butchered the Persian Fars at the Battle of Khoosh-Ab, and he had once more climbed the breach into the bloodstained streets of Delhi. Later, he had relived the day-long

battle on the slopes around Solferino in all its horror, and
marched once again in the midst of the blue-coated soldiers as
they tried, and failed, to turn the flank of the Confederate army
at Bull Run.

The memories had emerged with a power that had stunned
him; the images of battle so vivid that once again he had smelt
the tang of spent powder and the sour odour of spilt blood. Yet
the memories did not repel him as they often did. Now they fed
his desire to fight, and he used them, remembering the bitter
lessons he had learnt, preparing for the battle that was to come
with the dawn.

Around him, the recently awoken men prepared a scant
breakfast. Few had any rations left. They had been issued with
enough to last for five days, yet most had eaten them all within
three, lightening their loads as they slogged through the endless
march and counter-march. Jack himself had nothing left save a
few handfuls of desiccated vegetables and two lumps of rock-
like hardtack.

At last there was talk of the Union army awakening to their
presence. There had been rumours of skirmishes, scouts and
pickets clashing as the two armies came closer together. He had
overheard some officers talking of achieving surprise. He paid
the notion little heed. No army could march up on another
without being detected, and the clashes between the outposts
confirmed it. The Northerners would surely know that a large
Confederate force was coming their way. What they did with
that information was another matter. Complete surprise, to
Jack's mind at least, was nigh on impossible, but that did not
mean that the Confederates could not find an advantage.
Forewarned was not necessarily forearmed, and he had seen
enough of the world of soldiers to know that even with the best

and most accurate intelligence, armies could still be unprepared for what was to come.

The call to fall in echoed around the encampment. Three days of hard matching had brought them to this point. Now the tired and footsore army formed up in column for what for many would be their last march.

For the second time, Jack was about to go into battle on the Sabbath. The battle at Bull Run had been fought on a Sunday and had ended in defeat. He wondered if that was an omen. Just as they had at Bull Run, the men of both sides would inundate their shared God with prayers, begging him to spare them from death, or from a wound that would see them left in agony. He could feel fear in the air as though it was a physical thing, like the mist that shrouded the troops as they formed into long columns. He knew the men around him were wasting their time with their prayers. He had seen enough of battle to know there was no God present when two armies went to war. There was just death and suffering. Soldiers were forsaken by God until the last cartridge was fired and sanity was returned to His earth.

Jack rode around a regiment of infantry as it re-formed into the two-man-deep battle line in which it would fight. The men did not look much like soldiers. Some wore grey jackets, but not enough to give them the uniform look of a European regiment. Instead they wore a mix of browns and homespun tans, an eclectic selection of headgear, and every type of footwear you would hope to see. A few even formed up barefoot. Their one common feature was the muskets they carried. As he rode past, Jack looked over the weapons the men balanced against their shoulders. The percussion-cap muskets might have been woefully outdated, but every one was clean and well cared for. The Confederate troops did not look like much, but they knew what was important.

He headed east, riding past regiment after regiment. Experience told him that as the army concentrated for the battle that was now only hours away, the cavalry would be brought in to protect the flanks. For the first time in weeks, Jack believed he had another chance of finding Lyle and his raiders.

He pulled up as he passed the last regiment in a line. Ahead there was a small area of open ground. It was time to find some points of reference and begin to determine where he was.

'Captain! Are you the right of the line?'

'No, sir.' The captain had clearly assumed Jack to be a courier. 'I ain't sure what's to our right.'

Jack nodded his thanks, then pulled his horse around so that he took station behind the rightmost company in the regiment. It was the position he had fought in when a part of the 1st Boston. The Confederate army was drawn up in the same formation, a reminder that the two sides were officered by men trained in the same tactics of war.

A peal of laughter came from the middle of the company to his front. Two young soldiers were squatting down, much to the amusement of their comrades. At first, Jack thought the two lads were voiding their bowels, a not uncommon sight this close to an advance. It was only when one rose to his feet that he saw that they had been picking violets.

'Perhaps the Yanks won't shoot me if they see me wearing these, them being the flower of peace and all,' one of the young men proclaimed, much to the amusement of the men in the files around him. The pair each arranged a bunch of violets in their caps, causing the men around them to laugh still louder.

'Prepare to load! Load!'

The orders came one after the other. This regiment, like a few others Jack had seen, was armed with flintlock muskets, a weapon even older than the percussion-cap muskets he had spotted earlier. The flintlock had been the mainstay of European armies for centuries, and the ones these men held were little different to those that would have been used on the field of Waterloo nearly fifty years before. Not for the first time, Jack was glad that he had taken Pinter's rifle. The Henry repeater was in a sheath attached to his saddle. He had the Navy Colt revolver on his right hip, and his officer's sabre, now on longer slings as he was mounted, on his left.

To his front, the men were loading their muskets. In unison they tore open the paper cartridge with their teeth, then emptied some of the powder into the musket's firing pan before locking it in place. They then carefully emptied the remaining powder into the barrel. The cartridge paper followed and then the musket ball itself. With the whole cartridge now loaded, they withdrew the ramrod from its slings underneath the barrel, then rammed the ball and cartridge paper down so that it sat securely on top of the powder charge.

Jack watched them carefully. To his eye they looked dreadfully slow, and he spotted some not putting enough powder in the pan, whilst more than one dropped their ramrod or the cartridge as their clumsy, fearful fingers let them down.

A courier galloped across the front of the regiment, the officer whipping his horse hard as he raced to deliver a message. As he passed, the regiment began to move forward. Jack followed them as they crossed a field, the grass withered and shaded with the grey tones of winter. On the horizon, the sun was just starting to rise, the light beginning its long fight to push back the darkness. Dawn had arrived, and with it came the first signs of battle.

The sound of musket fire came from far ahead. Without being ordered to, the regiment picked up the pace. Jack could see their excitement in the briskness of their movements and the sudden alertness in their bearing. The sound of gunfire came again, sharper this time. It did nothing to deter the men in the homespun uniforms.

The regiment plunged onwards, entering the fringes of thin woodland. Jack went with them, picking his way through the trees and bending low in the saddle to avoid the lowest-hanging branches.

An odd snickering sound came then. It was as if an enormous insect buzzed over his head. It was followed by another, and then another. The air around him hummed as still more of the strange missiles zipped by. They pattered through the treetops, bringing down a steady shower of leaves and twigs onto the heads of the men marching towards the sounds of battle.

As quickly as it had started, the odd storm passed. Jack knew what it was well enough; he had been under fire too often to mistake it for anything else. There had been little danger from the musket fire, the shots too high and coming from too far away to concern him. Yet it did awaken a part of him that had lain dormant for many months.

The infantry regiment he followed pressed on. If the men had been deterred by the flurry of musket balls that had passed over their heads, they did not show it, moving forward at a brisk pace. The woodland thinned, and now beams of early-morning sunlight broke through the thin canopy to light their path as they emerged into a wide swathe of parkland.

'There they are!'

Jack was close enough to the leading ranks to hear the men cry out as they spotted that there was now nothing between them and the Union army. He smiled. They had just caught their first proper look at the enemy they had talked of fighting for so long.

The infantrymen were ordered to halt. The command came from the mounted colonel stationed at the very centre of the regiment, the instruction relayed by the captains commanding each company and reinforced by the beat of the drum.

To Jack's front, the men in the long ranks pulled their muskets into their shoulders.

'Let's kill them Yankees!' hissed the company captain in the pause between orders.

'Aim! Fire!'

As one, the regiment opened fire. The sound was tremendous, the great roar deafening as hundreds of men fired at once.

And Jack laughed.

He did not mean to, but the sound escaped his lips before he could hold it in. He saw heads turn, the scowls and glares sent his way enough to silence him.

'Load!'

The regiment stuck to their routines, the series of commands they had learnt now being used in earnest for the first time. Jack peered through the cloud of powder smoke that now smothered the line. What he saw confirmed his first thought. The enemy was too far away for the volley to trouble them. The men were wasting their powder, the muskets they carried useless at any distance over one hundred yards. He had laughed because the men were fighting so earnestly and with such great seriousness. Yet they were pissing into the wind, the long-range volley as effective as a small boy trying to hold back the tide by flinging stones into the waves.

More orders followed. The men lurched back into motion, moving out of the cloud of foul-smelling powder smoke their volley had left behind. The tang of rotten eggs lingered in Jack's mouth as he followed; he leaned far out in the saddle and spat. The stink was just as he remembered.

Ahead, blue-coated soldiers were forming a line of battle across the path of the Confederate advance. Jack could see tents in the distance behind them. The Confederate army might not have achieved complete surprise, but it was clear that they had caught the enemy unprepared.

The newly formed Union line disappeared behind a cloud of powder smoke, the roar of their first volley reaching Jack's ears a heartbeat later. A moment after that, the air above his head was stung repeatedly by fast-moving missiles.

'Lie down!'

The command came from the captain commanding the rightmost company. The men did not need to be told twice, and they went to ground, the command and the action repeated along the length of the line until the whole regiment was lying on the damp earth.

Jack stayed in the saddle. The enemy were far away and he knew there was little chance of his being hit. He could not help chuckling as he watched the distant Union line reload. The day was starting strangely. It was as if both sides were going through their drill like actors trying to squeeze in a last-minute rehearsal before the curtain went up. That could not last. They were there to fight; to kill or be killed. Neither side seemed ready to grasp that bitter fact.

He was still pondering the strange notion when the first artillery shell roared past overhead. The sound was tremendous, like an express train thundering down the line. He saw men around him flinch, but for Jack, the noise brought on a feeling that he could only describe as happiness. The oddness of the sensation made him laugh again, louder this time. Men turned to stare at the madman behind them, but he did not care. He was back where he belonged. He was back where he was master.

A shell landed a dozen yards to the right of the line, throwing up a great fountain of earth, the violence of the impact shocking. More enemy fire pattered past, the shots zipping through the air around him. And still Jack laughed.

Another shell landed, smashing into the company directly to his front. It hit with appalling destructive power, tearing men apart as easily as it churned the soil beneath them.

Jack heard the cries. Men shouted the names of those hit, whilst the wounded screamed as their flesh was ripped and torn apart. The smoke cleared to reveal the mangled, twisted bodies. One, a boy, lay spread-eagled on the ground, his arms thrown out beside him. His upper body, head and face were untouched, yet the entire lower portion had been reduced to so much offal. His hat lay on the ground beside him, the bunch of violets still in place in the band that ran around the centre.

Jack pulled on his reins and kicked his mount into motion. It was time to move on and continue the search for his quarry. The sun was up and the day's dying had begun. And he had never felt more alive.

# Chapter Forty-four

———◆———

 ack rode through chaos. He forced his horse into a
canter past the right of a Union line that was trading
volleys with a Confederate regiment coming against its
front. In the confusion, neither side seemed able to grasp where
the other was. It was quite unlike any other battle he had seen.
Much of the action was hidden from view, the trees and thick
sprawls of heavy undergrowth blocking lines of sight so that
men fought not knowing that an enemy unit advanced no more
than a few hundred yards away from where they stood. There
was no great battle line this day, no grand spectacle covering
miles of open parkland. This was a brawl on poor ground, men
fighting and dying where they happened to be, rather than as
part of some premeditated plan.

He slowed as he reached a Union encampment. There was
no sign of the men in blue uniforms amidst the ordered lines of
canvas tents. Instead Confederate soldiers ran around in
disorder as they ransacked the place. He brought his mare to a
halt and watched men stuffing rations into their haversacks and
taking Union equipment and uniforms, either as souvenirs or,
for many, out of necessity.

He rode away from the disorder, following a road to the east. Yet he could not escape the bedlam. Regiments were hopelessly intermingled, and whilst some advanced, others sat by and waited. All the while there came the sounds of battle, the roar of cannon fire and the rattle of musketry now ever-present.

Jack came off the road and attempted to steer around the confusion as best he could. As far as he could tell, the Confederates had forced the Union line back, but from the sound of it, the Union soldiers were not giving in and were fighting hard.

'Where's the cavalry?' he shouted at a courier who was mimicking his own actions by picking a path around the fringes of the infantry columns. 'I have a message for General Forrest!'

'Thataways!' The man was moving in the opposite direction to Jack, but he still flung out an arm and pointed back the way he had come. 'On the right flank, least they were an hour or so back.'

Jack pressed on, hoping that he would be lucky enough to find Lyle's Raiders on this flank and not the other. He had passed the worst of the scrimmage so returned to the turnpike. He now found himself riding alongside men going in the same direction. The men were fresh to the fight, their bright faces free of the stain of powder smoke. He had no idea why they would be heading east when to his mind they should be going north and pressing home the attack. Yet little was making sense that day and so he rode on, picking up the pace as and when he could, his mind set on one thing and one thing alone.

Lyle.

Jack stood in his stirrups and peered over the heads of the men in front of him. He saw no way through. There were too many of them, and they blocked the turnpike entirely. He faced a choice. He could go north towards the fighting, or south away from it. Or he could turn tail and return the way he had come.

He made the choice instantly. He was a soldier. He would go where the fighting was hardest and hope to find the cavalry doing the same.

He rode north, picking his way through a thick clump of trees then kicking his mare as it slowed on some softer going. Within minutes of leaving the road, he caught glimpses of the rear ranks of a Confederate regiment advancing in column. They were moving fast, their equipment thumping against their bodies as they double-timed. Jack watched their flags lead them on. One was clearly the regiment's own unique colour, whilst the other was a flag he had not seen before, even at Bull Run. It was square, a blue St Andrew's cross with white borders against a blood-red background. On the blue cross were twelve white stars. To his eye it looked rather poorly made, and he could not help wondering what condition it would be in when the day was through.

'Forward!' An officer shouted the encouragement as he double-timed alongside his men. His sword was drawn, and now he pointed it forward as he called for them to advance.

Jack followed, drawn to the action. He could see a little of the Union position about to be attacked. The area had once been a dense thicket with heavy brush underneath, but it had been chopped low by the storm of canister and rifle fire that had come from the defenders. Ahead, he could just about make out what looked to be a farm track, its fringes lined with tangled undergrowth and a scattering of timber. It was a natural strongpoint, and it did not take a military genius to know that the Union army held a good defensive position.

The regiment he was following was moving faster now, and

he knew they had to be launching an attack. They were not the first to do so. The ground they began to cross was already littered with the dead and dying, the sickening sight evidence that the Union line was gutting any unit that came against it. The bodies lay in the grotesque poses of the dead and the soon-to-be dead, backs broken, flesh ravaged, arms and legs ripped from torsos.

Jack reined in as the regiment launched their attack. It was only then that he recognised them. It was the same regiment he had watched march into Corinth. It took him a moment, but he located Denton, the officer he had spoken to. He was with the regiment's colour party, and Jack saw him raise his sword and shout to the men around him.

The regiment charged, the undulating rebel yell breaking out as they pounded forward. It was bravely done. The men would be able to see the bodies of those who had gone before them, just as they could see the Union line waiting for them. Yet they did not hesitate, ploughing across the broken ground, their ranks becoming more and more disordered as they charged.

Then the Union line opened fire.

Jack had not spied the artillery that waited on the farm track. The guns boomed out a heartbeat before the first volley of rifle fire. Men in the attacking column were cut down as the storm of canister and Minié balls ripped through their ranks. Whole lines of men were scythed down like wheat.

The screaming began.

The men in the column pressed on, clambering over the bodies of the dead and the dying. Yet the momentum of their assault had been shattered.

Jack caught sight of Denton. The major was hauling the regiment's colour from underneath the body of the man who had carried it, his mouth working furiously as he called for his men to keep going. They did as he asked, stumbling forward, their bodies bent over as if they advanced into the teeth of a gale, the high-pitched yell increasing in volume until it drowned out the shrieks of the dying.

The Union line saw them coming and poured on the fire, striking man after man from his feet. Still the Confederates advanced, a display of raw courage the like of which Jack could not recall seeing before. Denton went down. The major would surely have known that taking the regiment's colour would draw fire towards him, yet he had still carried out the brave act, and now he had paid the price. He crumpled to the ground, the flag falling so that it shrouded his body.

The men around him could take no more. They had given everything in the attack. Now those left standing turned and ran. The Union line fired on without mercy, killing without pause as their enemy fled. Jack saw a man grab the flag from Denton's corpse. That man died a moment later, a Union rifle bullet buried deep in his spine. Another took the colour before it even hit the ground, the men refusing to forsake their pride even as they broke.

The Union fire finally died away as the remnants of the regiment went to ground in a thicker area of woodland, the men who had tried so valiantly to take the farm track joining the survivors of the other regiments that had already failed to complete the same bloody task.

Jack turned his mare around, thinking to ride away and press further east. It was only when he was on the point of kicking back his heels that he saw a familiar face amidst a huddle of men sheltering behind a thick tangle of brambles wrapped around a fat tree trunk.

Corporal Hightower of the 65th Virginia stared back at him.

It was Hightower who glanced away first, breaking the momentary contact. He turned his head and looked at one of his men. Jack followed his gaze and saw a slight young soldier with his head buried in the crook of his arm. He was small, frail even, the musket he hugged close to him far too large for his tiny frame.

The young soldier looked up as he sensed the scrutiny.

'You!' Jack could not hold back the exclamation.

Martha stared back at him, her eyes bright against the powder streaks on her skin.

'What the hell are you doing here?' Jack fired the question at her.

Martha got to her feet. Her uniform was filthy. 'Doing my duty. Same as these men.'

Jack slid from the saddle and stalked towards Hightower. 'You know who she is?'

The corporal said nothing.

'You know she's a woman?'

'She wanted to fight,' Hightower replied in a flat tone.

'And you didn't tell her no?'

'Didn't think it was my place to stop her.'

'What about her husband? Didn't he have something to say about it?'

'It's not up to him to tell me what to do any more,' Martha interjected. 'He lost that right the last time he blackened my eye.'

'Shut up!' Jack gave the order without turning his head. 'I asked you a bloody question, Corporal.'

'Her husband don't know she's here. Least I don't think he does.'

'Christ on his bloody cross,' Jack muttered. He was not given a chance to say more.

'On your feet! Come on now, boys.' An officer was rousing the men who sheltered along the treeline.

Jack glared at Martha. The fury he felt was all-consuming. War was no place for a woman. He grabbed her arm and hauled her to one side. She came easily. She weighed nothing.

'You shouldn't damn well be here,' he hissed. 'Get yourself away. Now!' He twisted her around before shoving her in the direction of the rear.

Martha stumbled, the weight of her musket almost dragging her down. 'Don't you dare tell me what to do!'

There was fire in her words. But he did not care. He would not let her stay. He would not allow her to be sullied by the same filth that contaminated his own blackened soul.

'Go away! You hear me, Martha? Go away!'

'I ain't going nowhere.' She stood her ground.

'You there.' An officer came towards them, pointing at Hightower. 'Corporal, get these men on their feet and fall them in.'

Jack ignored the man and kept his eyes on Martha.

'On your feet. We're going to whip them Yankees, you hear me, boys? They won't stand. Not again.' The officer was moving quickly, stirring the men. All along the line, other officers were doing the same.

Hightower did as he was told and got slowly to his feet, followed by half the men around him. 'You heard the officer. Come on, boys, let's get this done.'

Jack took a step towards Martha. 'Get away from here, Martha, you hear me? You can't be here.'

'Why the hell not?' Martha hissed the words, keeping them for him alone.

'This isn't the place for you.'

'Yes, it is!' Her eyes blazed with passion. 'Don't you see? I believe in what I am fighting for, same as these men here.'

'You don't know what you're saying.'

'You're wrong. You think I spent my whole day in that there ditch? I've been with these fellows all morning. I was with them when we pushed back the Yankees south of here, and I was with them when we tried to cross that goddam field.' She searched Jack's gaze, her eyes flickering back and forth. 'I'm not leaving them now.'

'On your feet! Let's go! Form up!' The officers rallying the troops barked the orders one after the other. Already men were gathering around them, their ranks ragged. The smaller column was joined by what looked to be a fresh brigade: four unbloodied regiments forming up in the thickets and swathes of brush too far from the Union position to have been destroyed by canister and rifle fire.

Hightower looked around his small group. 'Come on, boys. Time we were going.' He said nothing more as he led them towards the ranks that were growing with every passing moment.

Martha moved as if to go with them. Jack gripped her arm.

'Let me go, Jack.' She did not fight him.

'You can't go out there. Not again.' He tried to understand the emotions surging through him.

'I can and I will. I ain't afraid of dying.' She kept her tone calm. 'Now let me go. Let me do what I want to do. Don't you be like him, don't you be like my John. I ain't yours to control. It's up to me what I do now.'

Jack held her there. 'You want to fight, is that it?' Anger spewed forth, violent and uncontrollable. 'You want to see this war? You want to kill a man?' He shrugged his knapsack off his back and dumped it on the ground. He would not need it where he was going. 'Well, come on then!' The fury had taken him. He moved, grabbing his repeater from its sheath then hauling her after him. He did not care that men stared. He did not care that an officer shouted a command at him. He cared only for the fight that he was choosing to make his own.

He frogmarched Martha towards the column, then shoved her forward. 'Get in there.' Paying no heed to the men he barged past, he buried her deep in the column several ranks from the front, then pulled her to him so that her face was inches from his own. 'You want to be here? Then fine. Stay. Die if you want to, I'm not going to stop you.'

He released her then. But still he stared at her. 'I'll see you in hell,' he hissed, then turned on his heel and forced his way out of the ranks.

'You boys want to fight?' He yelled the question. 'I said, do you boys want to fight?' He turned to face the ranks.

'Hell, yeah!' The first voices answered him.

'You want to whip them Yankee sons of bitches?'

They roared back at him louder this time.

'You want to kill them? You want to send them running back to their goddam fucking mothers?'

'Yes, sir!' the men responded, bellowing their agreement from deep in the pits of their stomachs.

'We're going to show them Yankees how Southerners fight! You hear me, boys? We're going to beat those bastards. Are you with me?'

'Yes, sir!' The roars of approval came back at him. These men had tried once to take the Union position and they had been beaten back. Now Jack fanned their anger so that it mixed with their shame and fear to produce the volatile cocktail that would throw them back into the fight.

The fury had him fully in its grasp now. It was the madness he knew well. Nothing else mattered. Nothing save the need to fight. Martha had summoned the devil, and now Jack would show her, would show them all, what he was.

For he was the master of war, and he would not be defeated.

# Chapter Forty-five

'Advance!'

The order came from a major who had taken station at the head of the column. He led his command forward. There was no room for manoeuvre, the flanks of the Union position secured by other blue-coated troops. The Confederates had no choice but to mount another frontal assault.

The column lurched into motion. Its ranks might have been uneven, but they were all brave Southern men. They did not shirk from the fight ahead.

The rest of the assaulting columns were on the move too. Yet this was no grand attack on good ground. The troops were advancing through heavy brush and thick undergrowth. Little could be seen other than fleeting glimpses of more men marching in the same direction. It gave the attack an eerie feel, enhanced by the clouds of powder smoke wafting through the trees.

The column pushed into the brush cut low by Union fire, the ground beneath their boots now carpeted with the dead and the dying. They cheered then, the sound coming deep from their guts. They knew what was ahead, yet they went forward willingly.

Jack had taken position at the end of the row where he had left Martha. Hightower was to his left, with the other men from his group scattered around them. As one, they began to yell.

The noise of the war cry wrapped around the column. To Jack's ear it sounded eerie, as if it were made by animals, or creatures from another realm. Yet there was something hidden in the series of yips and cries that fed his fury. For the first time he joined in, matching his pitch to the men around him. The sound filled his head, intoxicating and powerful. He was one of them now. And so he gave the rebel yell, the unearthly shriek in tune with the searing madness in his soul.

He looked ahead and saw the men that waited for them. They were little more than shadows, their forms hidden behind the tangled greenery that lined the farm track. He knew that he would kill them without question. They were his enemy now.

'Charge!' He shouted the encouragement. The pace of the advance was increasing as the madness took them all. They raced forward, screaming like men released from the dungeons of hell.

The Union guns opened fire with canister. The storm of musket balls ripped into the column, cutting men down in droves, the leading ranks torn apart. The men behind charged on regardless. They roared their devilish cry as they stormed forward, their boots crushing those that had fallen. Jack went with them. He was yelling constantly now, the sound spewing out. He thought only of the fight to come, of the men he would kill.

The Union soldiers held their ground and now opened fire. More Confederates fell. Hightower went down, a Minié ball smashing his face into so much pulp. Others fell around him, their rebel yells transformed into despairing cries as Union bullets found a home in their flesh. The pitch of the yell changed, the sound now punctuated by the screams of the dying. Yet still the men pressed on, rushing into the face of the fire no matter how many of their number were cut down.

The treeline was just yards ahead now. These were the hard yards, the cruel yards. Men died in their dozens as the defenders poured on the fire. It was as if the air was under attack from a thousand deadly hornets. The passage of time slowed so that the ground crawled past under the boots of the men rushing the Union line. So many died, their bodies falling to stain ground that so far had been left untouched. Still the soldiers in the bloodied and battered column pressed on, their raw, desperate courage holding them to their task even as the Union fire butchered the men around them.

Jack pulled his rifle into his shoulder. He had been here before. He fell silent, no longer yelling like the men around him. He fought against the battle madness, refusing to let it take command of his being. It would have its time, but he knew how to tame the wild, searing emotion; how to use it so that he could be the killer he needed to be.

He fired, snapping off his first shot even as he ran forward. He cranked the handle then fired again, revelling in the power of the modern rifle. He saw a man dressed in blue directly in his path, crouched down as he reloaded his rifle. He looked up as Jack charged towards him. For a moment the two men locked eyes, then Jack aimed his repeater and fired. The bullet took the Union soldier between the eyes. He crumpled, his body falling over itself as he died in an instant.

Jack fired again and again at the enemy pressed tight into the trees and bushes that lined the farm track. A man raised a rifle. Jack saw the muzzle lift towards him, then the flash as it fired. The bullet snickered past so close that he felt the snap in the air an inch from his cheek. He twitched the repeater, cranked the handle and fired. The man with the rifle fell, Jack's bullet taking him deep in the gut.

Jack had already looked away. He had slowed and so was behind the leading ranks of the column as they stormed into the Union line. It was a brutal impact. At such close range, even the outdated muskets the Confederates carried were horribly effective. For the first time, Union men died, the Southerners shooting down those who had killed so many of their friends.

Suddenly Martha was there. The Union fire had thinned the ranks ahead of her so that she was close to the front when the Confederate charge hit home. She plunged into the chaos, following the men ahead of her as they drove into the enemy line.

Jack ran hard, skirting past men rushing towards the Union soldiers so that he could get close to her. Already the sounds of the fight were changing. There was less rifle and musket fire now as the two sides engaged in brutal hand-to-hand fighting. In its place were the shouts, cries and shrieks of men fighting for their lives. He ducked under a low-hanging branch, then kicked his way through a bush and into the lane. He arrived to find chaos.

A soldier with the pale blue chevrons of a sergeant on his sleeve swung a musket at Jack's head. He swayed back, nearly losing his balance but avoiding the blow. He fired a moment later, immediately cranking the handle on the rifle then firing again. Both bullets hit the sergeant, twin eruptions of blood spurting from his chest. He fell away, his despairing shout of horror lost in the storm of sound that filled the air.

'Martha!' Jack called. He fired once more, the bullet shattering the skull of a Union soldier raising his rifle ready to fire. 'Martha!'

She spotted him then. She stood with her musket held out in front of her, staring at the scene that swirled around her. Jack saw her fear. Nothing prepared a man, or a woman, for this moment, not even being in a column flensed by enemy fire. The brutality of the struggle between men fighting for their lives was like nothing else on earth.

'Behind me!' Jack stepped forward. He fired as he moved, then cranked the handle again before snapping off more shots, gunning men down so that they died without ever knowing where the death had come from.

The confused melee swirled around them. A Union soldier reeled past, his throat torn open by a Confederate bowie knife. Another man, a Southerner, writhed on the ground, his guts ripped open by a Union bayonet.

Martha did as she was told, stepping sideways so that she was behind Jack just as a Union corporal rushed towards them, his lips pulled back in a snarl. Jack saw him coming. It was too easy. He raised the rifle and fired. The bullet hit the man in the centre of his face. His head snapped back and he fell backwards as if his legs had been whipped away from under him.

'Stay close!' Jack hissed. He felt nothing as he killed. He cared more for the count of shots fired, and the fact that he now had just one bullet left in the rifle.

It was bedlam. Death came from every angle as the two groups fought hard. Yet there was no doubt that the Confederates were gaining ground. More and more Union men were falling, the defenders starting to lose the fight.

Despite their casualties, though, the men in blue refused to break. Two Union men attacked a Confederate soldier, driving him towards Jack. The Southerner tried to counter the bayonets that were thrust towards him, battering them away with his musket, beating them back time and time again. But still they came for him, the men in blue uniforms screaming abuse at him with every strike.

Jack stepped to one side. One of the Union men saw him. There was time for him to stare before Jack fired. The bullet hit him in the chest with enough force to knock him from his feet. The second soldier's head twisted to look at Jack in horror as his comrade tumbled to the ground. Jack stepped forward and drove the brass-hilted butt of his rifle into the man's neck. It was a cruel blow, and it crushed the man's throat. He dropped his weapon, his hands scrabbling around his ruined windpipe. Jack gave him no quarter. He pulled back the rifle then smashed the butt into the centre of the man's face, bludgeoning him to the ground.

'God bless you,' the Confederate soldier gasped. He drove his bayonet into the man Jack had knocked down, stabbing the blade into the man's heart and finishing what Jack had started.

'Oh my Lord! Here they come!'

The man Jack had saved shouted the warning. Around them men still fought, the soldiers of both armies sticking to their ferocious task. The violent struggle was chaotic, but there was no doubt now that the Union soldiers were losing. There were too few left on their feet to hold the position for much longer, and those still fighting were backing away, surrendering the ground they had held for so long.

Yet the fight was far from done. Jack saw blue-coated re-inforcements rushing towards the track. The Union commanders would not let the position go.

He saw what had to be done. 'Stay here. Do not follow.' He hissed the terse command at Martha, then handed her his now empty rifle.

'To me!' He gave the command to the men around him as he started to move. The last vestiges of his control fell away and the wild madness of battle seared through his veins. He let it have its head, forgetting Martha, forgetting everything.

He drew his sword and revolver as he began to run. The feel of the weapons gave him power. It was how he had always fought. The memories of those fights flooded through him, feeding his fury. No man could stand against him. No man could match his skills.

'Charge!' He released the madness. Nothing mattered now save the need to kill. 'Come on, you bastards! Charge!'

Men came with him. The bloodied and battered remnant of the Confederate column charged at the fresh Union men. It was bravely done. These men had endured the destruction wrought by the Union volleys. They had fought their way into the Union line, driving the defenders back. Now they would fight to hold what they had so nearly won.

'Kill them!' Jack gave his final bitter instruction, then raised his revolver and fired at one of the men leading the Union soldiers forward, before changing his aim and shooting down an officer in mid stride.

Around him, Confederate soldiers ploughed into the fight, yelling as they charged, the cry even more inhuman than before.

A Union soldier ran at Jack. The man died with the revolver's third bullet buried in his brain. Another came at him with a bayonet, but he battered the musket away with his sword with contempt. It was too easy. He laughed then, the sound loud even amidst the screams and yells. He raised his left hand, the barrel of the revolver just inches from the Union soldier's face. The heavy bullet blasted the man's skull apart.

A Union captain came at him with a sword. The officer thrust with the sabre, aiming the tip at Jack's gut. Jack saw the blow coming. It was easy to parry it, the power in his counter sending the Union officer's blade wide. It left the man open. Jack barked another short laugh, then rammed his sword forward, stepping into the blow so that his full weight was behind it. He drove the sabre's steel tip deep into the Union captain's chest, then twisted the blade so that it would not get stuck in the suction of flesh. He was close enough to feel the rush of air on his face as the man's last breath left his mouth, and to smell the blood that followed.

He stepped back, tearing his sabre free. The Union captain stayed on his feet, his eyes locked onto Jack's face. Then he fell, his sword tumbling to the ground as his hands scrabbled at the hideous wound torn in his flesh.

Jack threw back his head and laughed. He felt invincible. He was a killer, and there was no one alive who could stand against him. For here, in the bloody hell of battle, he alone was master.

# Chapter Forty-six

---

The Confederates fighting for the lane battled hard, but the Union men came on with grim determination. No quarter was given and dozens died in the vicious, deadly melee filled with screams and the stink of blood and torn flesh.

Jack fought like a man possessed. He emptied the bullets in his revolver, firing blindly into the mass of bodies rushing towards him. He barely noticed the men he killed.

A Union soldier came at him, bayonet thrust forward just as the manual dictated. Jack blocked the blow then sliced the front edge of his blade across the man's face, taking his eyes. Another man filled his place, rifle lifting to fire. Jack ducked low then pushed up fast, coming up under the man's rifle, his sword taking the man in the groin.

The red mist drove him on. He backhanded the sword, slashing it deep into a man's neck then thrusting it forward so that it ripped through another man's throat. He made not a sound as he fought. He was a killing machine; an automaton that delivered death. Everything he had done, everything he had been had led to this point, to this fight. And there was no man alive who could stand against him.

A Union officer fired at him with a revolver. The bullet snapped past, stinging the air. Jack singled the man out, his first thought to close with him. Yet the Union men were swarming forward now, overwhelming the last Confederates still on their feet and blocking his path to the man who had so nearly killed him.

'Run for your lives!' A Confederate soldier sprinted past, his face a mask of blood from a wound to his forehead.

He was not alone. Everywhere Jack looked, Confederates turned to run. Many died as they went, the men in blue cutting them down without thought of mercy.

'Stand!' Jack shouted the command, demanding obedience. He hacked at a Union corporal, cutting his sabre deep into the junction between neck and shoulder. The man fell away, but three more elbowed one another as they tried to take his place. Jack swept his sword across the bayonets coming at him, then punched his left hand forward, using his empty revolver to club a man to the ground. The wild mania was beginning to fade, the futility of the fight overwhelming the madness that had driven him to this point.

Two more bayonets came at him. He battered one aside, but the other thrust past his parry and sliced across his hip, scoring through the flesh. He barely felt the pain. He slashed his sword back, slicing it down the man's face, ripping away a great chunk of cheek. Yet already more men were coming forward and another bayonet jabbed at his side, missing him by no more than an inch.

'No!' The cry was torn from his lips. He fought on, no longer attacking but just battering away the bayonets that came for him. He gave ground, stepping backwards, unable to turn for fear of getting a bayonet in the back. There was no escape. He stepped back again. His heels caught a corpse and he stumbled. Bayonets reached for him the moment his sword dropped. He recovered his balance, then beat them back with a desperate, hurried parry, but not before one had gouged a deep crevice in the back of his left hand.

The last of the madness left him. He no longer fought to kill. He fought just to stay alive. Yet there was no respite from the men coming against him. Around him, a handful of Confederates still fought on, but they were dying fast, the sheer numbers of Union troops sealing their fate.

Jack saw his death coming. He hacked at the men seeking to kill him, his sword knocking away their bayonet-tipped rifles for a moment longer. He would not allow himself to die here. Not this day. Not after so long. Not after so many battles.

A Union sergeant was shouting at his men, goading them with insults, calling them children for not finishing the lone Confederate officer. Jack heard every word.

The men tried to obey. They thrust their bayonets forward, faces twisted with hatred. Jack hammered them back. The blood running from the wound to his hand made his grip loosen on the revolver and it fell away, leaving him just his pitted and notched sabre.

He knew what was to come. He knew the end was in sight. There were just too many of them.

And then, at last, he saw the truth.

He was no god of war. He was just a man with a sword. His fate was to be no different to that which befell all such men.

He was just a soldier.

And soldiers died.

'Fire!'

The command came from behind him. He could not turn, even as he heard the cough of half a dozen muskets firing as one. The storm of musket balls seared past him. They hit the men he was fighting, knocking two from their feet.

'Come on!' Hands plucked at him, pulling him back.

He needed no more urging. He turned, the short-range volley buying him the time he needed. He saw Martha immediately. She was the one tugging at his clothing. A handful of other Confederates were with her. They were her comrades, the men he had seen huddled around her in the treeline, the same men she had fought alongside all day. They were the men who now saved his life.

'Run!'

One of them, a thick-bellied man with a wild grey beard, shouted the command. Together the small group ran past the heaps of shattered bodies. Jack reached out to Martha as they raced across the blackened, bloodstained ground. He held her arm with his free left hand, his fingers leaving bloody stains on her sleeve, and they ran together, tired legs threatening to buckle at any moment, backs twitching in expectation of a rifle bullet in the spine.

The Union soldiers let them go. The fight for the farm track had been hard fought, the men from both sides battling with ferocious courage. The Union men had held the line, and now they held their fire. They knew they would need their bullets if they were to defend the lane.

'Jesus Christ!' Jack hissed the oath as he broke into a thick tangle of greenery. He stopped running, dropped his sword to the ground and bent double, sucking air into his tortured lungs, dragging it down in great gasps. The pain came then. His side was on fire where the Union bayonet had scored his flesh, and his left hand was sending shooting twinges up and down his arm.

'Form up! Fix bayonets!'

Around them, another column was being formed. Fresh regiments had been summoned to the fight and now men with clean, pale faces prepared to cross the ground that had already claimed so many lives that day.

'You there! Join the ranks!' An officer with a loud, pompous voice shouted the command at the stragglers in the treeline. None responded to the command.

Jack sucked down one last breath, then straightened up, wincing at the pain as he did so. Martha handed him back his repeating rifle. The weapon felt impossibly heavy. He saw the dark marks on the brass hilt, and dozens of scratches and notches all along its length. He could not recall how many men the weapon had killed.

Martha's face was grey with exhaustion.

'Thank you.' He reached out to her, laying his bloodied hand on her shoulder. 'You saved me.'

She had no breath for a reply.

'I was going to die.' He said the words softly, as much to himself as to her. He had been a fool, an arrogant fool. And he had been one for a long, long time. 'You saved me. And now I'm going to save you.'

He took her by the hand and led her along the treeline until he found his knapsack. There were dozens of Confederate soldiers around them. Some lay slumped on the ground, whilst others sat and stared at faraway objects only they could see. These were the men who had crossed the field.

The next attack was about to begin. Officers shouted and drums rattled into life. Bright colours led a fresh brigade forward in another frontal assault on the farm track and its nest of deadly defenders. Some of the men who had fought before joined the ranks, swelling the column's numbers. Jack could understand why they did it. He knew the fury of battle as well as any. But this attack would go on without him. The lesson had been a long time coming, but it had been learned.

'You ready to get out of here?' he whispered as he led Martha towards his horse, which had remained where he had left it. The animal whinnied in recognition.

'Yes.' Martha gave the reply firmly.

'You saved my life,' Jack said again. He sucked down a breath, then boosted himself into the saddle.

'I didn't nurse you back to health just to see you die.' Martha stood next to the stirrup and looked up at him. 'My pa wouldn't have wanted that. He'd cuss me out for the wasted effort.' She reached up a hand for him to help her.

Jack grunted as he swung her up into the saddle behind him. 'I'm in your debt, Martha.' With her behind him, he could not see her face and she could not see his. He was glad of that. He would not want her to witness his emotion. She had done something incredibly brave, rushing back into the fight when any sane person would have been running for their lives.

'Why did you do it?' He could not hold back the question.

'Because you'd do it for me.' Martha slipped her hands around his waist.

'But . . .' Jack clamped down on the words that had sprung to his lips.

'But I'm a woman?' Martha pulled her arms tight, squeezing with enough force to make him gasp.

'Yes. You don't belong here.'

'No one belongs here, Jack, 'cept maybe the devil hisself.'

She released the pressure. 'Now get on with you. Get us out of here.'

'Yes, ma'am.' Jack felt her weight settle behind him, then he kicked back his heels and forced the horse that would carry them to safety into motion. It was time to do as he was told.

Behind them, he heard the rebel yell as the fresh column tried to take the farm track. He rode away from the fight as the first Union volley drowned out the attackers' cries and the screaming began once again.

# Chapter Forty-seven

———◆———

Jack sat and stared into the darkness. Martha lay close beside him, sharing his blanket. He could see little of the world around them, but he heard the sounds of other men. The Confederate army had made their camp on the field of battle, the men sinking to the ground wherever they happened to be. They were exhausted, but they were confident. Jack had heard whoops and catcalls as the tired men had made their camp. The Yankees were as good as beaten. The Confederate army had fought all day and they had fought hard. They had taken heavy casualties, but what was left of the Union army was now trapped with the Tennessee river at its back and the Confederate army to its front. The men from the South settled to their rest certain that the morning would see one last push, one more fight, and the hated Yankee army would be destroyed.

Jack and Martha could not have gone more than a mile when they had stopped for the day. The roads leading away from the battle had been clogged with men and wagons going in the other direction, as the great Confederate host pushed the Union army back towards the river. To slow their progress still further, other officers, desperate for knowledge, had stopped them at least a dozen times. Jack had shared what he knew, then asked questions of his own.

He had discovered that the farm track had eventually been taken. A Confederate column had broken through the Union line in a peach orchard to the east, turning the flank of the men holding the blood-soaked ground. Still the Union had held, even as their line had been bent back like a horseshoe. A Confederate officer, sickened by the bloodshed, had massed every piece of artillery he could find. Jack had heard that more than fifty cannon had brought down a bombardment on the Union position. He had not been there to see it, but he had heard it. The roar of the massed guns had created a wave of sound so powerful it was as if the very fabric of the world was being ripped apart. Under such a bombardment the Union line's hold on the lane had become untenable, and a stand of nearly seven hours had finally been broken, the bloodied remains of the Union forces pushed back towards Pittsburg Landing.

There they would spend a desperate night. From what Jack had heard, their army was in tatters, with a huge number of men deserting. Those that stayed formed a final line of defence, the battered, stubborn defenders sure to be beaten within hours of the sun's rise.

It began to rain. The water was icy on Jack's skin, yet he relished the sensation. It was a reminder that he was alive. He looked up, letting the frigid raindrops run across his face, and searched the sky for a glimpse of the stars. He saw nothing but blackness, the battlefield smothered with a thick blanket of cloud. He reached out a hand and rested it gently on Martha's hip. He had no idea if she slept, or if she too passed the lonely, cold hours of the night thinking on what might have been.

The fight over the farm track replayed itself over and over in his mind. He searched the memories, looking for something that would give him comfort. He failed. Without Martha and her comrades rushing to his aid, he knew with utter certainty that he would now be dead.

He felt the touch of death on the nape of his neck and shivered. The notion of his own death appalled him. He had believed that he did not fear it. He had watched the light of life leave a man's eyes on so many occasions that it had become commonplace. Yet now the thought of oblivion terrified him. The idea of not being, of not existing, was almost more than he could bear.

'Are you cold?' The voice came from beneath the blanket. 'I can feel you shaking.'

Jack did not answer. He was lost in thoughts of nothingness. Fear seared through every fibre of his being, the sensation like nothing he had ever felt before. He was no master of war. He was no hero, no great warrior. He was just another soldier. That realisation had changed him, and he wondered how he could go on knowing what he now knew. Could he fight again, burdened with this fear, or would it unman him? He had witnessed other men lie down and refuse to fight, no matter what punishment they were threatened with. He understood them now and feared he would prove to be one of them.

'Here.'

The blanket lifted and a hand reached out, the touch warm on his cold flesh. He took hold of it, engulfing it between his own, savouring the warmth. He did not move for a long time.

'I'm sorry.' Again the voice came from beneath the blanket.

'What for?' The words struggled out of Jack's throat.

'For what happened. For making you join that fight.'

'Don't be sorry.' Jack was finding it hard to speak. It felt as if his mouth was disconnected from his mind. His thoughts lingered on the notion of his own mortality. The fear of death would not let him escape.

'So are you still going to try to find that man?' Martha wanted to talk.

Jack could not answer. Shadowy faces flickered across his mind's eye. Rose, Lyle, Pinter, Hightower, Denton, and last of all, Martha herself.

'I'll help you.' She filled the silence.

'No.' The word came suddenly and without thought. He released her hand and returned it to her.

'You don't want my help?'

'No. I'm not going to try to find him.' Jack paused as the thought settled. He ran it through his mind, testing it to see what emotion he felt. There was only one. He felt relief.

'What about Rose?'

Jack took in a long, slow breath before he replied. 'I can't see her any more. I can't picture her face. Not like it was.' He paused. 'I've lost her.'

He said nothing more and Martha left him to his silence. His quest for revenge was over.

# Chapter Forty-eight

*D*awn came slowly that morning. It spread lethargically across the sky, as if it too were too cold and too drained from the effort of the previous day to want to start another. Yet slowly, reluctantly, the light pushed away the darkness. It left the Confederate army smothered in shadow, but there was light enough to see, and so begin another day. Yet the Southerners did not move. They lingered in whatever meagre shelter they had managed to find, reluctant to get on with the second day of fighting.

It had been a long, wet, cold night. Few men had slept. Union gunboats moored on the Tennessee river had shelled the battlefield through the hours of darkness. The noise had been constant, the bombardment a grinding misery that had to be endured, just like the fear it inspired that gnawed away deep in a man's gut. It had rained all night, preventing many of the soldiers from lying on the ground. The dawn put an end to the wretchedness of the darkness, yet brought with it only the promise of more pain, and more death

Eventually a few men emerged from their makeshift shelters to cook what rations they had, the first fires doing little to shift the cloud of miserable gloom. Most, though, stayed where they were, too tired and hungry to stir themselves.

They were left to wallow. No summons came from the fife and drum to force them to their feet. Instead the troops greeted the day in lethargy, and not one man, not one officer, was concerned. For the Union army was trapped and almost beaten, and there was no need to hasten their end. They had been too badly mauled by the previous day's fighting to put up much resistance. The Yankees could wait.

Jack worked on his sabre. He had already cleaned and reloaded Martha's musket, and he had loaded the Henry repeater with the last of the cartridges. Now he ran a whetstone up and down the blade's edges. The weapon was battered from the previous day, the steel pitted and scarred. But if it were needed, it would still do the job for which it was intended.

Yet he had no intention of using his weapons that day. He would bide his time and stay far from the fight. When the moment was right, he would get away from the battle, and away from the army. He had the vague idea of taking Martha home. From there his plans grew hazy, yet for now the simple objective was enough.

'Fall in. Come on now, men. On your feet.'

A lone officer finally arrived to stir the soldiers who had camped nearby. He gave the order in a mild tone of voice, like a clergyman asking unruly Sunday school children to listen. Some men obeyed, but others simply carried on with what they were doing. To Jack's eye the men were in no condition to fight. The long, exhausting march followed by a full day's hard fighting had taken its toll on them. Now they would have to find the strength to fight again, and he did not envy them one bit.

It took a long time for the regiment to form. The men's reluctance to rejoin the fight was obvious, and they were only spurred to greater efforts when the first sounds of battle broke the quiet of the morning. They came at a distance, yet there was no mistaking the opening salvos of cannon fire. The second day's battle had begun.

It was only when the regiment moved off that Jack got to his feet and began to gather his things. Martha had been up before him, spending her time tending to the mare they would both ride that day. The animal was as exhausted as the men around it, but Jack would not spare it. It was their one chance of salvation, and he would ride the beast into the ground if he had to. Nothing would stop him from getting Martha away from the battle.

'Are you ready to go, Jack?' Martha stood facing him. She still wore her soldier's uniform, but her musket had been left on the ground. Instead she just had the holstered revolver they had taken from the fight at the cabin in the woods.

Jack nodded, then paused. The sounds of battle were intensifying. Long-drawn-out exchanges of gunfire were interspersed with the roar of artillery fire. Somewhere not so very far away from where he stood, men were dying.

'Let's go.' He strode over to the horse and boosted himself into the saddle before helping Martha up. 'We'll look for a road heading south.' He spoke without turning around, his tone even and steady even as she wrapped her arms around him and pressed close to his spine.

'No.' She spoke the single word firmly. 'There is something we need to do first.'

'What's that?' The authority in her voice took Jack aback.

'We need to find my John. He's out there somewhere. I

cannot leave without knowing what has happened to him.'

'Yes, you can.' Jack sighed. 'He beat you. You remember that?'

'That doesn't matter.' Martha reached out and slid her hand onto his. 'We're married in the eyes of God. I can't just leave him.' Her voice was tight with emotion. 'He wasn't always so bad. We had good times. At the start we were happy and he was good to me. It was only after Joshua passed . . .' She did not finish the thought. When she spoke again, her tone was firm and steady. 'He's my husband. It don't matter what he did, or why he did it. I made a vow to God to stay with him until the end of our days. So I mean to find him.' She took her hand back from his. 'You don't have to come with me.' Her weight shifted as she started to get down. 'I'll go by myself.'

Jack reached back with an arm and held her in place. Martha had saved his life the previous day. He owed her. 'When did you last see him?'

'Yesterday morning. He didn't know I was there, but I knew where he was. I heard he got hit early on. Then things got kinda busy. Later on, me and Hightower asked some men from his company, and they reckoned he was back at the brigade aid station. He was still alive then.'

'That was then. A lot of men die.'

'Uh huh. He could be with the Lord.' Martha's tone did not change even as she contemplated her husband's death. 'But I need to know for certain.'

'Are you sure?' Jack could not see her face, but her tight grip around his waist betrayed her tension. 'We can ride on and get away from here. We don't ever have to look back.'

'No. I can't do that. I have to find out. I need to know what's in my future.'

Jack inhaled a deep breath. He did not know where he would find the strength for what lay ahead if he did as she asked, or where he would find the courage to fight if that was what it took to keep her safe.

'I'll go alone if I have to.' Martha whispered the words as she sensed his hesitation.

'No. I can't let you do that.' He let out the breath he had been holding, then kicked back his heels and let the horse walk for a few paces before pulling on the reins and turning it around. They would head back towards the battle that showed no sign of abating as it went into a second day.

The Confederate army had been slow to rise, but now they had gone back on the offensive, and Jack could hear the sounds of battle coming from all along the front. If things were going as the Confederates had predicted, then he was listening to the final stand of the Union army.

He rode towards the sounds, keeping to a cart track that led past a series of tangled thickets made of brush and young trees. He could see little, and not for the first time he wondered at the choice of battlefield. Soldiers could not fight what they could not see.

Martha had said little since they had left their overnight camp. He did not mind the silence. She had only spoken to give him directions as she tried to follow the ground the 65th Virginia had taken the previous day.

The noise of battle got steadily louder. At one point, they were forced to halt as they came across a Confederate regiment beginning an advance. Neither Jack nor the regiment's officers could see the enemy, the thick undergrowth and saplings blocking their line of sight.

Once again Jack heard the eerie rebel yell as the Confederates charged, and something of its unearthly madness resonated deep within him. Yet he felt no compulsion to join the attack, and he pulled his horse's head around and kicked his heels back so that they trotted across the rear of the regiment.

The yell was cut off abruptly as a storm of canister and volley fire ripped through the advancing ranks. Men dropped, shot down by an unseen foe. As Jack rode away, he saw the regiment's attack repulsed, the men running back and going on the defensive, their broken ranks forming a battle line in the face of what he was certain could only be a determined Union counterattack.

There was to be no easy victory on that bloody ground. By rights, the remains of the Union army should have been destroyed or captured, yet it appeared no one had told them that.

Instead they were launching an attack of their own.

# Chapter Forty-nine

---

*J*ack and Martha rode through an army thrown into disorder. They were forced to halt as another regiment hurried forward, blocking their path. It gave them the chance to run their eyes over the tired men and their thinned ranks. These were the men who had marched at dawn the previous morning and then fought all day. It was obvious they were in no condition to fight again, yet here they were, double-timing forward as attack turned to desperate defence.

Jack watched as the regiment took up a position beside a battery of guns that was already hotly engaged. Every gun was firing as fast as it could be reloaded. Each shot drove the cannon backwards, the heavy wheels gouging great crevices in the dirt. The men serving them had no time to reposition them, simply loading them where they stood before firing again, the guns spitting great gouts of flame as they flung another salvo at their unseen target.

'We're going to have to make this quick.' Jack had seen enough of war to recognise the signs of an army fighting for its life. He could only surmise that somehow the near-beaten Union army had been reinforced. He had seen it before, at Bull

Run. Then it had been Southern reinforcements arriving to save the day, the fresh troops brought to the battlefield by railroad in time to shore up the Confederates' battered left flank. Now the Union army must have conjured up support enough to turn the tide of the battle.

'Over there.' Martha tapped him on the shoulder, then pointed at a small group of tents, a yellow flag flying from a pole in their midst.

The aid station should have been far from the fighting. Yet the battle had turned so fast that it would soon find itself on the front line. As Jack rode towards it, the regiment they had seen taking position around the battery of cannon went into action.

He reined in, bringing the horse to a stand.

'Go on then.' He gave the curt command. He had no intention of getting down to join the search.

Martha did as she was bid. She was out of the saddle and running across the ground as the sound of the regiment firing a second volley seared through the air.

Jack watched her go, hoping she would not take long. The aid station comprised no more than four tents, and even at first glance he could see that it was overwhelmed. Temporary shelters had been rigged in all directions, with blankets draped over tree branches to provide some shelter for the wounded.

Bodies lay all around. Some were clearly dead, and more than one corpse was sprawled in a pool of bloody rainwater. The dead were surrounded by the most badly wounded. Some were whole, but many were missing whole limbs, or hands, or even faces. Those still living were swathed in blood-sodden bandages. A few orderlies tended the long lines of wounded, removing blood-soaked dressings or passing around a bottle of whiskey, the harsh spirit the only way of easing the men's pain.

Some men screamed as the agony wormed its way through their broken bodies. Others wept, or called for their mothers, or simply for a bullet to end their suffering. Many lay in silence, or else murmured prayers for deliverance from the hopeless misery in which they found themselves.

To one side of the largest tent, Jack saw a hideous heap of amputated feet, legs, arms and hands. Yet even that revolting sight was better than looking at the great pile of dead bodies next to it. The dead had been dumped without ceremony. Now they lay in a single monstrous mass, their bodies stuck in grotesque, unnatural poses. Sightless eyes stared out of the pile, faces frozen in expressions of agony for all time.

He turned his head and spat as the stench of the place wormed its way into his gullet. The air was polluted by the foul miasma of blood and shit, the fetid stench of torn and ruined flesh catching the back of his throat. He spat again to try to scour the acrid taste from his mouth.

'He's not here,' Martha called out as she returned, breathless.

Jack had not heard her approach. He helped her into the saddle, doing his best not to look at the dreadful place in which she had searched for her husband.

'There's another aid post about half a mile from here. An orderly told me that some men from the 65th are there.'

Jack accepted the grim news without another word. He kicked the horse back into motion.

Behind him the gunners and the infantrymen fired without pause.

The second aid station they approached was in no better condition than the first.

The ground around the huddle of tents was littered with the

bodies of the dead and dying, and just a glance towards the tents revealed another shocking mountain of corpses and body parts.

More wounded were arriving all the time. Some walked in, hands pressed to the rents in their flesh, their uniforms bloodied to the elbows from where they had tried in vain to staunch the bleeding. Others hobbled in, or else used their muskets as crutches. A fair few were carried in by friends. There were always men eager to quit the battlefield, and the act of assisting a mate was a better reason than most. More rarely, a man was brought in on a stretcher, the bearers attached to each regiment overwhelmed by the sheer numbers being wounded in the fierce fighting that had begun the second day of battle.

A covered ambulance came by. It was pulled by a pair of mules and carried two men. One glance told Jack that the men were officers, their insignia securing them passage to the rear and the more substantial aid stations. Yet their rank had not spared them the reality of battle, and Jack saw blood trickling down the sides of the ambulance.

He looked for more ambulances, or for farm wagons pressed into service to take the wounded away from the field of battle. There were a few, but nowhere near enough to bear the hundreds of men who needed them. The ones he saw were all filled with officers, the men with the gold braid on their uniforms guaranteed a berth away from the fighting.

'Come with me,' Martha demanded as she slid from the saddle.

Jack did not demur. He vowed this would be their final search. If they failed to find Martha's husband this time, he would force her to quit, even if he had to knock her down.

He tied the horse's reins to a tree branch, then followed

Martha through the lines of bodies. He did not look at the suffering that surrounded him, just as he paid no heed to the men who begged for him to stop and offer aid.

He said nothing as Martha spoke to an orderly who was working his way along the line of bodies, offering each man the choice of a mouthful of brackish water from an iron pail or a slug of whiskey from the bottle he carried. Few chose water. Her enquiry was met with a pointed finger, the orderly gesturing towards one of the tents at the centre of the aid station.

Martha walked away with whatever answer she had been given to her enquiry. Unlike Jack, she did look at the wounded, her head moving slowly from side to side as she searched for the man she had married.

One of the men started to scream. The heart-rending cries went on and on, each one longer than the one before, until they were cut off abruptly. Somewhere else a broken soldier was praying, his voice loud as he beseeched God for aid in his hour of need.

Martha walked on. Jack saw her arms clamp around her chest, as if she were holding in a scream of her own. Yet her pace did not alter, even as men begged for her to stop.

'Shoot me!' A man reached out to pluck at Jack's ankles as he walked past. 'I beg you.'

Jack looked down. The soldier had been shot in the groin. The lower half of his body was sheeted in blackened blood. There was no saving a man with a wound like that, and so he had been laid on the ground, the orderlies who had brought him there not even bothering to waste a bandage on his ruined flesh.

'You hear me, friend?' The man's fingers scrabbled at the hem of Jack's trousers. 'You hear me?' His voice vibrated with desperation and fear. 'Shoot me, friend, please, I beg you. I beg you!'

Jack stepped away, pulling his leg from the man's grasping fingers. He forced himself to feel nothing.

Martha ducked inside one of the tents. She came out a few moments later, her face the colour of old milk, and looked back at Jack. He was close enough to see the tears that streamed down her face.

She turned and walked on, then ducked into another of the tents. This time she did not come back out, so Jack followed her.

The air inside was foul. The stink of canvas mixed with the raw odour of sweat, blood and shit to create a hideous stench that made him want to gag. He saw Martha immediately. She was crouched down next to a man Jack had once beaten bloody.

She had found what she was looking for. She had found her husband.

# Chapter Fifty

---

Martha's husband was alive. He sat on the ground, his back resting against one of the tent's supporting poles. He was in his shirtsleeves, and the entire right side of his body was stained black with old blood.

'John?' Martha reached out a finger to touch his cheek. 'John, it's me.'

Life flickered into red-rimmed eyes. 'Martha?'

'Yes, I'm here.' Fresh tears streamed down Martha's cheeks, scouring clean paths through the grime that covered them.

'Thank the Lord.' John breathed the words. 'I got hit, Martha. I got hit bad.' He spoke like a child, the words simple. 'I lost my hand.' Like a toddler displaying a special pebble, he lifted his right arm to show the evidence. There was little of it left below the elbow. The amputation had taken off his hand and most of his lower arm. The stump was bound in a blood-soaked bandage.

'I see that.' Martha reached out and gently set her husband's ruined arm back in his lap. 'Now don't you worry none. I'm here now. I'll take care of you.'

'You will?' John's voice betrayed his confusion.

'I will.' Martha spoke calmly; the voice of a mother to a child scared by a nightmare. 'It's going to be all right.' She rocked back on her haunches. 'We're taking him with us.'

'How the hell are we going to do that?' Jack had known this was coming the moment he had seen her crouching next to her husband.

'We put him on the horse.'

'He's in no fit state to be moved.'

'We can't leave him here.' Martha pushed herself to her feet and came towards Jack, her eyes blazing. 'I won't do it.'

'You have to.'

'I won't. If you won't take us, then I'll stay here with him.'

'The entire Union army is headed this way. God alone knows how, but it is. We try to ride away with him and none of us will make it. Do you understand that?'

'He's my husband. I ain't leaving him for them Yankees.'

'You'll do as Jack says.' This time it was John who spoke. His voice was steady and firm now, the contrast to moments before stark. 'You'll do as you're damn well told, woman.'

'I'm not leaving you, John.' Martha shook her head.

'No. You need to go.'

'It's not your decision.'

'Goddam you, woman, will you never do as you are told.' The words came back at Martha, hot and angry. John lifted his good arm and pointed a bloodied finger in her direction. 'You'll leave right this minute, you hear me? I don't want you here. I don't want you at all. So you do as you are goddam told and get out of here.'

Martha recoiled from the anger in his harsh words. The memory of a hundred beatings was written in her expression.

'You heard him.' Jack was watching John's face. He was

lucid now, the confusion that had greeted their arrival replaced with what appeared to be anger. But Jack had been an impostor and a liar for a decade or more. He knew when a man lied.

'Let's go.' He reached out and pulled at Martha's elbow, only for her to shake him off.

She stood still, her spine straight as she looked at John for several long moments. Then she turned towards Jack. 'Carry him to the horse.'

Jack could see the determination in her eyes. She was no longer the woman who would accept what she was told with blind obedience. There was no fear left in her. She had seen too much to be frightened of a single man. The display was impressive, but he was still not risking both their lives for this wife-beater. There was another way.

'Wait. Hold out your hands.' He unbuckled the belt around his waist that carried his sabre and deposited it in her arms, then started to undo the buttons of his grey jacket. It was the jacket he had taken from Pinter all those months before. It had done its job, the officer's insignia it bore giving him the freedom he had needed. Now it would serve another purpose.

'There's more than one way to skin a cat.' He offered Martha a thin-lipped smile as he shrugged the jacket off. It did not take long to bend down and slide it over John's shoulders. He took a moment to force John's good arm into a sleeve and to wrap as much of the jacket around the man as he could.

'There.' He stood back and admired his handiwork. It would do.

'Hey!' He spotted an orderly on the far side of the tent. 'There's an officer here.' His voice was full of authority. 'God-dammit, man, why has Captain Joseph been left here?'

'I'm sorry.' The orderly walked towards them, half stumbling over a wounded soldier's leg on the way. The man was clearly exhausted. He had likely been tending to the wounded since the battle had started the previous day. A night without sleep had left his wits fuddled. 'I didn't see him there. Officers are supposed to be in the other tent.'

'I know where they are supposed to be, goddammit. I want Captain Joseph on the next ambulance, is that clear?'

'Yes, sir.' The orderly blinked hard as he looked at Jack, who was buckling his belt back around his waist. The lack of insignia clearly confused him, but the sabre made it obvious that the man shouting at him was no ordinary ranker.

'If I come back and find him still here, I'll be tearing you a new bloody arsehole, is that clear?'

'Yes, sir.'

'Good.' Jack glanced at Martha's husband, who had his eyes closed and his head rested back against the tent pole. He understood the thought behind the act. Clearly John did not want his eyes to betray him as Martha left.

He reached out and pulled Martha towards him, keeping a firm hold on her arm. 'Right, come on. High time we left. They'll take care of him now. It's better he stays with the doctors than that we drag him to God knows where.'

Martha took one last look at her husband, then nodded in agreement. They had secured John a place on the next ambulance. It was a better option for him than a desperate flight on the back of a horse.

'John. I'll find you, you hear me?' she called out to him. 'I'll find you.' She repeated the vow even as her husband failed to react to her words.

She said nothing more as Jack led her from the tent.

\* \* \*

Jack and Martha had been riding for no more than a few minutes when they saw the first grey-coated men heading south. The sight brought Jack up short, and he stopped the mare and watched as the broken ranks of at least two Confederate regiments poured across the field he had been about to cross.

They were running hard in complete disorder. Even as he watched, he saw men discarding their equipment, the ground soon littered with knapsacks, ammunition pouches and even muskets. This was no ordered retreat. It was a rout.

The thunderous roar of a regimental volley ripped through the air. It sounded so close that he could not help flinching in expectation of coming under fire. This time no musket balls or rifle bullets stung the air around him, but it was clear that the Union army had to be close by.

'What's happening?' Martha leaned forward and hissed the question directly into his ear.

'I have no idea.' Jack stood up in his stirrups, searching the ground as he tried to make sense of the situation he had ridden into. He saw nothing, his line of sight blocked in every direction. 'Shit!' The oath escaped his lips. Through a gap in some trees he caught a glimpse of a Union regiment advancing.

'What is it?' Martha repeated.

'It's a fucking disaster.' Jack felt the stirrings of fear. He did not linger to explain more. He turned the mare's head, then kicked back his heels and forced the animal into a trot. He had wanted to find a road so that they could make fast progress with some notion of the direction in which they were headed. That was no longer an option; the Union counterattack had seen to that. It was time to ride away from the battle taking any route they could find.

He did his best to keep them away from the shattered ranks

of the Confederate infantry. Yet it was not easy, the broken ground forcing him to move more slowly than he would have liked. An artillery shell roared by overhead, landing in the midst of the running men and sending up a great fountain of earth. Men screamed as fragments of red-hot shell casing ripped into them. They were left where they fell, the men around them callous and unfeeling. They thought only of flight and of saving their own lives.

More shells followed, ripping into the earth with shattering violence, each one killing and maiming indiscriminately.

Jack rode on, trying to ignore the knot of fear that was tying itself tighter and tighter deep in his gut. He pushed the mare hard, kicking it without mercy to force the pace.

He rode past a group of Confederate soldiers drawing breath behind a clump of trees. They carried Enfield rifles and were looking at one another for guidance. He was certain that an officer could get them to stand. They had fought long and hard, but he could see they were not yet done. With the right leadership, these well-armed men could still make a fight of it. He knew he could be the one to provide that leadership. It would be easy enough to stop his horse and shout the orders that would hold the men in place, the act likely summoning still more men to join them to hold their ground and perhaps even halt the retreat on this part of the line.

Yet lessons had been learned. He was not the man he had once believed himself to be. So he kicked back his heels and rode on by. With not an officer in sight, the men turned and ran.

The ground to Jack's front opened up and he pushed the mare into a canter. He could feel the animal struggling, but he did not care. He kicked repeatedly, forcing it to keep going. It picked up speed, and finally he spotted what appeared to be a farm track in the distance.

It was then that he saw the Confederate cavalry for the first time.

The men were riding directly towards him. There were no more than twenty of them in total. An officer with a bright shock of grey-white hair led them, and he spotted Jack and Martha in the same instant that Jack saw him.

Jack recognised the officer at once. For months, his life had been devoted to finding this man. Now he saw Major Nathan Lyle and felt nothing but fear.

The two men stared at one another. They had once fought sabre to sabre. No man forgot the face of one who tried to kill him.

Jack did not wait to see if the cavalrymen would change course. Instead he turned the mare around. He did not care that he now headed back towards the chaos of what might prove to be an entire army in retreat. He thought only of fleeing from the man he had once sworn to kill.

His horse was game. It stretched its neck and started to run. He could feel the power in the body beneath him as the mare raced away. Shouts came from behind him. Lyle had identified the man who had once tried to kill him. Now he gave chase, the hunted turned hunter.

The ground raced past underneath the hooves of Jack's horse. They galloped back the way they had come, flashing past groups of Confederate soldiers, the men paying them no heed as they ran from the Union forces that had somehow snatched victory from the jaws of defeat. Jack heard the roar of battle even over the drumming of his horse's hooves on the ground, but it meant nothing. He cared only for speed.

He risked a glance over his shoulder. He could see the pack of cavalrymen in the distance. They were giving chase, but it was clear that they were too far away. In a matter of minutes he would lose sight of them completely. Then he could think about slowing the mare and finding a new route away from the ever-changing tide of battle. He felt relief surge through him. It was Lyle's turn to be thwarted as his quarry escaped.

He opened his mouth, thinking to tell Martha that they would soon be safe.

And then the mare stumbled.

# Chapter Fifty-one

---

The mare tried to run on, but her gait had changed dramatically. Now she lurched and staggered where once she had thundered across the ground. Her right foreleg buckled under the strain of every step, and she slowed.

Jack heard the shouts from behind him. Lyle and his men had seen the mare stumble. The chase was over before it had barely begun.

It was the second time Jack had been pursued by these men. The first time he had been on foot. Then he had run, and he had fought, refusing to give in, his body and mind fuelled by rage. Now there was a different emotion surging through him. Now there was just fear, and it consumed him.

The mare hobbled on, still obedient to her master's commands, yet it was a futile effort. There would be no escape that day.

Jack pulled back on the reins, bringing the animal to a stop. He looked at his hands, wondering at the way they now shook. The sensation was like nothing he had felt before. Ice ran through his veins, whilst his stomach churned, his guts twisting themselves into knots and his bowels threatening to void. Then there was the urge to run, to howl or to cry. His emotions ran wild, uncontrollable and raw.

'Hold that whoreson there, boys!' The man who led the gaggle of cavalrymen bawled out the order.

Jack choked down fear. He forced himself to breathe, then slowly turned his horse around. It moved awkwardly, gimping on its right foreleg, but it did as it was told. It left Jack facing the man he had chased for hundreds of miles.

Lyle pulled up. He looked exactly as Jack remembered him, the image he had carried for all these months proving to be flawless. The heavy beard was the same, as was the wild and unkempt hair. Lyle's uniform was filthy, with mud, sweat, rain and blood staining the grey fabric.

Jack's eyes took it all in, just as they saw the revolver with the ivory grips that had once been his own in a holster on Lyle's hip. He had almost forgotten the weapon existed. It was a beautiful gun, the best a rich woman could purchase as a gift for a future husband. Once Jack had hungered after it, almost as much as he had hungered after the woman who had given the gift. Now he looked at it and felt nothing, the flame of that old desire extinguished by the coldness of the fear that now surged through him.

Lyle's men swarmed around them. Most pointed revolvers or carbines at the stranded pair, fingers held close to triggers.

'Get down.' Lyle had ridden forward so that he was no more than half a dozen yards from Jack and Martha. He looked over his shoulder as he gave the order, checking his surroundings, alert to any danger. They were in the middle of a grassy slope, with woodland to the east and west and open ground to both north and south. The view to the south was open, the grassland sloping away downhill for several hundred yards. To the north, it sloped upwards before turning sharply downhill and creating a patch of dead ground just under a hundred yards distant. The dead ground was the danger. Union troops could approach unseen, the only warning the Confederate cavalrymen would get of their arrival likely to be the first shots fired in their direction.

Jack thought about disobeying Lyle's order. For a fleeting moment, the urge to fight pushed away his fear. His hand twitched towards the sword on his hip before the thought was fully formed. It stopped short. The fear returned, swamping the heat of fury with a wash of icy terror.

He moved slowly and carefully, easing his body sideways, the action made difficult by Martha's closeness. He hit the ground hard and his knees buckled. For a moment he thought he would fall in an ignominious heap, but somehow his legs held him up. Martha followed him down. She edged towards him.

'Take the whoreson's sword,' Lyle snapped, before twisting in the saddle to stare towards the dead ground. He knew where danger lay. It was not with the man who had once tried to kill him.

Jack looked at the dirt in front of his boots. One of Lyle's men slid from the saddle, then scampered over. Rough hands pulled his sabre from its scabbard. At no point did Jack look at the man stripping him of his pride.

'And the other one.' Lyle ordered the same man to take Martha's weapons.

Jack's gaze did not leave the dirt. The overnight rain had turned the ground to muddy slurry. A single stone stuck up from the ground. It pointed towards the heavens like an ancient fossilised finger. He focused his gaze on it as he fought the fear that consumed him.

'Major Lyle?' The man sent to collect the weapons called for his commander's attention.

'What is it?'

'Sir, this one . . .' the man paused before continuing, 'this one's a goddam woman!'

Lyle tapped his heels back to ride closer to where Jack stood. 'You brought a woman to battle, whoreson?' He sounded incredulous.

Jack choked down the fear. He felt the need to puke and spew out the noxious cocktail that had stolen his courage. It took everything he had to look up and meet Lyle's baleful gaze.

'She came to fight.'

Lyle's eyes narrowed. 'Oh, she did, huh?'

'Let her go. She's on your side.'

'I don't think so.' Lyle shook his head, then glanced north again. When he looked back at Jack, there was a crease of a smile on his face. 'Now then, whoreson, I don't think we've got long. There's Yankees not far over yonder, and I reckon they'll be coming this way any minute.' He sat easily in his saddle as he loomed over Jack. 'You tried to kill me back at Donelson. I want to know why.'

Jack closed his eyes. The fear was fighting for control of his soul. He could not speak.

'Look at me, you son of a bitch,' Lyle spat the words, 'or so help me, I'll shoot you where you stand.'

Jack's eyes snapped open. 'You tried that before. You failed.'

Lyle rocked back in the saddle as if he had been slapped. He looked at Jack then, searching his face.

'Major?'

One of his men called across, but Lyle silenced him by raising a hand. 'I know you.' He spoke softly, as if to himself. 'I know you, whoreson, don't I?' He repeated the words, louder this time. Then he laughed.

Jack lifted his chin. He felt something stir. It was not fury. It was not the soul-rending madness that threw him into battle. It was something else. Something new. Something sharp and clear and cold.

Lyle stopped laughing. 'It was after Manassas. You were running with a black bitch.' The memory was coming back to him, and he whooped as more of it arrived. 'You shot me! With this very gun.' He slapped the revolver in its holster. 'You came all this way. Now why would you bother to do that?'

Jack was barely listening to Lyle. He wanted to turn to Martha, to look at her one last time, but he didn't. Instead he strained his hearing. He could hear something.

'You hurt me that day, you remember that, whoreson?' Lyle asked the question mildly, as if chiding Jack for knocking his shoulder in a busy thoroughfare. 'Not as bad as that black bitch did, of course, but I've still got the scar from that bullet of yours.'

'You killed her.' Jack spoke the words without emotion. It was as if everything had gone still both around him and inside him.

'Killed her?' Lyle sounded affronted. 'Hell, I wish I had. That bitch of yours escaped, but not before she gave me this.' He lifted his chin and pointed to a thick scar. 'She tried to slit my goddam throat.' He shook his head. 'You thought I killed her? Hell, I would've done if she'd given me the goddam chance. But like the fool I am, I wanted to take my comforts. So we left you to bleed out where you were and I took that bitch of yours into the woods. I got her ready easy enough, stripped her as bare as the day she was born, but before I could make a start, she stuck me with that little knife of hers. She made off too, left me with my gizzard slit and my pecker hanging out.' He chuckled at the memory. 'I should've just killed you both and been done with it.'

Jack absorbed the revelation, refusing to let it take hold of his thoughts. There would be a time for that. A time that would only come when Lyle was lying cold in the ground.

'So that's what all this is about?' Lyle fired the question at him. 'You came after me for revenge?'

Jack ignored him. The sound he had been listening for was louder now. The men around him heard it too.

'Major Lyle?'

'Be quiet.' Lyle had eyes only for Jack. 'You chased me down because you thought I killed that black bitch of yours.' He sneered as he spoke. 'She's been free all this time, yet here you are, chasing my tail.' He shook his head again. 'You've just wasted your life, whoreson, you understand that?' He cackled, displaying his contempt for Jack's actions.

'Boys.' He rocked back in his saddle as he brought the one-sided conversation to a close. 'We'll decide what to do with the woman later on,' he pulled on his reins, preparing to move, 'but do me a favour and shoot that merry little fucker right where he stands.'

The men around Lyle did not need a second command. At least a dozen of them raised their weapons, every barrel pointed directly at Jack.

Then the bullets started to fly.

# Chapter Fifty-two

*B*ullets snapped through the air before any of Lyle's men could open fire. As one, every head turned, the cavalrymen alive to the sudden arrival of danger. More bullets snickered past, hot on the heels of the first. One of Lyle's men hollered as a round hit him in the shoulder. A heartbeat later and another gave an odd cough, then tumbled from the saddle.

'Return fire, goddammit!' Lyle reacted first. He pulled his horse's head around so that he could face the threat that had burst out of the dead ground to the north, then snatched the Colt from its holster and fired, snapping off shots at the Northerners who had come to ruin his fun.

The Union cavalry kept firing even as they charged. The fire was wild, but the storm of bullets took down the man who had been disarming Martha. He hit the ground, his carbine falling next to his body.

Jack saw the men in blue uniforms and started to run. There was no burning desire to fight or desperate need for revenge. There was no fear. No courage. There was nothing in his soul save ice.

Lyle's men were no raw recruits. Even with bullets whipping

around their ears, they fought back, returning fire, then raking back their spurs and charging at the Union cavalry. They were outnumbered, but still they threw themselves at the enemy.

Jack pumped his legs hard. Pain, exhaustion and fear were forgotten as he concentrated everything he had on Lyle.

He closed quickly. Lyle never saw him coming. The Confederate officer emptied his revolver at the horde of men coming against him. As soon as the last bullet was fired, he thrust the Colt back into its holster and felt for the handle of the sword hanging on long slings at his side.

Jack grabbed Lyle's hand before it could pull the blade more than an inch from the scabbard. Lyle's head whipped around, his eyes meeting Jack's for a single moment before Jack grabbed his boot and pushed upwards with all his strength.

Lyle tried to resist, but Jack had the advantage of surprise. He grunted with the strain as he lifted Lyle's leg up, then pushed hard to topple him from the saddle.

'Martha, lie down!' He shouted the order, then darted around the horse to see Lyle sprawled in the dirt, his revolver thrown from the open holster.

Lyle scrabbled across the ground, snatching the Colt up from where it had fallen. He was still half on his knees when Jack reached him. For a big man, he moved fast. He lunged at Jack, using the revolver as a cudgel, forcing Jack to dance to one side to avoid the blow. It gave Lyle a moment's grace. He lumbered to his feet, then put his head down and charged at Jack whilst he was still off balance, crashing into him with enough force to send them both flying.

Jack hit the ground on his back with bone-jarring force, Lyle half on top of him. Yet even as the air rushed from his lungs, he twisted around and lashed out, smashing his left hand into the side of the Confederate officer's head. The blow rocked Lyle around and Jack pushed hard, twisting him onto his back.

Before Lyle could react, Jack straddled him and punched down, driving his right fist into the centre of Lyle's face, pulping his nose.

Yet Lyle knew how to fight. Even as the blood started to flow, he threw the revolver to one side, then reached up and took Jack's throat in both hands. He spat out a cry of triumph as he dug his fingers deep into the soft flesh under Jack's chin.

Jack punched again, smacking his left fist into Lyle's face, but the blow lacked its full force. The pain was brutal. Lyle's fingers were like claws, and Jack choked as his windpipe was crushed. Desperately he thrust his hands towards Lyle's face. They slid across the blood pouring from Lyle's nose until they found his eyes. Without hesitation, he dug his fingers in, driving his nails into Lyle's eye sockets with cruel precision.

Lyle's cry turned to one of pain. He bucked underneath Jack, his body convulsing in agony, and let go of Jack's throat. Jack felt his weight shift as Lyle writhed beneath him. He did not fight it, but went with it, using the momentum to slide to one side then roll away from the man he fought. The moment he was free, he levered himself up, and was on his feet in an instant. There was time to see Lyle's blood-streaked face as he lumbered to his own feet. His eyes were bloodshot, the skin around them gouged and bleeding from where Jack's nails had dug deep.

'I'm going to kill you.' Lyle had breath to hiss the threat before he charged.

Jack saw what was coming. Once he would have skipped aside, using his speed to keep him from harm. But he was older now. He no longer had the agility of his youth. But he had experience.

Lyle threw himself forward. Jack hauled down a deep breath and braced for the impact. When it came, the contact was violent, the thump of Lyle's head into his chest like being kicked by a mule. But he did not fight it, and he went backwards fast, grabbing hold of Lyle's hair as he back-pedalled.

His balance failed and he started to fall. But he saw the nape of Lyle's neck exposed, and so he clasped both hands together then brought them down on the top bones of his opponent's spine with every ounce of strength he had left.

It was a brutal blow. Lyle's legs buckled and he went down, still grasping Jack around the midriff. Jack had no choice but to go down with him, but this time he was prepared for the impact and he tensed, bracing himself. When it came, it hurt him badly, but he fought his way from beneath Lyle's body and staggered to his feet.

Lyle was slower. The blow to the top of his spine had stolen his strength, and he lay face down in the dirt for long enough for Jack to drop down onto his back.

Jack sucked down a breath, then grabbed a handful of Lyle's hair and pulled his head up from the dirt. The body beneath him tensed, but before Lyle could move, Jack slammed his face down into the ground. There was a sickening crunch before he hauled Lyle's head back up and drove it down once more.

'This is for me, you hear that, you fucking bastard?' Jack shouted the words as he smashed Lyle's face into the ground over and over again. He did not pause even as he felt the body beneath him go still. 'It's not for Rose.' He kept going, slamming Lyle's face into the ground repeatedly. It was heavy now, but he did not care. 'It's for me. You hear that, you bastard! It's for me!'

At last he let go of Lyle's hair. Every muscle trembled in the aftermath of the vicious fight, and the emotions surged through him, but he did not cry out. He rode the wild, searing tempest in silence, then looked up. Lyle's men were galloping for the rear, the short, sharp fight with the Union cavalry now over. One of them rode straight at Jack, sword drawn and tip pointed at his breast. There was no time to dodge. All he could do was sit on Lyle's body and stare at the blade that would surely rip through his chest.

The roar of a gunshot exploded from behind him. The bullet took the Confederate rider in the centre of his face. There was a spray of blood and brain, then the man fell backwards out of his saddle, the sword that had been reaching for Jack falling harmlessly to the ground.

For a moment, Jack could do nothing. He could see the Union riders charging towards him, but caring what would happen in the next few minutes was beyond him.

He leaned forward and picked up Lyle's head by the hair, then turned it to one side so he could inspect the face. There was nothing much left to see, the bloodied, distorted remains barely recognisable. A single rock shaped like a finger pointed upwards. The ground around Lyle was smothered with blood and gobbets of flesh.

Satisfied, Jack let the head drop, then pushed down with both hands on Lyle's back to lever himself to his feet. He stood there swaying, his legs almost lacking the strength to hold him upright. He refused to let them fail him. It was only as he stepped away from Lyle's corpse that he saw Martha sitting on the ground behind him, the carbine she had fired still in her hands.

The first Union soldiers galloped past. They ignored the pair on the ground, their attention concentrated on the Confederate cavalry trying to flee. Jack felt the ground shake as the horses thundered past. A rider shouted something, but the words were lost in the noise of the hooves thumping into the ground. He paid them no heed. Instead he bent down to retrieve a single fallen object, then walked towards Martha, forcing his battered body to obey him.

Martha still did not move. She sat where she was, watching him, her eyes focused on his face. Only when he came close did she toss away the carbine and reach up to him.

Jack fell to his knees beside her. He had nothing left. She drew him towards her, her hands cradling his face, and held him close, clutching him to her, her strong arms pulling him down so that his head rested against her chest.

He closed his eyes. Nothing mattered to him now.

The battle was not over, but his part in it was done.

He had found his revenge.

And it had not been for Rose. It had not been to avenge her death.

It had been for him.

# Epilogue

---

*The Beehive Tavern, Virginia, May 1862*

Jack sat near the open window, his eyes closing as he relished the fresh, cool air that rushed inside.

'You want another one, Jacko?'

The question was asked in a London accent. Lawrence, the owner of the Beehive Tavern, hovered near Jack's chair, a stack of empty glasses in his hands.

'Whenever you're ready. There's no rush.' Jack did not bother to open his eyes as he replied. He had been in the tavern for just under a week, paying for his stay with money Martha had retrieved from Lyle's corpse. It was not the only thing they had taken. The Colt revolver with the ivory grips now sat in the holster Jack wore on his right hip. He had picked it up with the last of his strength, and now it was back where it belonged.

It had been a long and fraught journey to reach the tavern. The Confederate army had been thrown into chaotic retreat and the roads leading south had been hellish. Even now, far from the battle, Jack had only the scantest picture of what had happened. He had heard tales of thousands of Union reinforcements reaching the battlefield. These fresh soldiers had been thrown into the fight, and they had turned the tide in the Union's direction.

He had also heard of the death of the Confederate commander Johnston. The general had been shot in the leg at some point in the afternoon of the first day and had been replaced by a general named Beauregard. If the stories Jack had heard were true, it had been Beauregard who had called off the Confederate attacks on the first day, and ordered the army to retreat when faced with a resurgent Union army on the second.

Yet Jack was sure that the true story of the battle would never fully come to light. In years to come, other men, who had likely never set foot on the field of battle itself, would try to piece together the events of the days of fighting, and attempt to stitch them together into a cohesive tale. It would likely be based as much on myth and hearsay as it would on fact. The notion did not bother Jack. He was in no better place to tell the tale of the battle, even having been there. He did know that the defeat had left the Confederates in dire trouble, and the entire western theatre of war was in turmoil as the invading Union army pressed steadily south.

But the state of the campaign was no longer his concern. He had been present at the battle for one reason only, and now he had taken his revenge. And that was what it had been. *His* revenge. It had never been about Rose, he understood that now. Avenging her had been a part of its genesis, for sure, but he understood now that it had been just as much about the shame of his own defeat, of being bested by Lyle. Now that man was lying in the cold earth, and Jack was free of the burden he had carried since he had awoken to find himself in a Confederate hospital.

He thought often of Captain Pinter, the man whose identity he had stolen, and who had told him that Lyle had killed Rose. He understood why Pinter had lied. He had seen Jack's need for an answer, and so he had provided the cruellest one he could think of, one that was designed to inflict pain. It had done that, but it had also done something that Pinter would likely never have intended. For that one spiteful lie had given Jack a purpose when he had none. What would have happened to him without that need for revenge? Would he have forced himself to heal? Or would he have simply succumbed to his wounds? He would never know the answer, but he did know that he was glad he had been the one to kill Pinter. The Confederate officer had paid the price for telling that most malicious of lies.

He was glad too that Rose was free. He had thought long and hard about trying to find her. But he had had his fill of chasing shadows. The fact that she was alive was enough. He was not concerned for her safety: Rose was the most capable person he had ever met. She had escaped from slavery to get to the free North, and if Lyle's account was true, now she had escaped again. She could be anywhere, and he was sure that she would be thriving wherever she was.

'Jack? Are you done there?' Martha called across to him. She was standing at the bottom of the stairs, her hands on her hips.

Jack placed the tankard carefully on the table.

Martha had changed. She was no longer the timid woman he had met all those months before. She was confident and sure, where once she had been hesitant and fearful. War had given her as much as it had taken away.

He got to his feet and walked towards her. The temptation to take her in his arms was strong. A part of him wanted her badly. She represented something he knew he desired. He could make a home with Martha. And he could be happy. But that was not to be his fate.

'Are you sure about this?' He posed the question he had already asked her a dozen times since she had told him of her plan.

'Yes.' Martha nodded.

'You sure he's worth it?'

'He's my husband.' She did not shirk from Jack's searching gaze. The sound of footsteps came from the stairs behind her. A man appeared and stood waiting patiently. 'We were joined together by the Lord.'

Jack held Martha's stare for a long time, then he sighed and looked at the man standing behind her, a man he had once beaten bloody. 'If you ever hurt her again, I vow I will come back, and I will kill you.'

'Jack.' Martha admonished him immediately.

The man behind her lifted his gaze. 'I understand. And I won't. I swear to God.' He paused, then offered a thin smile. 'I know how lucky I am.'

Martha turned and reached out to her husband. She took his left hand in her own and pulled him to her side.

Jack glanced down to the fused stump of mangled flesh that was all that was left of John Joseph's right arm. They had found him in an officers' temporary field hospital a fortnight after the battle, the fact that he was still alive due at least in part to the care he had been given because of his supposed rank. He had been with them ever since. He bore little resemblance to the man Jack had met before the battle. His suffering and experience of war had changed him. Martha had seen it and she had taken him back without hesitation. Now the pair would return to her father's cabin, where they would make a life for themselves.

'Have you got everything you need?'

'Yes.' Martha smiled. 'Thank you, Jack.'

Jack shook his head. 'I should thank you. I'd be dead if you hadn't saved me.'

'Twice.' She reached out with her free hand and tapped two fingers against his chest. 'I saved you twice.'

'That you did.' Jack forced a smile onto his face. 'You'd best be off.'

'We had.' Martha stepped forward to kiss him on the cheek. 'Thank you for giving me my life,' she whispered, then she led her husband across the tavern and out of the door.

Jack knew he would never see her again.

He turned and walked back to his table. Martha's husband was not the only one much altered by the events of the last few weeks and months. Jack himself was not the man he had once thought he was. He now knew that he was no master of war. He was just a killer, a soldier who, no matter how skilled he was, would likely share the same bitter fate as so many of the men he had fought alongside. But that day would not be today. For today he was alive, and for the moment, that was enough.

And once again he was alone.

# Historical Note

———◆———

If you have read any of the previous Jack Lark novels, you will know that I have something of a fascination with impostors. It was the inspiration for the series, and is an idea that I cannot resist returning to. It should, therefore, hopefully not come as a great surprise to see Jack masquerading as a Confederate officer as he embarks on his self-enforced quest to find Lyle.

Jack's presence in the South is not unusual. Thousands of Britons took part in the war on both sides, and of course the ranks of many regiments would have been filled with recent immigrants from across the British Isles. As to Martha's role, the presence of women fighting on both sides is well documented. There are many examples to read about, including the fantastic tale of Loreta Janeta Velazquez, who, rather like Jack, impersonated an officer, becoming Lieutenant Harry Buford, a Confederate soldier and spy.

General Bedford Forrest and his cavalry regiment existed, but Lyle's Raiders did not. Forrest's Cavalry was one of the most famous Confederate units to fight in the war. There are a great many resources available to anyone wishing to read more about their exploits, and I was able to base some of the dialogue spoken at the time of Forrest's departure from Fort Donelson on the account of the event by Private John S. Wilkes of the 3rd Tennessee Infantry. Anyone wishing to read more of Forrest's exploits will find a wonderful resource in *The Campaigns of General Nathan Bedford Forrest and of Forrest's Cavalry* by General Thomas Jordan and J. P. Pryor.

I also chose a fictitious regiment for Martha and her husband to serve in. As ever, I have tried to tread lightly over the history of the battles Jack experienced, and I never want to be accused of abusing the history of any real regiment that fought in these terrible conflicts, and so the 65th Virginia Infantry have found their place in the story.

The attack on Fort Donelson happened much as described. General Forrest did lead his men out of the fort the night before it surrendered. It was not the most glorious affair, and the battle for the fort is largely remembered for General Ulysses S. Grant's first use of the term 'unconditional surrender'. Numbers vary across accounts, but around 12,000 Confederate soldiers surrendered that day, a significant portion of the army the Confederates could put in the field in the western theatre of the war. There is no doubt their loss was to be felt keenly in the weeks and months to come.

There is much written about the battle of Shiloh, and I am very aware that I offer scant coverage of what would prove to be the largest loss of life on American soil to that point. There was a great deal more to the battle than Jack sees, and I would urge anyone interested to read more about this hard-fought contest. What is especially fascinating is the number of myths and legends that have built up around it. There are numerous articles and online journals that debate this subject. My particular favourite is an excellent article on the website of the Civil War Trust (www.civilwar.org) titled *Battle of Shiloh: Shattering Myths*, which is also where I first discovered the following wonderful quote from the commander of the victorious Union army, General Ulysses S. Grant. Grant wrote later that the battle of Shiloh 'has been perhaps less understood, or, to state the case more accurately, more persistently misunderstood, than any other engagement . . . during the entire rebellion'.

The action at the farm track, part of an area of the battlefield that would become known as the Hornet's Nest, is by far the most famous part of the battle, and I could not resist throwing Jack into the fray. It is worth noting that the sunken road that is so often talked of as being the basis for the strong defensive position was, perhaps, not as 'sunken' as myth would have us believe. The Civil War Trust article mentioned above elaborates on this argument, and tells us that the phrase did not appear until long after the battle. In addition, the photographs I have seen do not show a deeply sunken path, and so I have chosen to refer to it here simply as a track. I was also interested to read a document produced by the National Park Service about the Hornet's Nest at Shiloh, which tells us that the fighting there was not as significant as popular retellings of the battle would have us believe. However, the narrative of *The Rebel Killer* needed the fighting to be fierce, and so the action at the not-so-sunken road remains faithful to the more traditional rendering.

I also decided not to make Jack aware of the death of General Johnston, which came mid-afternoon on the first day of the battle. At the time, his officers removed and covered his body, hiding it from view lest it have a negative effect on the army's morale. It therefore seems reasonable to me that most of the men on the field would not have known of his death until well afterwards. I should note at this point that the letter Jack hears being read to the Confederate troops prior to the battle is the actual message General Johnston wrote and had read to his men before they went into action. I do confess to finding such things fascinating, most especially the language Johnston used to inspire his soldiers. A copy of this message is widely available online, but I first found it in the excellent Time Life book that covers Shiloh, which I shall acknowledge again later.

I was very interested in the notion that the Union army was taken by surprise by the Confederate attack. I confess I find it hard to believe that the Northerners were completely unprepared. There had been skirmishes between the two armies in the days leading up to the battle, and the initial phases were fought well in advance of the Union encampments. Therefore I have allowed Jack to doubt that the Confederates could achieve the complete surprise that some of its officers and men might have wished for.

As ever, there is a wealth of information available for those wishing to know more about this campaign or read original speeches and letters for themselves, and many of these resources are freely available online. I have already mentioned the website of the Civil War Trust, and this is a great resource that covers the entire war. I also made full use of the website of the National Park Service (www.nps.gov) which has an excellent series of articles about the battles, as well as a great range of maps and virtual tours of the battlefields. Once again, I turned to the Osprey series for research; they have some terrific books that cover the individual battles, as well as insights into the two armies that fought them. I have also found that the Time Life book series *Voices of the Civil War* give a fascinating glimpse into what it was like to be a soldier marching on the field of battle, and the book covering Shiloh is one of the very best. It is there that I found an anecdote from a certain Private Henry Morton Stanley, he and the man who would go on to find such fame as the explorer who found Dr Livingstone Stanley was serving in the 6th Arkansas Infantry, and it was a friend Henry Parker who put violets into their hats in the hope that it would somehow keep them safe in the tempest that was to come.

Jack has now survived another battle, and there can be no doubt that he has been much changed by the experience. Yet for once, he is almost at peace. But America is a troubled land, and he will need employment if he is to survive.

# Acknowledgments

---

I enjoy writing the Jack Lark stories immensely. However, they are not my work alone, and I am incredibly fortunate to have the assistance of three talented people to help me. The first, my agent David Headley, supports me at all times and I can never thank him enough for everything that he does. My editor, Frankie Edwards at Headline, is simply brilliant, and her enthusiastic and knowledgeable input makes these novels so much better than I could ever hope to make them by myself. Finally, Jane Selley has the unenviable task of copyediting my manuscript and making it into something more readable, and I must thank her for the work she does.

As ever, my final thanks goes to my family, and in particular to my wonderful wife, Debbie.

Want to know where it all began for Jack Lark?

# THE SCARLET THIEF

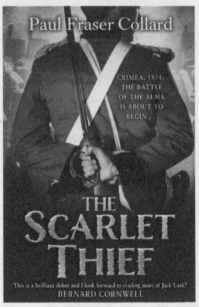

1854: The banks of the Alma River, Crimean Peninsula.
The men of the King's Royal Fusiliers are in terrible
trouble. Officer Jack Lark has to act immediately and
decisively. His life and the success of the campaign
depend on it. But does he have the mettle, the officer
qualities that are the life blood of the British Army?

HEADLINE